SONG OF THE STARLINGS

SHADOWS OVER AFRICA

T.M. CLARK

SONG OF THE STARLINGS

Published by Wilde Press

Edited by Creating Ink

Cataloguing-in-Publication details are available from the National Library of Australia www.librariesaustralia.nla.gov.au

ebook D2D © Published 2023 ISBN

Paperback D2D © Published 2023 ISBN 978-1-923129-15-3

Hardback © Published 2023 ISBN 978-1-923129-27-6

GENERAL FICTION

This is a work of fiction. Names, characters, places, and incidents are either the product of the author's imagination or are used fictitiously, and any resemblance to actual persons, living or dead, business establishments, events, or locales is entirely coincidental.

This book is written in English as used in the United States of America.

ABOUT THE AUTHOR

Zimbabwean-born T.M. Clark combines her passion for storytelling, diverse cultures, and wildlife with her love for the wild in her captivating multicultural books.

Writing for both adults and children, T.M. Clark is the author of Shooting Butterflies, Tears of A Cheetah, Child of Africa, Nature of the Lion, Cry of the Firebird, and the critically acclaimed My Brother-But-One, nominated for a Queensland Literary People's Choice Award in 2014. Her children's picture books, Slowly! Slowly! (a 2018 CBCA Notable Book) and Quickly! Quickly!, are beloved by young readers and are companion pieces to Child of Africa.

When she's not writing thrilling adventure stories, T.M. Clark is dedicated to helping other writers. As the coordinator of the CYA Conference (www. cyaconference.com), she provides professional development for both new and established writers and illustrators. She also co-presents at Writers as Sea (www.WritersAtSea.com.au), guiding writers on their creative journeys.

Tina Marie loves mentoring emerging writers, indulging in chocolate biscuits, and collecting books for creating libraries in Papua New Guinea. Her new novel, Daughter of Africa, is set to release later this year, continuing her commitment to captivating stories with an African heart.

Visit T.M. Clark at tmclark.com.au and follow her on social media.

facebook.com/tmclarkauthor

instagram.com/tmclark_author

amazon.com/stores/author/B018N3D2QY

bookbub.com/authors/t-m-clark

goodreads.com/tmclark

linkedin.com/in/t-m-clark

mastodon.au/@tmclark

pinterest.com/TMClark_Author

tiktok.com/@tmclark_author

threads.net/@tmclark_author

bsky.app/profile/tmclarkauthor.bsky.social

ALSO BY T.M. CLARK

ADULT NOVELS

- Child of Africa
- Cry of the Firebird
- My Brother-But-One
- Nature of the Lion
- Shooting Butterflies
- Song of the Starlings
- Tears of the Cheetah
- The Avoidable Orphan

PICTURE BOOKS

- Slowly! Slowly!
- Quickly! Quickly!

DEDICATION

As always, to Shaun, my love, my life.

PROLOGUE

Saliebos Farm, Thabazimbi, Northern Transvaal, South Africa

1987

Lightning split the African night sky and cracked through the bushveld. It shimmered; then the rumbling could be heard, tumbling over the *koppies*, growing in volume. Rain lashed the windows in sheets, rattling the panes of glass held in wooden frames by old putty.

Ben sensed his grandchild's presence in his bedroom before he heard the floorboard creak, despite her three-year-old featherweight and the storm raging outside. Having her in the house was enough to keep him awake.

He found he was always listening to ensure she was alright in her new room, and not trying to run away. Three years of her life had been stolen from him, but now that he knew about Chrystal, there was no way he would let any harm come to her.

They could start afresh and make good memories.

Ben wouldn't make the same mistakes with her that he had with her mother.

This time around, he would get it right.

He'd been given a second chance at parenting, and he was going to embrace it.

"You can come in." Ben lifted himself and turned slowly toward the door, pushing the photo album he'd been flicking through only moments before onto the quilt.

Chrystal stood there in her little white nightdress, a tatty knitted horse, which had once belonged to her mother, held firmly under her arm, and his heart became even more broken than it already was. Her blue eyes were too large and sunken deeply with black circles, her face showing more bone than was healthy for a girl her age. Her pallor was almost translucent. A vein throbbed in her forehead.

He could see the resemblance to his daughter Avril, and his darling wife, Ella. The same silver-blonde hair that they had both had. He knew it would change into a more golden color as Chrystal grew older.

Her hair was neglected, wild, and matted. Another sin to lay at his drug addict daughter's feet. Chrystal was as skittish as a newly born foal. There was no way she'd let a social worker near enough to touch her hair, and she certainly wouldn't let him.

God knew she didn't trust anyone. Of that, he had no doubt.

The social worker had said that it would be more traumatic for her hair to be brushed than left unruly, so they had left it.

So much had changed in her little life so fast.

Her mother dying.

Him collecting her from Cape Town this morning and bringing her home to live on *Saliebos* in the Northern Transvaal. He wished he'd been able to bring Avril home alive too. He had tried often enough and never gave up hope.

How could it all have gone so wrong?

A week ago, when Avril called and begged for his help, it was already too late. For Avril, but not for his granddaughter. He could still help her. Bring her into his life and give her the childhood she should have had. Not the life she'd had to endure with her mother in the decay of the city.

It was almost four years since Avril had disappeared from the last rehab center he'd paid for in Johannesburg.

Four years of no contact. A constant void.

Four years of total anguish.

During that time, she'd given birth to Chrystal.

Of all her betrayals, that was the one that hurt the most.

He had a grandchild he'd been denied knowing.

Avril had been found dead in the tiny flat in Woodstock outside of Cape Town. He'd never expected the call from the child services welfare officer contacting him about his granddaughter. The social worker was adamant that Avril had been clean for her pregnancy at least, and that while Chrystal was neglected, she didn't appear to have had any drugs forced into her little veins.

Chrystal shifted from one foot to another as if waiting for something. She bit her lip.

Waiting.

He cursed his daughter for keeping this little girl away.

"I can see that Mr. Nag there is a bit scared of the storm. Do you think we should tuck him in this nice big bed alongside us? We can protect him. I can put my hand over his ears to block out the noise, and you can stroke his mane to calm him," he said as a deep roll of thunder shook the homestead.

Of all the days for nature to unleash its fury on the African landscape, did it have to be the night I brought her home?

Chrystal nodded slowly and walked to the side of the bed, but she didn't climb up. Instead, she put the knitted toy in the air, as if expecting him to take it from her.

Ben frowned.

The welfare workers had told him that she hadn't spoken since the day the police had found her sitting next to her mother's body. They weren't even sure if she could talk.

When he'd first seen her in the flesh, all he'd wanted to do was hold her close. Hug her. His little gem that his screwed-up daughter had left behind. His last precious glimpse of his darling Ella. His grandchild.

Lost and alone.

But he was here now, and he would help heal those uncertainties and those nightmarish memories. Replace them with happier ones. Push them far back in her little mind until they were forgotten. He took Mr. Nag and put him on the bed.

"You want my help to climb up here next to Mr. Nag? I bet he would like that."

A loud clap of thunder had her scrambling up the side of the bed. Ben tucked her stuffed toy between them and made sure that the sheets and blankets were pulled up high under her little chin, her head on the large white pillow.

"When your mom was young like you, and the storms would roll in, she would hop in this bed with Grandma Ella and me. We would look at the photo albums of where we had been on holiday together and plan our next great adventure. That's what I was doing when you came in. Do you want to see the photographs of your mom when she was a little bit older than you are now? She was five when we traveled to England."

She nodded her head.

A louder and closer bolt sizzled as it struck near the house; the room lit up blue momentarily as the electricity transferred from the heavens to the earth.

Her eyes grew larger and she bit her lip while clutching Mr. Nag tight. Her attempt to control the fear that threatened to overwhelm her body and her soul was both disturbing and heroic to watch. He remembered Avril at that age; her emotional outburst would have been visible to all.

His grandchild was already strong.

His heart wept when he thought about how much she must have already witnessed to be able to control fear like this.

"Your Grandma Ella and I took your mum with us and we traveled to England on a big airplane, like the one we flew in today."

She silently looked at the ceiling as if studying the knots on the wood poles that supported the thatched roof.

"If you look here, you can see a picture of your mum," he said, opening the page for her to look.

Chrystal peered at the photo album.

He smiled. He had her attention. He continued, pointing to the pictures as they went through. "See this one here, she is standing with one of the lion statues in Trafalgar Square, and you can see the pigeons all over her. Can you see how big those pigeons were compared to her hand?"

She sat back up in the bed and leaned forward, looking at the pictures.

He brought the album closer to them and pointed to the next picture. "See here, this is a highland cow. We were in Scotland. That's your mum feeding it with a bottle. It's a calf, mind you. There's its mother standing close by watching, making sure everything is okay. Your mum loved those cows. When we got home, she asked me to buy her a Nguni cow with big horns, which I did. It took a lot to say no to your mother. She was my little girl. I wanted to give her everything, even the moon if I could have. I still have Nguni cows out there on the farm. Would you like to go look at them tomorrow?"

He watched as Chrystal reached hesitantly toward the album. "You can touch the pictures."

She traced the large horns of the strange shaggy cow as he carried on. "From that day on, your mother collected anything to do with cows. Remind me to look in the old barn, and we can find her figurine collection in there, one of these days. I packed them up and put them away when she got older. I didn't want her to sell…" Ben trailed off, not wanting to upset Chrystal more than she already was.

They continued their journey through the yellowed album, Chrystal silently turning the pages when each story had been told.

On the last page was one of his favorite pictures that Ella had taken. Avril had been ill and running a fever with a twenty-four-hour tummy bug while they were still in Cardiff. He'd been sitting in a chair next to her bed and had fallen asleep from exhaustion, having spent the night awake watching over his daughter. While he'd been dozing, Avril had climbed into his lap and eventually fallen asleep there.

"Your mum would always sit on my lap when she was scared or lonely," he said. "She always said it was because I had a bit of padding on my bones, unlike your grandma. She was thin as a willow tree but strong like ironwood. Your grandma said it was because your mum could hear the sound of my heart beating, and it drowned out all her worries, so she didn't have to think about being sick or lonely."

The storm had been building in intensity and was still unleashing its fury on the ranch. The lightning glowed blue once more, and a loud crack shook the house at the same time.

"The storm is right on top of us. Once this lot passes, it should start to calm down," he said. The thunder rolled loudly. Chrystal jumped, her whole body moving in a jerky motion.

"You know, I bet that if you snuggle up here, you can hear my heartbeat louder than that thunder like your mum used to do. You want a listen?' He tapped his chest, indicating where his heart was.

She looked at him, hesitant.

He held his breath as Chrystal got on her knees on the top of the bed and leaned toward him. She put her ear against the white T-shirt that he wore to bed.

He could hear the blood pulse through his own body as he held still, not wanting to frighten her. Not wanting to move in case she bolted.

He felt the moment that she trusted him, and climbed into his lap, like her mother had done in the picture, and snuggled closer. She put her arms around him and held tightly, her ear against his chest. Only then did he slowly wrap his arms around her and hold his granddaughter for the very first time.

"It's okay, Chrystal. You're safe here. I'll watch over you. I swear it with my own life. Nothing bad will happen to you ever again."

"Can I stay here forever?" she asked.

His granddaughter had spoken. "This is your home. You can stay here, forever and ever," he whispered as a tear rolled down his cheek. His heart felt like it might burst, from love for the grandchild he finally held in his arms and a deep grief over the daughter he'd lost.

CHAPTER 1

Saliebos Farm, Thabazimbi, Limpopo Province, South Africa

18th March 2016

The American was bang on time. He'd buzzed at the main gate and been let in to drive through the farm to the homestead. His Land Rover Discovery, with its shiny red paint and fat tires that would be the envy of anyone owning a 4x4 *bakkie*, drove up to the front of the building where Chrystal and her grandfather, Ben, waited.

Chrystal ground her teeth as she clenched her jaw.

Very discreet.

Not.

A top of the range rental, the Land Rover screamed wealth, tourist, and *hijack me*.

"Khulu, we never got to why he wanted to chat — specifically to me?" she said quietly. She'd started calling Ben Khulu, grandfather in Ndebele, when she was in preschool, and it'd stuck. He'd said she could call him whatever she liked, as long as she'd always remember that she could tell him anything and share any secret. He would be her best friend.

The friendship was still there.

But now that she was older, there were definitely secrets between them.

Some things were better left unshared.

A tall man climbed out, his black Stetson already on his head. He wore a teal green shirt, with its sleeves rolled up, and she watched as he stowed his sunglasses in his top pocket. His blue jeans looked new. He wore pull-on boots.

Obviously, a pen pusher. After all, everyone in Thabazimbi wore lace-up veld shoes, right? Chrystal snorted.

Ben dug her in the ribs with his elbow and murmured, "Watch your manners." Louder he added, "Rowan, good to see you again." He stepped forward and shook his hand. "This is Chrystal."

Rowan Zackery removed his hat and held his hand out for hers.

Khulu's reminder about manners had her putting out her hand. But as Rowan slid his hand into her, she looked up and into the greenest eyes she'd ever seen, surrounded by thick black lashes that any girl would covet. His hair was sable brown, with golden streaks through it, and worn slightly longer sitting on his collar. His easy smile seemed to come naturally.

Rowan nodded his head. "Nice to meet you. Ben's told me a lot about you." A strong American accent accompanied the deep voice.

"I wish I could say the same," she said, removing her hand from his larger one, fighting the urge to scratch it as he'd left a tingling in her palm.

Ben's phone rang. He looked at it. "Excuse me, I need to take this."

Chrystal continued to size up Rowan with an unexpected awareness. Standing up close, she could tell he was at least six foot three against her five foot eight. His broad chest accentuated in his tailored shirt. His arms were muscular, and his hands had been calloused as if he was used to hard work.

That was a surprise.

His scent surrounded her, masculine and strong. He smelled of new leather and something spicy. If she'd been meeting him under more favorable circumstances, she might've been happier to meet him.

He was no pretty boy like Eric. More of a man like Wes.

He didn't fit the picture she had in her head of what someone trying to "fit into a community" should look like. He moved with the grace of a leopard stalking.

Definitely military.

The hairs on her arms rose up.

Too much like Wes.

She knew nothing about him; there hadn't been time after Ben had dropped the bombshell at breakfast that Rowan was arriving and wanted to talk to her. And that he was offering a great deal of money to do it.

There was something about him that unnerved her.

She had to find out what it was that had her feeling off-centre.

And she was at a disadvantage — he seemed to know about her.

Distracted, she concentrated on what Khulu was saying as he stepped back toward them. "I'm sorry to have to run. Game fence is down in section twelve. I'll take some guys and go mend it."

"Let me know if you need me and the team," Chrystal said.

He nodded, then turned on his heels and whistled for his working dogs. Zulu and Themba ran to his side, sprung into the back of the *bakkie* and were already barking at the wind before Khulu even started the engine and roared toward the barn, the back of the *bakkie* doing a little fishtail in the loose gravel.

Shaking her head in disbelief, she turned her attention back to the man of the moment. Her 'guest' that she knew nothing about.

As Ben left in a cloud of dust, Rowan noticed Chrystal take a step back from him.

"One day I swear he'll drive off like that and those dogs will go flying off the back."

"I think the saying might be something along the line of not separating a man and his toys, even when both man and toys grow in size?"

Chrystal laughed. "Too true. And whomever decided that wisdom comes with age, had not met Khulu."

"Some people never get old, and I believe your Grandfather might be one of them."

"Perhaps, in his mind, but physically, he's slowing down.' She paused a moment and looked as if lost in a memory, then added. "Not that his dogs would ever admit to it, they are devoted and adjust their speed instead."

Rowan nodded and took the opportunity to study the legendary South African warrior, known only as Savannah. She looked every bit the typical rancher, in her button-up khaki shirt and jeans with leather boots, but it was her attitude that defined her as the heir apparent. The real confidence about her was unmistakable.

Her grandfather had said she was restless, and while she was a farmer at heart, he thought that she'd return to paid security work when she found out a little girl's life was on the line.

Rowan had been intrigued.

His job wouldn't only be convincing her to help him, but also that Ben was okay with it. Ben had said that she thought that the stress of her 'job' was too much for her elderly grandfather and was part of the reason she'd retired.

It was obvious to Rowan that it was a simplified version of the story rather than the whole truth.

He knew that she was intelligent and efficient at her job. Her comments had shown that she was funny and caring too. Someone he could work with, and perhaps enjoy her company while he was at it. And he hadn't missed that she tried to hide her attractiveness under oversized clothes.

He reminded himself that he was only in Africa to find Akina Wilson.

If he found Henry's mole while he was here — then that was icing on the cake.

He looked to where a horse whinnied out in the paddocks alongside the barn, and his eyes followed a magnificent specimen. Its black coat shimmered in the morning light. The horse snorted, turned from the fence, and trotted away with a buck, but continued to hold itself proudly.

An enigma in the environment he was in. Surrounded by wild game, wildebeest, sable, and buffalo. *I hear you, buddy.*

Ben had said Chrystal would be the key to unlocking the secrets in the Waterberg area's underground, but she was going to be a reluctant recruit. As old men do sometimes, he'd refused to elaborate. Actually, Ben hadn't given much information on her, as you'd expect from an ex-combat veteran protecting someone.

Her personal file had also been light on details. He knew that was the way with security companies, the less on paper the better. The special ops file had been a bit more detailed regarding her combat experience, and yet it still felt inadequate. His friend, Henry, who happened to be her ex-employer, had given Rowan both of her work files when he'd recommended her.

As far as they were concerned, without her, Rowan didn't have a hope of finding Akina alive.

Add to that, his faith in his ability to find stolen and lost children alive, was starting to waiver. His last job back home had ended badly: Three dead kids, their parents' lives forever shattered, instead of happy reunions.

He hated to admit it. He needed Savannah's help to find Akina.

Curtis Wilson had been through enough without losing his only daughter too. Rowan and Curtis had become friends fifteen years ago while traveling together in the Middle East. Curtis had been involved in a corruption case against a private company for water rights. Back when he was in the core and had the might of the USA army behind him.

He glanced at Chrystal, wondering what was going on inside her head at that moment.

"He's a beauty, that one," Rowan said. "Doesn't quite fit with the rest of the animals here, but he's a magnificent horse."

"Interesting. Of course you know horses," Chrystal muttered, but began walking towards the horse. Her back straight. Guarded.

Ben had said that it would be simple to convince Chrystal to take the job. After witnessing them together today, Rowan knew that the old *codger* was wrong and he had deliberately misled him.

Chrystal wasn't going to 'be simple' at all.

From the moment he'd stepped out of his vehicle, she'd bristled.

She was hiding something from her family.

Something big.

He thought he knew what, but he couldn't be sure.

He might be wrong.

He hoped he was wrong.

But as for Akina Wilson, his theory was well-formed: He hadn't come halfway across the world to find another body.

He truly believed she was still alive.

When Ben had left him alone with Chrystal, he hadn't been surprised. After all, he'd asked for her — well, Savannah. Tracked her down, so to speak.

Ben might have been out of the military for many years, but it was clear he still knew what was going on in his granddaughter's life. Apparently, he also knew how to attempt to make her face her demons head-on.

The only thing Ben didn't seem to know was what had driven her away from private contracting.

What had made her turn her back on a successful career?

He glanced at Chrystal, trying to ignore that captivating 'something' about her.

The way she'd strode out as he was driving in to meet them, not letting his vehicle come up to her, a slight step ahead of her grandfather. A protective move to the trained eye.

The way she moved, like a jaguar, despite being away from active duty for a few years. A natural gracefulness of someone who was sure of themselves, and fully aware of their surroundings.

Chrystal was guarded.

Thinking before she said anything. She was a straight shooter.

Without Savannah and her skills, he was pretty much up shit creek and running out of time too.

She stopped and turned around to face him. "I agree. He's stunning. Like most dangerous beings, you can't help but notice him, the wild edge he possesses," Chrystal said, dragging him back from his thoughts. He wasn't sure if she meant him or the horse.

"That's Snowflake," she said. "He's still green-broke and extremely headstrong. Our horse manager is working with him. I'm hoping that soon he'll be ridable, although I'm not sure if I'll pass him on to the stables for horseback rides in the reserve area. He seems too used to his freedom and own space."

Rowan frowned. She was still analyzing him.

He would play along.

They had all day to talk.

She smiled. "Ben thinks he's too spirited and will break my bones, but we have one of the best trainers in South Africa. He'll make sure Snowflake won't throw me." Chrystal shook her head as if dislodging a memory. "I don't bounce as easily as I once did."

He nodded.

Her admission of weakness caught him a little off guard. Realistic was added to his list of characteristics he was making of her.

"Unfortunately, none of us do," Rowan said. But his attention had shifted, and he was no longer looking at the horse. Instead, he studied the Chrystal. She was more like the horse than she realized. Her hat in her hand, her hair golden blonde, with lighter streaks in it from hours spent in the sunlight, a full mouth, and a smattering of freckles across her nose. There was an exhausted look to her too, of someone who had seen so much. A fragility waiting to implode.

Battle-scarred.

He'd seen that look before.

"Come," her voice interrupted his thoughts. "Let's go and say hello. I promise you, Snowflake's gentle to talk to, despite his attitude. He was a pet and got to be almost five with no saddle training at all. The family who had him became scared of him as he grew bigger, and he was left to run wild with their cattle. He doesn't seem afraid of buffalo or rhino either, so he'll make a good addition to our stable.

"We can do a tour of the farm while we chat." She glanced around, as if to make sure that no one could hear her, and seemed to be taking her time, contemplating her words.

"But before we do. Let me be straight with you, I didn't even know you existed until a few hours ago which really doesn't sit well. I would've liked to have done a bit of research to find out why you need to talk to me."

She certainly was direct. He thought about how Ben had said she'd want to throw his ass off the farm the moment she knew who he was. That he was linked to the mercenary world — the world of private contractors that she said she so desperately wanted to escape from. Until he explained why.

But, before he said anything, she continued.

"Khulu said he hoped that I'd help you. I know that my granddad is a crafty soul, but I also know that there's more going on here than he's letting on. You need to level with me or leave. Because nothing will save you if I find that you are here to do something illegal or to put this farm or anyone here at risk."

He was going to have to tell her and trust that she would make the right decision.

Once that was in the open, they could get on with finding Akina. "Your grandfather thought if you got to know me a bit, then you would be more open to why I'm here," he said, running his fingers through his hair. "I need your help. Well, Savannah's help."

She took a deep breath. He could hear it, but other than her chest lifting slightly, she gave no other indication that she was listening.

"Please hear me out—" he went on.

She stood still, seemingly relaxed. He could see the stance was deceptive.

Ready to fight, like a caged wild cat facing an electric prodder.

He watched closely for other 'tells' that she wouldn't be able to return to battle.

He'd seen too many good men go down with PTSD and recognized most of the symptoms — if she showed any of them, he would find another way.

She would be useless in the field if she was suffering. But even knowing that he felt drawn to her. Willing her not to show weaknesses.

"I run a private investigation firm in the US, specializing in child retrieval. I'm in Thabazimbi looking for the only daughter of a prominent American businessman. It was all over the news a few weeks ago. Akina Wilson is only eleven years old and was abducted in Cape Town. The South African strike force believes she's dead. I don't. I've already tracked her further north than they assumed she'd survived. But I've lost her trail. I know she was alive when they moved her into the area. I have a witness that said he saw her handed over to an old woman. A sangoma. He said the witch doctor lives in the bush around Thabazimbi, but he didn't know where."

She frowned. "Traditional sangomas sometimes move around."

"As I found out — and it's why the trail went cold on me. I got to interview a number of them that were on a register. None of them had any useful information for me. That's when I began thinking differently and came to find you instead."

He saw her roll her shoulder as if it hurt. The last report hadn't said she'd been injured, but the reports often had the barest information in them, for the sake of the operative's safety.

The report indicated that Savannah had retired after her last op had gone to shit. The thought of going back in was taking its toll on her, but she was handling it well on the outside. He was going to push on.

He had to.

He needed to know if he was going to be able to rely on her.

If it came down to just the two of them, could he trust her not to crumple?

"I'm still on the hunt, even if the trail is cold. By now I should have found a body. I've unfortunately come across a few of those before today." He took a deep breath; he should tell her about the last three dead kids too, but now was not the time.

"I believe she's still alive. Contrary to what the task force said. I believe that the people who kidnapped her either knew exactly who they have or Akina told them. Once the news broke, her value increased because of what her father's done to so many corrupt people all over the world. They removed the GPS tracker from her arm. Her kidnapping might have been revenge on him, but if it wasn't, they were simply lucky to get someone so valuable. This is not your standard kidnapping. There have been no demands. I believe they've taken her for the slave trade."

He watched her take a breath in and let it out quite slowly.

"If I'm right, whoever's got her will try and break her spirit, make her compliant. She has added value because she's super intelligent and multilingual. An added asset in their market, pushing up the price of their commodity."

He saw her flex her fingers, but she caught him looking and instead held her hands together in front of her.

She was still in control.

Good.

Control here meant control under pressure. And under fire. So far, she appeared okay.

"They've had to hide her until the heat dies down. Problem is, it's turned so quiet out there now and she's not showing up on any of the usual gossip vines." He rubbed the back of his neck.

"There is 'usual' chatter about abducted children?" Her face twisted in disgust.

"Let's call it 'usual' for the sake of this case. You know the side of the internet civilized people don't want to venture into. I know that as an ex-private contractor, you're aware of the dark web. I know you're retired, but I need your skill." He hesitated. Looked downwards, then lifted his head again to look at her. "I've spent the last two precious weeks coming up with exactly nothing. Fourteen whole days wasted while that poor kid has been subject to god knows what. I came here to hire you. Will you come out of retirement and help me find my client's daughter?"

He saw her open her mouth to talk, then close it. He rushed on before she could refuse. "I've heard a lot about Savannah, how she gets the job done, no matter what. That you know Africa well, speak several African languages, and have contacts to tap into. I'm an American. I usually work in America, sometimes across Europe. I'm good at my job, but I have never operated here. It's surprisingly difficult.

"I need you to help me save Akina from the horrors that await her if we don't." He changed the pitch of his delivery of the next sentence. Dropped his voice deeper. "Even now I'm worried I might be too late. Her father needs — no, he deserves to know either way. This is personal to me. Curtis

15

Wilson and I have worked together before. He fights against injustice and corruption. He's a good man, a great father."

As if waking from a trance, she turned around shaking her fists. "I'm going to kill him. Literally. From the little he told me, we were getting some extra cash for *Saliebos* for having a visitor, stay a few days with us in the house, not dismantling everything I've done to help me settle into civilian life again. I walked away. I survived. Did he know this is what you wanted?" Chrystal's voice was raised as she flayed her hand around in the air. "What was Khulu thinking?"

Rowan frowned. "I think you misunderstand. I'm not asking you to leave the ranch and go overseas, I'm asking you to make it look like you're showing me the area. I'm asking you to help me dig around here in Thabazimbi. Help me to find the sangoma and where Akina went. You'll still be sleeping in your own bed at night — but I could use some help infiltrating some of the shadier areas."

She shook her head. "No. You're asking me to return to something I walked away from. You're asking more of me than W—" She hesitated. Blowing out the rest of her lungs full of air noisily. She inhaled again before she said flatly, "You're asking me to become a vigilante in my hometown."

"I'm asking you to help me find one scared little girl. To stop her being traded as a sex slave."

She took a few deep breaths, and he could see she was beginning to get her emotions under control. He didn't think he'd ever seen a woman physically pull herself back from an outburst like this before so calmly. Controlled again, she rolled her shoulders and looked him right in the eye.

"You paid for the chance just to speak with me? Before you actually even knew what my answer would be?" Her frown cast a million doubts.

Rowan nodded. "It's only money. And if I can get you to help, then it's worth it." He took his own deep breath. "My client is prepared to pay whatever's needed. Name your price. I hate to admit this, but I'm out of my depth. I'm short on contacts. I reached out to Henry Thompson, your old boss, and he's of the opinion that if I can get you to come out of retirement, it'll be the greatest chance of finding Akina. He believes you're the best. And Ben said the hardest part would be convincing you he's okay with you helping me. She's just a child."

He watched a small frown form on her forehead. "Henry's involved?"

"No. I work for myself, but we served together years ago. He gave me your name and file and told me you were among the elite. The one chance little Akina had if you chose to take this case and find her."

She took two steps backward.

"I'm not trying to sway you with money, but I expect to pay you the contractor going rates per day with the comforts of home close by."

She put her hands on her hips and shook her head. "You're barking up the wrong tree. Did Henry's precious file, which he has no right to have just 'given you', tell you most of my private security work was done outside of South Africa? I don't have a network here in Thabazimbi." The way she stood made her appear more feminine, not larger than life as she had obviously intended.

"This is your hometown. We can say that I'm looking to purchase a farm, have heard about the biodiversity of Stud Game Farming, and want to invest. I'm an American with the dollars. South Africa is still an ego-stereo-typical-chauvinistic society that most males we encounter will dismiss you. They'll never suspect you to be investigating anyone, and if we get into trouble — well, you know how to handle yourself."

"Make sure you understand that our Stud Game Farming is not for the hunting trade, it's to restock game reserves and populate new ones. Our days of breeding beautiful specimens to be trophies are over."

She raised her eyebrows at him and pulled a face as if biting the inside of her cheek.

He rushed in before she shot him down on the more important issue. "Let me be straight with you. I know that things went wrong on your last mission."

"Let me guess — Henry?"

"Yes — but I don't think he gave me all the facts. There are holes the size of the Grand Canyon in the last report. He said if I find out who the mole was then, it would be great for him too, but right now, I'm not that interested in what happened on your last mission. I need the Savannah in Henry's file. The one who walked out of the jungle."

She blew out a breath through her pursed lips.

"I need to know that you'll be fully committed to finding Akina. If your heart isn't in it, it wouldn't be worth our time." He pushed further. "Your last team were all killed in action. They didn't come out of that jungle, except you and the 'mark'. You survived against all the rolls of the dice. I came looking for that Savannah. I believe she's the only way I'll find Akina."

She was shaking her head. Without thinking, he put his hand out and touched her arm.

She didn't push it away.

Chrystal was quiet. Then she appeared to straighten up as if she was facing an enemy. She looked at him, and he noticed that her eyes were the same blue as cornflowers.

Henry's file hadn't mentioned that. Eyes like hers were harder to hide in combat.

He dropped his hand.

"Before I decide, I want to see your file. What scheme you've come up with, and exactly what you expect of me. I need to know that I'm working with a professional. I'm not going to lie and say the money wouldn't be useful, but I have to believe that there's a chance this girl is alive. And know what you're prepared to do to get her back. There's a thin line between a vigilante and a home-grown terrorist. A line that I'm not going to cross."

Rowan nodded his head. "Fair enough."

There might be hope for Akina after all.

"Let's go work through your files. There's no way I can let a little girl disappear into the slave trade. I'll be fighting to the end, no matter where that is in the world, to get her back. I guess Khulu will have to be okay taking the farm on full time again."

CHAPTER 2

Waterfront Shopping Mall, Cape Town, South Africa

4th March 2016

Akina increased the length of her stride. She glanced at her smartwatch.

3:25pm.

She knew how to walk fast without making herself look panicked. Besides, what did it matter if anyone saw her running?

No one would care.

Except for the big security guard who seemed to be following her.

The concierge at the hotel had told her father that this was a great mall with a panoramic view of the harbor, and world-class restaurants. It was full of designer-brand stores, but it also had a lot of local boutiques. He had come with her but chosen to sit in one of the restaurants, catching up on his emails, and given Akina permission to explore alone so long as she checked in on the hour and met him back there at four.

New York was home, but Akina liked being wherever her father was, so was happy traveling. She understood that the one item that her father's money had never bought her was the space to be totally alone. But lately her father had started letting her have time by herself.

She hadn't done any shopping today, but that was because she hadn't seen anything that took her fancy. Her father always said that it was her Japanese heritage that she didn't spend for the sake of spending, and she was like her late mother.

She'd been browsing for almost three hours and needed to check in again. She still had thirty-five minutes to go before she'd return to her dad and they would get ready for their meeting with his work colleagues for dinner at eight. That'd be enough time to take the dessert she'd made out of the fridge. She knew there'd be leftovers she could give to passersby. There were always people in the streets going hungry in South Africa. They accepted the free food with gratitude, unlike in some countries where it landed in a bin.

A few years earlier, when they had been in a restaurant in New York, and the South African Minister of Social Development, Health and Welfare, Thulas Masutha, had asked her if she cooked. There had been much conversation about the quality of the meal that night and how good it was.

The next day, she attempted cooking for the first time.

It was a disaster.

She was better at it now.

She looked over her shoulder.

The man was closer. She needed to make sure she was right, that he was following her.

She looked around before entering the Guess shop on her right. There weren't many people in the store, a group of four adults were inspecting the denim jeans, and a girl around her age was by the T-shirt racks.

Akina reached for her phone and typed: *I'm being followed.*

She looked at her phone and decided not to press send. She shouldn't be getting paranoid that someone was going to steal her. Her dad's warnings were always in her head. Still, she also heard him saying he was an overprotective parent because Akina was all he had left after her mum had died. And there was no reason to steal her; after all, she was simply an ordinary kid.

One of the ladies started to leave the store. Akina followed close, glancing behind as they left the shop.

The man pushed off from the wall and followed.

Damn, she hadn't lost her tail.

She was opposite the toilets. She could duck in there and wait for her dad.

She walked into the restroom and into a cubical. Using some of the toilet paper wrapped around her hand, she closed the toilet lid. Wiped it and then sat down. Throwing the paper on top of the dispenser, she pulled her phone out.

3:35pm

> Akina: Plz come and get me. In the toilets by the Guess shop — a weirdo security guard following me

> Dad: Probably thinks you stole something. You didn't, did you?

> Akina: Not funny. Come get me!

> Dad: Stay there. I'm on my way.

> Akina: Hurry!!!!!

Her dad was on his way. She could feel her shoulders relax.

She'd learned early on that she didn't lead a normal life. Her father was ultra-rich. The GPS chip implanted in the top of her arm was proof she lived in a different world to others her age. Because of his success, and his stand against corruption in the international business world, she was a target.

She rubbed where the tracker lay under her skin. When the insurance company's doctor had put it in, he'd said that the likelihood of them ever having to use it was so slim that she might as well forget it was there.

An easy thing for a man who didn't have a tracking chip in his arm to say.

3:40pm. She watched her dad's tracker on her phone stop outside the ladies' toilets entry.

She tucked her phone into her pocket and unlocked the cubicle.

The door burst inwards.

Akina was knocked backward onto the closed toilet, her head hitting the wall behind with a sharp thunk. A large woman stepped inside the small enclosure, and before she could react, the woman shoved a rag into her mouth and injected something into her neck.

"No!" she tried to scream, but the sound was blocked.

This can't be happening.

Fight a little voice in her head shouted at her.

The toilet stall began to swirl around.

She tried to pull the rag out.

She couldn't breathe.

Gasping. Choking.

The face of her attacker became distorted and her vision blurred.

Fight.

She raked her nails over the hand holding the rag in place.

The woman swore, but the sound came from far away in the distance.

"Daddy! Help me!" Akina screamed silently as blackness overtook.

CHAPTER 3

Hartbeespoort Dam, North West Province, South Africa

6th March 2016

Levi slammed the phone down.

"Fucking hell!" He punched both his fits into the new mahogany desktop hard, causing the ornate desktop lamp to fall over. He smacked it with his hand and it bounced off the desk and skidded to a silent stop on the thick carpet.

No satisfying smash.

He picked up the vodka tumbler next to his keyboard and, spinning around, threw it at the glass-fronted picture behind him. The splintering of glass was music in his ears, but it fueled his soul with wanting more.

The door burst open. "*Skattie*? What happened? Are you okay?" The heavily accented Afrikaans voice asked.

His wife stood there, her blonde hair perfectly styled and blow-dried, her trim figure covered in a designer mini dress.

He liked the hemline short like that, so he could touch her pussy whenever he wanted.

She always wore designer clothes.

He paid for them. He paid for everything. His trophy wife. Sharlene Marietjie Louw. Or as he called her, Chris.

She made sure that she always looked good. Her figure was perfect, shaped with hours spent in the gym.

He looked at her face.

She was almost the replica of the old picture he held in his safe, only matured. The plastic surgery lines didn't show at all. Not on her nose, or eyes, her cheek implants, not even on her chin. She had already resembled his Chrystal when he'd seen her all those years ago. That was the only reason he'd allowed her near him, as a substitute. It had still taken a lot of work to improve her to anything near Chrystal's standard.

He'd gone looking for Chrystal after being released but had been too late. Chrystal Booysen had trained with the police.

Hell would freeze over before she'd accept him.

He could never go near her.

He had checked on her over the years and found she'd become a private security contractor. By then, he'd been married and moving quickly up the ladder in his new profession. Rocking the boat would draw unnecessary attention to his activities. Sales and marketing were interesting, and he'd learned much. He had needed a wife, on his arm for work functions, and Sharlene Marietjie had been the answer. But he always felt like he was stuck with second best. With fake tits, bleached hair, and re-sculptured looks. His wife was an imitation of the real thing.

"*Skattie,* you can't go breaking things. I only finished re-decorating from the last time you trashed this room," she said.

"You think I give a flying fuck?"

"*Skattie,* you don't mean that. Oh Jesus. You've been drinking vodka again. I can smell it..."

"I'll fucking well drink vodka if I want to. I work for every cent in this house and I'll drink it if I'm in the mood. You hear me, you stupid bitch," he said, walking toward her.

"Don't, *Skatt.* Don't. No. This isn't you talking. This is the vodka."

He grabbed her hair. "Look around, from that expensive Italian land-scaped garden you insisted we have, with that hideous fountain, to the new carpet in this room, I have paid for it all."

"I know, *Skattie.* I know and I appreciate all that. I do. I promise," she pleaded as he let her hair go. "And I love you for it all. You work so hard."

He smacked her.

Hard.

The crunch of her nose breaking was satisfactory but fueled him for more as he rearranged her artificial face.

His money could pay for the reconstruction. It wouldn't be the first time.

She dropped to the floor. Screaming. Her hands covered her face.

"No, *Skattie*, no. Don't hurt me again. Please stop. Please, I love you."

"You don't love me. You love my money," he said, as he started to remove his belt.

"I love you. I love you. You don't need to do this. You don't need to hurt me. I didn't do anything." She attempted to get up and scramble away.

A blood trail smear showed on the new carpet.

"Why should I believe you?" he said, raising his arm and bringing the belt down.

A welt formed on her perfect legs. He came closer.

She kept still, her hands holding her nose.

He traced his finger over the ridge of purple skin.

"Stop. Please stop. *Skattie*, please," she begged.

"Why? Tell me why I should stop?" He smacked her again, keeping the buckle in his hand, and feeling the bite as it pierced his palm.

"Because I love you. I love you."

He lashed the belt one more time, but she'd pulled her legs up and wrapped herself into a tight ball, her whole body locked down. He reached out and grabbed the back of her neck, pulling her slightly up, and turned her, put both his hands around her throat, and squeezed.

"I love you." She clawed at his hands. Her artificial nails breaking. "Please don't kill me. I love you. Think. The police will send you back to jail." She managed to grip his thumb and attempted to lessen the pressure. "The–gangs…get–you… again. You–worked– so…hard—" she said, but the last words choked out.

She lay there, not moving.

He pulled back and then rocked back onto his feet, still kneeling.

The gangs would get him.

He spat on the carpet.

Fuck – she was right.

A wife beaten to death would be noticed. The whores he'd killed along the way, no one cared about, but his wife, the woman he married…the gang

25

would find him again, and pull him back in. Despite the years, you never got away from a prison gang. Not unless you were smart like he was.

"Fucking hell," he said, dropping the belt and running his bloody hands through his hair.

He brought both hands down on her chest, and jerked her head back, breathing into her mouth. Six breaths. He rocked back to thump her chest.

She coughed and took a ragged breath.

He moved to let her go.

She turned on her side, drawing her legs back up into a fetal position.

He ran his hands over his chest. For so many years he'd covered up his roots, but he had nearly blown that. And for what?

Because of his latest trade. The one side of the transaction.

His client had wanted a young Japanese Geisha Doll to play with.

He had told his team to go get a tourist's kid. Easy money.

And his incompetent employees had snatched an anti-corruption billionaire's daughter.

Levi remembered the day he walked away from the correctional services facility of Polokwane and breathed the air on the outside of the tall fences for the first time in years like it was yesterday.

He climbed into the back seat.

The taxi driver was obviously a regular — he could see the thick wooden knobkerrie next to the driver. Solid wood. He suspected there was an illegal handgun stashed in the door too. Loaded and ready. Just in case. Given he was a prison pickup, there were no other people in the taxi — a rarity in South Africa.

Levi cleared his throat. "Change of address. Take me to the China Motel on 2nd Avenue and I'll give you an extra few rand."

The taxi driver shook his head. "My instructions from the prison are to take you to the halfway house. I'll start a new fare when you come out. I can take you wherever you want to go as long as you pay upfront. That's how it works."

Levi nodded and sat back.

Not worth reacting to the taxi driver or his arrogant nature.

He was another wanker who thought that he could tell Levi what to do.

He had earned the spider tattoo in prison for a good reason.

He would wait. Plot revenge. Finally get it. He was ultra-patient.

It was best to keep calm, fit in and lay low until he could disappear and make a new life for himself.

Reinvention was going to be the key. He was going to become Levi Louw. No one would ever remember Lukas Le Roux.

He needed a computer. That was the way to get people to do everything. He had seen the future while serving time for poaching in the Marakele National Park.

It was time he became more than the bullet.

He needed to be the gun — the kingpin.

After he sorted out his father.

He'd paid with his soul in prison for hunting bush meat to sell, taking the blame for his own father.

But it was not all in vain.

He took a picture of the woman from his pocket. Eric Garner was a dipshit and didn't even realize what he'd thrown away when his love of easy money got the better of his dick. Taking the picture from the ex-conman had been easy.

If he wanted something, he got it.

Simple as that.

But getting Eric to talk about her. That'd taken time and patience. Eventually, he'd known every sordid detail of Eric's miserable life. He knew all about Chrystal: the amazing woman of the land, who could rope a buffalo like a cowboy, dressed like an angel, and could fuck all night like she couldn't get enough.

Eric would never return to sneak-a-peak at his lost love. The spineless wimp was dead without a single tattoo. Never rebelling against authority, that was the "system" that attempted to hold the men. Even in jail, not everyone was designed to wear stars of authority, *Tjappies*, as epaulets on their shoulders in prison.

He had three to go with his original hidden fangs tattooed on the inside of his lips that signified that he could bite, and later, his spider web for patience. Every outlined character on his chest showed his quick escalation in status while a prisoner. Dug in with scraps of an old guitar wire sharpened on the bricks, and ink made by mixing brick dust, with burned paper and rubber with his own saliva.

Eric died with no *Tjappies* art. Choosing not to join a gang was dangerous.

27

Joining a prison gang was dangerous too. It was said you never left.

He would test that now that he was out. Fuck them too.

"I'm coming to you, my Chrystal. One day you'll know me. One day."

He looked out the window but got distracted by the reflection of himself instead. He traced the tip of his finger over his latest tattoo at the base of his neck, still red around the edges, the black ink raised with swelling.

Anyone who knew rocks would think it was a facetted diamond.

He knew better.

It had been no sacrifice on his part to mark himself for her already.

One day, she would be his.

CHAPTER 4

Cape Town, South Africa

"Time to get out. My boss wants to meet you," a man said as he pulled her from the animal crate she'd been locked in. At first, she'd rattled the cage door and tried hard to move it so she could get out.

She'd screamed until she had no voice. The hoarseness hurt, bringing blood into her mouth.

She had cried. Until she had no more tears left to wring from her body.

No one heard.

No one came.

It was all in vain.

The hours and days blurred past. Her only glimpse into the outside was through the door when it was open to let in the woman who fed her. She could see that it had thick bolts in the concrete floor and a thick padlock on the bolt that kept her inside.

Caged.

The crate was only just tall enough for her to stand up in; it brushed against her hair in one place where there was a dent in the metal bars. It was longer than it was higher. She could almost lay herself twice across, but not quite. She had measured. She suspected it might have previously been a pig's cage. She'd seen a TV program about pig production and how a farm used to keep the mother pigs in such a crate to keep her nice and fat, and how they'd then let the mums out into a bigger space, as well as outside when the farm went organic and free-range. Her father had said, "One person's opinion and actions can change the world," and she'd believed him.

Now, not so much.

No amount of caring how much space a pig or a chicken had when you were being held captive in one of their cages would make a difference.

The man half-carried, half frog-marched her up the stairs and into the room above. His body odor was strongly mixed with herbs of some sort.

Her legs were wobbly, for while she could stand in her cage, she seldom bothered, sitting instead on her blanket. Waiting for the next time the door opened and she could get a glimpse of her surroundings before everything went dark again. Hoping that soon her father would send soldiers to find her, and she would be home. Safe.

She shielded her eyes as she struggled to adapt to the bright light.

The man was dressed in long loose trousers and a tunic top, and he didn't wear any headgear. His beard was grey. On his black skin it shone like silver.

He shoved her forward.

She fell on her knees.

A white man pulled her up by her arm. His fingers bit into her skin. She could smell his expensive cologne. She recognized its musky scent, but not well enough to name it. His boots were polished with a black shine to them, as if he took great pride in his appearance.

She lifted her head and looked up at him. He was cleanly shaven, and his hair was slicked back, accenting that it was thinning in the front. The suit he wore wasn't hand-tailored like her father's, but she could tell it was expensive.

The man had money. Or the illusion of it.

She glanced around the room. It didn't say money at all. A shabby sofa sat to one side with a TV on a stack of pallets. There were lights strung up without being properly installed, and a musty unwashed smell.

"Is it true you're Curtis Wilson's daughter?" the white man asked.

She kept quiet.

He smacked her across her face with the back of his hand. The force dropped her back to her knees.

What just happened?

He had hit her.

No one had ever struck her before. No one.

Disbelief that he'd slapped her made her freeze.

Her ears rang.

The burn on her cheek was nothing like a bee sting. This was a new type of pain she had never known.

She could feel where her neck muscles had pulled from the viciousness of the smack.

Her knees hurt where they had connected with the concrete.

She lifted her head.

He backhanded the other side of her face. This time it was even harder and she fell sideways. There was instant pain on her cheek. Like fire.

"Shit!" he said. "Do you think I wanted to scar that face with my ring? Answer me!"

She lifted her hand, and the searing pain in her cheek intensified. She brought her hand away and could see red. Blood.

Akina struggled to form words to answer, unable to comprehend exactly what was happening. She was trying to answer, but it was as if her voice had been stolen from her.

"Answer me, Akina. That's your name, isn't it? Answer me or we can keep going with the discipline."

She looked at the floor. Tears that she couldn't control rolled down her face. Realization that he'd actually struck her.

Not once.

Twice.

Only bullies turn to violence when they are unable to win any other way, her father's voice boomed in her head.

These men were larger than her. Stronger.

This round she knew she couldn't win. Now was not the time to fight.

She nodded.

The salt from her tears ran into the cut on her face and burnt the shame into her cheeks for submitting to him. Humiliation for being treated like an animal.

"Is it true that you can speak multiple languages?"

She raised her eyes to look at him. His hand was ready for another backhand.

Another cut.

She quickly answered. "Yes."

"And you're eleven years old?"

She nodded.

"Fuck!" he said.

She looked down at the bare concrete floor. In the corner of her eye, she could see a skin of some sort covering part of it. Its brown and white speckled hair wasn't from an animal she was familiar with. A little further along were two guns propped up in the corner. From the TV, she could tell one was a shotgun because it had two barrels, and the other one she thought perhaps was an AK47 because it had a curved magazine. Not that it made a difference to her, she didn't know how to use either, even if her legs were stronger and she could get to them. As she was, she could hardly hold herself upright, even though she was in a heap on the floor.

"Don't do anything stupid, or I will hurt you more," the white man said. "I might not like doing it, but it's for your own good."

She looked at him; his face showed no emotion when he said it.

The man was a liar.

He enjoyed hurting her.

The tell was the throb of his skin beside his eye. She had seen that tell in a man playing poker with her dad before. He'd been lying too. Blood and pulsing in veins always gave someone away. That was a visceral reaction the man couldn't control. Her father had taught her that.

"Get her out of here. Keep her locked up for now. Don't attempt to move her until the media frenzy dies down. They'll give up eventually, and then we move her north. Make sure that wound is cleaned; we can't have this type of Starling damaged. And make sure she starts doing some exercise, we can't have her so weak she can't stand up. Increase her food; she looks like an Ethiopian from the 1980s. I need to contact someone about moving this Starling. Now we know who she is, she'll be even more valuable in the long run, to the right people."

"My daddy will send soldiers to kill you," she said, lifting her chin.

"Really? And how will he find you?" the white man asked.

Akina stared at him.

The white man looked at the silver-bearded man. "What did you do with her watch and phone?"

"Tossed it in the sea, like you said."

There was silence, and when the white man spoke again his voice was pitched higher in excitement. "She's too sure that she'll be rescued. She must have a GPS tracker implanted." He clicked his fingers together and pointed to the dark room. "Get her back underground. Go get a microchip machine from a vet. Find it and cut it out. And make sure she gets a bath — she stinks."

CHAPTER 5

Leopard Hill Farm, Thabazimbi, Limpopo Province

12th March 2016

Nosipho Calio grinned. The old barn on Leopard Hill looked perfect for what she needed. She could bring in some long tables and stack the wooden cases against the back wall. There was plenty of space to build *ikhayas* outside for her workers, for the people assembling the weapons to live and not have to leave the farm. Loose lips created problems and the less reason her small staff had to leave the farm and talk to the locals the better.

She was no stranger to farm life. There was a time before she became maCalio, before she had money and power when she lived in Gazankulu, the apartheid government's black homeland for the Tsonga people. Before she had become maNtuli's second in command.

Power. It was a fickle thing. She only had power because people feared her.

Because she could control their money.

And she could control them with threats and violence.

Her track record proved that. Her position ensured everyone knew it too.

Holding the old *knobkerrie* tightly, she pulled the big corrugated iron door open. She would never go anywhere without her grandfather's fighting stick. She flooded the barn with as much natural light as she could, as the salesman had told her that the electricity was off. He also had said that one old *úgógo* lived on the farm in her own rondavel, and he'd suggested that even if maCalio bought it, the old woman be allowed to remain, as she was rumored to be a sangoma.

Even *she* didn't mess with the spirits and the ancestors.

A sangoma needed to be shown respect, or that would bring problems of its own.

Anyway, having a sangoma on the premises might prove useful. If the rumor was true, she would have to step carefully with the woman and ensure a few changes took place while keeping the witch doctor on her side.

maCalio walked inside and her skin goose-bumped at the temperature change.

She held her finger up under her nose, blocking out the smell. There were piles of bird poop splatted on the concrete floor. She looked upwards and noticed the exposed beams and the hole in the roof. Big enough for a medium-sized bird to come in, use the barn as its own private sanctuary, and big enough to destroy her merchandise if she didn't fix it first.

Dung could be scrubbed off. Sunlight soap and elbow grease never hurt anyone.

She walked around the perimeter of the inside of the building, making sure it was secure and made with bricks from the bottom to the halfway point the whole way around. Everything looked intact, there were no gaping holes that any inquisitive child could climb through.

At the back of the barn, an assortment of hand tools for farming still hung on the wall, their black outline drawn onto the grey concrete blocks. "Safe place if those haven't been stolen," she said aloud.

Her voice didn't echo. There was a muffled quality to it instead as if the room was ready to keep secrets.

A good sign.

She nodded slowly and walked back to the large doors. Pulling them closed behind her, she walked along the path between the sheds and the farmhouse. She glanced left when she heard a rustle and looked into the blue eyes of an extremely matted ragdoll cat. It had no collar to identify that it belonged to anyone. It had a chunk of its ear cut out, a sure sign that once it had been neutered or spayed. Marked by a vet.

"Here cat-cat," she said, clicking her fingers.

The cat looked at her and meowed with a broken yowling sound, but it did not come toward her.

She pushed the key that was labeled 'front' into the door of the house and it didn't move, but a shoulder against the door to shove it inwards was all it needed. Dust fairies danced across the room from the curtain-less windows and descended toward the wooden floor. It was as clean as could be expected, and the place looked structurally sound.

She would have a place to stay when she visited here to check firsthand on things when she wasn't busy doing maNtuli's business in Johannesburg.

Another yowl came from behind her as the cat brushed up against her legs, welcoming her into its territory. Then it walked toward the kitchen. It hissed and ran back to her, threading itself between her legs. She reached down to pet it but instead of purring and becoming friends, it swiped a paw, scratching her hand.

"*Eina, bliksem* you cat. Get out." She stamped her foot and clapped her hands making a noise to scare the cat.

The cat yelled again and moved away between her and the kitchen cupboard. It hissed again before it ran back toward her. It growled. She stepped backward.

It turned toward the door, making its way out.

"Typical cat," she said, "as fickle as anything, even if you are a beautiful thing."

Still holding her hand and dabbing at the blood with a tissue, she took a few steps toward the kitchen, but the cat ran in between her and the kitchen door again.

Growling.

"Cat?" she said, "I need to look inside, see how much I need to renovate in there as the property agent said that the kitchen is old and needs some attention."

She took another step forward and the cat growled again. It turned and the hair on its back that was not matted, stood on end as it hissed.

She stopped.

Something was wrong.

Very wrong.

Slowly she backed up as the cat did too. Still growling, although it had turned from a loud vocal growl into more of a soft, steady sound of happiness now that she was doing what it was telling her to do.

She looked past the cat into the kitchen and saw a large snake slipping over the lino floor toward them.

The rock python was the biggest she'd ever seen.

Its dark, painted skin rippled as it moved. Hypnotized, she watched the dappled markings. Its black tongue flickered in and out of its fat head, scenting the air then tasting it. Dull eyes unmoving.

Snakes were one of the reasons she hated living rural.

Even in a city, people in South Africa had the occasional snake in the garden, but the chances of seeing one here were much greater.

Slowly, she backed out the front door.

The cat turned, dashed out across the wooden floor of the entry hall, and out, only it didn't stop on the small veranda as she had, but went up into the fever tree close by, despite the thorns. Climbing high to the top branches where the weight of the snake wouldn't support it. Among the many weavers' nests.

The birds erupted in chatter and came out of the nests, dive-bombing the cat.

"You and that snake have crossed paths before I take it. So that's what you were trying to tell me, that the *nyoga* was in the house!" she said, her heart still thumping and her hands a little shaky.

Keeping the snake in her sight, she watched as the fat reptile inched out the door, slid down the three steps, and onto the ground. It sashayed over the sand and gradually disappeared into the knee-high grass. Without much help, it was soon camouflaged by the brown and green stalks. Other than leaving its tracks of passage in the dry loose soil, she wouldn't know it was there if she hadn't seen it with her own eyes.

"Guess we will have to deal with him another day," she said, and the cat howled again. "You are very talkative for a cat."

The cat looked at her and climbed down the tree. Picking its way back through the branches, it at last jumped to the ground, then swishing its tail, it walked back into the house as if it knew it was now safe and a place they could enter. The birds continued to sound their alarm calls.

She followed the cat. "I guess I will have to forgive you for the scratches. You were trying to warn me. You remind me of a story I got to read with my daughter, Rulleh. It was about a snake and a Mongoose. Rikki-Tick-Tavi. It's from the story of the Jungle Book." She followed the cat into the kitchen. The cat purred and jumped on the counter. "I am really glad you did not try and fight that *nyoga*. He was too big. Sometimes, waiting is a good thing, not acting and living to fight another day is wise."

She reached out her hand and the cat knocked its head against it. If it was possible, it purred louder.

She looked around the kitchen. An old Esse stove and no cupboard doors, with a cement polished floor. It would need to be replaced if she was going to live in the house. The cat jumped off the counter and walked through to the dining room.

She followed. "You knew that *nyoga* was in here, maybe you are a good cat, and you keep the *tokoloshe* away," she said, looking out the window at the barn, at how it blended into its environment. It wasn't about to stick out and scream illegal behavior to anyone — it looked like any other farmhouse.

This place could be perfect for the ghost guns operation. Perfect.

She was glad that she had insisted on coming alone and not with the salesman. She could tell him it was bad and see how much more he would knock off.

The cat looked at her as if it could understand her thoughts. Then licked its paw, cleaning itself, disinterested in its human once again.

Farms like this, they were too large for a hobby farm, too small for a real farm, but the space — it was what she needed.

The ideal place for the weapons part of the business.

"Come on, my good luck cat Rikki. You and I have the rest of this house to look at. I could do with some time away from the rat race of Johannesburg."

She clicked her fingers and walked purposefully into the bedroom section.

Once she'd finished the tour, she could see that while it was old, it was functional enough. She locked the house up behind her and the security gate, then taking the *knobkerrie* from near the door where she'd left it, she looked out at the barn again and saw a small building next to it that she hadn't noticed before. Walking over slowly, she tried the wooden door.

It was locked. There was a bolt on the door and a new shiny padlock. She looked for the keys on the bunch the salesman had given to her but couldn't find one that would fit. She walked around looking to see if there was a window.

There wasn't.

She put her ear to the door and listened.

No sound.

But she had a feeling deep in her stomach, one that told her that it was important that she know what was inside this smaller building.

On the outside she could see a tap, and while there was no water dripping, there was bright green grass from the runoff and a patch where there had obviously been a puddle. A few buckets, a cooking pot and pan, and a few enamel plates rested against the building and a small cooking fire with a grid on it was close by. Two blankets spread to dry on the low bushes that had been recently washed — they were new, she could still see the soft pile.

Putting her hand above the coals, she could feel a slight warmth, it had been used within the last twenty-four hours or even less. She wouldn't want to dig in the ashes as they might burn her.

She looked along the well-worn path leading away and saw a traditional outhouse built from sticks with thatch making a roughly round shield with no roof. Walking to it, she covered her nose with her hand. There was no door, just a roughly constructed long drop toilet that flies buzzed around, signaling it was still in use.

The sangoma was a resident of the farm.

She had something that needed protecting locked in the barn.

It didn't matter for now, but maNtuli and she would know everything that went on here when the place was bought.

The cat trailed behind her as she walked back to her 4 x 4.

"Rikki, are you coming to be cleaned up or staying here until I buy the place and get you brushed locally?" she asked.

The cat jumped into her open door and went to sit on the passenger seat as if it was used to vehicles and going places.

Driving away, she smiled, not a little one, but one like the Cheshire cat from the book about the Queen of Hearts that she had read with her daughter before she died.

Now there was a woman of power.

She even changed nature to suit herself, by painting the roses red.

CHAPTER 6

Pandora Timbers Mission Orphanage, Thabazimbi, South Africa

21ˢᵗ March 2016 — 40 days until auction

Mother Stella-Rose Naude knelt on the polished floor in her office, bent over at the hips, her head bowed into her arms that rested on the cool cement. The hands of the analog clock on the wall were pointing heavenwards. It was precisely 12:00. It had been drilled into her since she joined the Zuga Mission Church as an aspirant years ago to pray at midday.

She raised herself up until she was only on her knees. Slowly she took one bead at a time on her *perle sacre*, the beautifully made purple-plated prayer necklace. Praying on each of the three beads. She bowed her head before her simple wooden cross on the wall. She didn't need to look at it to know it dwarfed both her and her humble office. It constantly reminded her that she was a sinner.

Her lips moved slowly as she mouthed the words, "Forgive me. Forgive me for wanting to be *Divina-Saint*." While this meant divine saint in Italian, her church had adopted it to mean saint-like — one to be forever remembered and exulted, and she was fine with that definition.

Perhaps then her family would take more notice of her, and less of Chrystal.

Perhaps if she amassed enough money for her church, made enough of a difference to the good of the congregation, like Mother Theresa, they would forgive her small trespasses.

Mother Theresa saved the babies from the gutters in Calcutta but didn't give the mothers the contraception needed to stop them from happening.

She was saving the children. Sacrificing the lives of a few, to give many more a better life.

"Forgive me for my ambition. For wanting to be near you in the eternity. I know that I suffer from greed and want to make a better place for myself and my sisters, and I know that I must work harder to create forgiveness here on earth and pay penance here before I can join you. Because of your mercy and love, despite my faults and failures, I am forever your servant."

Stella-Rose waited for a while. Contemplating her prayer. If she was a *Divina-Saint*, she would forever be acknowledged by all. Not only by those at *Saliebos* who didn't see her.

But to get there she needed devoted and dedicated followers on earth. She needed to grow them and make them believe in what she was doing. Those who would bring attention to the good she did.

She would be remembered forever.

While Chrystal would be forgotten.

"Sister Mary-Jane's a good person. Please forgive her for all her trespasses. Forgive her for her over-indulging in food and showing a gluttonous sin. It's not her fault. She hasn't learned yet to trust you that you will provide for those who believe."

She gave a passing thought to how she could help Mary-Jane understand that there would always be food with her in charge.

"Forgive Sister Marguerite for over-indulged pride. Wanting to make everything pretty and beautiful for you. Forgive our visiting Brother Andrew, for being deceitful and pretending to be oblivious to the heat, even though he's obviously hot and not used to the altitude and sun.

"Forgive Sister Vannini, for her blind faith in me, and thank you for sending her to help make my job easier. Our Sisters serve you. It's only through your grace that we can ascend to heaven. Everything I do, I do by the grace of God. Everything in the name of the Father, Son and Holy Spirit."

She crossed her hand over her chest and made the sign of the cross from top to bottom, left to right. She kissed the last bead at the end of her *perle sacre*, placing it around her neck, and pushed up, letting her dark blue robes

0

fall. Waited while the cramps eased out of her knees before walking toward her desk. There was work to be done, the mission, orphanage and school didn't run itself, and the administration and coordination of it all was her responsibility.

Striving to be a *Divina-Saint* and ascend into heaven to be with her God didn't come easily.

It took hard work.

Courage.

Sacrifice.

A knock at the door interrupted her thoughts.

"Come in."

Sister Vannini entered and then bowed deeply. "Mother Naude, there's a Mr. Levi Louw here to see you."

"You may show him in." Stella-Rose said brightly as she put her hands underneath her work desk. Damnation, why would he be coming to her office in broad daylight? "And Sister, please bring us some tea."

Sister Vannini bowed again.

The man who walked into her office was of average height — he was one of those men who would fit into any crowd anywhere. His hair was cropped short and he possessed an ordinary face. His clothes were expensive and classic cut and hung well but nothing to suggest overly what type of person he truly was.

If you looked closer, you would see a small section of a tattoo sticking up above the collar of his pinstriped blue shirt where his tie was done in a perfect Windsor knot. Despite the heat, long sleeves covered arms she knew were covered in tattoos. Just as he'd covered up his criminal past with his new name, his prison brands were carefully concealed.

But people didn't change that much, though they tried to hide behind a facade of money and possessions. This man was still a poacher, it was the animals he hunted that had changed — and where in the pecking order he believed himself to be.

Behind the blank stare was a complicated man, fighting his own immortal demons. A man drowning in his own sins. His soul bargained to the devil a long time ago.

One of her many marionettes necessary to run her mission.

He was the means to the end.

The man who controlled the muscle; who did what she was unable to do in her exalted position, but what needed to be done for the good of her church and the community that it serviced.

She took a deep breath and let it out slowly.

This man shouldn't have disobeyed a direct order — never to come to the farm in the daytime. While he was known to travel, her mission was far from convenient to visit.

He should have picked up a phone and called.

He was becoming disrespectful.

His attitude was changing. His ambition to assert his control, slowly poking its head out above the dung pile.

She needed to slap that back down. Reconfirm exactly who was in charge.

Unfortunately, he was a man who knew too many of her secrets.

A man who would deliver more Starlings for her today. But in doing that, would create more of a possibility that she could be seated on the right hand of God, as a *Divina-Saint*, if she kept her cool around him.

She took another deep breath and purposely did not stand as he walked up to her desk. "Levi Louw." She didn't bother putting her hand out in greeting. He hated to be touched.

She knew he loathed her using his full name too. He preferred to be addressed as simply Mister, if she gave him a choice.

It was time to start bringing him back down to size. One small act at a time.

"Mother."

She was used to one-word sentences from him, it had been that way since he'd entered her life.

"Sit." She motioned to the visitor's chair.

"Obliged," he said, pushing an envelope that he'd removed from his pocket across the table toward her.

She didn't insult him by looking inside while he was there. She knew it would be correct to the last untraceable US dollar. In all their dealings during the previous six years, he'd never once shortchanged her. If there was one thing she could trust him with, it was that he always brought her complete share of the Starlings' spoils. Always cash. She slid it into her top drawer and silently closed it, before looking at him. "You'd better have a good reason for coming to Pandora Timbers in daylight."

"Leopard Hill farm has sold. The Doll needs to move," Levi said, still not sitting.

She knew that he was trying to be intimidating by towering above her. She held her ground. "And this news couldn't have been told to me on a telephone?"

"It must be done now. Today. The one who bought it, her name is Nosipho Calio, people call her maCalio. She's the right hand of maNtuli's crime syndicate in Johannesburg. She's feared by all, even the Nigerians."

"And?" She put her hands back under the table where they wouldn't betray her anger — she wanted to bash the top of her desk, instead she stayed silent, waiting for him to talk.

"maNtuli and maCalio run guns, drugs and prostitution, and don't deal well with competition. More importantly — she's openly opposed to child trafficking." He appeared to want her to acknowledge that phrase, but she kept silent.

"Starlings," he said.

She nodded. This was her term, she never uttered the first one.

"She's been known to interfere in other shebeens and brothels, not owned by her, to save the younger kids from working there," he finished.

Stella-Rose rolled her eyes. "She seems like a bit of a contradiction to me. A gangster with a selective conscience."

"She's …dangerous. You'll also need to move that sangoma on. She cannot stay anywhere near maCalio. That one, she's strong for an old woman, but not as forceful as maCalio. maCalio will find out what was happening there, and she'll break us."

"Break me?" Mother Naude asked. "How exactly can this Calio do this?" Deliberately not giving her 'ma' as her title of respect.

"Those who don't die by her gang, die by her poison. She studied chemistry at university before she—"

She clicked her tongue. "She's an educated gangster?"

"More than that. Ruthless. Calculating. Mean, is what I hear about her."

She looked at his face, trying hard to see if the tell-tale tick in his eye was twitching like it always did when he lied to her. It wasn't.

She had to take this seriously. He was scared.

"Is that a threat to me?"

"A warning. I've seen what she can do. We need to be careful. What we have built, what we have achieved, she could bring it all down if she pokes her nose in."

"There is nothing to link the farm to us. This isn't a big enough threat for you to have shown your face here, in daylight. Why did you break the rules so blatantly?" Her voice-controlled and low, hiding the emotional turmoil she felt inside.

"I have visited The Japanese Doll. She's still defiant, not submissive like the other girls. I'm not sure of this plan you have to fly her out of Gaborone anymore. She's not compliant like the others before her have been. She'll expose us as soon as she gets a chance. She's not a typical child that one."

"Already we have kept her too long in South Africa. She needs to move," Stella-Rose said.

He shook his head. "She will not break. I don't think we have ever had such a headstrong one to deal with before."

She hated the children being referred to as anything but Starlings. And what happened was secret. Necessary. Referring to them as anything other than Starlings was dangerous. Levi was attempting to manipulate her again. "You have never had an educated Starling before. That's the difference. Every Starling has a breaking point." She emphasized the word, before she got up and walked to her window.

She knew how to control other children, she did it all the time in the orphanage. She had learned that lesson early in her life. Caring for someone meant weakness where they were concerned.

But giving this information to a man like Levi — there could be carnage.

However, this child was too valuable not to use the quickest method to get her under control. Her mind made up, she turned back to him, her hands hidden inside her robes. "When I was eleven, I would have done anything for my chosen sister. Anything. Has she made a friend at all among the other girls?"

"No, we have kept her isolated."

"Give her a friend to talk to. To bond with. Sometimes it's not force that breaks a girl's spirit. She obviously has a belief in herself that she's a good person. Give her a friend, and she'll think she's responsible for her too. Then make her doubt herself. Threaten harm to the friend's personage, and follow through with that threat, and you'll control The Doll."

"I'll give it a try," he said in the same flat voice.

Stella-Rose knew he wanted her permission to beat the girl, but her one stipulation after his initial attack on the American kid was that he didn't harm her in any way — she was too valuable. She hoped he understood that now, but somewhere inside, she knew he simply didn't care and was itching to take a *sjambok* to her and flog the snot out of the girl, like he did to the other kids who showed an inch of defiance.

But she would never give him permission to do that.

Not on this one.

The money they stood to receive for a perfect child was too great.

This child in particular had value.

He might have blundered into possessing her, but now that they had her... the bids would come in and they would be higher than any other child on the market.

"If we can't fly her, then you need to think about having someone leave soon and push through to Maputo," Stella-Rose said. "Have them catch one of the cargo ships there and go up through the Suez Canal. It'll take about twenty-one days by ship, give or take a day. Your alternative is to drive twelve thousand kilometers, around one hundred and eighty hours, to get to Tripoli on time for the original cargo ship. This might prove difficult. It includes trying to cross Sudan without any upsets. The auction is set for Saturday 30th April. Either way you have forty days to keep your end of the bargain. Get her to Venice and to auction."

"What about the other Starlings already in Gaborone?"

"Stick to the original plan. They go by air to Tripoli, and then cargo ship to Venice. Sister Vannini will accompany them as usual. We know that once they're in the church accommodation, they won't go anywhere on their own."

"And if The Doll gives Tahaan trouble while transporting her?"

"Deal with it. Get her to Venice, with no cuts, no bruises. She must not be harmed."

"Fine." His manner was sullen. He knew she'd stopped short of giving the permission he sought.

"Be warned, make sure you get everything sorted, because even with the transportation this month, there will be two Starlings to collect from the old ruins for the domestic market as normal. Their adoption papers were signed today."

"Two? On the same day?" he asked.

"It's not like we haven't done that before. There's an order that needs filling. Make sure you and your team are ready for both the pickup and delivery. None of us can afford any more hiccups. Understood?"

"Yes, Mother. I'll make it work. As always," he said. "My team won't let you down."

Sister Vannini knocked, then opened the door.

He strode out, leaving her holding the tray.

"Men!" Stella-Rose said. "Mr. Louw said he didn't want tea, he has to be at another meeting, but you're welcome to share with me, so we don't waste it."

An hour later, Stella-Rose sat on her chair staring at the Lord's cross on her wall. Questions running through her head.

Why now? When Minister Thulas Masutha was getting greedy, pressing me for more Starlings and faster delivery?

She needed him, and his diplomatic ties for the international auctions that brought in higher prices. It was because of him she'd turned a profit faster on her commodities.

He was the one with the contacts.

The one who at first had known about the auctions overseas and the highway up Africa for trading.

But times were changing on that too.

Soon he too would be obsolete.

The sacrificing of a few for the good of many.

Her path to heaven was clearing even faster.

The number of legitimate international adoptions was up, so her little mission orphanage looked good.

But with Leopard Hill closing its access, she was going to lose one of her safest holding areas. False information spread about that farm had worked well to engrain in the local population to keep away. Superstitions were just as strong today and always in South Africa, witchcraft was both revered and feared. They could find another place...

Her mind went into damage control.

Where can I move my latest precious Starling?

Unfortunately, it was only because of Levi that she even had that cargo to trade — this time. He'd come gloating when he'd snatched a valuable one, instead of a ragdoll for his disgusting client.

But it was Sister Vannini's words at teatime that swirled around her head next.

The same words that Chrystal had said. *"You can always count on me."*

Years blurred as she raced into another time, when life wasn't as complicated as it had become as an adult.

They were on their first day of camping by the dam and the wind blew hard against the side of the tent.

"I'm going to the bathroom," Chrystal said.

Stella-Rose shoved the toilet paper and a small spade in her hand. "Remember what your grandfather said: dig deep despite the hard-dry earth."

Being teenagers hadn't meant they weren't still told what to do by Ben and her mother when they were out in the bush alone.

"Sure," Chrystal said, taking them and opening the zip on the front of the tent. She got out and went to find a clearing.

Stella-Rose followed her out. She made her way to the firepit from the night before. Their deck chairs had been blown over, and the blankets that had been on them lay on the ground. Chrystal had left her shoes there too.

Stella-Rose put her hand above the coals. Still warm. It wouldn't take too much to bring it back to life. She shivered against the strong wind and the cool morning air. She snagged one of the blankets, and wrapped herself, before she added some logs, pushed in kindling and paper, and watched the fire flicker to life.

She took the empty kettle to the table they had set up under the tree. Filling it with water, she decided that they could have cookies too and went hunting in the 'pantry'.

"In the last bag, typical," Stella-Rose said to herself as she went back to get the kettle. She turned around.

The fire was huge. Too big for the fire pit.

The chairs and blankets were on fire.

It was already in the trees behind the tent.

"Chrystal," she screamed. "Fire! Fire!"

She ran around the flames and called again. "Fire!"

Stella-Rose heard Chrystal call back, her voice a little distance away. "Where?"

She looked again at the fire and realized that the wind was blowing it directly toward her.

"Oh my god, run! Run! Chrystal, run!" Stella-Rose screamed as she sprinted toward where Chrystal was still pulling her pajama pants up, spade in one hand and toilet paper in the other. Her blue eyes were huge in her face as she stared at the fire closing in on them.

"Run!" Stella-Rose screamed. "Run fast."

Together they fled.

The fire gave chase.

The smell of smoke rolled before them, shrouding the bushveld and blurring her vision. Despite coughing deeply, they kept running.

They had no choice.

A stop would mean being burnt alive.

They came to the road. Stella-Rose stopped and looked left and right to orientate herself.

Chrystal said, "We head for the reservoir. Khulu will come find us. Run. Keep running."

Moving on the road was easier than through the bush, but the wind brought the flames closer as they ran almost parallel to it. Small pieces of thatched grass and twigs rained down. Embers were still alight as the wind pushed the flames and the heat ever closer.

The reservoir came into sight. As did a herd of cattle running toward them.

Wild with fright. Panicked by the fire.

"Faster," screamed Chrystal.

Slowly the distance between them increased.

"Don't leave me!" Stella-Rose shouted.

Chrystal slowed, reached back, and grabbed her hand. Chrystal dragged her behind, as she was the faster runner. Stella-Rose tried hard to increase the length of her stride and keep up.

The cattle were gaining ground.

They got to the reservoir and rushed to the far side, just as the cattle split around it, and continued to stampede into the bush on the other side.

Chrystal knelt down. "Stand on me and get up, then pull me up. We have to get in the water."

Stella-Rose clambered on top of Chrystal. She put her elbows on the edge of the concrete. "Higher."

Chrystal lifted herself up, and Stella-Rose walked her feet up Chrystal's back using the reservoir's concrete to help take some of the weight. Then she was on her shoulders and could climb up. She lay on her stomach on the edge of the water tank and held both her arms toward Chrystal.

Grabbing hard, Chrystal pulled. Clambered up the side of the concrete, and eventually, she put her arm over the edge. Stella-Rose clutched her pajama bottoms and pulled with all her might to help her the rest of the way.

"Get in!" Chrystal shouted as she dived into the water.

Stella-Rose hesitated.

"Jump in!" Chrystal called when she re-surfaced. "It's freezing cold but it's better than burning in the fire."

Stella-Rose shook her head.

Looked at the water.

Back at the fire.

The heat intensified. Her clothes felt like they would melt onto her body. "You know that I can't. I still can't swim."

"I'll hold you up. I promise. Trust me." She swam toward Stella-Rose and grabbed her leg and began pulling. "Get in or you'll burn."

A noise that sounded like a freight train coming toward them caused Stella-Rose to freeze.

Although they could see the fire approaching, they didn't expect to feel the heat so intensely when it arrived.

Chrystal tugged hard on Stella-Rose. She fell in.

Her head went under the water.

She swallowed mouthfuls.

The water was going into her nose. In her mouth.

It was everywhere.

Stella-Rose opened her eyes to try see and it was an opaque green.

She couldn't see Chrystal.

And then, her head was above water. Chrystal was holding her up — holding her against her chest as she made her way toward the side.

"You have to move your hands and feet like this, like what I'm doing. We can hold the side when the fire gets too hot, go under, and then come back up," Chrystal said.

Stella-Rose could feel the green slime that coated the inside of the water reservoir. The frogs that were there dived downwards and out of their way.

Chrystal put her hand higher on the concrete. "Grip the side with both hands."

Blinking. Her heart beat wildly. Stella-Rose held on.

"Kick your boots off, they've filled with water," Chrystal said.

Stella-Rose got them off and immediately felt lighter. They didn't float up but sunk to the bottom of the abyss.

"That's it. When I say go under you mustn't hesitate. I'll hold your hand while we hide. Take a deep breath and then we go. Count slowly to twenty and come up. Hopefully, the fire will pass over us fast. If it doesn't, take another breath and we keep doing that until we know it's passed. Okay?"

Stella-Rose nodded.

"We can do this. We can do it together," Chrystal urged, giving her hand a squeeze.

She nodded again.

"Here it comes. Feel the heat in the wind, take a breath—"

Stella-Rose sucked in a breath and felt Chrystal pull her under. One. Two. Three. She kept her eyes tight shut. Eight. Nine. Ten. Not seeing anything. The top of her head got hotter. Nineteen. Twenty. She was being pulled up again. She took another breath.

Chrystal dunked them under again.

Her chest burned. She opened her eyes to the greenness beneath.

Chrystal pulled them upwards.

They surfaced.

The fire was gone, as was the heat. Holding on the side, she looked around. They were behind the fire line. The fire had jumped over them and now tore through the bushveld, toward the farmstead. Around them, trees still burnt, but it was a gentler burn, not the inferno that was inside the wind of swirling fire and embers that had come through first.

"You okay?" Chrystal asked as she used her arms to lift herself out of the water and sat on the side of the concrete edging.

Stella-Rose didn't have the strength yet to hold tight, let alone clamber out. "I'm okay."

"Wow, that was scary. It could have killed us!"

Chrystal grabbed Stella-Rose's arm and helped her up onto the side. "Where on earth did that fire come from?"

Tears filled Stella-Rose's eyes. "I restarted the fire from last night, then went to get water for the kettle. When I turned back, it was out of the pit and onto our chairs and the tent—"

"You left it? In this wind? In the dry season? What were you thinking?"

"Of getting you water for your hot chocolate! I didn't think that the fire would cross onto the blankets you left by the fire."

"Oh no, don't blame this one on me. Look at the fire, it's going to burn out the farm. It's burning everything."

"It was an accident. I didn't mean for it to get out of the fire pit. All I wanted was to make some hot water—" She hiccupped.

"But it has. Look at that fire. You shouldn't have turned your back on it. This is your fault."

Stella-Rose blinked rapidly.

Despite the years she still couldn't control the hurt. Tears stung in her eyes and rolled down her face, into her robes.

The beginning of the end.

Eventually Ben had come looking for them, and Chrystal had put all the blame on Stella-Rose.

It was all true.

She'd turned her back on the fire. It was her fault.

She had only been the housekeeper's child. Her mother was in charge of the household staff but wasn't the wife of the owner. Her child was a no-one on the farm. Her best friend was the owner's granddaughter, who'd already taken all her mother's time away from her when they were younger. And Stella-Rose had wanted Chrystal to protect her now, to take some of the responsibility for the fire, and save her from everyone's wrath.

Share the blame. Make it easier. Even a little.

Crystal never did.

Because of that, her mother had sent her to boarding school.

Ripped her away from the only home she ever knew and made sure she hardly ever darkened the *Saliebos* farm gate again. Even when time had come for university, she had been sent to Cape Town, to the one furthest away from home. And Chrystal never protested against her leaving, not once.

She knew deep down that Ben was the main influence, he wanted the firebug off the farm as much as her mother wanted her bothersome daughter gone, out from under her feet.

"It turned out I couldn't count on you as a friend after all, could I Chrystal?" she said into the quiet room. "Not then. Certainly not now we walk different paths in life. I wouldn't change my path toward my God, not ever. And you're a paid soldier. Killing for a living. You walk toward the dark."

CHAPTER 7

Thabazimbi, South Africa

Akina had been in the darkness for so *long*, days and nights blended together. She clung to the belief that she would be okay, having watched enough TV programs to know that ransoms would be paid, and she would be returned, or some marine from somewhere, paid by her father, would come and rescue her.

As long as she was alive, they would find her.

He would never let them stop looking.

Not her dad.

She heard the soft whimper coming from somewhere across the room.

She wasn't alone.

"Who's there?" she asked.

No answer.

The whimpering stopped for a moment and then it became a sob.

Muffled, as if they were trying to quiet themselves.

The cold in the room gripped her again in its icy fingers. Akina rubbed her hands together and over her arms, clawing at the thin blanket that was wrapped around her.

The person hiccupped, and a louder sob broke through the darkness.

A sound of helplessness.

Someone who'd given up hope. It rattled through her body, and for a second she contemplated giving in to the fear again too, but she knew better.

Crying did nothing.

Unless she put in the effort to lift herself up, no one else would.

She missed her dad, like a part of her heart was absent from her body. She could hear his voice, loud and clear. "No use crying, Akina, pick yourself up, and try again. Tears are for the weak who don't have options. Strong women make their own options. They create change and pathways of choice."

Akina began to sing softly. It was what always helped her since she'd first been put into the little cage. It made her not feel so alone, singing the song her mum had always sung to her when she was younger. After her mum died, her dad continued to sing it to her. It was their song, and somehow singing it always made everything seem better.

"Lift your voice skywards, that way your mum will hear you, wherever you are," he said.

She did that now.

"Sunflowers, sunflowers growing up so high

We're all pretty maidens

We all have to die

Excepting Akina-Aster

Because she's the only one,

Such a shame, such a shame

We'll never see her face again."

The whimpering in the corner subsided and a quietness returned to the room.

"Ngabe ungumuntu omubi?" the voice asked.

Akina couldn't understand the language, but she could hear the quiver in the voice of someone young.

Another child. It was hard to judge in the dark. She guessed the child was younger than her. Those who'd passed through already had all been younger than her.

"I don't understand you," Akina said. "Do you speak English?"

"I not so good English."

The small voice came from closer than Akina had first thought. There was little light in the new place they had her locked up in.

"That's okay, we don't need to speak perfect English. My dad speaks

English, but my mum used to speak Japanese to me. My dad made sure that I could also speak a few others too."

"I talk Zulu, and little bit English. Only few Afrikaans talk."

Akina settled into her blanket. "What did you first say?"

"You bad person?"

"I'm not bad. My name is Akina."

"I is Cherri. You talk funny."

Akina smiled. "I'm from a place called America. My mother was Japanese and my dad's American. I guess I do have an odd accent."

"Yebo."

There was silence.

"I think the people who took me are bad though," Akina said.

"Someone tooked me. I do not know where I is." The sobbing started again.

"We can be lost together. We have to stick close and wait for my father to send someone to rescue us."

"Is your *ubaba* a policeman?"

"*Ubaba*? What is that?" Akina asked.

"Daddy," Cherri said.

"No, he's a businessman. He'll pay for the best soldiers to come get me. Like in the movies."

"Your *ubaba* will do that?"

"My father would never give up looking for me. My dad would search the whole wide world to find me. Everywhere and anywhere."

"How he find you? It's dark," Cherri said.

"Because I know that he'll stop at nothing to get me back home. I know that he'll send someone. He can afford to pay the best soldiers in the world, and they'll find me and take me back home." She lifted her chin. It was true — he would. Even with the GPS tracker cut from her arm, he would find her.

She rubbed where the thick scar continued to heal. Even with the bandage tied on top of it she could feel the ridge on her skin. They had moved her again since cutting her. They injected her with something, and she'd woken up in a different cage with the cut.

The room had smelled better and wasn't as cold as the last one. The cage was bigger.

The old woman who was looking after her was gentler than the previous woman. She dressed weird, with skins and lots of beads that clunked together with a dull thud when she moved, and she chanted all the time so there was never silence between them. The old woman gave her a bucket of water to bathe in daily, and while it was cold, it always smelled good, as if she added herbs or something.

She wouldn't give her name, and she asked Akina not to talk to her because then she would get into trouble.

"How long we here?" Cherri asked.

"I don't know. It's always dark. As long as the old woman brings food and water and empties my toilet bucket, I can stay alive and wait. She's kinder than the woman at the last place they held me and feeds me better. She even gave me a small Bar-One a few days ago. The first time I've had chocolate since they took me."

"She *cha* let you go?"

"*Cha?*"

"mmm. Maybe stop."

Akina shook her head, even though she knew Cherri couldn't see. "No. But I know my daddy won't leave me here. I know he won't give up. He won't."

"*Cha*. Is No. I go also when soldiers come?"

"Of course. Where's your dad? Isn't he going to send someone to save you?"

"My ubaba dead, and my mommy—on Saturday. The chief took me orphanage before úgógo comes. I don't think anyone save me." There was the high-pitched whine again as Cherri began to sob. "I don't know my úgógo."

"Don't cry. I won't let them leave you behind. We're friends now. Pinky swear, I won't leave you." Even in the darkness she put up her hand and put her little finger out and could imagine Cherri doing the same.

Cherri said. "Pinky swears."

CHAPTER 8

Saliebos Farm, Thabazimbi, Limpopo Province, South Africa

22ⁿᵈ March 2016 — 39 days until auction

Rowan looked at the property listing they'd collected from Frik, the real estate agent, in town. It was part one of their plan, which involved looking for local information on more sangomas.

He still couldn't believe that Chrystal had drunk Frik under the table in a bet at the local shebeen. All to get her hands on all the listings that were now spread across the dining room table.

He held a yellow highlighter. "Color any features like basements, wine cellars, and any outbuildings that were a distance from the main farmhouse."

"Not many basements in this part of the country. Extremely few under-ground wine cellars," Chrystal said.

"When she first went missing in Cape Town, her phone and smart watch GPS locators were silenced within moments of her being taken, but her GPS tracker flashed on for a while, then disappeared again. Later it was found traveling in the sewerage system. I suspect they stored her below ground or in an enclosed heavy steel and concrete place, so they will keep doing that if they can. Basements are good hiding places."

"Not in rural Africa. You'll see how few underground storage areas we have. Unless it's a mushroom farm, we don't bother digging into the dirt. Too labor-intensive and time-consuming. Also cost in concrete to build it up again, easier as a farmer to slap it on top of the ground."

"Right," he said, a small frown on his forehead.

Without looking up from her plans, Chrystal said, "Look for anything that mentions lockable in the adverts. That's what we want."

Rowan looked at her. "Lockable?"

"*Ja*. The biggest problem most farmers have here is theft. If it's not bolted down, it walks. Having reliable lockable storage is important. And dogs if we're unlucky. They wouldn't put her just anywhere. It'd have to be remote, not where others can hear her scream."

"She might not be screaming anymore. They might have broken her," Rowan said, his voice low and filled with emotion.

"Don't think like that," Chrystal said. "We'll find her."

"True," Rowan agreed.

Chrystal frowned as she pointed at one of the places in front of her. "It'll need to be secure, because they wouldn't want to chance someone walking through the bush, coming across it, and finding her. Most corrugated iron sheds are out. Too flimsy, and too hot. Someone would cook in them. You said they wanted her alive. So, we look at concrete structures."

She drew a line through the page she was on then threw the paper to one side.

"What's wrong with that one?"

"It's a smallholding too close to town." She massaged the back of her neck. "No one would keep a prisoner there. Too many nosy neighbors and do-gooders in the city. We need to look at the farms a little further out."

"Fair enough."

"Also, no garage. Single dwelling, not even a maid's *ikhaya*." She pointed out the window to the staff quarters. "Most houses in South Africa have servants living near the main house. It's convenient for your maid to always be there when you need her. Not so awesome for the maid to be on call twenty-four-seven. It's a throwback to colonization."

He nodded. "What about this one?"

She looked at it. "*Buffelshoek* farm. I know that one, it's a commercial vegetable producer. They have chemicals in that shed. I did some crop spraying for him about a month ago. That's in the clear."

"Fair enough," Rowan said, and continued in his pile before he pulled another one aside. "This one? It has a dwelling, but it had a big structure on it, that would fit about six cars, and looks like it has a small annex that looks like it's dug out."

Chrystal took the pictures and the blueprints. "Looks promising. This one says it sold recently; we will have to step carefully on this visit. That's interesting, I know that name — Jacaranda Industry Holdings."

"You know it as you or as Savannah?"

"Savannah. I came across them in the Congo. It leads back to a South African, maNtuli. It's a good practice to know everything you can about who you're sourcing your weapons from when you contract. If they're trustworthy or not. It's one of the fronts for her gun-running cartel. A few years back she went through a bad patch and almost landed in jail, it was rumored she overstepped the line and killed some man in front of witnesses in a sports stadium. All the witnesses disappeared, so they couldn't bring charges against her. She has a thin veil, but a good one, between her and all her illegal business activities, with several legal companies operating too—"

Rowan sat looking at Chrystal. "And? What happened?"

"After that, she dropped out of the news and concentrated on her businesses. Weapons, taxis, shebeens and nightclubs. There's a rumor she's shifting drugs after her rapid expansion up Africa, but I haven't seen any proof. She's like a cat, lands on her feet every time. She only puts females in top positions locally, but as you go further north, she's had to make some exceptions and give some men a little authority. The women take the *ma* term into their names."

"No intel on moving into human trade instead?" Rowan asked, flipping the highlighter in his hand from side to side.

Chrystal watched the strong hand control the pen and shook her head. "Prostitutes of consenting age only. I've never heard of her being involved with anything that would harm children. maNtuli has a sad story about being sold as a child, and many of the women who head her companies have a similar background. She's rescued and empowered them. I heard about one of her lieutenants, maCalio, her husband took their daughter and sold her to someone, and she killed herself before maNtuli or maCalio could save her."

"Some husband."

"Rumor has it maCalio threw him off the same balcony the kid jumped off, as well as the man who bought the child. Of course, nothing was proved, no witnesses. maNtuli's vocal against child prostitution, and runs an unofficial orphanage for homeless kids, out near the Kruger National Park. Not one to tangle with if you can help it. Last I heard she was still running ghost stock."

"3D printed guns?"

"This is Africa — stolen guns, all disassembled and then reassembled with all the different serial numbers of multiple parts, making them untraceable. Add to that the millions of live rounds that go missing from the police stores, and you can bet she has a hand in it somewhere. The farm will be worth a visit. I tapped into maNtuli's supply chain near Virunga National Park on a mission, she proved to be a reliable resource. Let's hope she's as reliable on her home soil if we need firepower."

"You're putting her on the pile to look at?" Rowan asked in a surprised tone.

"For interest's sake. To keep tabs on what she's doing, more than what's on her farm that I should know about from an anti-poaching point."

They continued for a while until Chrystal broke the silence again. "This is Pandora Timbers. It's not on the market, and Ben and I have the first option if the Mother Naude ever decides to sell. Why would it be included in here?"

"Let me look. It's either a mistake or a coincidence and I don't believe in those."

She passed the paper pack to Rowan. A stillness followed and all she heard was the blood beating through her own head.

"They have a dugout underneath their church. They also have one in the area which says 'the rectory' and in a building marked 'mission', and another in this building here." He pointed to a little square that was slightly away from all the rest—separated by a field with a label on it saying: 'Curing barn ruins'."

"That's going to be tricky, asking the sisters if we can look in their place. It's holy, no matter what religion it is, mostly unless you are a terrorist. Any holy ground is treated as such. A church, a mission, a mosque, a synagogue. Those are historically left alone in South Africa."

"Might be so, but we'll need to take a look. I'm not leaving anywhere unsearched; I have to find Akina. We can probably rule out under the altar, too much traffic. There might be a cellar in the living quarters. It looks like it has a chimney near it, so was probably originally part of the kitchen area." He ran his fingers through his hair. "The curing barn ruins. That's where we should start. The rectory could also potentially be looked at if we are careful. These are really old plans." He lifted them to look at the other side of the papers to make sure they were indeed blank.

"This is Africa, the trees here have eyes; there's no way we can sneak into a mission unnoticed." Chrystal was shaking her head.

"Any idea who lives in the rectory?"

"I don't know but guess we're going to find out. For full disclosure, there's another complication."

"What?"

"Mother Stella-Rose Naude and I used to be best friends when we were growing up. Our paths took different forks in the road. She's the daughter of our elderly housekeeper Nicola."

"You know her? That'll help — you call her and arrange a visit—"

"I wish it was that easy. We don't talk anymore, and you know the saying, 'a woman never forgets where she buries her hatchets'. I think between us we have more than a simple ax, we have a whole arsenal of weapons."

CHAPTER 9

Saliebos Farm, Thabazimbi, Limpopo Province, South Africa

23rd March 2016 — 38 days until auction

Chrystal knelt down in the veld and touched the faint outline of a shoe print. "A single man, carrying an uneven weight in his backpack, or he's favoring his right leg." She pointed to the ground where black ants ambled over the boot prints, going about their everyday business. "Whoever cut the game fence here in section twelve hasn't bothered to even attempt to cover their tracks. They walked in from the game reserve, and then walked back out again. Now that we are past where our herders have gathered up our ear-tagged sable from inside the reserve, there is no mistaking that we're on his trail."

"I will take your word for it," Rowan said.

Zenzele laughed. "Believe Miss Chrystal. She has been tracking with my father since before she could tie her shoes."

"Is that so?" Rowan said, lifting one of his eyebrows.

"*Yebo*," Zenzele said, grinning, then he smacked Rowan on the shoulder. "Our Misses knows lots about the bush, she does not tell everyone that she knows."

"Thanks for nothing Zenzele," Chrystal said. "Come on, let's follow this guy. He's heading that way." She pointed, then straightened slowly and arched her back, her buttock and thigh muscles protesting.

Rowan might not know about tracking through the African bush, but he was right about some of her skillset being rusty. Simply carrying a pack again today, something she hardly ever did anymore, was hard. Already her muscles were protesting about the weight, a sure sign that they needed more training, and not only a few days of it.

She held her hand up as a single kudu bull walked silently in front. She loved seeing the shy antelope as he turned his head toward them. His black nose shiny with health, chewing the grass, his big ears twitching as he listened. There was no tag to say he'd once been a breeding animal. He must be one of those that had been born in the wild since they'd started adding to the reserve.

"Must be a nice pool of water nearby, he's been for a mud bath, trying to make himself bigger, have thicker horns. Must be someone in the area worth beefing himself up for," she said, and as they watched, a clump slid down from his twisted horns, dropped onto his grey-flecked coat and then slid to the ground.

An oxpecker perched on his back, clearing ticks and other parasites from his skin. Its large red and yellow eyes looked at her with disdain for disturbing their walk through the bushveld. With a flick of his tail, the kudu started to slowly walk away, as if it knew that they were no danger to it.

She heard the low rumble of Rowan's laughter behind her, obviously finding the idea of a male kudu bulking up to attract a mate funny, as they continued walking through the long grass between the acacia trees.

The sound of the bush washed over her, the melodious calls of Egyptian geese chattering, and distinctive sounds of a nearby common quail, along with the love calls of the doves. A pied barbet's haunting repeated call. Her shoulders relaxed and she turned her face to the sun.

While she was glad that they had been doing extra training together, getting her body back into peak condition, she dreaded the next floor mat training she knew was coming with Rowan, but looked forward to it at the same time. Although she sparred with her anti-poaching team, they were always respectful of her, both as a woman and as their boss. They never went hard at her, no matter how much she insisted they give it their all.

In the last few days, Rowan had thrown her to the floor more times than she cared to count.

Beneath the T-shirts that he wore were muscles corded with lead. When he moved them, the strength they had was extensive. She could both admire and identify with that body for what it was: a honed killing machine.

She eased her weary body back into motion. It was always harder getting it to move than keeping it going when her body was in this state.

Rowan fell into step behind her. She knew that Zenzele came next as the leader of the anti-poaching squad on duty.

She smiled. Zenzele had reminded her of days spent in this same bush with his father and Khulu. Back then, she never knew it would be a life skill, back then, looking for animals to hunt and eat was simply part of growing up.

She never had a choice really. She always did what Khulu did.

Khulu hunted: so did she.

Khulu handled firearms: she'd learned the good and the bad of them. How to clean them and respect them.

Khulu patiently showed her how to weld in the big equipment workshop and ride a horse — and then when she was older, a motorbike. To drive the tractor, then the *bakkie*, then the ten-ton truck. He also showed her how to service each and every vehicle she could drive.

It was how it was.

He was her grandfather. She idolized him.

At one stage he'd called her Shadow. But after they'd seen Peter Pan, she'd stopped him from calling her that — she didn't want to be stitched to his shoes.

She laughed aloud, breaking the silence.

"Share the joke?" Rowan encouraged.

"I was thinking of what a pain in the ass I must have been to Khulu growing up. I was at his heels the whole time. Learning all these skills as part of growing up on the farm and living on the land. I even went to the same agricultural college he went to." She looked back to see Rowan smiling.

She grinned too. Then looked forward, watching the ground, the trees, aware the whole time of the horizon and her surroundings.

"The police force was different though. It taught me how to fight in hand-to-hand combat. Khulu never laid a finger on me. Not to inflict pain, nor to save me from pain. He wasn't a grandfather who believed 'spare the rod and spoil the child'. Thank goodness."

"Never?" Rowan asked.

"Not once. I remember he would caution me, but always verbally and with kindness and reason. I didn't do bad things. I never wanted to do anything to make my grandfather mad at me. He was all I had from when he rescued me at three years old."

"You're lucky." His voice sounded closer than before, like he had closed the distance to better hear her.

"*Ja*, but the thing is," she said quietly. "Sometimes when you're so lucky, it all needs to be questioned and almost taken away before you appreciate it."

"Someone taking something away I should know about?" Rowan asked.

"*Ja*, you." She looked back at Rowan and grinned. "Taking away my sanity. What was I thinking — letting you live in the same house as Khulu and me for mission control and that in a few days I'd be back up to spec? I have been a farmer for two whole glorious years. Different muscles used for different jobs." She moved her shoulders under her pack and massaged her neck.

"This walk is probably a blessing in disguise, it'll help with the distribution of all those acids settled in your muscles already," Rowan said bluntly.

She glared at him over her shoulder. "Easy for you to say, it's not you hurting. And right now, I need every ounce of energy to find the son-of-a-bitch who cut the fence. Not only is the fence supposed to be a deterrent to keep people out of the reserve, it also protects the animals inside. Avoids human/animal conflict. What isn't normal is to have someone drive our stock into the reserve — that's what's sounding the alarm for me. This is not about poaching. Something else is going on here."

"Any idea what?" Rowan's voice held a hint of interest.

"Not yet. Once we find this sucker, there're going to be some interesting questions."

They came to a road within the reserve. "What? Why?" Chrystal said, turning in small circles, spiraling outward. "Dammit."

Rowan had stopped when she motioned and was looking at her. "What?"

"The prints stop here. He got into a vehicle and left us only the treads of his tires to say that he'd been here." She pointed to the ground and the overlay of tracks. Zenzele stepped around Rowan and followed her circles, shaking his head, clicking his tongue in a disapproving way.

"He cuts the wire, drives the sable herd into the reserve and then hitches a ride?" Rowan asked.

Both Zenzele and Chrystal shook their heads.

"It looks like he came back to his own vehicle that was hidden here. Look," she said, pointing to where there were the ends of bushes showing they had been cut and were already wilted and dying in the hot African sun.

"Shows investment in the crime." She widened her circle. "Now that is even more curious," Chrystal said, stepping toward a tree.

Etched into the bark was carved: *Stop looking or she dies.*

Chrystal put her fingers on the bloodwood tree. They came away covered in fresh red sap. She saw something further down the trunk, flies buzzing around. Using her hand, she shooed them away. They lifted up for a second and then settled again, but not before Chrystal saw what was nailed to the tree: a small human ear.

"Fuck," Rowan swore.

She couldn't breathe. The pain that slammed into her chest was like a freight train. It squeezed her like a python and caused her breath to come out. She couldn't get any air in.

Pain slashed down her left arm — pins and needles stabbed downwards from her shoulder into her wrist and then her fingers.

"Chrystal?" Rowan said.

His voice came from far away. Muffled by the blood thumping in her ears.

She bent over and threw up. Then gulped in a breath as she attempted to put her arms above her head, to help the air get into her lungs.

They refused to cooperate, and her lungs scorned her efforts.

All she could see was the blood on the ear. The blood on the tree.

Human blood.

Behind her eyelids she saw blood all over Wes. So much blood.

All over her hands.

Her hands were inside his chest, and the blood covered them.

She couldn't get any air. The python was back and his body rippled around her chest. Crushing. Pain in her neck, up into her lips.

"*Inkosazana*. It's okay. You're home. You're safe." She felt Zenzele lay her down and put something under her legs, to elevate her feet.

"*Thula thul, thula baba, thula sana, Thul'ubab uzobuya, ekuseni—*" The words of the traditional African lullaby washed over her, the deep voice of Zenzele and the rhythmic patting on her arm. *Hush, hush, hush-a-bye little man, be quiet baby, Be quiet, Daddy will be back in the morning.*

67

The tears leaked out and ran down into her hair. She sucked air into her lungs, and slowly the python uncoiled. There was still a pain in her chest, and she rubbed at it, trying to get rid of the vice grip.

"Kukh'inkanyezi, zi-holel' ubaba, Zimkhanyisela indlel'e ziyak-haya." Slowly the drumming in her ears quietened and Zenzele's voice got louder. There's a star that will draw him home. It will illuminate his path home too, where we are.

She lifted her hands to look at them.

They were clean; there was no blood.

She looked at Zenzele. "*Siyabonga.*"

He nodded.

"You okay?" Rowan crouched near her.

She looked at her fingers again and drew in a deep breath.

"That's it, all clean. No blood. Breathe," Zenzele said.

She felt Rowan's hands on the opposite side of her body. Warm. Confident. Pulling her back from the pain, the blood and redness and into the bush again.

Zenzele's soothing voice resumed singing. "Sobe sikhona ka bonke bashoyo, Bayathi buyela. Ubuye le ikhaya. Thula thula thula baba, Thula thula thula sana." All will urge on, they'll say, go back. He returned to this home. Hush, hush-a-bye baby. Hush, hush-a-bye baby.

She took another deep breath.

She heard Rowan's voice talking quietly to Zenzele. His hands were still touching her.

Bringing her home. Calling her back.

Another breath and the python was beaten.

Only the dull pain of her heartbeat remained.

"Definitely a message for us," Chrystal said.

Ben looked at the photograph of the tree on the phone screen. "You sure you're okay?"

Chrystal nodded. "I'm fine." She shut down the fussing from her grandfather. "This is one sick bastard. To do that to a child? Why? Break the fences, herd the sable into the reserve, and then leave us a gruesome present in their retreat. How did they know we'd be the ones to find it?"

"They know you and your routines," Rowan said. "They know that you'll bring the anti-poaching guards and come running if there's a problem. I guess the silver lining is we have proof she's still alive. You don't warn people to stay away from a dead child."

"You think this is good news?" Chrystal's voice was raised. "That someone already knows that we're looking and is trying to tell us to back off by mutilating a child?"

Rowan straightened his shoulders. "I don't believe that belongs to Akina. With her mixed heritage, it's the wrong skin tone. That ear had been out in the sunshine for a while, we couldn't tell yet if it was from a live body or removed from a corpse. Whoever it was, they know that we're gathering information on Akina."

Chrystal asked, "The question is, how did they know we were looking?"

"I'd guess from when I was asking questions of those sangomas I had on the list," Rowan said, rubbing his temples with his fingers. "But now we do know that they're watching our every step and will move her again. One thing I do understand after being in this business for so long is to never discount anything along the way. We need an analysis of that DNA. Maybe the kid's in the system, maybe we can get something from this horrendous situation."

"System? You think we have a DNA system in South Africa of children? You do know this is a third-world country, don't you? Most mothers battle to simply vaccinate their kids against the diseases they know about like tuberculosis, diphtheria, and polio and you think they have money to submit samples to a DNA catalog? You're about to learn how old-school our systems really are."

"South Africa is not as backward as you think," Rowan said, a frown creasing his forehead. "You have one. I've used it. It's not extensive and only records some stolen kids, where there is blood to use as a specimen. Unfortunately, it's mostly for murdered kids, but sometimes, there are others. Akina's DNA is on her medical file, held by the insurance company in America, so we'll have the blood analyzed, but I certainly don't believe that ear belongs to her."

"Call the police and ask them," Chrystal said.

Rowan was shaking his head. "That's not so easy. You saw the files. We aren't working with the police. They went on to something fresher. To them, Akina is another statistic. For us to get their involvement we must have proof she's alive. I suspect they'll agree this is real enough if this ear belongs to her, but once they reopen the case, that's the end of us. If we do anything in their jurisdiction, they'll consider us an interference."

Chrystal nodded. She knew that from her time in the police force. "If they reopen the case, I really am going to be a home-grown vigilante."

"True."

"Next we'll be fighting out there in someone else's country and they can label me a terrorist too." Chrystal smiled. "A mercenary if I'm lucky."

"There's always that possibility," Rowan said.

Chrystal clicked her tongue. "Man, I lived without this shit for two years. But there you go. So much for being a model citizen." Chrystal pushed some wispy hairs out of her face. "A little girl is counting on us, so one psychopath and his threats are not going to stop me. Call me what you like, this isn't preventing me finding Akina. She needs help and we're going to get it to her."

He smirked. "Sometimes you have to take a gift when presented with one. We know she's alive. They won't kill her. If they were serious, they would've given us her ear. They probably need her whole so they can sell her. I vote we leave the police out of it as much as we can. We've obviously ruffled their feathers. Now, we just have to find her."

"I'll leave you to it then," Ben said. "You know where I am if you need me, but you two seem to have this under control." He left the room.

There was a long pause while they both took stock of what had been said.

Rowan reached out and slowly turned her office chair toward his, so they were facing each other. "You realize your panic attack raises questions for me."

"I know, but you came to me. You're the one who asked me to come out of retirement to help you," Chrystal said.

"I wasn't aware that you had panic attacks at the sight of blood."

"*Human* blood."

"You kept this from me when I asked if you were okay."

"With or without it, you needed my help. One of the oldest rules in live animal husbandry is that the goods need to be in perfect condition. In the human trade, what happened to not soiling the merchandise?" Her chest heaved.

"Can you control them?" Rowan asked, concern in his voice.

"Some are worse than others. Today's came a little out of left field — how was I supposed to know that your children traffickers are sick fuckers who'd cut off a child's ear?" She thought about what really caused her attacks, and then forced it from her mind. Some things were better left buried deep inside. They were simply too dark for the soul to comprehend.

Rowan reached across and put his hand on hers. "Zenzele was good at getting you to calm down again. Like he's used to them. Can you tell me about that, at least?"

She nodded.

He removed his hand.

Her intake of air before she started was loud. "We grew up together here on the farm. Nkosi, our old maid, used to sing that song whenever Stella-Rose and I had any bouts of tears. She would hug us and pat our backs. Much like when a kid is being carried on his mother's back, and she dances a rhythm with her body to calm the child. Zenzele is only five years older than me, and I can't remember a time he wasn't here with us. He would push us around in cardboard boxes and play with us, even when we started school, he would sit with us at the dining room table doing homework. Zenzele was with me when I had my first one — about a month after getting back home. We were training in the anti-poaching barn, and one of the guys accidentally drew blood. It splashed on me and I had the attack."

She looked at him. "He sent Zane to fetch Khulu and then started singing to me while patting my arm. By the time my grandfather got there, the men were all singing, and I was conscious again. Embarrassed as hell, with no idea what had happened."

Frowning, Rowan asked, "Is blood the only trigger?"

"Human blood. Yes." She took a deep breath. "I've seen animals in snares, and blood after the sable bulls got into a fight — that wasn't pretty. I can cut up carcasses in the abattoir without a problem at all."

Rowan frowned. "Why do they happen?"

She shook her head and pushed her chair away from his a little, creating more space between them. "If I knew why then I could stop them – don't you think?"

He took her still being snarky as a positive sign. Not as damaged as she could be. "You never had them before your last mission?"

"I wouldn't have survived my last mission if I was having panic attacks of any sort."

Her voice held steady.

This was simply a fact to her.

"What about photos with blood?" Rowan asked as he watched for any reaction in her pulse rate at the bottom of her neck. It wasn't changing.

"No reaction."

"Can you tell me what happened? There's no mention of PTSD in your file. We both know only you and your mark walked out of the jungle on your last mission."

"That's none of your business." Her voice was icy.

He could tell by the slight tilt of her head that she was locking him out. Sealing him off again. "Whatever happened is obviously still inside your head. Talking about it might help—"

"I've lived with this for over two years, and here you come in telling me all about how to handle it? You think I don't know I've got a problem? That I'm no longer a good soldier? A soldier who can't take the sight of blood is useless. Kind of like a surgeon with Parkinson's. Not a great combination."

Her voice was rising. And he watched the throb in her neck as her breathing changed, becoming more rapid as she spoke.

He'd pushed her to her limit.

She'd drawn her line and was not going to budge.

He had no right to push her any further now that he knew she had a weakness; it wasn't going to change her as an operative.

He had the urge to reach out and calm her, but he immediately put that thought away. *Business agreement. Off-limits.*

She'd joined him in his search for Akina, and that was what he needed to concentrate on. He took a deep breath. "Sorry. I'm not usually so insensitive. You caught me off guard."

She looked him in the eye and held the contact for a moment, then blew out a ragged breath. "Me too. At least I have exposure to the people we're dealing with. They're sick and twisted in their heads, not just perverted. I guess now you're aware of my aversion to human blood, we can deal with it if we need to."

He nodded, fully comprehending the gravity of her position with her panic attacks. Better to find this out now, before they got into a combat situation.

CHAPTER 10

Traveling away from Thabazimbi Area, South Africa

"Please don't put me in the box," Akina cried.

"The journey is long, and you must stay quiet. Remember what happens when you do not listen? Now, the other girl. She is your friend? Yes?" the man with the silver beard said in English, but his voice had a tinge of another accent that Akina couldn't put her finger on yet.

She had met him before.

When she had first been kidnapped.

She remembered him. His body odor was unique from all the others that had handled her since then.

Akina nodded.

She remembered the rich white man who beat her, and this man had done nothing to help her.

He was not a friend.

He would not help her.

"If you make a noise, I will kill her. Understood?"

She nodded again. "Please don't put me in this box. I'll be quiet," she pleaded.

The man hesitated for only a moment, then he shook his head. "I mean what I said. I will kill her..."

The man closed the box and banged a nail in to keep it shut. The sound of the hammer on the lid was loud and each knock vibrated through her.

She was sealed in.

Akina struggled against the rising bile in her throat.

She didn't want to throw up, not in the confined area she was now in. She knew that she would have to smell it for a long time if she did. Already she was well acquainted with the acid aroma of her own urine and the smell of not having washed.

She hated being wet with her own pee.

There'd been light when they had put her inside the box, she could see it, little holes in the roof of the box allowing the sunbeams through. She could move her hands and cover them if she wanted to.

She hadn't. She wanted to make them bigger.

They had put something green over the box, and the man with the silver beard had been shouting at the other man to make sure it didn't cover the breathing holes.

Now, it was dark.

She could still feel that they were moving, the vibrations through the box raked her body.

The temperature in her wooden box was dropping. She rubbed her own arms to try and get the friction to warm her a little.

"Cherri, can you hear me?" she whispered. "Cherri, you okay?"

Nothing.

They had obviously spaced her and Cherri apart or the wind was drowning out her words, or it might be that now Cherri had a bandage wrapped around her head, she might not be hearing anything.

She hadn't said much of anything since they'd cut her ear off.

Cherri had even stopped crying.

Akina closed her eyes again and started to sing quietly to herself, trying to gain a tiny bit of comfort from the sound of her own voice, to help her be brave. She knew it would be harder for her daddy to find her now that they were moving again. "Sunflowers, sunflowers, growing up so high, we're all pretty maidens, we all have to die. Except Akina-Aster, for she's the only one, such a shame, such a shame, we'll never see her face again…Sunflowers, sunflowers, growing up so high…"

. . .

The tone of the engine that pulsated underneath her changed. Light flooded over the tarpaulin, making the green hue that had been there during the day return.

She listened.

Sounds were all around. The slamming of doors, the truck beeping as it backed up.

The crunching of someone walking close by on loose gravel or stones.

Distinctive sounds of animals. She didn't know what they were, but they murmured and bellowed. She could feel the weight of the truck changing, and the sound of the animals increased.

Something jumped on top of her crate, the noise loud.

She screamed.

It bellowed.

A clatter as something slipped and then she couldn't hear it on top of her anymore.

More bleating.

The aroma of animals defecating and urinating in stress.

"Close the back, we go." She heard the distinctive voice of the man with the silver beard. She felt the vibrations of the truck, as they started to move again.

Akina woke to raised voices.

Someone was shouting over the bellowing of the animals. They were kicking her box. The silver-bearded man. "It is the law that at a border post, customs move those trucks carrying livestock the quickest. We jump all the queues. Can you not see that these animals are stressing? They need to get out of here. Take pity on the animals in the heat. I have been here for over three hours."

"Wait your turn. The trucks transporting giraffes arrived here at the same time. We are working as fast as we can. This is not a large busy border post usually; you should have gone to a bigger one if you wanted to move faster. For now, you wait your turn."

"Do you know how much these cattle are worth? Do you? You need to move us through. I can't have any dead."

"What is inside with the *mombies*? There is a section that has a green tarpaulin over it. Up the front, I can see it."

"Bags of pellets and feed. Hay. I can't have them pooing all over their food. When we are through here and get to Gaborone to unload them, I'll unload their fresh breakfast with them, so they settle faster because they know that feed. They won't get the squirts and shit all over their new owner. Are you stupid that you don't know that you always transport—"

The animals chose that moment to bellow and she couldn't hear what else was said.

"Stay with your animals. I have to check your veterinary certificates and then I can stamp your papers. It should not be much longer."

She could hear the man walk away and the animals moved again.

"Japanese Doll, you alive?" the silver-bearded man asked.

She didn't answer him.

"If you don't answer, I kill her. I can easily stop the air going into her box. Easy—"

"No! No! Please. Akina, tell him you're okay!" She heard Cherri's muffled pleading. "Don't kill me!"

No wonder she hadn't been able to hear her when the vehicle was in motion.

"I'm alive, but I can't hear well in here," she shouted.

"Good. Not far to go now, a few hours," the man said. "Your little friend is not dead."

The next time Akina woke up, the truck was backing up again, the annoying beep-beep-beep of the reverse sound ringing loudly in her ears. Drowning out the noise of the animals as they knocked against her box.

She could no longer smell the cattle over the stench of her own urine. She could hear other voices as they were offloaded. She sucked at the water bottle they'd given her, but it had been emptied miles ago.

Something thumped down on her box. "You keep quiet now."

She knew that voice.

"They take their cows, and we drive away. I am taking you to a different place. Remember your friend? You choose if she lives, or she is killed." He laughed.

She wanted to try to kick off the top of the box.

She wanted to punch him.

But she couldn't.

She held her hands by the little holes and kept quiet.

Mostly, she wanted her dad.

Tears leaked from her eyes. She let them roll out unchecked and into her hair.

A picture of her dad flashed in her head. A memory from earlier in the year when she was having a bad day, and now she couldn't even remember what it was about.

"Akina you are strong." His voice was so real it was as if he was there. "My daughter, you're brave and can achieve anything you want to, it will take a little hard work, and sacrifice," he said. "You are so my child. You're like me. We hold everything in here," he had pointed to her head. "Here," he pointed to her heart. "This is where you must never show your enemy you hold anything."

It was so real as if he was there with her, yet he wasn't.

But it helped reinforce her: She must not show any weakness.

Akina dashed the tears away, sniffed loudly as the truck started up and began the next part of their journey.

"This is really hard, Daddy. Before they kept us in cages, and we hardly moved around. Now, we are traveling every day and sleeping somewhere strange each night. I'm leaving your phone number behind in the sand, telling them that you're rich, hoping someone will call you. Someone will be a decent human being. I'm trying Daddy; I'm being so patient. I'm trying to be compliant, so Cherri doesn't get cut up anymore. It was my fault they took her ear. If I hadn't tried to fight them—" She took a shuddering breath. "I'm not fighting or making a scene anymore now. Why haven't you sent someone to find me yet? Why is it taking so long? Please Daddy, send someone to save me. I can't do this alone."

CHAPTER 11

Thabazimbi Area, Limpopo Province, South Africa

24th March 2016 — 37 days until auction

Chrystal tried hard to focus on the road ahead to Hetty's Holt, a farm on the north side of Thabazimbi that they had on their list. They'd both thought it looked worth investigating, but Grace's voice kept interrupting her concentration on the speakerphone.

"I heard a rumor that you have a guy living with you — like in your house. Keeping news like this from Frik is understandable, but why've you kept it from me?"

Chrystal groaned inwardly. If her best friend Grace knew half her secrets, she wouldn't come near her anymore.

Most people who knew her secrets were dead now.

Besides, there was no way she would ever taint Grace's life by telling her about Savannah and what she'd done.

Damn Rowan to hell and back for dredging up the past.

She glanced at him sitting next to her in her Land Cruiser. If they'd only taken his hire car then Grace would've been on the phone, not on the speaker where he could hear too. She saw him lift an eyebrow at her, but thankfully he kept quiet.

Damn Akina for going shopping and not simply staying at home to begin with.

Damn.

Because now she knew she would have to lie to Grace again. She silently admitted that even the omission of the news was a lie in the long run. Misleading and misguided.

Grace knew she went away and worked in security contracting, but she had no idea what it was that Chrystal actually did. To her it was glamorous, she went away and came back richer.

"It's not a rumor, Rowan Zackery is staying with us, he's looking to invest in this area and buy a game farm." She fed her the lie they'd come up with, best to stick to that. "But I would love to know who's feeding the gossip mill on *Saliebos* so I can shut that leak down. I thought the days of doing things and the whole town knowing about it were over once we got out of our teenage years." She mentally crossed her fingers knowing that Grace would forgive her for more lies. Perhaps when they found Akina, and everything was settled, she might tell her why Rowan was visiting, but until then, even a childhood promise had to be broken.

Again.

"Not your farm. Don't be hard on Frik, he has your best interests at heart and is still complaining about a headache." Grace's voice sliced into her guilty thoughts.

Chrystal groaned.

"I should have known that Frik would tell you, but — put your mind at rest, Rowan's a true gentleman and you don't have to worry about me." Another mental image of crossing fingers, because when they had sparing matches, he wasn't gentleman enough to pull the punches.

He went hard.

Fast.

And made her body pay for every ounce of adrenaline that pumped through it. Not that she was complaining, but being battle-ready was taking too much time. She didn't mind those sparring matches either, his body was angled in all the right places a male body should be.

And fitted her perfectly...

She balked at the direction of her own thoughts. Shut them down.

She had absolutely no intention of thinking of his body in anything other than a professional capacity. She'd never mix work and pleasure again. She'd sworn that to herself in the Democratic Republic of the Congo two years ago, because ultimately, the work had taken priority, and she'd lost too much, personally.

Wes was gone.

Now there was a blackness inside her so dark, no one and nothing could ever scrub it away. She didn't deserve any pleasure.

Taking a much-needed breath, she tried hard to stop the darkness rising.

"When do I meet him?" Grace's voice interrupted her thoughts.

"Why would you want to meet him? It's not like we're dating."

"Why wouldn't I want to meet him? How long will he be living with you?"

"He's here for—" She took a breath... another lie but laced with truth. "As long as it takes. Until we find what we're looking for."

She looked at Rowan, he grinned at her and gave her the thumbs up.

"Yes, but—"

"Grace, he's sitting next to me in the Cruiser — he can hear you."

There was a short silence then Grace laughed. "Oh. Hello Rowan."

"Hi Grace, nice to meet you," he said.

Chrystal rolled her eyes.

"Guess you can't talk lots then. I also called to tell you we have to beg off dinner tonight."

"Thank goodness, because I forgot."

"Reschedule to next week?" Grace said, her voice still full of perkiness, showing no signs of ending the conversation.

"Can I get back to you on that one?"

"Sure."

"While I have you on the phone, do you know if there's ever been any anthrax at Hetty's Holt, Hammers Drift or Leopard Hill?" Chrystal said.

"No, but I'll check for you. You know there's a resident sangoma on Leopard Hill? You might need to tread carefully there," Grace said.

Chrystal looked across at Rowan, who sat up straighter and leaned forward, frowning.

"Why?" Chrystal asked.

"You need to get out more. Locals say that that place is cursed. Everyone knows that Eaton Sanderson's was a rotten apple. Really *vrot*. He killed his wife Morag. Shot her multiple times and tried to blame it on her being an invader, much like the Pistorius case, only he wasn't famous, so he never got the fancy lawyers."

Chrystal said, "Cursed?"

"That's why the sangoma is there," Grace said, her voice filled with conviction. "Eaton went to jail and the farm went fallow. That was when this sangoma moved in. Anyhow, she lives there. Apparently, you visit only if you want to see her for bad *muti*."

"Then how did the new owner buy it?" Chrystal asked.

"Ask Frik, he would know the full *skinder* but I heard that Eton died in prison, and it became a deceased estate. You can bet that the sangoma isn't going to be happy about being asked to move on. She's had the run of that farm for many years now. Could probably put in a land claim."

Many black South Africans were in litigation for land claims on land they had resided on for generations. It was becoming difficult to know if there was an indigenous claim on a property when purchasing a farm. Chrystal glanced at Rowan. "We'll be sure to take her a chicken when we visit then."

"Good luck with that. I heard she's not a pleasant one," Grace said. "Lots of cursing happening because of her."

"It's Africa. Who are we to judge who believes what?"

"True."

"Listen, sorry to cut this short but, we've got to go. I'm at the turnoff for Hattie's Holt. Chat later," she said, putting her indicator on before turning off the main road and onto the dusty farm track. She slowed even more as she hit a large pothole.

"Sure. No problems. Take care." Grace hung up the call.

Chrystal let out a big breath. "I believe you have 'met' Grace then."

"Guess so."

"We might be in for dinner next week. Believe me, she's going to grill you. I'll try to get you out of it if you want, or you can come, that's your choice."

"Okay," Rowan said.

"Okay? As in yes?" she asked, raising her eyebrows.

"Yeah, I'm visiting with you, and if you have dinner at Grace's, then we go to dinner."

"Okay," she said, not totally convinced she'd heard right.

"What's Grace to you?" Rowan asked, then smiled at her.

"Knew it was too good to simply be a yes," Chrystal said, laughing. "Best friends. Grace and I probably bonded because we had both lost our parents and were being brought up by relatives."

"Seriously?"

"Sure. Penny adopted Grace, after her sister's death, when Grace was one year old. Stella-Rose and I were a done deal because she was our housekeeper's child, and Amy and Frik we met on the first day of kindergarten. I believe that if Penny hadn't intervened, I might still have been dressed like a boy until I went to police college. Khulu was not ready for a grandchild, let alone a little girl. It was fine before I started school, but once I was there, and my fairy godmother Penny came into my life in a more influential way — life became a lot more girly." She glanced at him. "For both me and for Stella-Rose. Don't get me wrong. Nicola is awesome, it's just she's old fashioned too, and not fashion conscious at all. Serviceable is good enough for her. But Penny: she had style, pizzazz and understood little girls so much better."

Rowan smiled. "Must have been nice to have all of you living so close."

"It was, but sometimes people forget you grow older — people change."

"A sangoma on Leopard Hill who wasn't on the register. Definitely worth moving up the list to next." Rowan looked at her, and she flashed a smile.

"Totally."

They reached the driveway of a huge, thatched roof house. The property was vacant, the lawn was recently cut, the garden beds were clear of weeds, and it all looked neat. Maintained as a property on the market should be. Chrystal drove slowly to the side where there was a three-birth car park. They could see both the house and the sheds.

"This it?" Rowan asked.

"Guess so — no fresh tracks in. No dogs, not even a guard to meet us. An empty property, like Frik said," Chrystal said as she jumped out her Cruiser, then checked her 9mm was strapped securely to her hip and the keys for the property in her hand. "Come on, let's go take a look at that cellar we saw on those plans."

Chrystal stood next to her Cruiser's bonnet, one foot on the bull bar in the front as she re-tied her lace. "Nothing here. My vote is that we visit Leopard Hill next. We need to go through Thabazimbi to get there, so we might as well grab lunch. We'll need a chicken, and perhaps a blanket to soften her up, get her to talk. That is if we can even find her on that farm. I don't think she'll be sleeping in the main house."

"Why not?"

"That's squatting," Chrystal said in a 'don't you know anything' tone. "By now she has a right to have laid a land claim, more than twenty years on that farm, but I think that since she was brought up during the apartheid era, and she won't go take something that doesn't belong to her. She's old school. Has respect. We show her the same."

"Ah. And the chicken is to make sure she doesn't curse us after she tells us everything?" Rowan said, raising his eyebrows.

Chrystal smiled. "Something like that."

"The chicken is for her to sacrifice, and the blanket to wrap the poor chicken's body in after the deed is done?" he said, now realizing that Chrystal was only half-listening to him.

She laughed. She was listening. "Don't get your hopes up. You know that there's more than one sangoma in this region, just because we have located another one we didn't know about and who's in the bush doesn't mean she knows anything useful—"

"I know — but it's hard not to think maybe it's a step in the right direction," Rowan said.

"I understand your enthusiasm, but maNtuli's not someone we want to tangle with and something about her owning this new place isn't sitting right in my gut."

"I hear you. Let's get there and have a look."

Chrystal stopped in front of the farmhouse on Leopard Hill farm. The chicken balked softly in the back, letting everyone know about its dissatisfaction.

She could already see that no one was living there. There were no curtains in any of the windows, which were all shut tight. There was nothing special about the sprawling federation style farmhouse, with its rusted iron tin roof. Everything looked like it was frozen in time. Deserted for so many years, it had taken on an almost haunted vibe.

"Interesting. Everything left alone. The windows haven't been stolen to put into shacks. The effects of having a sangoma living here keeps things safe," Chrystal said.

"This place has potential for hiding someone," Rowan admitted as he looked around the yard.

"Potential?" Chrystal frowned.

"If you had something to hide, wouldn't you have it where there is a resident witch to protect it?"

"Fair point. I wonder where she is?" Chrystal asked.

"Who, the witch or your legendary maNtuli?"

"The sangoma. The chances of maNtuli being here are slim. Let's get out and see. Leave the car open so that chicken has some air."

They ambled around the house, tried both the front and back doors, which were locked. "Let's check the sheds."

The small building had a new lock on the door. The larger of the sheds had an unlocked door, which they pushed open and walked inside. It smelt of old bird droppings.

There wasn't much in the machinery, but there were a few tools on the wall. "Definitely someone watching the place, or this place would've been stripped, including any plumbing in the house. The scrap metal people in Africa don't ask where the metal comes from; they pay the going rate. That's the reason people can 'recycle' the pylons from the power lines."

"Kind of dangerous taking a power pylon," Rowan said.

"When there's load shedding and they know the power is off, they steal all the pylon scaffolding, leaving enough to hold up the structure, and they're gone before the power comes back on. The danger is if there's a storm, those power lines will come crashing down, and have to be replaced. And now ESKOM is saying they're broke and they can't replace the pylons. The people affected have no power."

"This is a strange country. Steal the thing that helps you?" Rowan said, shaking his head.

"If your choice was between your kid starving because you can't get a job, and you probably having no power in your cardboard shack already, wouldn't you steal too?"

"I guess," he admitted.

"It's easy to look at our country with first world eyes and go, it's crazy. Most problems are rooted in not enough jobs, not enough money and too many fat cats skimming off the top to care about those people needing to steal every day to survive."

Rowan coughed. His eyes fixed on something over her shoulder. "That has to be the witch standing in the doorway," he said as he motioned with his head and stared.

Chrystal turned, and sure enough she could see her.

The sangoma had on traditional robes of skins, and a tattered T-shirt with a skirt that had seen better days. She carried a walking stick that was intricately carved, and while her hair was in dreadlocks, it looked more 'birds-nest-unkept' than stylish. She wore skins around her waistline and a necklace made from chunky sea bean seeds, and tractor shoes on her feet.

"*Salibonanie*," Chrystal said, greeting her as she walked closer. "I'm Chrystal from *Saliebos* Farm." She stopped when she saw that the old woman's eyes were blue — she suspected they were covered by cataracts.

"I know who you are," the sangoma said. "Why are you here on Leopard Hill? You are trespassing." As she moved, the necklace made a dull knocking sound. Slowly she moved into the shed.

"We're looking at farms for Rowan to buy. I know this farm has recently been bought by maNtuli, but we came to see if we could find you. If she was around, we'd ask for permission to take a look and see if Rowan wants to make a re-offer to her for it. We visited the farm next door, but it's too small. We need both, if he's going to do some game farming."

The sangoma looked at her. "You speak true?"

"We brought you a gift to say thank you for passing the message onto maNtuli. It's inside my *bakkie*."

The sangoma nodded her head.

"Can we look in the little barn while we are here? Save us coming back," Chrystal asked.

"Locked." The sangoma shook her head.

Chrystal nodded. "We wanted to know if it would be good for mushrooms?"

"Only half in the ground," the sangoma said. "Not cold enough for mushrooms. The new owner, she will not want to sell. Her worker, she took kitty-cat with her last visit, she is coming back soon. Kitty-cat says she is coming back."

As if on cue, they heard another vehicle drive in. Together they all walked outside.

The silver Land Cruiser had already stopped. It looked brand new and was loaded with boxes inside and had crates on its roof racks. The red dust in the area attempted to cling to it, but instead made what looked like rivulets down the paint. A woman got out — she was built like a rugby player. All muscle. Short, shaved hair, with small gold earrings in her lobes. She carried a panga at her hip on one side, and a sjambok on the other. Her V-necked shirt revealing scarring on her chest. Chrystal wondered where her gun was hidden.

"Busi, are these your visitors or mine?" The voice was stern, and not impressed, heavily accented.

"Neither, maCalio. They are for maNtuli. Madam Chrystal is from *Saliebos* Farm, a few farms away, by the national park, and he's looking to buy your farm."

"This farm is not for sale," maCalio said, a frown visible on her forehead. "You have wasted your time."

A cat, shaved to look like a poodle — with length on its dark stocking legs and around its head, but short everywhere else — meowed as it jumped out of the vehicle and ran to the sangoma. She reached down and stroked it. "You have a nice holiday with maCalio? Of course, you did. Look, you are so soft. All your protection is gone."

"Of course he's soft now," maCalio said. "Do you know how long it took the vet to get rid of all that matted hair? The poor animal needed to be shaved, not brushed. Do you know how much pain it was in?"

"It is not my cat; it belongs to the farm. It chose to come live here. It has always looked like that," Busi said, stroking it again.

The cat purred loudly.

maCalio shook her head. "He's mine now. Come Rikki."

The cat stayed with the sangoma.

maCalio dug in her pocket and showed the cat a treat. It ran to her. "Farmers. Prospective farmers, you can leave now, we are not selling," maCalio said in a dismissive tone.

"Thank you for letting us know," Chrystal said. "Just let me give your sangoma her *bonsella* because I came uninvited and need to pay respects."

maCalio eyed her with interest but nodded.

Chrystal fetched the chicken from its cage, and holding it by the legs, she tucked the blanket under her arm. She handed them to Busi. *"Siyabonga mama."*

The sangoma smiled at the Xhosa blanket being presented to her, and her live chicken. She dipped her chin in thanks, her gnarled hands reaching for the gifts as she bobbed in an old-fashioned curtsey of respect. It was something Chrystal hadn't seen performed for many years. Then Busi turned and walked away, her movements slow but determined as if trying to put space between them and herself.

For a while they all watched, as if waiting for the old lady to be out of hearing distance.

"Now that she is gone. What are you doing on this property? Anyone can see that man is a soldier and not a farmer," maCalio said, pointing a finger at Rowan.

Chrystal smiled; maNtuli's lieutenant's reputation was deserved.

She didn't waste words, simply called a knobkerrie a knobkerrie.

"We came to ask for permission to look at the farm. We meant no disrespect," Chrystal said. Then she waited, and when maCalio didn't add anything, she continued. "This is Rowan. He's a private investigator from America. Rowan, meet maCalio. Lieutenant to maNtuli. In our line of work, she's known for being one of the best gunrunners in Africa with a network to rival the Russian spies of the eighties."

Rowan put his hand out to shake hers. maCalio just stared at him.

Chrystal spoke again. "I know that your boss and you are both passionate advocators against underage children being taken into whore houses, so I can tell you why we're here. We're looking for a little girl. She's eleven years old. Even younger than maNtuli was when she was sold. And much the same age as your own daughter would have been—"

maCalio bristled. She hugged the cat closer. It meowed in protest. She lessened her grip.

Chrystal knew she had hit a nerve.

"You know much about my life. I know nothing of yours. I will find out soon enough," maCalio said, picking an imaginary piece of lint from her shirt.

"Like you, I too have many faces. I show one to the world, and another that is known in the private security contractors' circles. We are not strangers. maNtuli's goods helped my team before, when I was in the Democratic Republic of the Congo. You gave us the weapons we needed for the fight up there. And to bring a man out of the jungle alive. I know who you are and what you do, but I'm not here to talk about things in the past. I'm here to talk about an American child who's being hidden in Thabazimbi. A little girl whose life we're trying to save."

Her cat meowed again, and this time, it leaped out of her arms, his tail swishing, as if she'd squeezed it extra hard.

maCalio nodded once. "I am your ally in this. However, I am afraid I already scared the perpetrators away. Something was going on when I got here just over a week ago. I found that something had been kept in my small shed, but the cages were already empty when I got to see in there. I did not give it much thought. I assumed it was some *muti* that Busi was up to. If you say there were children involved, that changes everything." She reached into her Cruiser and drew out a pen and pad from her over-sized handbag. "This is my number. Do not come here again, unless you have made an appointment with me first. The next time you come there will be guards at the new fence I am having put up, and they will not be friendly."

"Thank you," Chrystal said, taking the paper and putting it in her back pocket. "I'm lucky to have you on the same side of this fight as me. I think we both know that we need to talk to Busi. If we don't go after her now, she'll leave tonight. She isn't stupid, after all, she's a sangoma."

"This is true too. Follow me, we can drive to her *ikhaya*. We should meet her on the way, she is an old woman, how fast could she have walked through the bush?"

"You would be surprised," said Rowan in a soft voice that was still clearly audible.

"Come Rikki, inside now." maCalio clicked her fingers and the cat jumped into her vehicle.

They drove through a farm that was overgrown with thorn trees and weeds. Where once it had been rich soil used for maze, and cattle that ate the sweet grasses, now it was choking. The wild invasive species was thick and prohibited the growth between trees, the ground beneath held no grass, only bare soil. The fences that had once stood proud, lay on the ground, the wire rusting, and the wooden posts eaten by termites, some entangled into the thorn trees as they grew through them and took over.

They crawled after maCalio as she used a single well-worn path as one of the tracks for her wheel, and bundu-bashed with the other. It was obvious that while she was dressed as a city slicker, she knew her way around 4 x 4ing.

"She doesn't care much for the paint work on her new Land Cruiser. We're getting scratched to hell, and she's breaking the trail in front of us. Her Cruiser is going to show damage," Chrystal said, breaking the silence.

"I don't think she cares. She's thinking she should have reacted sooner, and didn't and feels guilty now," Rowan said.

"Her? Guilty? Please. She doesn't possess a bone of culpability in her body."

"Every person has a weak point," Rowan said, his voice serious. "That small thing that they believe keeps them thinking they are a good person. I think you touched on hers. I was watching her face. She wasn't a happy camper knowing that there was a possibility that some kid had been held here, and that she hadn't done something about it. Hadn't reacted."

"I hope so. I took a chance confiding in her. It was lucky she arrived today while we were here."

She hit a massive hole in the road. What had obviously once been an ant bear hole had been expanded into burrows beneath the surface, that had over time collapsed. Driving out of it, without going directly into more thorn bushes, took concentration.

Ahead they could see what looked like an old stone residence, with a thatched roof, a little saggy in one section, but it had recently been patched with fresh grass. To the side of that stood a single traditional *ikhaya*. The rondavel construction was standard African style; however, the paintings on the outside were clearly Ndebele. The hut was whitewashed, with the decorations of shields, eyes and geometric shapes in bright bands of colors, marked it as a house that was something special.

"Busi's house?" Rowan asked.

"Guess so…"

The old woman had stopped on the path as they came out of the tree line into a clearing and spoke to maCalio through the window.

"I hope she doesn't blow it with the sangoma," Chrystal said.

Busi walked to the passenger door and climbed inside to sit with maCalio.

"Interesting move. Right, let's hope we get to her house and can have a good look around. I sincerely hope she isn't using human parts as part of her *muti*. Some old traditional sangomas do that, especially albinos, and when they don't have access to that, they will substitute a white child," Chrystal said, almost snarling at the repulsiveness of the practice she didn't believe in.

"Africa has a sick side to it that authorities keep well hidden from the tourists," Rowan said.

"Trafficking happens all over the world." Chrystal pointed out.

"It does unfortunately, as does witchcraft."

"Africa is no better or worse than places like China who use our animals' parts, like rhinoceros' horn and lion bones. Or, what about America's New Orleans, where they still practice voodoo?" Chrystal said defensively.

"I don't agree with the trade in humans or animals but you're probably right," he said, not rising to her bait at all. He already knew she was passionate about Africa, and it was okay for her to say something against her country, but not for him to.

He was the outsider.

He smiled, thinking about her behavior. In America he would have compared her to a porcupine.

They would back up when threatened, signal with noises sounding like they had breathed in helium gas, both verbal and by shaking their smelly oil-coated quills, and then when all that failed, smack you with their tails, leaving barbs behind as they made their escape.

Chrystal had done that when he had questioned her about her last mission — gone on the defensive and rattled her quills. And he didn't want to be around when the full force of her 'quills' were actually implanted into the person provoking her.

He knew that at some stage it was coming, he had to hope that when she blew, it was not in his direction.

maCalio stopped outside the house and they pulled up alongside her.

"Busi looks terrified," Rowan said. "Only a moment ago we talked with the all-powerful witch doctor, but now she looks like someone's granny who's in trouble."

"She's not an innocent here. She's the only one on the farm, and will know what was kept in those cages, and if it wasn't her, she'll know who it was who kept them," Chrystal said.

They reached maCalio. Busi was gesturing to her table on the outside where a whole heap of harvested herbs was stored. Some were hung from above, while others were piled onto the wooden shelving that rested on cement bricks.

Bulbs from different plants, thick and thin stems, lay together in neat rows. Small rodents, frogs and rats, were drying pegged to a board at the back of the shelf.

Rowan put his hand over his nose. The decomposition smell was putrid.

"I'll fill you in when I can," Chrystal said as she listened to maCalio and Busi speaking Ndebele. Many of the words were similar to Xhosa and even Twana, so she could easily follow. "From what I can gather, maCalio told her you were interested in seeing a real sangoma's house and where she healed people."

"Good that we could use me as the excuse, hope the poor old woman doesn't hex me because of it," Rowan said, crossing his fingers on both hands.

"Curses only work if you believe they do, get real. Now *shoosh*, I need to listen."

Busi smiled. "The white man doesn't speak our African languages. We must speak English so that he can understand that we are not talking about him. In our tradition, it is rude to speak softly, because you might talk of your neighbor, but it is also rude to speak when there is one who does not understand what you say in their company when you can speak his language."

"Fine," maCalio said, switching to English. "I have a problem. I need you to throw your bones and make medicine for me."

Busi nodded. "I knew that one day you would come and ask that of me. You have much trouble around you."

maCalio nodded. "No kidding there. Where do we do this?"

"My *ndumba*, the *rondavel* outside. This is where all the healing takes place."

maCalio nodded and followed Busi. "I want Chrystal with me, you need to throw her bones too."

"There must be big rain in the clouds if you and the white farmer want your bones thrown together. Trouble coming. Come inside, sit."

Rowan walked into the round building. Inside, tables were lined with different containers of medicines, most looked like dried teas shoved into coke bottles and jars. Nothing was labeled that he could see. A buck's skeleton head hung on the wall, its white bone contrasting with the brown mud. A photograph of a child, her large blue eyes dominating her face looked free of dust, as if it was looked after with pride, unlike the rest of the paraphernalia around. There was a cattle hide mat covering most of the floor, showing its age where big patches of the hair had rubbed off from continued use.

She looked at Busi again. Perhaps not cataracts. If they both had a genetic mutation, the girl was obviously related.

Busi got a grass mat from under the table and passed it to Rowan, pointing with a gnarled finger. "You go off the skin. Over there."

"Come, the women, you sit here with me," Busi said, signaling to come closer with her hands.

Chrystal sat cross-legged on the skin, maCalio sat like a Xhosa woman with her legs out straight in front of her looking strangely out of place in the rural setting.

Busi retrieved a black-backed jackal skin and unwrapped it, spreading it as if it was a table on the floor skin.

She grabbed what to others might look like a short broom handle with hair, but Chrystal realized it was an *ishoba*. She had seen them in the markets. People used them as fly swatters, but in a sangoma's hands, it had a different purpose. Held together by a handle, decorated with beads, Busi flicked it over both Chrystal and maCalio.

Then she sat on the mat with them. Her legs stretched out in front of her, like maCalio's and she said, "What is this problem that you need help with?"

At that time, maCalio's cat sauntered in, and went up to her. It sat in her lap.

maCalio stroked her cat. "I'm having a problem with vermin. If I was this cat, I would hunt them. Kill them."

Busi stilled. Slowly she whispered into the leather bag in her hands, and then she shook them before opening the top wide. The insides scattered over the jackal skin.

An odd mixture of conch shells, animal knuckles, old coins, cut pieces of wood, and some sort of skull.

Busi picked up the *ishaba* again and skimmed it down maCalio, from her head to the mat.

"This shell means there is trouble coming. This coin, this is minerals. Something with maybe rocks or iron or steel. This feather, it means that you will have to move from a place to another. The lion bone says something is being hidden from you. This skull, it means that there is death."

Immediately she threw some powder onto maCalio and then she swept her again with the hair.

Busi put her hand into one jar next to her, sprinkled it over the hair and then swept maCalio a third time. The cat yowled and sneezed. Putting its paw out, it caught the hair. "No kitty-cat leave the wildebeest tail alone; the *ishoba* is not a toy."

The cat dropped its paw.

"You need to ask your ancestors for help," Busi said. "You need to get a white cloth and a black cloth, put two hundred-rand notes inside the cloths and sprinkle some of this." She passed her what looked like an old glass jar. "Then you ask your ancestors to help you to clear the way for this problem to be sorted. You throw it all in the fire, and you sleep next to the fire. The next day, you put this green powder into a bathtub of water, and when you are soaking, you ask your female ancestors aloud about the solution and how they can guide you. When you are finished talking with them, drink this yellow powder in a glass of water, while still sitting in the bathtub."

She sprinkled the two different colored powders onto newspaper, and wrapped them up neatly, tucking the paper into itself so that nothing would escape.

"This will help protect you when there is danger." Busi was nodding and passed her the feather from the jackal skin. "Carry this with you, it will protect you."

maCalio nodded. Her cat got up and walked under the table, stalking as if looking for something.

Busi brushed over Chrystal with the *ishoba*. "What is it you need help with?"

"To find someone," Chrystal said.

Busi gathered her reading equipment up again, threw more trinkets from the table next to her inside, and spoke into the bag. This time she blew into it, before letting the knickknacks fly.

Most of them stayed on the jackal skin, but the skull skidded off, and away.

"This tortoiseshell, here near the ear, means you have unhappiness from something that died. The skull, it chose not to be in the reading, and death is not wanting to show its face to you. The marula seed here on the back, says you need to be careful. Beware of the one who wears you on his skin. He is a *nyoga*, and he watches you, always. But he hides behind another." She spat on the ground. "This leopard knuckle, by the tail, it means that you will find what you search for, but it will not be easy as you must look in the shadows."

She threw some powder into the air and swept it over Chrystal.

Busi got up and went to fetch a bottle from the end of the table before she came back and sat down.

"You need to visit The Smoke That Thunders. Take the thing that is valued with you, the one you keep from the person who died. Put this powder on it and throw it in the water. Return blood to the earth. You do not need this item anymore. It is time for it to be set free. The great god will give you the forgiveness you seek, even though the bones tell me it was not your fault to begin with. This person who died, he wants you to be free from the agony now. It is time to let him go."

There was quiet in the room. Chrystal looked at Busi and then maCalio, Rowan, and back to Busi. "That's it? No more powders or anything?"

"*Haaa*. You are not a believer. You will not take my *muti* even if I gave it to you. You do not need anything else, the *tokoloshe* runs from you, but the veld and all its creatures, it knows that you are its friend, and it will be there for you on your journey."

Chrystal smiled and nodded.

"And what about your bones? Do you read your own?" maCalio asked.

Busi shook her head. "I do not need to. I know that you found the cages. I understand that now you want to know what was in them. I did not kill those Starlings. I do not use humans in my *muti*. It was my part to keep them safe, keep them fed and away from any men who might hurt them. If I do not, they will kill my own granddaughter." She motioned to the picture on the wall. "They took my Liyana anyway."

maCalio huffed. "If you knew this was what I was going to ask, why did you read the bones for me?"

"Sometimes, a sangoma can see that someone is struggling with the *tokoloshe* she battles. The sangoma can see that it needs to be slain, even if the person cannot even see they have a *tokoloshe* riding on their shoulders. But not when the sangoma isn't allowed to help." Busi's face was serious.

"What am I supposed to do with you? You should have told me what you were hiding when I first came to this farm," maCalio said.

"I did not know you would be a friend then. It was my duty to the children to protect them from those who would harm them."

maCalio nodded.

"Do you know if there was a young Japanese looking girl kept in there?" Chrystal asked.

Busi nodded.

Rowan leaned forward.

"Do you know where they took her?" Chrystal asked.

Busi shrugged. "Information like that is not important to each in The Circle. We look after the Starlings, or they will harm our own. I have told them this place is no longer safe, when the white man in the expensive car came for new pictures for a sale after all these years. I will have no more children. They sent me this from my grandchild." She went to her table and from the shelf above, she took a box and passed it to Chrystal.

"Is there blood in here?" Chrystal asked.

Busi shook her head. "Not now. Now it is dead. Dried."

Chrystal opened it.

Inside lay the first joint of a small finger, complete with its nail. She put her hand over her mouth.

"They told me if I talked to anyone that they would cut her throat next. But the bones told me about today. They told me that maCalio, she needs help, and I need to be strong for that friendship, and that this stranger was coming from across the sea and would visit with the *Ingqwele*. The Champion." She pointed to Chrystal. "You will be there to help save my grandchild. I should not receive any more bones. I am a believer in the bones — even if you are not."

"We won't tell anyone you helped us," Chrystal said.

Busi threw some different powder onto *ishoba*, and brushed the hair over Chrystal, and then she stood in front of Rowan. She brushed him too.

maCalio stood up. "You stay on this farm, do not move away into the bush. I will protect you too because you helped those children, but if I ever hear that you have anything to do with child trafficking again, only the vultures will find your bones to eat off. There will be no crossing over. Understood?"

Busi nodded.

"Come Rikki, we have other things to do today." maCalio clicked her fingers and the cat came out from under the table, a lizard hanging from its mouth. He put it at maCalio's feet. "Good boy. Now, let's go hunt something else, shall we?"

They walked outside, and as maCalio went to get into her vehicle, she turned to Chrystal. "I meant what I said about trespassing here again. Let me know when you find the child and shut them down so they can never traffic again. Children are one commodity that maNtuli will never trade in. If you need anything on your journey, contact maNtuli's network, as you know it already. I will tell her what is happening. Find the children. The one you seek and the one who belongs with Busi."

CHAPTER 12

Thabazimbi Area, Limpopo Province, South Africa

The Legend of the Golden Inkonkoni

Deep in the soil, under the canopy of the big ironwood tree, Busi's spade hit something hard. She bent down onto her knees and scooped the sand out with her hands instead. At last, she felt the outside of the sweet tin she had used. It was still safe.

Using her fingers, she gouged the soil away from the box. Slowly, she freed it of its soil tomb, until she could pull it up toward her. Buried for its protection, she brushed the sand from the lip and then settled onto the ground, her legs in front of her, holding the rusted tin.

She closed her eyes and remembered another day, when she had been as young as her granddaughter.

Inside the cave, the fire crackled, lighting up the walls painted with hunting scenes of large elephants with tusks that touched the ground, buffalo with wide thick horns and mighty chests, alongside thousands of wildebeest, their bodies elongated and their circular horns distinct. The lions waited in grasses, hunting the zebra, while tall giraffe with long legs looked out over the herds, sentinels to watch for the spotted leopards. There were depictions of a river crossing, the scaly crocodile in the water capturing animals as they migrated to fresh and nutritious grasslands.

Busi crept closer to the fire.

The sangoma spun around one last time. The different weighted beads on her skirt caused the fabric to balloon outwards at different heights so that she looked like a giant butterfly before she sat down on the rock. She stopped the beating of her drum and silence returned.

"The children were all in the village with the old sick people, and their sangoma. The hunt had taken all the parents farther away from the village than ever before. It was almost time to move again, but the new chief, he was worried. He had heard whispers on the wind of strangers.

"Of men who came in the night. Hidden in darkness and killed everything they found like wild dogs. Stealing the children."

Busi smiled. Of all the stories the sangoma told, this was the most real, the one that gripped her.

"The men, they hunted in packs of hundreds. No one had been able to stop the wave of fire and death that came with the warriors," the sangoma cautioned with one finger outstretched, motioning from side to side.

Busi looked around her at the faces of the other children. The boy nearest her had his mouth open. The girl next to him held her hands tightly together on her chest, both their eyes following the sangoma's every move.

"The herd boy looking after the cattle had been watching over his blind sister that day. His sister said that she could see the line of strangers walking along the riverbank. Through the water with crocodiles, and not one tried to eat them. Past the spotted leopard, who did not pounce. Past the cobra, that did not strike. Not one of the animals could see them. The men were hidden. Like a *tokoloshe*. The boy looked to where his sister pointed and he could see nothing. But he trusted his sister.

"The children ran into the village to warn that the warriors were coming and tell them what the blind sister had seen. At first, the old people laughed.

"How could this be? A blind person cannot see," the old man said.

"Only the sangoma listened to the children. She reminded the villagers that there was no way the village could fight off such men filled with so much spirit power. The old people began to cry and gathered their grandchildren close. The sick put their heads down and refused to lift them. There was a deep sadness that came over the whole village.

"But the sangoma, she was a crafty woman. She called to her ancestors and all the spirits of the land. She called on the elephants for their strength and wisdom. She called on the buffalo for their tenacity to fight and never give up, and for protection within their herds. She called on the eagles above for their sight that she too would be able to see the warriors and know where they were. And she called on the cheetahs for their speed so that she could run fast. Lastly, she called on the springbok for its ability to maneuver from tricky situations and jump out of the way where there was danger. She asked them all for their help. She begged them to come to her."

Busi smiled as the sangoma imitated each animal as she mentioned them. Finally, when she jumped to the side, like a springbok, she laughed with the other children.

The sangoma nodded and threw another branch of wood onto the fire. It crackled and popped as the dry leaves caught fire quickly, and the cave glowed brighter for a moment. Then it settled again. The sangoma clapped her hands to bring the attention back to her.

"She knew that no animal would give part of their spirit to a human without her providing something in return. She promised that if they sent a champion to help them, she would give her life to save the children in the village, that she would be the sacrifice. And she began to dance and chant.

"Slowly, she transformed, and when she was finished, there stood a mighty golden *inkonkoni*." She pointed at the wildebeest, painted in orange and larger than the rest, where it stood alone, away from all the others.

The kids began to laugh. It started as small giggles, but then exploded into belly laughter as it always did when she told the story. Busi wanted to tell them to stop laughing because she wanted the story to carry on. Sure, the color was off in the ancient rock art, but it represented gold. They knew that.

"No, she was not an ordinary *inkonkoni*. She was bigger than any of the other animals and had a golden hide that could reflect the light and blind her enemy, with eyes that were like the eagle's and could see everything, even in the shadows. She could even tell the difference between the heat of a body from the cold stone they sat on. The golden *inkonkoni*, she pawed the ground with her hoof and dug a great hole. Water flowed up. She had been given the memories and intelligence of all the matriarch elephants. Inside her, she could feel the strength of the mighty buffalo, and when she looked into the river, she could see the muscles like his broad chest on her body. She had a golden beard and mane, and her tail was so long it almost touched the ground. The golden *inkonkoni* could see that the spirits were happy with their choice because her horns were big, wide with sharp points, but they curved inwards a little so that anything inside could be protected.

"The people covered their eyes and cowered in corners, but she told them not to be afraid. They had to climb up into her horns and onto her body, and she would take them all to the cave behind the village. And when each one was loaded and holding on tight, she raced with the speed of the cheetah to the cave behind the village where the water was sweet, and she knew that they would be safe while she battled the warriors."

"And used her strong horns," one child said.

"We will come to that part," the sangoma said with a patient smile, and the children leaned in, wanting to hear more of the story. Busi crept closer again.

"She ran back to her village where her own human body returned. The golden *inkonkoni* was gone; she was an old woman with grey hair and wasted muscles, shriveled over with age and weariness.

"She sat on the ground and she waited for the warriors.

"Too soon, she could hear them in the grass nearby as they surrounded her village. She could hear each of their heartbeats. And she could see each of them with her eagle eyes, even when their chief walked toward her and laughed. 'Look, it is only an old woman. How can she do anything against the might of us? She cannot even see us or hear us.'"

"And the sangoma, she stood up and poked him in the chest. 'You are not welcome here,' she said. 'Take your warriors with you and return to the land you came from, or you all die here today.'

"The chief got a huge fright. His eyes showed white in his face with fear. But he still underestimated the sangoma.

'"You are old. Look at you. A woman.'" He pushed her back down to her knees.

"The sangoma gave him one last chance. 'You are not welcome here. This is your last warning.'"

"The chief laughed, and he lifted his big, curved panga and cut off her head, in one big swipe."

Busi gasped and put her hands over her ears. "I hate this part. I don't want her to die."

The sangoma smiled and continued.

"And when her blood touched the sand, the golden *inkonkoni* emerged. The gold of her coat was so bright that the soldiers lifted their hands to their eyes so that they might not be blinded. Using her big horns, she speared them through their dark hearts. Using her strong hooves, she cracked open their skulls. She used her long tail to strangle them when they cowered from her. The wildebeest hunted each of the warriors down."

"Good," Busi said as she crept right up to the sangoma.

"But some of them, they had managed to stick their spears into her side, and her very lifeblood was discoloring the sand. The wildebeest kept fighting. With the tenacity of the buffalo, she did not give up until every warrior of the dark *tokoloshe* was dead. Only then did she walk back to the cave to tell her people that they were safe. But she was too weak, so much of her golden blood was staining the earth.

"Outside the cave, the *inkonkoni* fell to her knees. The blind girl with the blue eyes ran out and she put her arms around the beautiful beast's neck.

"'Thank you. You have saved all of us,' the girl said."

"Awww," Busi and all the children said in unison.

The sangoma lifted her pointer finger. "But the sangoma and the will of her ancestors, and all those of the animals of the land knew that the children would always need protection, that the *tokoloshe* would return again.

"'Pull from my mane some of my hair so that you can keep it with you always and pass it to the next sangoma and those after her so that for all time the children can be protected. My spirit will never die, even though today I will turn to dust. When the need is great, I shall return, with all the spirits of the ancestors, and the spirits of the animals, to protect the children once again.'

"'I will do as you ask,' the blind girl said. 'I promise.' She pulled out a handful of golden hair, and with tears running down her face, she felt the big strong *inkonkoni* crumble to dust in her arms. The great golden *inkonkoni* was gone."

Tears ran down Busi's face now, too. She had crept closest to the sangoma, who gathered her up into her arms.

"The blind girl kept her promise. With the help of the new sangoma, they made a sculpture of an *inkonkoni* and placed the knot of hair from her mane inside the statue. The sangoma taught the girl in the ways of the healer, and the dance of the spirits and the songs of the mountains and all the spirits, so that she could pass those onto her children, and they could pass it onto theirs, along with the story. They would always look after the golden *inkonkoni*, because a dark time would come when the golden wildebeest would return to once again save the children.

"And to this day, it is passed from sangoma to sangoma. It is our duty to protect the golden *inkonkoni* so that one day, the golden *inkonkoni* can return when the time is at its darkest the children's champion will return."

From her bag she carried on her chest, the sangoma brought out the golden *inkonkoni* statue that had been passed down from one sangoma to the next in her family for as long as the stars had watched from the sky.

"One day, someone else in this cave will be the sangoma, and they will guard this golden *inkonkoni* statue and make sure it is ready to fight for the children."

Busi smiled as the sangoma looked at her. She too had those same blue eyes, but she wasn't blind.

Busi touched the tin box and was brought back to the present.

"For many years I feared you were only a story, and yet I could not sell you for money. From the minute my mother gave you to me, I have carried you around, as a heavy secret."

She dug her nails into the side of the tin and managed to lever it open. Lifting the object inside, she peeled the layers of newspaper and cloth that wrapped up what it held safe inside. Until she came to the last layer. A soft cloth that protected it.

Taking a breath, she slowly lifted out the statue.

It was exactly the same as when she'd seen it twenty years ago, before she'd buried it.

The golden *inkonkoni* shimmered in the afternoon sun. It was deceptively heavy for its size, but then she had always suspected it was made from real gold. She ran her hand over its cold exterior. The *inkonkoni* stared at her, its eyes bulging, its horns as sharp as they had always been, its facial expression one of a snarl.

She looked at it again. It looked normal, its facial expression blank, like every other *inkonkoni*. Perhaps she had imagined that snarl, or perhaps its spirit wasn't happy for being underground.

"Come on, *inkonkoni*, you are needed. The children of our tribe are in trouble, my little grandchild included. I'm sure I have now-now met the one who will be the great-wildebeest in this time. I need your spirit to accompany her, keep her safe, and to save the children."

CHAPTER 13

Botswana

Through the crack in the door, Akina saw the inky night sky, and the stars that stood sentinel over the ancient earth. The night noises from a settlement close by wafted in on the breeze. Music from a radio that played loudly, its beats and rhythms being shared with all the neighbors, but she didn't recognize the tune at all. A man and a woman arguing. The smell of fires and food being cooked.

In the darkness of the room, her eyes slowly adjusted to the muted light and the whole place came into focus.

Far from being dark, the room boasted sparkles of light in the tin roof above, where holes had rusted through the corrugated iron. Creatures scratched somewhere inside or outside the iron-clad hut.

"Is your head feeling okay?" Akina whispered.

"The nanny put *muti* on it. She said for healing. It make me itch."

"I still can't believe that man cut off your ear."

"I don't want talk about." Cherri's voice cracked as if she was about to cry again.

"Okay," Akina whispered, reaching for her arm and stroking it. "We won't. No cage tonight. At last a little space to stretch out, and they didn't even tie up our hands."

"I glad. I hate cages," Cherri admitted.

"Me too."

Both girls huddled together on the single mattress that was thrown onto the mud floor. Cherri moved slightly. "Did he speak where he take us?"

"No," Akina said. "But we have to get away. We are close to other people tonight. Can you hear them? Listen—"

She held her breath as the sounds wafted to them, like gentle music. The voices were too far away to make out words, but the people were talking, not shouting. Sounds of everyday life close by, not monsters like the man who was transporting them.

"I hear, but he will hurt me two times. He talk he cut off my other ear."

The girls fell silent at the sound of a voice right outside the room.

"Make sure you checked those kids are locked away safely," the silver-bearded man shouted. He got up and came toward the *hut*.

Cherri whimpered.

Akina could feel Cherri's whole body shake. "Stay still. Quiet."

She hoped if they were motionless, they would not attract any unwanted attention. She had moved their mattress to hide in the shadow at the back of the room. Taking a breath to be as still as she could, she shrank further into the corner, a blanket covering her body. Cherri snuggled into her side, clutching her own threadbare blanket to her chin and putting her hands over her mouth so she wouldn't make any noise.

They were both naked under their blankets. The woman had taken their clothes, apparently to wash them.

Akina was grateful if that was true. She hated the smell of herself and missed the deodorants that she'd started using, and the lovely scents. She longed to have green-apple shampoo and mint-flavored bubble gum.

The man blocked the sliver of light from the door, peeking through the crack. Moving around trying to see where they lay.

A mosquito bussed around Akina's head.

She dared not swat it, as even that could bring unwanted attention to them. She didn't want that man near them.

The man shook the door, ensuring that the chain held, but didn't open it. Finally, Akina could hear him as he walked away.

Akina tip-toed to the door, her blanket wrapped around, and peered out the crack.

He had gone back to the fire that danced in a cut-off drum. The woman who was looking after him sat nearby on a block of wood.

He pulled her closer.

She seemed to shrink away, even though physically he had drawn her to his side.

Akina frowned. It was interesting that she was scared of the silver-bearded man too.

"Don't even think of screaming. You make any noise and I'll slit your throat," he said.

Akina froze.

He began trying to hug the woman, and hold her, but she shrugged him off. He smacked her. The sound sickening in the night.

Akina put her hand over her mouth. She dared not cry out.

He pulled on her clothes and Akina wanted to cover her eyes with her hands but couldn't.

The man hit her again and knocked her to the ground. He had ripped off her top and as the woman tried to cover her breasts, he batted her hands away with a laugh.

"Look at those titties. Bet you really want a good fuck."

Then he took his trousers down, and she could see his bum.

She didn't want to see what was going to happen next. She fled back to the mattress, next to Cherri.

But she could still hear the woman protesting. The sound of flesh on flesh, loud and grotesque in the night that slowly turned to grunts, and then his, "Fuck you are so tight I will have to fuck you again."

Akina put her head onto her knees and used her hands to block out the sounds. Softly, she sang her Sunflower song.

It was quiet. Nothing moved. Akina looked to the roof to see that dawn light now shone through the holes, and a promise of the sunlight to come. Around the crack in the door frame, a slight blue hue was replacing the blackness.

"Cherri, you awake?" Akina asked, glad that while the younger child's

SONG OF THE STARLINGS

speaking English was getting better, her understanding of it was much better than when they had first met.

"*Yebo.*" She reached for Akina's hand on the mattress.

"I know it's dark, but it's when they are sleeping. It's time to try and run away. My father is trying his best, but we are going to have to help him. We need to get out of here."

"Your *Ubaba* not coming," Cherri said, pulling her blanket higher up to her chin.

"My father won't give up. He will find us," Akina said, still quietly but with conviction.

"We lost."

"Even if they take us further away, he will find us. We have to give him crumbs to follow. Remember the story of Hansel and Gretel?"

"*Cha.*"

"The crumbs of bread left to find the way home?" Akina said.

Cherri shook her head. She could feel the vigorous shaking against her body.

"It's a story about a boy and a girl who leave a trail of breadcrumbs when they go into the forest, so they don't get lost. But the birds eat the crumbs as food, and they can't find their way back. Finally, they find a house — you know what, eventually because they stay together, they find their way out of the forest again and live happily ever after," Akina said, hoping Cherri didn't ask for more of the story right then, because it was a bad example now that she thought about it. "What if we get away and then tell him where we are? That way we could be helping him. The white man's not here so he can't hurt us. Last time I made him angry, he cut off your ear, and made us start traveling—"

"Talk about happy thing?" Cherri asked, her voice flat. She sniffed. Clearing unshed tears.

"I don't know anything happy right now. Except trying to get away," Akina said softly.

"*Yebo,*" Cherri said again, her voice monotoned.

"We need to see if there is a way we can get out of this room. There are no windows. We can check around the bottom of the hut and see if there is a place we can squeeze out. Come," she said, standing, then pulling on Cherri's hand to help her off the mattress. Her legs were not as good as they had been, they still cramped from hours spent in cages and traveling in her box, but she'd make them work. Dropping Cherri's hand, she forced her traitorous limbs to listen to her. She stumbled to the iron side and began pushing on the bottom.

Cherri went with her along the edge of the hut looking for some small escape route.

There was nothing.

"We stuck," Cherri said, her voice defeated.

"For now. But maybe when they go to load us in the truck, we run, fast," Akina said. "Get away when he isn't looking."

"*Yebo*," Cherri said. "We go two." Showing two fingers close together.

"I won't leave you behind," Akina reassured her.

There was movement outside.

Akina froze.

"Wake up the cargo, get them in the truck. The sun is about to rise, time to go," the silver-bearded man said.

"Their clothes are not dry yet," the woman said.

"It'll keep them cooler in their boxes. Get them fed, quickly."

They scrambled back to their blankets and pretended to be asleep as the woman unlocked the padlock and took the chain off the door.

"Wake up," she said in English. "Here are your clothes. Get dressed. I will bring you something to eat. Make sure you go to the toilet in that bucket before you get into your boxes."

Akina nodded as she looked at the woman. She was dressed in ordinary clothes, a T-shirt and a long skirt. Both items had seen too many washes and were faded. Threadbare. Tatty. She had beads in her plaited hair. She moved as if she was in pain as she closed the door behind her.

She didn't lock it.

"Quick, get dressed. Hurry, Cherri."

They threw their wet clothes on as fast as they could but sliding wet clothes over their bodies wasn't easy. Cherri, who was in a skirt and top was dressed before Akina, who was still trying to wiggle into her jeans when the woman opened the door again.

She carried two bowls. "Eat." She put them on the floor and reached out to Akina to help her with her jeans. With the extra set of hands, Akina was able to get into them, and zip them up.

Tucking in her shirt, she said, "Thank you."

The woman looked at her and nodded her head in acknowledgment.

. . .

They walked out in front of the woman, with only one of her hands on each of their shoulders, toward the truck where the silver-bearded man waited. Ready to take them somewhere else they didn't want to go.

"Run," Akina said.

Both girls broke away from the woman.

"Go left!" Akina shouted. They turned and ran across the small, cleared patch of ground, and onto the path between some trees.

"Stop! Stop you idiots," he shouted.

Akina ran faster.

"Wait," Cherri cried.

Akina glanced behind her.

Cherri was falling behind, and behind her lumbered the man.

She held out her hand and Cherri grabbed it. Akina dragged her as they ran along the path, picking up a little speed, but Cherri still slowed her down.

Akina could hear the man's heavy footsteps approaching behind them.

She could hear his breathing.

Looking around wildly, she looked for shelter. Safety.

"Help us, anyone help us!" She shouted at the top of her voice. Surely someone would hear her.

"Come on. Cherri run. And scream as loud as you can," she said, increasing her stride again, pulling Cherri with her.

Cherri screamed.

Her heart beat fast in her chest. Her fingers hurt where she held Cherri's hand in a vice grip.

At last, she could see another hut through the trees — the woman outside had started her cooking fire. A skinny dog barked at them. The woman looked up.

"Help—" Akina screamed.

The silver-bearded man grabbed Cherri, ripping her small hand away and out of Akina's with a jerk. "Call out again and I'll kill her right here," he warned, his voice icy, his willingness to hurt Cherri clear.

Akina stopped.

For a moment, she contemplated seeing if he really would.

"Pinky sweared," Cherri cried. "Don't leave me."

"Who is there?" the woman asked, now walking away from her fire and closer to the bush. A large knife in her hand, raised in a threatening manner. Her dog was in front of her. Its menacing warning growl gave Akina goosebumps.

"Go back to your cooking woman," the silver-bearded man said. "We are just passing by."

The dog barked more. She could see the hair on its neck bristle. Its white teeth flashed as it pulled back its lips and snarled, protecting its owner.

Akina looked over her shoulder. Cherri was bundled under his arm. Her small body shook, her face pulled in agony as she sobbed, one arm held at a weird angle by the man. He dug in his pocket of his pants and drew out a Swiss army knife.

He was serious. He'd kill Cherri.

She couldn't live with the thought that Cherri was dead because of her.

Akina walked toward the silver-bearded man. He stepped out the way so she would be in front of him on the return journey and smacked her on the top of her head as she walked past. Hard. Causing her to stumble forward. But she didn't fall on the ground, saving herself in time. She didn't give him the satisfaction of seeing her lying on the ground and having mud on her clothes for the day. Her head rang as if he'd struck a giant bell over her and she could feel waves of every vibration of the heavy metal, even though it was just his hand. She glanced at him.

He was glaring at her. "Keep walking, you snot-nose brat, all the way to the truck."

CHAPTER 14

A hoopoe drilled into a tree somewhere close, a quick rhythmic knock, knock, knock noise as it searched for caterpillars or whatever other insects it could find under the bark.

Chrystal smiled.

Their resident bird was a constant source of amusement to her. She couldn't remember when they hadn't had a beautiful golden and black hoopoe hanging around the farmhouse. They had always been there, like the grey go-away birds bathing in the water feature and the blue faces of the guinea fowl scratching in the flower beds and roosting in the trees at night.

Chrystal heard Rowan moving around in his room. She'd been up since four, as usual. She'd already visited the stables, given instructions for the horses, and spoken to the farm foreman, to ensure that everything was running smoothly, and that they had their instructions for the day.

Now she made the coffee and put out a packet of biscuits.

"Morning," he said, walking into the room.

"Good afternoon. Sleep well?" It wasn't his fault that farmers got up before the sparrow farted, it was her routine.

"It's not that late, not even five-thirty in the morning. And no, I didn't sleep particularly well. I've been going over what that sangoma said, and I have a lot of questions."

"Me too, but most I probably can't answer. Right, let's start with something in our stomachs, shall we?" Chrystal said.

"Romany creams?" He read the box as he sat down.

"Sure, they're not rusks, but they will do."

"Hey Khulu, got coffee ready. Want some?" She greeted her grandfather as he walked into the room.

"Where's the rusks?" Khulu asked.

"Finished," Chrystal said. "Nicola called in for another week off. She said her sister is worse, and she thinks she's not going to make it."

"That's too bad, but it happens when we get old, and we've had our threescore and ten years," Khulu said.

"Don't tell me it's the circle of life bullshit—" Chrystal said.

Khulu laughed. "Don't need to, you said it first."

Chrystal smiled as she put the coffee in front of Khulu, pulled out her own chair and sat down. "To fill you in Rowan, this is the longest Nicola has ever taken off."

"How long has she been with you?" Rowan asked.

"Since I got to the farm. I was three. Twenty-nine years. Nicola was knocking on the kitchen door the day after I arrived. She told Khulu he should employ her to manage the house now that there was a child in residence. She had a daughter my age, and we could be friends."

"That's something special," Rowan said.

"No. Special was it was only 1987 and apartheid was in full swing. We had a white housekeeper, and while we had maids, like my dearly departed Nkosi, Nicola was the one who 'ran' this house. Khulu's always been a progressive thinker, and he knew he needed help when I came along. She supervised the house, made sure a child could live here. Nkosi looked after me."

"That's interesting," Rowan said.

"Nicola was the one who got everything done for me, while Khulu was running the farm when I was little. She taught me those nursery rhymes kids love so much."

"Does Nicola live in your house when she's here?" Rowan asked.

"Goodness no. She has her own little house on the farm. We pay her a pension now; she's the one who insists on still looking after our house. Beauty is technically our housekeeper now, but she can't cook for peanuts, despite how many hours Nicola spends with her trying to teach her. Beauty does all the work already, but Nicola still supervises her to stay useful."

"Nicola still works?" Rowan asked.

"*Ja*, only because I could never ask her not to come into the house. She would be shattered if I asked that of her," Khulu said.

"If she's retired, why work? Why ask for time off?" Rowan asked.

"It's her way of letting us know where she is, and that she's alright." Chrystal took a breath. "Nicola's husband was the foreman in the feedlot when we were still doing cattle, but he was killed in a car accident coming home from a bull sale. Khulu almost died that day too. Nicola and Stella-Rose moved in here with me while he was laid up in hospital, and then she looked after him when he came home."

She looked at Rowan. "After that, when he was well again, they moved back into their own house that she'd shared with her husband. I used to have romantic notions that her and Khulu would get together, but one day I went into her house and saw that her lounge area was a shrine to her late husband, and I knew that anyone who loved someone so deeply, even beyond the grave, would never love my grandfather enough in this world."

"Wow, that's something I never knew," Khulu said. "Interesting what comes out when your grandchildren get older. But you were right in a way. I think I'm the obstacle. I'll always be a one-women man and your Grandma Ella was enough for me."

Chrystal stopped talking. She couldn't believe she had revealed so much about her family to a stranger. Rowan had been here for a week, and she'd told him more than anyone other than Amy and Grace knew.

Khulu coughed. Helping her over the awkward moment. "What's your plans for today?"

"I want to check up on something that's bugging me about our fence line break. Then we're going to Weltevrede farm near the Botswana border. They have a huge underground storage area we want to look at. Ideal place to stash a kid. When we were in the shebeen last night, we also heard that there's a sangoma that works by the river there and baptizes people in the water. We'll try to find her too, perhaps she's part of The Circle that Busi, the Leopards Rock sangoma spoke about."

"And Pandora Timbers when we come back," Rowan added.

"Visit Stella-Rose at the mission? You sure?" Khulu said.

Chrystal nodded. "I know that while her and I don't talk much anymore, we still keep silent tabs on each other. She'll know about Rowan being here. I know that she's all about religion and making a better place for herself in the afterlife now, it'll give us an 'in' to Pandora Timbers — and we really need to look there."

"How'd she become involved in religion?" Rowan asked.

Chrystal shrugged her shoulders. "I don't understand it. She was always smart like, more super smart. We'd had rough times, even before she went to boarding school and then to varsity. After the fire, where she burnt out over half of our farm, she didn't seem to trust me as much. She didn't confide in me like she used to. She was angry at me for telling the truth, that she let the fire go, and I wasn't near it. She started studying to be a psychologist in Cape Town, I always thought that it was because she wanted to understand people better.

"But next thing, she flew overseas. Nicola said that she'd been called to God and went to Italy to train. I never got it then, and I still don't. It was as if she always wanted to be as far away from *Saliebos* as she could. But as long as we are not at each other's throats, I'm happy."

"You two never talked about it?" Rowan asked.

"A long story short. As primary kids we were inseparable, but then we were teenagers and Nicola decided Stella-Rose needed to go to boarding school in a bigger town, better school. She wasn't at the farm hardly at all anymore. She went from there to residence in varsity. I remember Khulu arguing with Nicola about her being so far away. But when she went overseas, she simply left. No goodbye, nothing. She was just gone. No letter for me at agricultural college, nothing. I chose to let it go. Now, all these years later, when she took over as Mother of the Mission at Pandora Timbers, we have a tentative truce because we are in the same neighborhood again."

Rowan frowned. "That's sad."

"That's women for you," Khulu said. "And don't dare try to interfere. It makes it worse."

"I have a sister, I know exactly what you mean," Rowan said.

Chrystal rolled her eyes. She wasn't going to be baited by their chauvinistic banter. But the news of his sister was — interesting.

"Khulu, even you said that when she came back after her training, she was different. Judgmental. I have to admit, she made an amazing transformation of that place though. It was derelict, and now it's a modern version of what it was back in its heyday as the local mission station, and she even now does international adoptions from there. She's really helping the community, her church and the children."

Rowan frowned. "The cash injections began when she arrived?"

"I don't know, but I do know that since she's been there, the mission looks more prosperous than ever. She's grown the orphanage side, got nice signs up. The only thing I hate about her doing so well in her church is that she won't sell to us so we can expand. She won't lease the land either. Which is weird, because when she started the place needed so much, it would have been easy money, but she said she wanted to preserve the land and keep it all private. An isolated retreat for her Sisters and her orphans, where they're in their own cocoon of space."

"Interesting," Rowan said as he stood up and went and put his mug in the sink.

"I'm dreading this meeting already," Chrystal said, putting hers next to his. "I need to brush my teeth, then I'm ready to *waai*."

Rowan frowned.

"Go. It means ready to go," Chrystal said, smiling.

Rowan watched from the passenger seat as Chrystal edged slowly into the herd of golden wildebeest that slept in the road. Some of them sat, chewing their cud, staring at her. Their golden eyes glaring, out from golden fleeces.

He wondered if perhaps the Greek mythology story of the golden fleece coming from a sheep had the wrong animal in it, and maybe it could have been one of these animals in front of him instead. They really did shimmer golden in the light.

They got up and moved out of the way begrudgingly, snorting as they did as if in disgust that she had the audacity to ask them to move. Their long tails intermittently swished at the flies, the sunlight shining through their raised manes.

She put her arm out her window and banged on the side of her Land Cruiser. "Come on, you lazy cows, move. I don't have all day."

"Are they always so docile?" Rowan asked.

"These are mainly cows and last season's calves, so not too much aggression from them. Besides they know this vehicle feeds them, so they shouldn't turn on me, but they need to get out the way a little so I can get through to the gate."

She pushed the remote on a farm gate and drove through, watching in the rearview mirror that no animals followed her through before it closed.

"Before we head out, I wanted to take you to the top of that *koppie* there, show you the fence line," she said, pointing directly in front of her at a small hill.

She navigated the overgrown bush road and slowly made the climb upwards, before she stopped her Cruiser and got out, leaving her door open. He did the same.

He could see across the green valley for miles. Nestled neatly inside tall hills and craggy rocks, with mountains in the distance. The smell of the freshness of the air made him feel alive. "It's beautiful."

"When I come here, I can almost feel my pioneer family's strength," she said, "as they navigated the untamed land. Their struggles to get here, their belief in creating a new life. That was even before they found iron ore in the area and the town exploded." She took in a deep breath and lifted her face to the sunlight. "I fall in love with it every time."

Rowan looked at her. She really did blend in with her environment, her blonde hair moving in the light breeze. She belonged here in Africa, along with her ancestors. She clearly had an affinity with the land.

He cleared his throat. "Where's your fence line?

"There." She pointed. "Can you see where this paddock backs onto the game reserve? That's the double predator fence," she said, pointing down to the north-east. "That's where we fixed the fence. From up here, above the tree line, we can see the roads running inside the reserve. Whoever he was targeted there, because it looks like a weak point, the only fence of ours that isn't electric.

"Whoever left the ear had knowledge, or access to information, of *inside* the game reserve, the official National Park. Not part of our reserve that adds to the park. That is the weak point in our fence line. Not here. I think I need to get Zenzele to start talking to some of the game guards in the reserve. Before this bastard leaves us any other messages."

"Let me see if I've got this right. You think the person who left the ear knows the area inside the game reserve, but not outside?" Rowan asked.

She was nodding. "*Ja*. He doesn't know who owns what. He's working from a line on a map, not local knowledge."

"Change of plan," said Chrystal, hanging up her cell phone. "Do a U-turn."

"Another one?" Rowan asked.

"Probably okay to call this one a detour. Khulu said there's a truck rollover right outside Frik's estate agency, it almost hit into his front window. Apparently, a mining truck failed to stop, and plowed into a goods truck. The Zambia truck driver was killed instantly, but he had two kids in the cab with him. They're being transported to the hospital. The one child was screaming about being taken away and kept asking to be taken home. Not to be left with the bad men. Khulu thinks we should get to the hospital as quickly as we can and talk to the kids."

"The likelihood of the police letting us talk to those kids is probably zero, but I'm willing to try," said Rowan, a new excited tone in his voice that she hadn't heard since the time spent with Busi.

"I agree." She nodded and smiled.

"Even if we don't get to speak to the children, we should be able to find out about the truck from Zambia. This might be the break we need to look at the trans-African roadwork network and find out how they are shipping these children," Rowan said. "Perhaps they are trucking them somewhere, like they do in America."

"Maybe." She bit the inside of her lip, not wanting to get her hopes up to have them dashed again.

"Or it could be an isolated incident," Rowan admitted. "We shouldn't get excited. We're aware that many of the long-distance truckers have a child that 'services' them while they're in one country. They ditch them before they cross the border, and a different trucker will pick up those same chil-dren for their route. It's all organized for them by an agency. Not all children are trafficked out of each country — crossing borders requires money, inge-nuity and time. Often the truckers aren't the ones dictating things. In the

USA, it's the traffickers who set up border crossings if they occur, and from what I gather, it's the same here."

Chrystal shivered. "You say that with such clinical coldness."

Rowan was silent for a while before he said, "It's like a knife. In there all the time. Turning. Slicing. But I can't let the emotions out until I have her back safely with her father. I have to believe she's still alive. She's too clever — too aware of the world, and how it works for them to have simply killed her. The fact that she can speak several languages, and picks up others fast, might be the thing that keeps her alive. I lost the last three kids; I don't want to lose her too." His voice almost broke as he swallowed the emotion.

"What do you mean you lost them?" Chrystal looked at him, frowning.

"I mean I was too late. Despite saving hundreds previously, the last three together cut deep. I retrieved bodies..." He stopped talking and looked into the distance.

"I'm sorry. I had no idea."

Rowan opened his mouth to talk, then closed it. Reluctant to tell her more.

"What happened?' she asked quietly.

His voice was strained when he continued. Filled with emotions. Broken. "All suffocated to death. Three little kids holding hands, huddled together for comfort in their last breath, stuck in a container because some fucktard put them in an airless tomb to move them from Houston to Miami." He took a deep breath in and out then looked at her directly. "It's the shit part of the job, for every happy reunion I get to do, there are far more deaths than you want to know about."

"That's harsh. It must be constantly on your mind. I had no idea. I'm sorry for being so flippant." She reached her hand out, then drew it back, unsure whether he would accept the contact.

"I probably owe you one too. I should've told you about it earlier. How far to the hospital from here?" asked Rowan, sitting up straight as if now ready to take on the world again.

"Half an hour."

"Did Ben mention the name of the trucking company?"

"No. You want me to call him back? Ask if he's still hanging around there? He can have a look for us."

Rowan nodded. "Switch with me. I need to use my laptop." He slowed and pulled over, then walked around the Land Rover and got back in the passenger seat. He took his laptop from his bag and searched for any news already coming out of Thabazimbi as Chrystal jumped behind the wheel and pulled the vehicle back onto the road, and dialed Ben.

Checking the Facebook community page first, then a search for any news items mentioning the accident, he concentrated on his screen.

Chrystal hung up the phone again. "Khulu said the name on the vehicle was Dhow Limited Transport Company. He's hanging around in case anyone other than the police approach the vehicle."

"Fantastic. And look here, we've got a tweet: 'Having a coffee. Suggest you avoid the center of Thabazimbi.' There's a photo, complete with a number plate."

He googled the transport company. "Their site says they truck copper down from Zambia, through Zimbabwe and Botswana, to South Africa. They also do routes north from Zambia, through to Dar es Salaam, some push through on the Trans-Africa highway all the way to Tripoli in Libya. There is a connecting highway in Zambia that cuts through and then crosses to Lobito in Angola, through to Tripoli eventually. Much of that road is still in disrepair or incomplete. Then there's the chance that this truck might not be connected at all. We can't get our hopes up."

"No, but we can be happy that these two kids are now found, and out of their clutches."

"We're here," Chrystal said as she turned the Land Rover into a small parking lot at the hospital. She nodded to the car guard as she walked away from her vehicle. "Come on. Emergency is this way — I know one of the doctors here. He's a friend."

"Another contact you have that I would need to try and get to know," Rowan said reassuringly.

"There has to be one good doctor I can call on when I need one. My anti-poaching guys can get pretty beaten up sometimes."

"Only the guys? He never had to patch you up?"

"A few times," she admitted, then smiled. "Not too much, I've been lucky."

They pushed through the doors and entered the hospital. The air-conditioner was working, and it was cooler inside. Sitting on the benches outside emergency were some two dozen people, quietly waiting their turn.

A woman held a child to her breast, feeding it.

An older man held a grubby cloth to his eye. She looked away before she saw any blood from his affliction. Another man sat with his child, sleeping in his arms. Another had a snot trail being wiped away from his nose, she couldn't tell what ailment the child had, but she was thankful that there was no blood for her to see.

Chrystal walked to the glass partition. "*Dumela*. My name is Chrystal Booysen. May I speak with Dr Carlo van der Westhuizen please?"

The black woman behind the counter kept her head down but looked above her glasses at her.

"*Dumela*. He is on duty. You must wait."

"How long must I wait?" Chrystal asked, ensuring to keep her voice light, and non-threatening. Friendly.

"Maybe two or maybe three hours, when he comes off duty."

Chrystal shook her head. "I don't need any treatment. I'm not jumping the line. This is an important matter; I'll only take a minute of his time. Please let him know I'm here to speak with him."

The woman gave her a disapproving look, then lifted her bulk from the chair and disappeared behind a doorway, reappearing a moment later. She buzzed them through and she said, "Dr van der Westhuizen said to go through into emergency, he is *baie* busy, but can talk to you between patients. Go to the red area. Follow the red tape that is on the floor. He says to tell you there is no blood."

"Thank you," Chrystal said.

"He knows?" Rowan asked quietly.

"Not now," she said calmly as they pushed through the security door and went into the actual emergency room.

Modern and clean, the room smelt like disinfectant. The cubicles were painted in a light sky blue, and surrounded by disposable curtains, on the walls were murals making the area feel a little less sterile. Nurses walked back and forth, going about their duties, ignoring the visitors as they followed the red stripe on the floor.

"I'll be out in a moment," she heard Carlo say through the curtain when she got to the red section.

"*Ja*, okay," she said.

"Take a seat," Carlo said loudly, then seemed to turn his attention back to whoever was behind the curtain.

Chrystal sat on a plastic chair. She bent down to take a look under the curtain. When she righted again, she looked at Rowan. "There are only his feet and a nurse's. Maybe we'll be lucky and he'll have a kid there."

Chrystal was instantly aware of Stella-Rose when she walked into the emergency room.

She kicked Rowan's chair to get his attention and motioned with her head as she hid it behind a magazine.

Another Sister was walking quickly behind Stella-Rose, the dark blue of her robe flapping slightly.

Chrystal hoped that Stella-Rose didn't notice she was there, before the nurse opened a different curtain to where Carlo was, and the sisters walked inside. The curtain was snapped closed behind them.

"That was Mother Stella-Rose Naude," Chrystal said.

"Why would she be here?" Rowan asked.

"She runs an orphanage. Remember?"

"The hospital called her before social services? That's an interesting move, even in South Africa," Rowan said. He stood up and walked quietly toward the curtain, Chrystal close behind him.

Rowan shook his head. Chrystal put her hand up as she listened.

They were talking Zulu.

"We do have runaways, we operate an orphanage not a prison," Stella-Rose said. "They ran away together, her and her sister Mthunzi. We filed the appropriate paperwork with the police department and social services when it happened. I'm delighted to get her back."

"There are still a few things to do. Social services need to be present, even though Nofoto asked for you. But we thought you could help her settle faster, and perhaps shed some light on this situation."

"It's been over six months since I reported them missing," Stella-Rose said.

Chrystal frowned. Stella-Rose was involved with the disappearing kids? Surely not.

That was a line she was sure her sister would never cross.

No matter how much she'd changed.

But what Stella-Rose was saying didn't add up.

From all the accounts of the orphanage, it wasn't a place that kids would run away from. Kids knew a good thing when they came across it, especially those who were already in their early teens.

Runaway kids made no sense.

Her frown deepened. Admittedly, she really didn't know Stella-Rose anymore.

And she didn't know Mother Naude at all.

"You can stay with her while we wait for social services," the doctor said. "She was lucky, she escaped with bruises — that's all. We have scheduled her to talk with our psychologist, losing a sister is never easy. We've also had a rape kit ordered, if you would like to stay with her for that, although Nurse Zeelie will be by her side constantly. She'll need lots of reassuring."

"Thank you, Doctor Ntebza. We're happy to see Nofoto, but we're sad to hear about the passing of Mthunzi. Believe me, we're relieved that she's been found."

"I'm not sure what's kept child services today. Excuse me," the doctor said.

Chrystal stepped back and grabbed Rowan, linking her arm to his and made like they hadn't been standing eavesdropping, but were walking and happened to be there when the doctor opened his curtain.

"Hey," Carlo waved. "Good to see you. What's up?"

"Thanks for sparing the time. I know you're super busy. Is there somewhere we can talk privately?"

Carlo pointed to a staff room, and they walked in before him. He closed the door.

"This is Rowan. He's an investigator looking for the American kid that went missing a few weeks ago," Chrystal said, speaking quickly as she knew time was of the essence. "He has reason to believe the little girl was brought to Thabazimbi and I've been helping him. Khulu was in town and saw the accident, so we know there were kids in that truck. I eavesdropped in on your Dr. Ntebza, talking to Stell — Mother Naude. We wondered if you knew anything about the kids?" She waited for him to reply, but he didn't, so she went on. "Or the accident? Could you arrange for us to speak with the doctor if she doesn't report to you?"

Carlo shook Rowan's hand then turned to Chrystal. "Whenever you're involved in something, there's always fireworks. It's a good thing I know you're on the good side."

Chrystal nodded. "I'm hoping you can bend the rules a little to help us, see if the kids in the truck are connected to the kid we're looking for."

"Dr. Ntebza's a locum. I'll get the file from her, have a chat and find out everything I can. I'll call you later." He went to leave but Chrystal stopped him, placing a hand on his arm.

"Carlo, you need to tread carefully," she said. "There's something really wrong with the kid's traffickers. We already had a child's ear pegged to a tree warning us away. Be careful, watch your back."

"That's fucked up — even by your world standards," Carlo said, his brows pinching together.

"*Ja* and getting weirder all the time," Chrystal said.

CHAPTER 15

Zambia

"See what happens when you try and run away," the silver-bearded man said. "The big boss-man comes to make you stay in line. Force you to behave."

"That's right," the white man said. "You get me joining you for the duration of your journey. Understand that no one is running anywhere. This beating on the black brat is for trying to escape last time, with a little extra, in case you two think it's a good idea to try again. Just don't."

Akina looked down as he grabbed hold of Cherri by the arm.

"Hold The Doll. Make sure she watches," the white man said, as the first blow connected with the side of Cherri's face.

Both Cherri and Akina cried out in pain.

"Stop. Please stop," Akina begged.

The white man ignored her.

Cherri's small body collapsed as his fist struck her stomach.

Akina saw the small bit of white spit at the side of his mouth, a sign of extreme excitement. He was enjoying hurting Cherri.

She tried to look away, but the silver-bearded man held her head and her eyes open with his big fingers.

When Cherri was punched in the stomach again, she threw up.

Akina vomited too.

The white man laughed. "You see little Doll; you feel every single blow to your little friend, don't you? Ah that religious zealot bitch was right. You have to find the soft place in your heart for a friend, then you can control any child." He dropped Cherri in a heap on the ground and gave her one more kick.

He walked to Akina and grabbed hold of her jaw. Hard. "Know that if you two ever attempt to escape again, I'll kill her. Her death will be on your hands. Is this what you wanted when you decided to try and escape? Your friend dead?" He smacked her backhanded hard across the face.

She tasted blood.

Whether it was hers from her cut lip, or Cherri's from his knuckles, she didn't know. Tears burned her eyes and spilled down her face, and suddenly she was free of the silver-bearded man, and she ran to where Cherri lay.

"I should have done this earlier, perhaps then we wouldn't be doing this fucking long drive, and we could have flown her, like the others. Bet you one thousand rands they don't try escape now."

Things had changed since they tried to run away.

Cherri took a long time to recover. Her little body had been badly beaten.

The bruising on Akina's chin from where the white man had gripped it had faded and was not as sore, but the memory of what he'd done to her friend was still fresh.

Cherri took a few days to be able to keep any of the food down that the women gave her, and she was having trouble sleeping. Akina had to hold her to comfort her. Often they woke when Cherri had wet herself.

Each night, the women who looked after them at each stop were different.

Sometimes younger, sometimes older. But they always had food, blankets, a cage or room to lock them in. Their clothes sometimes had been laundered and were sometimes dry, sometimes still damp. Sometimes they were given a bath in an enamel tub, but those had become a luxury, and were few and far between.

She watched as today's 'caregiver' made a cross over her chest before walking out of the room with the paraffin lamp sucking all the light with her.

Darkness.

They could hear the distinctive sound of a chain being pulled around the outside and through the corrugated iron and wooden doors.

"Did you listen anything?" Cherri asked.

Akina shook her head. "I keep listening for some of the languages I speak, but other than English I can't understand much they say. I think that the man with the silver beard and the white man speak Arabic to each other on purpose, so we don't understand them. The women don't seem to understand them either. I heard them say something about getting us to a port and it being an easy journey across an ocean from there, but that's all I have understood so far. The white man also said to keep off the toll roads and we're on this road to avoid the police roadblocks in Zimbabwe. Wherever we're traveling, there're still people about. You must not worry. My daddy will send someone to save us soon, it can't be much longer." Akina took a deep breath and whispered into Cherri's good ear, "Can you keep a secret?"

"I never tell. I swear. I keep secret," Cherri said.

"Pinky swear?"

They touched little fingers.

"Remember the bit of the story I told you of Hansel and Gretel? I've been leaving breadcrumbs like they did, only no birds are going to eat them. Since they started moving us around, I'm trying to help my dad find us. Every time we have a sand floor, I write his number in the dirt. I say: *Phone my daddy, he has $*. And I write his cell number on the ground. I keep hoping that one of the women will call him when we've gone. That they will not rub the number out without giving it a try."

"Cha. Scared of white man." Cherri said, shaking her head.

Akina smiled. "It'll only take one. He'll find us."

"We get free, we get home?" Cherri asked. "I no want stay. I go home."

"We don't have any money," Akina admitted. "And if we get caught again the white man will… I'm scared that maybe next beating he'll kill you. I don't want you to die." Her voice was quiet, and she had to swallow hard not to cry at that thought.

She did believe the white man would be true to his word.

Cherri was in real danger of being murdered.

"We not stay. We find help. Someone help," Cherri said.

"I don't think so. We're still kids. They would never believe us," Akina said, tears welling in her eyes.

"We get away, we find phone and phone your daddy. Then he send soldier," Cherri said.

Akina pulled a face her frustration evident. "Where are we going to find a phone? This is Africa, they're not on every corner, even in the cities, when I saw phones they were broken. Vandalized."

"Everybody has cell phone; we find one," Cherri said.

"Perhaps if we both know his number, and if one of us doesn't make it, the other one must phone. If we ever get the chance again, even for one of us to escape, we must so that my father's soldiers can come and save the other one," Akina suggested.

"I can't go. We promised."

"I know, but we have to. It's different now." Akina took a deep breath. She had to get Cheri to understand. "The white man hurts us, and he'll kill us soon. We don't have a choice; we have to get away or die."

"*Yebo*," said Cherri.

"You swear it?"

"Pinky swear," Cherri said, holding up her little finger.

They shook on it.

"You need to know my father's cell number. He always has it with him. Always."

Cherri nodded. "I learn numbers."

"Right, we start tonight. It's America +1 500 334 4555, Repeat it."

"+1 500 . . . umm."

"334 4555. It's easy, like counting numbers in sequence. Threes, fours and then fives."

"+1 500 334 455."

"That's it, almost, only three fives at the end." Akina smiled.

"I say it all the time and remember."

"Right . . ."

"Stop talking, go to sleep!" The white man hammered on the door.

Cherri jumped and pressed closer to Akina.

For a long time, they were quiet. Until they couldn't hear any movement outside.

"There are no windows tonight," whispered Akina.

"Maybe tomorrow," Cherri said.

"Perhaps we can find a piece of iron that's loose that we can sneak out of?"

"I look here," Cherri said, her voice raising a little above a whisper.

"Shoosh. Keep quiet or they will hear us," Akina warned.

Akina felt Cherri's whole body nodding before she scrambled away and went in one direction. She went in the other, pushing and pulling with all her whole worth against every inch of the *ikhaya* until she met back up with Cherri exactly where she had left their blankets again.

"Nothing," Cherri said.

"We can try again tomorrow. At the moment they are stopping every night. Sleeping somewhere. It's not like when they moved us first, where they drove through the nighttime. Maybe another stop we'll find something. What's the number?"

"+1 500 334 4555."

"Perfect." Akina wrapped the blankets around them both. "We'll go over the number in the morning and try again to escape."

It was so hot in her box.

Her bottle of water had run out long ago, but Akina tried to sip once more from it.

It was definitely empty.

They seemed to be traveling further today. She hadn't heard any cattle or anything else being loaded into the truck. From the drone of the engine she suspected they weren't carrying anything heavy. She'd begun to tell the difference and made it into a game.

Her legs cramped. "Ahhh," she screamed in pain. There wasn't enough room to turn her body and get to her legs to rub them. Her stomach hurt. She tried to breathe, but she couldn't.

The box was spinning around. She was going to be sick.

She hated the smell of vomit.

She rubbed her stomach, and her arms began to cramp too. The pain gripped her, and she could hear she was panting. Like a dog. The box spun more and then there was blissful silence all around her.

She was floating.

Someone was screaming and it hurt her ears. "She's dead! She's dead!"

She felt a cold splash on her face then heard a voice that she knew. "Get her out of there. Quick." This time he was speaking English.

She tried to turn away so water didn't go up her nose.

"Not dead. She moved," the man with the silver beard said.

"She's coming around. Good," the white man said. "More water. Cool her as fast as you can. You idiot Tahaan. With no animals or tarpaulin on, her box was directly in the sun and it was cooking her."

"You were the one to close her box this morning Levi, not me."

She heard the sickening crunch of flesh as people hit each other.

"Stop. Stop. You said two children?" A woman's voice, heavily accented

"Get her out and bring her here too," the white man, now she knew his name was Levi, said. She repeated it in her head so she wouldn't forget it.

The men returned. "Tahaan, help me open more bottles. Get some into her. She has heatstroke. Look at that rash on her neck."

The water was cool when the silver-bearded man — no, his name was Tahaan — when Tahaan lifted her head and let her drink. She gulped it down.

Her stomach cramped. Ripping pain through her, drawing her head down to her feet. It hurt.

She vomited it back up.

"Slowly, you need to sip it," Tahaan said pressing the bottle to her lips again.

She sipped.

Her head thumped.

Her eyes hurt.

Everything hurt. She tried to sit up. The world swirled.

"Keep her lying down," Levi instructed.

"The other girl is not so good, she's awake, but dehydrated badly," the woman was saying as she carried Cherri around and put her next to Akina on the ground.

"She was protected a little being on the side, her box would have been mostly in the shadows," Tahaan said.

"Bring their blankets. We need to wet them. They will help cool the kids down. Keep getting water into them both. Tahaan, see if there's a Fanta in the hep-cooler, not Coke, they must not have caffeine. Lots of sugar to get their electrolytes up. If we add some salt that would be good too."

Tahaan got up and left.

"Bring something to elevate their feet too," he instructed the woman.

She scurried away.

"Don't you fucking die on me brat. You're worth too much money," Levi said. "Besides, I think The Mother Bitch would slit my throat herself if that happened."

Another name she had to remember for her father's soldiers.

She closed her eyes and let the hammering in her head drown out his putrid voice.

Akina had the shakes.

She could feel her whole body shivering. Her teeth chattered. Freezing tendrils gripped her skin, despite the big fire nearby. She could see the orange flames. The woman was holding her, rocking her back and forth in a steady rhythm, her face sweating.

"She needs a doctor. Medicine for fever," the caregiver said.

"No doctor," Levi said. "She'll survive. She might be in a bit of pain, but she'll be fine. She's too stubborn to die, that one."

The woman increased her rocking. "The little girl needs another blanket; see she shivers. From the bunk. I get it."

"No. You stay there, the older one is your responsibility. Tahaan, fetch another blanket," Levi said.

Akina closed her eyes, the noise in her head too loud to listen.

Akina woke up. At last her body didn't feel like it was burning or freezing. She could feel something soft underneath her, something warm wrapping her up. She snuggled in. Her head no longer had a thunderstorm inside. Her tummy grumbled.

"She awake," the caregiver said. "No fever. She needs food."

"Thank goodness," Tahaan said, and she could hear him sigh.

"Can we continue our journey?" Levi asked.

"She weak, but keep in the air-conditioning. Should be okay — they need to be cool," the caregiver said, her English broken.

There was a moment of silence.

"That means that you have to travel too, until they are well. I can put you on a bus to get you back when they are better."

"What about my family? How many days?" the caregiver asked.

"Your daughter will be returned if you do this, as a thank you. They can stay behind the curtain all the time. It'll be your responsibility to make sure they don't try and move. Not for anything. Understood."

"I understand," the caregiver said.

"Hey, Japanese Doll." He poked her in the ribs. "You hear me? You don't move from behind that curtain or I'll cut off the other of your little friend's ears."

Akina nodded.

She knew not to argue with Levi.

Akina and Cherri were locked in yet another room.

But today's travel hadn't been as bad as expected. They were in the curtained off section of the truck.

Akina knew it was so they didn't die.

The caregiver looking after them had stayed by her side the whole night. Checking on her constantly, giving them both sugar water and salt. She was still with them that night when they arrived at the next caregiver's house.

They were transporting a massive amount of redwood in the back of the truck. Levi was giving the woman instructions. "Make sure they are dressed like boys. Tomorrow we push through to the border post, they cannot be found if we get stopped. With so many trucks on this highway, these border patrol guards are harder to bribe than others. Understood? We protect the assets at all costs. The Doll is too valuable to lose. Use the other as a shield if you have to. The Doll has to get to auction."

There's an auction? Akina tried hard to think of what that meant. This was the second time she had heard them refer to their destination as an auction.

"We look-see the room," whispered Cherri.

"Did you notice the window?" Akina asked. "I think it's too high for us."

"I stand," Cherri motioned to her shoulders. "Look-see."

"After we check the bottom. Must be an easier way than trying to get out the window. That man said tomorrow we cross to Malawi, so at least we sort of know where we are," Akina said, keeping her voice low. "Do you remember the number?"

"+1 500 334 4555. I told you I learn it," Cherri said with pride.

"Let's check around the bottom." The girls went along the hut's edge performing their ritual, looking for some small escape route out.

"Nothing. Try to stand on my shoulders," Akina said.

"But how you get up?" Cherri asked.

"You might need to go alone. Leave me here," Akina admitted, her voice showing the stress she felt, and the fear of being the one left behind.

In the dim light, Cherri shook her head. "*Cha*. Cha dark alone."

"Okay, then all you have to do is look out and see where we are. If there are lights close by or if we are alone in the bush. We can decide once we know. One step at a time. My dad always said that to me. One step. Then another."

"Your *ubaba* is nice. When soldiers come save us, I meet him?"

"I'm sure you will. You ready to climb?"

"*Yebo*," Cherri said, nodding vigorously.

They had a few false starts, then finally Cherri had her feet firmly on Akina's shoulders. "Walk your hands up the wall so we can balance, you are heavier than I thought...."

"I trying—"

Akina took the weight of Cherri and held her ankles.

"A little bit more, I see trees and lights. Far outside," Cherri said, a bit too loud.

"Shhhhh. Are there bars on the window?"

"Cha," Cherri whispered.

"Can you climb out?"

"I wiggle. I climb the wood here and out, but I how far to the ground? All dark outside." Cherri tried and wobbled on Akina's shoulders, but eventually admitted. "More higher. I can't hold on and get up."

Akina looked around. There were only the two old mattresses in the room, and a metal bucket to pee in, nothing else. "Get down; we can put them on top of each other, get the bucket, and try again."

They pushed the mattresses together and put the toilet bucket on top. Akina stood on the bucket which wobbled, forcing her to hold onto the wall to steady herself. This time Cherri could pull herself up a little and climb into the window. Akina's shoulders ached. She ignored the throb as Cherri stood on them.

Crouched over inside the window, one leg inside the room, one outside, with her hands protecting herself in the middle from the iron so it didn't cut into her, Cherri balanced. "It far down, but there is lights close-close."

"Can you get down on the outside? Are there footholds?"

"Nothing. *Cha* down." Cherri said, her voice even in a whisper low and filled with disappointment. Despair.

"Maybe we tie the blanket together, then we put it out the window so that you have some on the outside, and I have on the inside. I'll hold this side; you hold the other and climb down. Then you hold it strong so I can climb up and I can get out too."

"*Yebo*," Cherri said as once again she climbed down and then got off Akina's shoulders. When their blankets were tied together, she climbed back up and made sure that the blanket was halfway, with the knot in the middle and the blanket covering the sharp edge of the corrugated iron.

"Does it touch the ground on the other side?" Akina asked.

"Nearby," Cherri whispered.

"Go. Climb out."

"What if you too big?" Cherri asked.

"I'll fit. I can wiggle too. I'll come after you," Akina assured her.

Cherri was shaking her head. "*Cha*. Be far. Dark."

"Go ... once you're down, I can come after you. My legs are longer, I won't need the blanket to get down that side, so we'll be fine."

"I scared," Cherri said as she clung to the edge of the windowsill and to the blankets.

"Me too, but you're the bravest person in the whole world right now. Look at where you are and what you're about to do. You're going to get out the window, and then, we'll be free. Away from those horrible men."

Cherri disappeared out of the small space.

Akina held her breath and held tight to the blanket. Cherri's weight on the other side pulled the blanket. She heard a small thump as Cherri held, and then slid further down the blanket against the tin of the room.

"Shhhhhhh, Cherri you have to be quiet or they will hear!" Akina warned, then she heard a loud rip, and her side of the blanket fell on top of her.

There was a hard thud on the other side. Cherri didn't scream.

"Are you okay?" Akina asked quietly.

"It wasn't too nearby. I can't get up again. What we do?"

"Hang on, I'll climb up," Akina said, and she stood on the bucket and tried to grab at the ledge and find a hold she could use to get up.

But she couldn't.

There was nothing for her to cling to.

She was too short to even reach the ledge.

"I can't," Akina admitted. "Cherri I can't get up to the window!"

"I *cha* get back inside. What we do?"

Akina put her forehead on the metal barrier. "You're going to run to those lights and get help for both of us."

"But I naked. What if I *cha* come back?"

"Wrap yourself in the blanket, until you can find some clothes to borrow. Then make sure you get to call my dad. Tell him where we are. Tell him to send a strong soldier to fetch us. Pinky swear you'll get help for us both."

"I *cha* leave you. We promised. Remember?" Cherri said then hiccupped.

"Shhh… quiet. I remember, but we also promised after we tried to run away and failed, that if one gets a chance to leave to get a message for my father, then they have to. I can't climb up there, and if they find you outside, Levi will cut off your other ear — or kill you. You need to escape. Get us help. Remember to be very quiet... they mustn't know. You're very brave and the best friend I've ever had."

"But—"

"Run Cherri. Go for those lights. Find a phone. Don't come back," Akina pleaded. "Get away from Levi."

"I won't come back. Pinky swear."

134

The cockerel crowed, telling the world that in his territory, he controlled time.

A new day had arrived.

Akina woke with a start.

She looked at the ripped blanket that she was wrapped in.

Hopefully Cherri had made it away and was still alive. That someone where the lights were would help her.

She hoped that she would remain alive after Levi found out what had happened.

Because any moment now the new caregiver who'd locked them in would come back with their breakfast, and Akina was sure she'd raise hell even more than the rooster. The sun was about to rise, and so would Levi's temper.

Akina took a deep breath. "Daddy, I'm your daughter. I'll stand up to adversity and corruption, but this, with Levi and his beatings, is going to be really hard. Help me. Please help me to be strong like you."

She heard a noise outside as the door opened and the caregiver brought in the breakfast of mealie-meal porridge and meat, only this morning there was a jug of milk too.

She put the tray down. "Where is she? Where is the other one?" she whispered, her voice urgent.

"Gone," Akina said.

"No. No. Doesn't you understand? Now my own daughter will die. He's going to kill her."

Akina stared at the woman. Her face was one of despair. One who had suffered and was in shock.

They had learned early on not to ask anyone of them for help. They were all too scared of the men to do anything.

Now she understood the reason why.

"We didn't know about your daughter. The blanket broke—" Akina was still whispering. "You can get Cherri and sneak her back in here, if she's outside." She crossed her fingers behind her back to excuse her lie.

She knew Cherri wasn't coming back.

But perhaps in her distress the woman would make a mistake and Akina could make a run for it too.

The woman straightened her T-shirt she wore over a long blue skirt.

"They will take her and make her service the soldiers now." Tears filled her eyes and she wrung her T-shirt in her hands. "My daughter. My poor daughter. She will be dead."

Akina reached out and put her hand on the woman's arm. "Go find Cherri. It's okay, you have to do what you need to survive. It takes courage to do differently, and I won't blame you if you choose not to. I wrote my father's number in the sand behind the bucket. Please try to call him. Please try to make it right. He has lots of money and can help you get away from here and make a new home for your daughter far away. Go find Cherri, bring her back so they don't know she got out."

"There is no future for me and her, unless I do what they ask," the woman said. "If they catch me phoning him, they will kill me."

"Then don't get caught. My father is rich. He will pay you for helping me."

The woman shook her head. "My daughter. They will kill her now."

"Then don't help me, but quick, at least try save your daughter. Cherri will be outside, go bring her inside. Before they wake up!"

The woman ran out the room, but Akina still heard the chain as she put it back in place.

Locking her captive inside.

CHAPTER 16

Saliebos Farm, Thabazimbi, Limpopo Province, South Africa

3rd April 2016 — 27 days until auction

A soft but sharp knock on her door woke Chrystal.

"Can I come in?" Rowan said quietly.

"Sure," Chrystal said as she pulled the sheet up to her neck and looked at the time — 02:14.

Rowan walked just inside her bedroom. Like a leopard in the shadow, he stopped near enough so he could talk while still keeping a respectful distance from her. "Sorry for waking you but I got a call from Curtis Wilson. Long story short, he said he received a call and it was a young kid's voice. All she could say before her time ran out was that Akina is alive and needs help."

She pulled her cotton dressing gown closer. "Fantastic—"

"It sounds like she didn't have enough credit on the phone to make an international call. The number is registered to a Salin Jambga. Her location is listed as Mpika, Zambia. It's on the Great North Road, six-hundred and fifty kilometers north of Lusaka."

"I know where it is," she said, struggling her arm into one sleeve then the other.

"Confirmation of her being alive is good news. News that she's heading north through Africa, means we're closer than yesterday," Rowan said. "We're booked on a chartered jet. I'm kind of hoping that your guys have passports. I'd assumed that we'd be able to travel as a full strike team."

She nodded. "They all have passports. I'll leave a second team on call here, with instructions to follow should we need them. The rest of my teams need to remain at home. *Saliebos* can't be left unprotected."

"Our charter leaves from Lanseria airport at ten. We can update the names on the manifest when we get there." Rowan stepped away from her.

"You got this all organized already?" Chrystal frowned. "How?"

"Holly, my kid sister. This is what she does. She organizes. I've learned that she's really good at it, and now I trust things like this to her."

"You haven't mentioned your sister worked with you before, only that you had one," Chrystal said.

"Holly is three years younger than me, but anyone watching her would think she's the oldest. She's bossy as hell. But I love her dearly. She's a partner in my business, and I couldn't do without her."

"And here I thought you did everything alone," she said, tying a knot in the gown belt around her waist.

"You of all people should know, you go alone, it takes a long time, go together, the journey's achieved much faster," Rowan said. "I'm only a part of my company. There's a team working behind me — as with any good operation. A lone wolf is dangerous, can't bring down something big like a caribou. A pack is a much better idea."

Chrystal smiled. Hearing the American animals he used was a reminder of how different the worlds she and Rowan operated in were. "In Africa, we would have said being part of a lion pride could bring down a buffalo."

She was rewarded with a flash of his smile.

"But I have to give credit where it's due too," Rowan admitted. "A lot of this speed was also the Zambian air force. When they found out why we're in such a hurry to get there, let's say they were super cooperative. They'll meet us in Lusaka and take us anywhere we want to go. Apparently, they're moving helicopters from Livingston for us. There is no airport at Mpika, it's an airfield, and probably hasn't been used commercially for the last twenty years or so. From what Holly could gather, the air force controls all airspace in the country and the local police chief from the Mpika's Tazara Station was told to make ready for us."

"Interesting. The air force controlling the space is true, in a fashion. Zambia is really big, and the north isn't that well patrolled. Sometimes crafts fly over the border, and they know nothing about it, or rather they claim ignorance." She slid out of bed, trying hard to make sure that the gown was covering her.

"Talking from experience?" Rowan asked, but his voice was breathy as if he had been running.

"Fortunately for me, yes." Chrystal paused, checking what she was going to say next, before she continued. She didn't need to go into the details of her previous operations, and where she was or what had happened.

None of them were relevant to finding Akina.

She looked down, realizing that she'd just flashed Rowan probably more than she was comfortable with.

Tough. It was her room.

She lifted her head and looked at him directly. "We leave at sunrise. We can take my helicopter. Grace can bring it back and she'll do some of the mustering that I'm due to do with Khulu." Chrystal's mind started to race, constructing a list of what needed to be done. "I can take four in the chopper, so I'll get Zenzele to load gear and he can leave early with the men. We fetch Grace. It'll only take us about an hour to Lanseria. We'll need to make sure they have a landing pad available for us—" She was standing next to him now.

Rowan smiled and he didn't move any further from her. "Expected as much. The private company I use will have already begun notifying their ground staff."

"What type of charter?" Chrystal asked as she went past him and switched on the main light. The brightness made her blink as she got used to it, but she saw Rowan look down her body, then back up, before looking away.

"One who knows the urgency of what we're doing and has the flexibility to work around us the whole time we're out the country. They're good, but we won't get away with weapons on board. Not going into Zambia."

She stepped away a little. Putting some space between them. "That won't be a problem — I know a supplier. He works out of Kitwe, and he's become part of the maNtuli network. Her suppliers are like a spiderweb up that way, into the Congo, Uganda, Chad and Sudan. If there's conflict, believe me, there's a supplier of hers there. Once we know what's happening with the child who called, I can arrange the rest. We'll be limited on what we can do as long as we have air force and local police with us."

"It didn't look like we had an option but to have them tag along, at least for the initial meeting," Rowan said.

"Probably not. Depending on what this girl has to say, and how far behind Akina we are." She pulled out her dressing table chair and offered it to him. He shook his head. She sat there instead. She didn't feel as exposed as in the bed.

"One step at a time," Rowan said, but his fingers were already drumming a hurry-up-and-wait signal on his crossed forearms.

"If we don't find Akina, we'll need that arms cache drop. And I would suggest that we touch base with all the other anti-poaching businesses along the way heading north. They'll cover us. If the trail goes toward Congo and Sudan, the game guards will know where the rebels are and keep us clear of them. The weapons we pay for will need a home when we're done and handing them off to an anti-poaching group is better than destroying them. They're underfunded at the best of times, but those men and women have heart. They'll be there for us."

"We'll certainly need that cache before we go after the traffickers," Rowan said as he now paced her room.

Back and forth like a caged wild cat.

Chrystal watched him move. "It's possible, even in Zambia. Trust me. Hopefully we can catch Akina before they cross the border again. Mpika isn't that far from the Nakonde Border into Tanzania, six hours on a good day. If they get spooked, and turn left, then we'll be tracking through the Democratic Republic of Congo. That's hostile territory at the best of times. A beautiful but harsh place. Rather they go toward Tanzania. Easier route."

"That's positive thinking, but Africa is rather large, and you talk as if it's small. That's still a massive distance to cover from here," Rowan said.

Backward and forwards. He was getting ready for battle. Restless. An apex predator.

"But they have to cover it too. We'll catch up fast. I'll give you more on the trans-Africa route while we're in the air," Chrystal said. She took a deep breath and slowly let it out.

Out there on the road was some form of transport carrying Akina, now it was up to her and her team.

Like wild dogs, once they got scent of their prey, they were officially on the hunt.

Hopefully the odds would be the same, if not better than a painted dog pack: they would find her.

CHAPTER 17

Pretoria, Gauteng Province, South Africa

3rd April 2016 — 27 days until auction

"Davinia. *Wosa*," maCalio called and beckoned with her hand. "Show Velaphi the ropes. Make sure she knows them well."

"*Yebo*," Davinia said.

It'd only been six months since they'd moved into the new warehouse on the outskirts of Pretoria and at last, she could hire a few hand-picked people. There was too much work for the number of people who worked there now.

This new warehouse was good. There was more room inside but importantly outside too. She liked that it was removed from everyone, and in an older part of the town, away from the business of other factories and warehouses. maNtuli liked the location too, or she would never have shifted everything here.

"Come, Velaphi. I'll show you how we get this all done," Davinia said. "maCalio expects everybody to work fast, but you'll get used to it. A shipment came in last night, already they have all been unloaded from their boxes somewhere else and loaded into our own boxes and brought here. See the boxes are all stacked neatly over there to put things back in."

"Why?" Velaphi asked.

"Eish." Davinia shook her head. "You need to learn not to ask questions, to just do what you need to do."

maCalio smiled as she continued to eavesdrop.

"You're new, so I'll let you know that first of all, they're all checked to make sure that no one has hidden a cell phone or a camera inside to watch us. maCalio is worried, she said that they suspected that someone was trying to hurt maNtuli's business, so she changed the way we clear the weapons when we moved to this place."

Velaphi nodded.

"Now, in this warehouse we get these weapons stripped down. You do three or four of the same type at the same time. Always more than two. When you re-assemble again you take different pieces from each, never the same parts in the same gun. Assembling from different pieces from different guns. Never the same," Davinia stressed.

maCalio smiled again. Davinia was good at settling people in, making sure they understood their roles. Their new recruit was sharp. Hand-picked by maCalio herself. Davinia didn't tell her that many of the weapons came from the police, that they were redirected to their operation, instead of being destroyed, not only for the general gun amnesty the government had running, but from evidence too.

maNtuli had a deal going with the contractor at the police armory. Guns, millions of rounds of ammunition. Their source was good for business. As good as those rebuying at the other side of the transaction.

But that was an area that maCalio didn't have anything to do with. She looked around. This, this was her part.

"*Yebo*," Velaphi said.

She continued to eavesdrop.

"This table we each have a section of. We're expected to keep it clean, if we don't maCalio comes and she'll smack your head. Believe me she hits hard. Make sure you always keep your workstation tidy; you cannot afford to have any dust anywhere near the weapons."

This time, maCalio hid her smile.

"Okay," Velaphi said. "It looks simple enough."

"Don't be fooled to think it's simple. As you go, you check that every single part number is different. If she checks and one's wrong, then we'll pay the price."

• • •

143

She'd walked away from the Velaphi, knowing that Davinia had it under control, and was helping the older women in the polish and packing section.

"maCalio, *woza. Woza!*" Davinia called.

maCalio strode over.

Davinia handed her an electronic box. "That is not part of any gun."

It was sealed square and didn't have a light on it.

"Look. This was hidden inside the butt of this shotgun. When Velaphi took that rubber end off, it fell out."

maCalio moved the electronic box from one hand to the other, studying it. "Winston, *woza.* You worked at the train station up the road, yes?"

"Yebo."

"And you didn't get fired, you just left?" maCalio asked.

"Yebo."

"Take this box and go to the train station. You need to put it onto a train and make sure that it stays on the train. You must not throw it. You have to get onto the train and put it carefully or it might break." maCalio was wiping her fingerprints off the small box with a soft cloth. She then wrapped it up in another piece from the rag box.

"A train with passengers?" Winston asked.

"It is better if it is a goods train, but I do not care as long as it is moving away quickly. Don't worry that box won't hurt anyone, as long as it keeps moving."

Winston nodded.

"Davinia, take Winston and drive that *bakkie* over there. Go to the train station. When you two are finished, you take Winston back to the Joburg warehouse. I will send someone there in a day or so to fetch him. But you, you come back here, and you hide on the roof of that building up there, and you watch this place. You take photos of anyone who comes to the gates and you do not leave that roof until I tell you."

"*Yebo,*" Davinia said.

maCalio held out her hand. "Here are the keys and some rands for petrol, but do not stop before Winston gets that box on the train. Understood?"

"*Yebo,*" Davinia said, closing her fist on the cash, and she watched as Winston was handed the electronic thing in the cloth.

"Go," maCalio said. "Get rid of that thing, quickly. Your lives depend on it." She turned around to the warehouse and spoke loudly. "Everyone listen up, quickly, pack up. Fast. Reload all these crates and boxes, put all the weapons into the cattle truck. This place must have not one spring or anything to show that these guns were here. Collapse the tables and the chairs and put them in last. We leave here in half an hour. Do you hear that, thirty minutes? Pack this workshop up. Totally."

She strode out and lifted her phone from her pocket, already dialing maNtuli's number.

"You were right. Someone is looking for you or looking to double-cross you. They put an electronic tracker inside the last set of guns. I have sent it away, but we are clearing out. Just to be safe."

"It is a pity. I was beginning to like that warehouse, it is close to a big transport hub," maNtuli said, her voice calm. "It wasn't in the plan to close down that warehouse when I got the farm. It was meant as an expansion."

"We can come back in a few weeks, once the police have raided. They would not raid a place twice, if they see there is nothing here," maCalio said.

"True. Move the truck to the new farm." maNtuli said. "We should be safer there simply because it has its own sangoma watching over it. It is sooner than we planned to begin any work, but it will be the answer for now." The call cut off.

maCalio looked at the truck. It was half full, she could fit all the workers in too without any problems, and there was still her Cruiser to load. She walked back inside the warehouse, pocketing her phone. The farm was a better choice than the other warehouse in Polokwane. No other workers there for these ones to talk to.

"We are moving away. You will continue your work. Nobody stays behind. If you have to call your family, do it now. Switch your cell phone off after that as I am collecting phones for a week or two at least. You will have an *ikhaya* where we are going and food, but it is a little out of Joburg. We will look after you. Anyone want to stay behind?"

No one's hand went up.

Good, she didn't really feel like shooting anyone today.

Her phone rang. "We were lucky, there was a train about to leave the station. It is gone," Davinia babbled.

"You have done well. I will call with more instructions soon. *Humba Kahla*." maCalio hung up her phone.

She locked the warehouse door behind her as everyone was already sitting on the back of the truck. The old man Hunter and his son, Vitalis,

145

began closing the weather sides of the vehicle. His people and the guns would be dry and safe inside.

Hunter had worked for maNtuli longer than she had, and she trusted the old man. He had helped her settle into her place and been there while she rose up the ranks to 'ma'.

maCalio did not forget such things.

"Follow me. If you lose me, do not worry, I will find you again, keep driving toward the R510 and Thabazimbi."

Hunter nodded and then got in and started the truck.

maCalio knocked twice on the door next to the small spider motif that marked the truck as maNtuli's and the old man did a big circle in the yard, before driving the truck out the warehouse's gates and heading north.

maCalio stood outside the doors to the barn at Leopard Hill farm. The electronic control for the gate had worked, which probably meant that the whole of the electric fence was already working too. She had flicked on the floodlights that she'd had installed, and they were working perfectly. It was almost like standing there in daylight.

Not that she planned to use them often, people in the country would talk if they saw bright lights like a sports stadium lighting up the night sky, but if she needed them, like tonight, they were there.

Her contractors did not disappoint. They knew better to over-deliver and deliver fast.

And it was just as well.

She watched the old Mack truck drive in, slowly inch around the side of the barn, and stop next to her vehicle. When Hunter turned off the engine, she could once again hear the slight throb of the generator, because everyone knew that you couldn't rely on Eskom for power.

"Welcome to the new warehouse," maCalio said. "A few weeks early. We can offload now, and then lock the barn for the night. Probably better to cover everything inside with tarpaulins. In case we have a contractor who wants his throat cut tomorrow."

Hunter nodded.

"They still have another week's work before they are finished upgrading everything, but I will have a word with their boss."

"And our people?" Hunter asked.

"They can choose a house, we built enough for them. Just past the sheds is a new housing compound. They will need some sleep tomorrow, after their late night today. We will wait until the contractors are gone before they unpack the boxes and carry on working. And warn them about Busi, the sangoma. But I know our workers. A week out of the schedule will not make a difference on this order. We will still ship on time." maCalio smiled.

A cockerel crowed, then another.

How was it that even when there were hardly any residents on a farm, there was always still a cockerel?

The sun was lightening the sky from inky black to a cooler blue as it raised its yellow head above the horizon. maCalio was sitting at the kitchen counter in the main farmhouse, sipping tea. Rikki sat on the counter next to her hand, purring as she stroked him.

"Your hair has grown out nicely, almost looking like a cat again, and not a poodle," maCalio said as her phone rang.

Davinia was whispering. "The police came to the warehouse and raided, like you said. They were not quiet about it, even sleeping on the roof next door I could hear. They followed the tracker on the train, the policeman was not happy."

"Did you get photos of the policemen who were there?" maCalio asked.

"*Yebo*, but it is still a little bit dark. And they are far away, even with the zoom," Davinia said. "I'll keep taking more, they don't look like they are going away anytime soon."

"Send them to me. I'll talk to you later. Stay out of sight and remember, do not get caught," maCalio said, ending the call.

maCalio stroked her cat. "That one has been with us for a long time. She is solid. It is time to teach her more. Move her up in the ranks."

She flicked through the pictures on her phone. "Let us put them on my computer," she said. "Sometimes you can see better on a larger screen." She collected her device and the cord from the room she was using as her study, and they were soon looking at her screen.

"Look, that one is Constable Duma Tshabalala, I would recognize him anywhere," maCalio said aloud.

The cat looked at her as if it understood.

She smiled.

"That one looks like Detective Zweli Sithole. But I can't make out who is standing next to him, in the plain clothes."

More pictures came through.

"Look who that is standing in the background. There," maCalio said. "Eish. Elias De Waal, himself. He didn't even send one of his *lackeys* to look at what was happening in the raid. That double-crossing asshole."

Her cat yowled when she hit the countertop with her fist.

"At least we know who the problem in the supply chain starts with, but we do not know why he wants maNtuli out after all these years? Who is the one he wants to supply to?" maCalio said.

She sat still for a minute, staring at the screen.

Stay safe on the roof Davinia, because soon you are going to be busy.

She made a mental note to call her again and give her the instructions. Follow Elias De Waal. Everywhere. She needed pictures of who he talked to and anyone he met, both inside the police armory and outside in the real world.

She ran through Davinia's story in her head. She'd finished school all the way to year twelve. Her mother made sure she had an education, but Davinia was on the streets a lot while her mother worked hard for the money. Her and her brother. The brother wasn't so fortunate, he wasn't as clever as Davinia, and got caught stealing. He went to jail and died there. Davinia came to work for maCalio over four years ago because she tried to pick maCalio's pocket. She had a gift for not being seen.

"But does she have a stomach for what we have to do sometimes?" maCalio asked aloud, running her hand over Rikki's newly grown fur. "She is young still, only twenty-two."

maCalio smiled. At that age she had been running her own business for three years already. But she had no time to dwell on the past now.

Busi, the sangoma had been right, she had troubles.

And it was something to do with metal. Machines of war were definitely made of metal.

Someone was trying to muscle in on the gun running business and cause her trouble. There had been incidents up north in the Congo. Unexplained and unfortunate happenings. In Sudan, the same thing— ammunition caches going missing or being blown up.

Now the electronic tracker in the weapons from the South African police force armory. She had to find out who was the *nyoga* behind it all. And then, they would die.

She wouldn't allow any competitors to muscle in on her arm of the business that she ran for maNtuli.

She owed her too much to let her down.

Davinia was her eyes on the ground in Pretoria at the moment.

But she knew of other eyes that were unexpectedly looking north now, and she predicted that any moment, her nearly next-door neighbor would call on maNtuli's supply chain.

She needed to be doubly cautious. After all, they were sisters now. They'd had their bones thrown together.

Busi had bound them together with her reading.

Even if they were on different sides of the business.

CHAPTER 18

Zambia

Akina knew Levi detested her.

She understood why Levi hated that he couldn't break her, no matter how much he tried with physical force.

There had been chaos when Levi had realized that Cherri had run away, and despite them tracking her to the tarred road, she was gone.

Akina's relief had been short lived as Levi had turned his anger on the three of them, relieving his fury by beating them. Until calmness had been restored, and the calculating snake had returned.

Across the morning fire Levi boasted to Tahaan. "I'm telling you; no one is going to find The Doll today or any other day we have her in this overlander. I've smuggled many people across Africa like this for years — even during the apartheid war in South Africa. Name it, I've trucked it in and out. Guns, ivory, pangolin scales, humans, doesn't make a difference what the cargo is, it doesn't get found at the border posts. This is better than the Mack truck."

Akina looked downwards, not wanting to be caught listening. They hadn't realized yet that by keeping them with her in the front of their truck she'd been able to listen to their constant talking, and even started to add

Arabic to the list of languages she could understand. She hadn't attempted to speak it, but was following, and understanding their conversations easily now. Although some words were a mystery, but usually she could guess the meaning from the context of the discussion.

Levi seemed so proud of the fact that he could get away with breaking the law.

She couldn't wait until her dad's soldiers caught up with him.

But she was worried about what would happen to her now.

Unsure of where they were, or even what country they were in.

Akina wondered if Cherri had remembered her father's number and been able to get to a telephone. Even if she hadn't, she was glad Cherri got away. But there was a part deep inside her, that wished it was her too.

Wished they had escaped together.

Being the one left behind was hard.

There was someone with her all the time now, except when she went to the toilet. The advantage was she could eavesdrop.

"Any news from The Mother Bitch on the others?" Tahaan asked.

"They are due to fly to Tripoli," Levi said. "If this brat hadn't given so much trouble, she would have been on that flight too. The auction house in Venice knows we're coming, and that we have a particularly special package. They can't wait to get her photo in the catalog."

"Still makes no sense to me why we drag her all the way to Italy, probably to have to drag her back again," Tahaan said.

"You have that wrong. When she's sold, she's the buyer's problem. The auction house gives her a passport of the destination country, and off she goes with them. It'll take a few days, but the money will make us rich." He motioned toward her with his head. "That one will be our biggest score yet. Worth more than all the others put together. The best, most profitable mistake ever."

Akina frowned. Selling her. She knew that the slave trade had ended many years before, and she wasn't understanding exactly how he would be selling her.

Then the realization hit her: Levi thought he was above the law anywhere in the world — not only in South Africa.

He was everything that her dad fought against in his anti-corruption corporation, trying to help people against men exactly like Levi. She wondered why it had taken her so long to get it straight in her head what his problem was.

"Put that fire out and get ready. Iesha, have her ready to leave in ten minutes. There are still thousands of kilometers between us and collecting our fortune," Levi instructed, throwing the last of his coffee into the fire.

Tahaan immediately began putting the fire out and packing their few possessions into the overlander. Iesha walked with her to behind the trees to the toilet, toilet paper in her hand.

No chance to write her message in the sand this morning.

And by the time they returned, Levi stood by the overlander, clearly eager to get going. "Get in the box."

He reached toward her, and she shrank away, out of his grasp. "Listen up you fucking reject. Get in the box, it's time to go."

The look in Levi's eyes was pure loathing.

She was about to cop yet another beating. Even if she did what he asked.

She knew it.

He'd stopped trying to hold himself back since Cherri had gone and taken out his anger on her.

Tahaan had stepped in more than once when he hit her, reminding Levi that she was not to have any damage, that she was too valuable to them, that she had to be alive and well. He took a few beatings of his own from Levi in the process.

"Come on little one," Iesha said. "I'll get in first. My head will be the one to go into the darkness, and you will see the light the fastest that way around. Yeah-yeah?"

Iesha too had been beaten and made to travel with them for the last few days, since Cherri had escaped. Iesha's beating had been worse than hers. She knew that Iesha was still paying the cost of having Cherri escape on her watch.

Akina nodded.

"I'm not asking again, you half-breed freak," Levi said.

Akina shuddered.

Getting in the box was not easy. This box was not like the old one on the back of the truck where she'd been before with animals above her. She had to share, lying close to Iesha, and then when they got in, Levi would slide it closed so they traveled underneath the vehicle, for miles squished together.

He lit a cigarette, threw the match onto the ground, and took a deep drag. She could see the orange burn at the tip.

She climbed in next to Iesha.

Levi had burned her once on her stomach with a cigarette to show her what would happen to her if she so much as sneezed in her box now that Cherri was gone. The pain of burning had been beyond anything she'd experienced before. She put her fingers on the crusted scab.

It still hurt.

Tahaan pushed the box underneath the overlander.

The darkness was instant, except for small breathing holes where light followed oxygen in. There was a small slit where if she peered carefully, she could see out the side of the truck. She tried not to look out of it when they were moving as it made her feel sick.

She took deep breaths, trying to control the panic that threatened her every time she traveled inside the box.

Akina was glad Cherri had kept her promise and hadn't come back.

She wondered if they would have killed her, these men, if she dared to come back. She thought perhaps Tahaan wouldn't, but Levi, for sure would.

He did not mince words or emotions.

They had slowed down, the engine of the overlander changing pitch. When they stopped, Akina peered out her small window to the world. She could see a market on the side of the road, perhaps yet another truck stop, and watched a small child running with a bicycle rim and a stick in the distance before it disappeared. Voices wafted in.

She didn't need to look for Levi, she knew his voice, but the other voice was softer, strongly accented. They appeared to be arguing.

"I've had enough of this," Levi said. Quick as a cobra, his knife had sliced the man's throat. He opened the door above them, and he pushed the man inside the overlander. She couldn't see him anymore.

In horror she pushed back into Iesha.

"Whatever it was little girl, forget it. You can't win against these men. Not here." Iesha patted her on the leg. "We have got to stay alive. One day we'll get free again, and perhaps get revenge on them, but for now, stay calm. If your father is as rich as you claim, perhaps he can help me get my daughter back too, but we'll have to see, won't we?"

153

"What? You want to get away too?" Akina asked.

"You think I like being raped every night? And my daughter. What about her?" Iesha said. "Remember, you were the one responsible for sending her to the rebels—"

"I told you we didn't know—" Akina said, once again ready to apologize.

"It's still your fault that she's lost to me. Before you came, they already had her, but they promised she was safe. Now, after meeting the white man, I think they lied to me. I might listen to them and do what they say to avoid another raping and another beating, but that doesn't mean I like them."

She adjusted how she was lying, relaxing into Iesha's back.

If they were at a truck stop, then there was no way they were getting out of their box, even though they were stopped.

It grew colder, a biting wind seemed to seep into the box. She was glad for the heat of Iesha against her, and it felt especially good on her lower back.

Akina had taken two days to recover from the beating that she got when Cherri had run away. Physically anyway. Her ears had finally stopped ringing and her stomach no longer hurt when she ate food or went to the toilet. Before that day, she'd never experienced a beating with a stick, and she never wanted to again.

In losing Cherri, Levi had lost his tool to manipulate her.

He hadn't taken that well.

She'd heard Tahaan remind him constantly that The Mother Bitch would not be pleased that he'd hurt her. She wished The Mother Bitch had more control over him — perhaps she would beat him for hurting Akina.

Akina now hoped that her father would send somebody not only to save her, but also to kill Levi.

She couldn't talk to Iesha like she could to Cherri.

Iesha would tell Tahaan everything, even if she now pretended to be wanting to get away too.

Tahaan would tell Levi…

Now, instead she was cataloging every experience she went through in her head. Every single thing about the men.

She'd seen Levi's tattoos.

Levi had shown her the fangs tattooed inside his mouth and explained that they meant that he would bite and that he got them in prison. Akina didn't want to be near enough to him for him to be able to bite anything. Human bites got infected; she knew that from her time in school. She'd also seen the tattoos across his chest and over his arms when he took off his shirt in the heat.

In the middle of his chest and up his neck was a huge diamond. All the tattoos had messy shadowing as if the artist had spilled ink and smudged it around.

She closed her eyes and hummed her Sunflower song. The stillness of the truck, with the constant distant noise of people outside eventually lulled her to sleep.

Akina looked out, away from the campsite. They were in a game reserve somewhere. As the sky changed from blue-purple to black she thought she could see large mountains in the distance. What she couldn't see was any sign of civilization other than a fire pit and an ablution block she was told not to use. She could smell somebody else cooking dinner though, so someone must be nearby.

She knew that there was no way without a GPS tracker that her father would find her out here in the wilderness.

Iesha pitched a tent for them. Like last night, she would sleep next to her, probably tied together by a cord. Iesha was taking no chances.

Tahaan settled down in front of the fire that Iesha made inside the concrete barrier. She knew not to count on getting anything from him except what he was told to do by Levi.

Levi sat on the steps of the overlander with his computer open. Again.

She couldn't believe that Africa seemed to have really good internet coverage for a place that was supposed to be so third world. Did he have a satellite phone? She hadn't considered that. If she could find it, she could use it.

She'd watched the Africa Eco Race with her dad and seen satellite phones used all the time. But she had no luck trying to watch what Levi did with his, so that if she ever got a chance, she could call her dad. No opportunity had come up — yet.

Somewhere out in the wilderness she could hear lions roaring. A hyena laughed nearby making her feel like she was in a nightmare version of a

David Attenborough show. There were other noises that she couldn't identify that kept going throughout the night. She was wrapped in a blanket, her
clothes hanging on a line to dry for the night in front of the fire.

She stared at Tahaan. He had no tattoos.

"Where are we going?" Akina asked him.

"You'll know when we get there," he said in a gruff voice.

"How many more days do we need to travel?" she asked.

He grunted then looked around making sure no one could overhear him
before he answered. "Perhaps a few more days. You can do that in the box?
Survive a few more days?"

"I don't know. I'm still hungry," she said.

"You had your food; Iesha gave it to you."

"I know, but I'm still hungry," Akina said. She tried her best to make her
voice sound like a young girl. As Levi wasn't near them, she tested how far
Tahaan would let her go, see if she could get him on her side. Her father
used to say how well appealing to a man's good nature worked for other
people when he was helping them get out of bad situations, so perhaps she
could try and make it work for her.

The man looked at her and shook his head. "There isn't any more food
rations today."

"But—"

"No buts. No arguing. You don't want Levi to hear you arguing, do you?
If he hits you again, then you might have to stay with him always. You don't
want to have to stay with him, do you?"

"No." It was interesting that he'd threatened her with Levi, not that he
would do it himself. The worst he'd ever done to her was bop her on the top
of her head. Granted it had been hard, but it hadn't damaged her.

Not like Levi.

"Good. Then don't raise your voice and don't argue."

Akina's heart beat wildly.

Her father was never going to find her. They'd spent so many days on the
road, everything was a blur. And now if Cherri ever got through to her
father, they would be looking for a cargo truck not a tourist vehicle.

And if what Tahaan said was true, she needed to make sure she didn't get
another beating from Levi. She didn't want to stay with him another day
more than she had to.

She went to lay inside the tent.

If she could get up early enough, she could get to the toilet in the bushes behind the ablutions block alone again. To do exactly what she did each night when she went to the toilet. Write her father's number in the sand and *Save me, my dad has $*, but now that she had more information, she had started adding to it. Leaving more crumbs for the people her father was sending to save her.

CHAPTER 19

Pandora Timbers Mission Orphanage, Thabazimbi, South Africa

4th April 2016 — 26 days until auction

Mother Stella-Rose Naude switched her back one last time, feeling the bite of the leather strap.

She deserved the punishment.

The girl who walked away from the accident was going to be a problem.

Stella-Rose had paid the policeman a sizable sum to create the documents that said that she had reported the children missing months before.

She'd also paid the social worker to backdate her paperwork saying that these children had run away and that their escape was not due to a problem at the orphanage. Obviously, the social workers had never had those two children on their file. They came in, they were sold. End of story.

There was no further investigation needed.

At first the social worker had been adamant that it would be a problem to fabricate the papers. It was surprising how an opinion could be changed when a large sum of money changed hands.

All that remained now was the locum doctor to the area, who had made it her job to check on the girl. Not once but twice already in one week. She was the only one not in Stella-Rose's control.

"I have sinned my God. I failed to protect all the children within my orphanage from this one child who will bring trouble to our door. Forgive me as I have lied to the doctor, but it was all for the good of the children. Those that I have in my care still, and those whom only I will remember."

She brought the lash down on her back again.

"Forgive me, I have failed you. I have brought shame to our mission and our children, and all those who work here. I will not fail you again. This child I have will stay for now but, she will be traded again. She brings with her darkness that the other children here never need to know about." She brought the lash down on her back one last time. "Amen."

Stella-Rose put the switch down and slowly stood. She felt as if she was going to throw up and made to run to her small en-suite bathroom. She didn't make it before her stomach emptied on the tiles. Now she would need to clean that up before she could get into a bath.

By the time she got into the bathtub, it was icy cold. Thank goodness. It already burned her back, bringing the pain of punishment to the surface again. The water around her was rose pink.

"I wonder how you are involved Chrystal?" she said aloud.

She'd seen her sitting in emergency but had chosen not to acknowledge her.

It was easier that way.

The clock could not be turned back to undo what had happened between them.

But she was curious as to why Chrystal had been at the hospital. Her mother would usually fill her in on all the gossip from the farm and every-thing that was going on in Chrystal's life, but her mum was on a holiday, visiting with her sister in East London.

Stella-Rose knew that Chrystal was a paid soldier. She knew that Chrystal had come home and was now damaged.

Like her.

She wondered if the demons that Chrystal had in her head were as bad as hers, but knew that Chrystal would not spend time trying to purge her sins out with lashes.

If indeed they could ever be purged.

She sunk lower into the bath, and her memories.

. . .

159

Her second year at university had started so well. She had good tutors and lecturers and achieved good grades. When she'd met Dwayne, she had never expected to fall in love. She never thought she would let a man do the things he did. Or that it would feel so good to do them with him.

But like everything else, Dwayne had turned out to be a lie.

The perfect man had turned out to be the perfect cockroach, and she'd been left pregnant and alone. Stella-Rose had always told her mother what a modern woman she was but found herself unable to go through with the abortion when it came to the crunch.

Instead, she sat in her room pregnant and abandoned.

"Stella-Rose." She could hear Miriam's voice and a soft knock. "I'm one of the international third-year philosophy students. Can I come in?"

"Sure."

Miriam walked into her dorm and closed the door. "There is no easy way to say this, so forgive me, I hope you don't take offense." She sat in the only chair available and wrapped her arms around her legs. "I heard about your problem, and that you don't want this baby, and you don't want to be a traditional tribe's person either. I know that there is no shame in having a baby, but don't you feel it would ruin your life?"

Stella-Rose looked down.

"It doesn't have to." Miriam smiled at her reassuringly. "Come with me, we can go see the Zuga Mission Church sisters. They will help you. Their faith is all based on healing, and they help other women who feel they are in trouble or need a sister's shoulder."

She had rushed at it with two hands outstretched. A way out — and she wasn't sorry.

It had created her a path to God.

The child had died at birth.

At first she'd wished she'd died along with it.

But God had other plans for her.

The sisters were there to help her through. They'd stayed beside her bed praying for her, telling her that the loss of her child was not her fault. She wasn't to blame.

At the end when she'd recovered, the gynecologist told her that she would never have another child.

Now she was an empty vessel.

She'd had her chance at motherhood, and she'd felt like she'd destroyed it.

Stella-Rose felt that she deserved to have that punishment put on her.

For listening to other people and thinking that her child's life was not precious, and even thinking of an abortion.

God had known she wasn't one hundred percent committed to the preservation of life and had punished her.

The sisters were there to tell her that she was misguided, but if she felt like that then she should devote her life to saving others in her situation. Saving others who needed help and showing them that the way to redemption was through their God, and through song, dance and healing.

She didn't understand then that no matter how much song and dance and healing she would do, it would never fix the hole inside her heart from losing her baby.

Eventually, she found herself in Italy's beautiful hills doing her training as an aspirant in the Zuga Mission Church.

Committing to the sisters and the church became so much part of her; it had helped ease so much of her guilt. She never anticipated the duties she'd end up performing for her church.

Like finding inventive ways to make a few dollars donated by some kind soul last for a month and provide for everybody under her care.

She finally understood how Jesus and his feeding of the thousands worked.

It was ironic that she did not believe in the miracles they claimed he and every saint after him performed.

But she did believe that if you were a good businessperson and you had your head on right, you could take a business and improve on it.

Trading in children was a means to an end: providing stability for them all. God had shown her a way forward so she could make sure that her orphanage prospered, as did her status in this life and in the afterlife. While it sometimes played on her conscious, she knew she was being weak in those moments, and she would strengthen her resolve and her devotion.

She would be remembered, just like all the other saints.

· · ·

Goosebumps danced on her arms and belly. She climbed out the bath, she pulled the plug out, and watched as the blood that had been washed from her went down the drain. Like her precious friendships from her childhood had disappeared. Vanished.

Now all she had was her sisters of the mission and her devotion to God.

She felt cleaner.

She'd paid her penance for what she had done, and her part in the trans-action that had resulted in the girl being in the vehicle in the first place. Stella-Rose did not regret the transaction as it had helped feed all the chil-dren, kept them in good health with a roof over their head and the wolves at bay.

It ensured she was one step closer to the right hand of her God.

Sacrifice was necessary in the eyes of her Lord.

CHAPTER 20

Mpika, Zambia

4ᵗʰ April 2016 — 26 days until auction

Chrystal would never have imagined that she would be back in Zambia, using the skills learned to hunt down criminals and poachers, to look for an innocent child. And using her persuasive skills to make the Zambian officers see sense, that a show of force would startle and silence the little girl, more than help her talk.

They had driven into the tiny township in two official vehicles. Only Captain Desmond Kesha, who'd been in their helicopter, and Inspector Stevie Chilikazi, from the Mpika Police station accompanied them.

"We're looking for Salin Jambga," Stevie said to the old man standing outside of where the house was supposed to be. "We were told that this is her address."

The problem was there was nothing there except some buildings that were falling down, and a tractor with a grader attachment in the front which was being used to level the area. In a town of around fifty thousand inhabitants, people tended to make themselves scarce when government vehicles arrived.

"There," the old man said pointing to a small hut nestled between others, on the opposite side of the road. Then shuffled away.

It was a harsh reminder that this was a continent used to having people who asked questions resorting to violence when they didn't get the answers they wanted and that those who were not involved should get as far away as possible if they wanted to keep out of trouble. It was Africa, you didn't interfere with those who appeared to have more authority than you.

Chrystal took a breath.

Patience.

It was one of the first things she'd learned from Khulu at a young age: always be patient.

She knocked on the door and called out. "Hello mama. Hello!"

Silence answered.

"She can't be home. But it's almost dark, so she can't be far," Desmond said.

"Then we wait," Chrystal said as she moved down the road, before she sat on the ground away from the shack.

Shack was being kind.

A mud house with a tin roof, with cardboard covering where windows were supposed to be. Chrystal studied the construction going on and wondered what was being built when all around her was nothing but poverty and despair.

A woman walked toward them. She carried a bundle of sticks on her head for firewood, and behind her skipped a young girl. What was unusual was that the kid wasn't helping by carrying sticks on her head too. The bunch was too wide to turn within the small confines around the shacks. Once the lady had turned the corner, she had to walk past them, or she'd leave her precious cargo behind.

"Continue to chatter. Wait till she's nearer. We can't afford to spook her," Chrystal instructed.

The minutes ticked past.

Finally, she was at the shack. The young girl, who wore a dress that was too big for her, came forward and pushed on the door. Something looked off about her when Chrystal looked directly at her. She disappeared inside. The woman put the stick bundle down, and then maneuvered it through her front door.

While she was distracted, Stevie stepped close. "Salin Jambga?"

The woman seemed to get a fright, but she held her ground, blocking the doorway with her body, as if trying to stop him from looking inside. Trying to be brave in the face of authority. She nodded.

"You're not in any trouble," Stevie said in Bemba. "These people have come a long way, and they want to ask you some questions, that's all."

"What type of questions?" She didn't budge.

Desmond said, "We were told you helped a brave young girl after she ran away from someone who kidnapped her."

Chrystal could see that they were making a concerted effort to be polite.

The woman looked up and down the street. There was no one else other than them in her section walking around. Everyone thought there would be trouble and had hidden themselves away.

"I told the policeman at the station that. I have done nothing wrong," she said, and she drew the little girl closer to her, concealing the small child behind her.

"I promise, we mean you no harm," Rowan said in English. "We got a phone call from your number telling us that Akina was still alive."

With that, the child hiding behind her pushed past the woman and walked up to Rowan. "You her *ubaba's* soldier come to save her?"

Chrystal smiled. Then she realized what was wrong with the child's head. Her short-cropped hair couldn't hide the fact that she was missing her ear.

She shivered as if someone walked over her grave.

Chrystal bent down to her height. "What's your name, sweetie?"

"Cherri." She looked down.

"What a beautiful name. My name is C—Savannah. It's kind of long so my friends call me Savvy. These are my friends. That's Rowan, Zenzele, and Desmond kindly flew us in the chopper from Lusaka, and then this tall man here, this is the Chief in charge of your local police station, Stevie. He has the same name as Stevie Wonder, but he's way taller, don't you think? I hear that our Stevie has a little girl around your age, and a baby coming soon too. We've come to ask you about Akina."

Cherri looked at her.

"Can you tell me what happened that night?" Chrystal asked.

The little girl looked her in the eyes. "I called. I promised. I stole clothes and Salin's cell phone." She looked downwards. "I no clothes, and the blanket broke." She looked at Chrystal again, while constantly wringing her little hands. "I promised. I promised. Akina said promises important." Her eyes welled with tears. "We did pinky swear. I *cha* go back, to Levi. I stay Salin. I stay."

Chrystal watched in horror as Cherri peed herself while standing there. The urine pooled on the hard-compacted sand before running downhill.

Salin turned the girl and led her away. "Come inside. This poor child has experienced horrors no one should ever have to endure."

"We feared as much," Chrystal said as she followed Salin and Cherri into the coolness of the little shack.

"She's lived through hell." Salin pointed to her ear. "Come on Cherri, it's going to be okay; you're safe now. I promised to keep you safe, and I will."

Salin carried on. "It's okay, we have a clean dress and panties. You don't have to talk about it anymore. Come we can have a little wash. There's no shame, my strong girl. You got away and helped your friend. It's safe here. You hear me? I keep my promises too."

Chrystal shook her head. "I'm sorry. I know it's hard to talk about. Salin, can you tell us what she's told you."

"After she's clean, we can talk," Salin said, but her face was that of someone who wanted to close the door and protect her young charge.

"This may take longer than we thought, I didn't think she'd be so young," Chrystal said. "Rowan and Zenzele, please can you go grab something for dinner and some drinks. I should have thought about it, they need food. There has to be a takeaway open somewhere near here."

"Keys?" Zenzele said and put his hand out to Stevie.

Stevie shook his head. "I'll come with you. As much as I want to hear what's going on here, I can't allow you to drive my vehicle."

The men left, and Desmond and Chrystal sat in her small shack. Waiting.

Inside it was clean, but there wasn't much there. A rug made of woven recycled plastic bags covered part of the dirt floor. A paraffin stove stood in the one corner, with two pots on it. Two plates and two tin mugs sat neatly inside a small enamel bowl. The walls had been smoothed inside, to create the illusion of concrete, but were cracked as only mud walls could. A picture painted in bright earthy colors hung on the one wall in a chipped frame. There was a screen of woven sticks, separating the bedroom area where she could see a pallet bed. In the corner Salin was washing Cherri in an enamel basin.

"I talk. They save Akina," Cherri said, loudly at one stage.

Chrystal frowned and looked toward Desmond, who shook his head to tell her not to talk, that he was listening. His head at an angle, straining to hear.

Salin put Cherri on the bed, now in a clean dress, and she patted her back. Singing softly. About half an hour later, she came through to where they sat. "We will talk outside. She needs to rest for a while. She is emotionally exhausted."

They followed her through her house, and in her small yard outside was a mahogany tree. "I haven't seen one of these for a while. What a beautiful lucky bean tree," Chrystal said.

"I collect the beans and make jewelry with them, then I sell them in Lusaka and Livingston to the tourists. My neighbor is good; she lives in my home while I'm away so that no one can cut down our tree."

Chrystal nodded in understanding while crossing her legs and sitting on the ground under the tree. Rowan, Zenzele and Stevie arrived back, and came through the house carrying takeaway bags of fried chicken. They had also brought other snacks and drinks in cans that they could all share, and in Rowan's arm was a teddy bear.

Chrystal had no idea where he'd found that, but looking at him — the stuffed bear under his strong, solid arm, his expression hard, but with eyes that showed the compassion and grief he felt for the little girl — her heart melted. Something so small and yet, he'd taken time to go find something special for Cherri, and probably paid a small fortune for it too.

She smiled and he winked at her.

This was a man worthy of love and a family.

He was everything that should have scared the shit out of her. Instead, she found it endearing—

Now that did scare her.

Chrystal noticed that Salin put some food aside and covered it from the flies before eating her own, to make sure that Cherri was fed.

"Thank you," Salin said. "Cherri never got fried food like this while they had her, but she knows it from before. She's had some in South Africa, when we walk past the fried chicken shop, she told me about it."

Chrystal said, "Is there anything you can tell us about the night that Cherri came to you? It's crucial, we need to find out what happened."

"She doesn't sleep well that one. Even next to me she kicks and hits in her sleep. It is good she found me. I know what it was like to be lost and homeless. I did not always have this either. So maybe I can help her a little bit, and now you have come. Like she said."

Rowan passed the box of chicken around again.

"When I found her in my house, she had on my neighbor's shirt as a dress. She had my phone and had made a call until I had no credit left. After I had calmed her down and made her understand that I was not going to hurt her for using my phone, that it was good she did not steal it, she told me that she could not ask anyone for help with no clothes on.

"That was why she was in my neighbor's shirt, and she had called Akina's daddy in America. She told me she has to get Akina's daddy to send the soldier to save Akina from Levi."

Rowan nodded. "We've been sent by her father to look for her. But we're not soldiers."

Salin looked between them all. Shaking her head. "He is the police, and he is the air force. How can you not be soldiers?"

"I'm an investigator. It's my job to find her. Then we bring in the good guys like Chief Stevie and Captain Desmond, and all their men and women wanting to help, to bring Akina home too," Rowan explained.

"But you are so few," Salin said.

"You can only see a few of us, but there are lots and lots of good people out there helping us. Did she tell you anything special about Akina?" Rowan asked. "We need to make sure it's really her."

"Akina has a new scar on her arm. They cut something out of her. I do not understand what. Cherri said that is why it is taking so long for Akina's daddy's soldiers to find her — because it's gone. She told me the white man, Levi, calls Akina the Japanese Doll. And there is a big dark Arabic man looking after them as they travel — his name is Tahaan, and that Akina is starting to understand what he says, and there was something about an auction, but she was not sure of that. Cherri said Akina thinks they speak Arabic so that they kids couldn't understand. But Akina is learning their language fast. And they don't know that she listens to them."

"Anything else?" Rowan asked.

"She's only little. Cherri gets distressed every time she talks about her escape. From what I gather, Akina could not climb up through the window. She says that Akina made her leave her behind. She ran for the lights, after falling. She obviously came into this settlement, looking for help."

"Salin, can be outside with you?" a small voice asked.

Salin stretched out her arms, and Cherri ran to sit in her lap. She tucked herself in. "Look what Akina's daddy's friends brought you." She brought the covered plate around and uncovered the battered chicken and chips sitting next to it.

"For me?"

Salin nodded.

"Eat up. We can talk when you're finished." Rowan said. The teddy bear was on the ground behind him, and she hadn't seen it yet.

Too soon, she had consumed a can of coke and two pieces of chicken were only chewed bones left behind. Cherri was licking her fingers of the remnants of salt. She sighed.

The light under the tree was beginning to fade, and bats flew across the indigo sky as they made their night passage to find food in the bush.

Smells of cooking and smoke from fires around descended as mosquitoes buzzed around.

"You save Akina?" Cherri asked, looking around.

"We need your help," Rowan said, pointing to her. "We need the very brave girl who ran away to help us with some more things. Do you think you can be that brave girl again?" Rowan looked at her and raised his eyebrows. "I bought something for such a brave girl." He passed her the teddy.

Cherri hugged it tightly to her. "For me?"

Salin laughed and covered her mouth with her hand.

"Of course, it's a gift to you," Rowan said.

"You don't have to do anything that makes you sad or mad okay? If it gets too hard, you tell me before you wee-wee in my lap," Salin said, patting her lightly on the back.

Cherri was nodding, her arms around the teddy.

"Can you take us back to where you left Akina?" Rowan asked.

Cherri nodded.

"We did," Salin said. "I can show you the place. We went there the next day, but it was deserted. Even the police who we went with said that they were long gone."

"Do you remember the policeman's name who was with you?" Stevie asked.

Salin shook her head.

Even now she knew not to cast a stone at anyone, in case they got into trouble from their boss and came after her for revenge.

"I'd still like to see where they were, even if they have gone—" Chrystal said, then she looked at Cherri. "Zenzele and I want to look at the sand and see if it tells us any secrets. Have you seen footprints in the sand, like animal tracks?"

Cherri was nodding.

"We can still look at those, even if the animals have gone," Chrystal said. "We can look like that for Akina. In the dust."

"Can you remember exactly where it is?" Rowan asked.

The little girl looked up at Salin.

"We can show them. I promised you when I found you that I would help do everything to get you back to your own grandmother. And we would call Akina's daddy again."

"*Cha. Cha* go back." Cherri said hiding her face into Salin.

"It's okay Cherri, we stay here far away until Akina is found and you are ready. There is no race to go away from me." Salin said, patting Cherri's back, soothing the now sobbing child.

"But you haven't called him again, and it has been two days," Rowan said quietly.

Salin nodded. "The house where I do some ironing work for the man who owns the petrol station, only pays me on Friday. Then I can get credit in my phone and call," Salin explained. "This time I will call on the internet, so it does not use all my phone credit in a few seconds."

"We'll give you money for that call, and more," Rowan said.

Chrystal smiled. Rowan was finally starting to understand about Africa and her people's staggering within the depth of poverty, and how those trapped in it still showed such dedication to do the right thing, and be decent people.

The sky was dark blue and the stars shone brightly as they stood to leave. Chrystal noticed that Rowan was hanging back as Chief Stevie and Captain Desmond said their thank yous and goodbyes.

She watched with interest as Rowan checked that the authorities' backs were turned.

"We'll come back in a couple of days. This'll tide you over until then. Please, don't let her out of your sight." He shook her hand as he passed Salin an envelope.

Salin was silent as the envelope disappeared quickly into her bra, with a small nod of acknowledgement.

Chrystal squatted down. "Cherri, you're smart and brave, and we promise you, that Rowan and I won't stop looking for Akina. Thank you for being such a good friend to her."

CHAPTER 21

Kitwe, Zambia

7th April 2016 — 23 days until auction

Chrystal took a deep breath as she prepared to enter into the arms dealer's lair. She knew Zenzele was close behind. Even if she couldn't see him, he was a master of disguise, like a caracal she would not hear his feet as they touched the ground, and she would not know where he was as long as he stayed undercover. For all him saying she was good in the bush, one of his best skills was that he was excellent in urban warfare. He could probably win a parkour competition if he ever entered. He seemed to thrive on being on rooftops and running through small spaces, while she preferred the bushveld or jungle any day.

She raised her hand to knock, but the door opened before she even touched her knuckles to the wood.

"We're closed," a big man with a shaved head said.

"You'll be open for me. Tell J that the hyena always knocks at the door at drinking time," she said, giving them the password they had used a few years before.

The door swung inwards.

She had to duck to enter the doorway. She'd learned that short doors generally meant that the police force in the area did raids, and the extra split-second it took for people coming in to have to duck, then refocus, might be the second that patrons needed to escape from the room.

She looked around. Like most African establishments that sold guns, there was nothing to show that this was their trade; this was not a Walmart in the USA. To an untrained eye, this looked like an upmarket shebeen, with its bar, snooker tables and a little dance floor tucked in the corner.

A tall man wearing desert camo pants and a T-shirt came toward her.

"What can I help you with," he asked.

She looked at him.

He'd matured in the last two years. Silver grey hair sparkled in his beard and at his temple, but the merry blue eyes hadn't aged at all. "Jason Adams, I haven't got so fat that you wouldn't recognize me."

"No Savannah, I recognize you. I heard you only just got out of the jungle alive and have since retired. The fact that you're standing in front of me means the rumors were wrong. You're still active."

"Depends which rumors you're talking about. I did come out of the jungle. I am alive and I did retire. All true. I'm back, only this time I'm working on something somewhat different, and I don't have the same company backing me. It's a privateer. I met with maCalio a few days back; she said if I need anything I could tap into maNtuli's supply chain, and she'd sort it out."

"What've you got yourself into? Have to admit, never saw you for crossing over to the other side and working with those women. You were always about right and wrong. It's black or white with you."

"I didn't say I'm working with her. But let's say she also wants a satisfactory conclusion to this mission. She's helping out of the goodness of her heart."

"That woman doesn't have a heart."

"You say that and yet this is your livelihood, and she's part of the supply chain."

"Ah, that's different. Believe me, if I could do it without her, I would. Besides, I cooperated with her opposition. She took over when her predecessor mysteriously died of poisoning and maNtuli now reigns over her enterprise. You could say I inherited her. That bitch might be part of the chain, but she's a mentally damaged link. Good businesswoman, but unnecessarily cruel."

"Since when has cruelty made you wince?" She knew Jason was ex-marine, ex-merc now like most others, trying to get by in Africa, left alone to live how they wanted to.

"It always has."

"Ah, you're one of the good guys Jason — only you still don't know it."

"Ha ha... a good guy, now you're a comedian. It's good to see you, but I was hoping the rumors were true and that you were out for good. Was imagining you having a little family somewhere on your farm. Same color golden hair as yours. Fitting into civilian life, leaving all this shit a million miles behind you. You had a hard time on your last mission, and I don't want to know if you don't come out of the jungle this time. Knowing you escaped it then — and he didn't."

Wesley.

"He's still with me," she said, her eyes brimming unexpectedly with tears.

"One day, you'll wake up and you won't need his ghost walking beside you. I'm just sorry it was you who went with him. I was supposed to be on that mission, not you."

"I'm not sorry I was with him. I'm sorry I had to keep that promise. That's all," Chrystal said. Her mind quickly shut down the thought of the night she had given her word to bring Wesley's heart home if he died in a foreign country.

"So—you back in for real?"

She nodded. "We're heading toward Tanzania. Should make it a walk in the park compared to what we faced last time."

"Don't count on it. Some pretty vicious militia sprung up there over the last two years. Die-hard religious groups are now operating in Tanzania and up into Kenya."

"Shit." This was one of the reasons she'd come to see Jason. He was always on top of which factions were fighting, and where they were. Wes had relied on Jason's information in their missions, so she had come to him to make sure she wasn't making a mistake either.

Africa was fickle. Ethnic and religious violence was like the wind, it changed when you least expected it and blew in a different direction almost every day.

"Depends on what you're going after? You might not need the intel." He looked at her.

She took a breath and moved her arms to rest her fists on her hips. "I know you wouldn't normally ask anyone that, but you were Wesley's best friend, so I'll let that one slide."

"Tell me. It'll help me decide whether I'm going to give you extra help or not."

"Seriously, you'd think you would give me all the help I asked for because of our history."

"Doesn't work like that. I have a history with maNtuli too, that doesn't mean I would go out of my way to help her more than I have to because of our business dealings."

"You're a hardened bastard, Jason," Chrystal said, her voice steady, but with a hint of sadness.

"Yeah, I guess so," he said, walking behind his bar. He pulled out two glasses and a bottle of whiskey.

She raised her hand to say no. "I'm looking for a little girl."

He paused, frowning. "You serious?"

"Ja. She's an American kid who got snatched in Cape Town a few weeks ago."

"I saw that in the news. Thought she looked Japanese from her picture. Wasn't she like nearly twelve years old? That's old to snatch a child for anything but the sex trade."

"Let's hope we can save her from that then."

"Poor kid. What do you need?"

She passed him a list, handwritten neatly on plain white paper. He opened it and looked it over. "Everything on here is good, except for the helicopter. I can give you a smaller one, can still take six people but it doesn't have built-in weapons. You can always open a window or a door and use the guns you're going to be carrying to do what you need to out there. It's all I have at the moment. And it's going to cost your backer." He wrote the price on a paper and passed it to her.

"Is that only the helicopter, or the weapons included?" she asked.

"Everything."

"We'll take it," she said. "We need to get moving."

"Jeep is outside. It'll fit you and your man on the roof until you pick up the second vehicle. You'll find the cache at these coordinates." He took the piece of paper back from her, and wrote down numbers in neat clear writing, before holding it out to her. "Pleasure doing business with you as always, Savannah. I wish more of my clients were as lovely as you."

"I'm sure you do," she said, reaching for the paper, she smiled.

He kept it from her reach still between his fingers. "No actually, I don't. I'm lucky they aren't or we might have world peace and that's not good for business. You can collect the rest in four hours." Finally, he passed it to her. "Account number on there too."

"Great, so you said pick up will be ready in two hours?"

"You really are in a hurry. Fine, two hours," Jason said.

"Appreciated. Stay well." She turned toward the exit.

"You too Savannah."

Rowan watched Chrystal drive back toward the hotel where they had based themselves. Even from a distance he knew it was her, her golden hair giving her away as it flew haphazardly in the breeze.

She stopped at the front and climbed out. He could already tell that something was wrong. The slight drop in her shoulders, and she held herself stiffly. She was emotional. Zenzele walked beside her, chatting and continually pointing to things. To Rowan, it looked like he didn't realize that she was in distress.

They had repeatedly gone over the plan and written down the list of guns and other equipment she would ask the gun dealer for. By the time they landed at Ndola Airport, he had come to appreciate that she was entirely in Savannah mode.

She was efficient, calculating and he was reminded that she was exactly what he needed on his team to find Akina.

Now, she was back after organizing the weapon logistics of their mission. And she didn't look happy.

Mission. He snorted at his choice of words.

In a way it was a rescue mission, but then he didn't think that much about what he did in his life; he just did it. Now Chrystal was doing precisely what he would've done had it been his home turf, had they been his contacts.

She lifted her hand and waved.

Damn, she knew he'd been watching for her.

Zenzele continued talking and was still going when she opened the door and walked into the suite.

"Do you ever stop talking?" Rowan asked.

"*Yebo*, but only when my boss-lady says she's okay."

She smiled. "I'm fine. Seriously."

"No, you were not. You had marks down your face, like he made you cry," Zenzele protested.

"They were happy tears. I haven't seen him in a few years. He was the best friend of a friend of mine once," she said. "It was a happy-sad moment to see him."

"Wait a minute. The arms dealer here is an actual friend?" Rowan asked. "As in you know him personally? What about the whole maNtuli connection?"

"*Ja*. He wasn't always the man he is now. He used to be a security contractor. I didn't even need to threaten him with big-bad maNtuli. When I mentioned her to him, I can tell you that there is no love lost between the two of them, and we can leave it at that. He's given us everything we put on the list. Here." She passed the paper that Jason had given her to Rowan. "His bank account details are written on there, and coordinates where we fetch are on the back. You'll need to get it transferred before we can pick anything up."

"It's a fair price. I'm impressed."

"Smaller commercial helicopter than planned, no guns mounted."

"That might work in our favor if we end up going in hot," Rowan said.

"I don't know, I'm kind of partial to having guns on my helicopter. Zenzele, tell the team to be ready to rock and roll in fifteen minutes." She put the coordinates into her GPS. "Pickup is about forty minutes out of town."

"*Yebo*," he said, and disappeared out the door toward where they could hear the men.

"You want to talk about it?" Rowan asked.

"No."

"Fine. Then let's get mobile and get back to Mpika as soon as we can. I think we pay Ms. Salin Jambga another visit, and we can pass on more cash from Curtis to say thank you and also to start little Cherri on her journey homewards, hopefully to find her granny."

177

CHAPTER 22

On the road – Tanzania

Akina woke, gasping for breath. The small breathing holes where light followed oxygen into the box under the overlander were dark, and there was no air.

"Steady, we just stopped, that's all," Iesha said next to her. "Stay as quiet and as still as you can."

She took deep breaths, trying to control her panic.

She knew now that she was so far away that she didn't know how her father's soldiers were ever going to find her. She had left his number whenever she could, but now that Iesha was with her, the opportunities to be alone, without her looking at her all the time were fewer and fewer.

She was running out of time to get help.

Today they had passed through miles and miles of nothing. There had been the odd village they didn't stop at, but the drone of the engine in the overlander had been going all day, from before the sun rose to now, and she could see it was already late evening.

She didn't know how much longer she could hold on.

Silently she asked her father: *Daddy, come on, hurry up.*

The engine started again, and she braced herself against the side of the box to try not bump her bladder too much.

She desperately needed to wee.

She needed to drink something.

She needed her father's soldiers to perform a miracle and rescue her. She simply couldn't rescue herself.

CHAPTER 23

Mikumi Game Reserve, Tanzania

7th April 2016 — 23 days until auction

Chrystal landed the helicopter in the demarcated area of the Mikumi Game Reserve. She could see Rowan standing next to Desmond and the head game ranger. While she had spoken to them on the radio, she was still not sure of their commitment.

After Chrystal and Rowan had visited with Cherri and Salin again and seen the site where Akina had once again disappeared, they had found a witness to the traffickers' burnt-out truck, who had said the two men, a woman and a young girl had driven away in an overlander.

They'd taken a gamble that their target would use the highway through the reserve, as it was the quickest route through to Dar es Salaam. They had figured that they were now on the run and would no longer be bothered with disguises after switching vehicles.

Burning their vehicle had been a mistake.

It had left a huge footprint.

People in Africa noticed a burnt vehicle.

If Chrystal and Rowan were wrong, and didn't find them here, they would head northward.

They had two names and the word auction to work on so far, and Holly was exploring all options of where the 'auction' was on the dark web.

From the look on Rowan's face, she could tell things were tense on the ground.

She shut down everything, and as the blades came to a halt, Zenzele jumped out of the helicopter, the chucks for parking it slung over his shoulder, knowing his job was to secure both the chopper and its blades. Her hand lingered over an eye, which similar to the eye of Horus, was painted on the control panel as she did the shutdown checks. She'd seen it before, but she couldn't place it. When she looked up, she could see the group walking toward her. She recognized the head ranger right away, let out a sigh of relief.

Lawrence Apaza and she had 'worked together' before.

Technically, that meant that she'd worked with his anti-poaching units, and he'd helped to keep things quiet while she and her team tidied up an elephant poaching ring that was operating out of a village near the park. A Chinese diplomat and a Tanzanian politician had been brought down in the sting. They had increased the anti-poaching guards' training while there and donated all their rifles and spare ammo on leaving the area to them.

She only hoped that some of that goodwill was still around.

"Savannah, *As-salam alaykom*," Lawrence said, putting out both his hands and clasping one of hers in both of his. She put her left hand on top of his. Her skin looked very pale in comparison and they shook hands, completing the 'Peace be upon you' greeting.

"*Wa Alykom As-salam*," she replied automatically, returning the blessing.

"I trust your flight in was scenic?" Lawrence asked.

"You have such beauty here, it's hard to look beyond that to everything else happening around, isn't it?"

"Some days it's easier than others. Come, come, you need to tell me all about how I can help you this time. You know, many of the guards here still remember you and will want to say hello."

Game guards were a fraternity of their own. Two years ago, the game guards had put her on a mercy flight on a small plane from Virunga National Park, along with the oil rights negotiator she'd rescued. They had been shifted from national park to national park to hide her from the rebels.

If it weren't for the game rangers in the Congo, she would have been dead. Like the rest of her team.

It was them who'd seen her civilian helicopter shot out of the sky and, even though it was outside their park, had rushed to help. It was them who'd shot the rebels chasing her, dragging her 'mark' along through the forest. Running for their lives.

She owed game rangers her life.

And once again, she was about to test their integrity.

They had gathered in Lawrence's meeting room, which he affectionately called the War Chamber. Chrystal understood the origins of the name, as the national parks were at war with the poachers. Unfortunately, they were always outmanned and outgunned, the poachers being organized military groups, backed by big eastern money.

He pointed to the map on the fifty kilometer stretch of road that ran directly through his reserve. "This is where you need to look. It's the only public camping ground. If they're here, that's where you'll find them."

"Do you have men there?"

"A few. Permits are bought at the gate. Since you have no other information, other than they're driving an overlander, I can't help you further on that part. My guards do take down number plates, but we all know how useless that can be. They are so easy to change. I'd say if they are going to stop at the camping site, this is it. Take your helicopter and do a high flyover. If you see one, then the men can go in the Jeeps and have a look around. We can't have anyone knowing that you're not part of us. I'll open the uniforms cabinet for you and your team and have one of ours with you in each vehicle. I'll come in the helicopter."

Chrystal nodded. "Thanks for your help. I knew we could rely on you."

Lawrence threw his hands up. "You need to understand that I'll do everything in my power to help you, we owe you a debt. But I walk a fine line here. Don't make me and my men regret it. We can't have anyone pointing a finger at us saying we help mercenaries."

Chrystal grinned. "I don't know any mercenaries. I'm just searching for a lost girl."

Rowan touched her elbow. "You sure this is okay? He's with us in the chopper?"

"We'll be fine. Lawrence speaks great English so with my smattering of Arabic and Swahili we should be good. Besides, I want Zenzele on the ground with the other game guards because he's the best there is when it comes to spoor. If there is anything left behind by her, he'll find it. If she continues to write her father's number in the sand or leaves any item of hers behind, if she still has anything of her own, he'll be on it. It's a waste to have him in the air with me."

Rowan touched his hand to her shoulder. "I want more than fine. I want safe. I'm worried about your panic attacks without Zenzele there."

"I'm good. I think being active helps, but I'm not going out looking for human blood to test it if that's okay with you. Besides, you know the song, and you could sing it at a push," she teased, looking a little bit smug.

A smile tugged at the corners of Rowan's mouth. "Stay focused. You know that I'm thankful to you for getting us so far. Don't you? You have done so well."

She grinned. "What's this? Pep talk day?"

He looked so serious. She admitted that she preferred him smiling. His smile made her feel happier. Lighter inside.

He laughed.

Better.

"Take care, and remember to keep the chatter to a minimum, we don't know what scanner or coms they have available to them," Rowan said.

She blew him a kiss over her shoulder as they walked out to her helicopter. Then she shut down all personal emotions as she went into pilot mode and got her expensive bird into the sky.

As she flew over the beautiful reserve, her mind wandered to why she had done that. She used to blow her team a kiss when they were splitting, as a good luck gesture. Wes had always said it was their last lucky charm, before she left them somewhere hostile. It had all been casual at first with Wes, but then as their relationship had intensified, so had the nature of kisses. She took a deep breath.

But Rowan and her were not separating, he was sitting right behind her.

And they were just colleagues.

She might even say that in their short time together, a friendship had formed.

Why had she done that?

She felt him tap her arm, bringing her back to the present. Chrystal looked at where he was pointing.

Elephant meandered through the trees toward the sparkling water. The jumbo didn't like the helicopter's noise and obviously associated it with danger as they picked up their pace as she got closer to them.

She chose to fly higher. Climbing away and giving them space, she could see already they were slowing their run. She smiled.

Lawrence gave her a thumbs up. He did love being in the sky.

She watched the wonder on Rowan's face as he saw Africa from the air. Flying over a herd of buffalo, their sheer numbers caused the dust to churn up, despite the wet season. The one old cow in the front turned and lifted her head, pawing at the ground in defiance of them. It was good to see that buffalo all over Africa were still as cantankerous as hers on *Saliebos*.

She slowed their speed as they came up toward the road that snaked through the reserve, happy that she didn't have any guns to mark her as anything other than a commercial flight. People below might hear her and look up, but they would think it was some rich person trying to see as much as they could in a short space of time. She adjusted and flew near the road, to make sure it didn't appear she was following it, but it was always there, in view.

"There are no overlanders on this section," Lawrence said, taking his binoculars from his eyes.

"Rowan? You see anything?"

"I don't see anything, only kombis and lots of SUVs, a few big trucks."

Looking at the horizon to where the sun was, she figured they would get to the camp in time and have daylight enough to have a look around. Still, they would either have to land the bird and have a night out themselves while they waited for Zenzele and the rangers to join them, or head home to return the next morning. Zenzele and the boys already knew they would have to camp out. They were prepared.

She looked out the window as they flew over the trees — a flash of green vegetation passing underneath.

She let her mind wander back to when she'd last been flying so far up Africa. In such different circumstances too, where emerald green forest with thick vines rushed beneath her. She remembered loading the five men and their mark, a contractor who'd been negotiating mineral rights with the local tribe before he ended up a rebel forces prisoner. After saving his life, she later learned he was Samuel Patterson-Quinn, one of the mine's directors in Zambia. They had flown east for hours, and were almost out of the hot zone, nearing Virunga, when she saw something appear on her horizon. Another craft.

She forced her bird to fly higher and higher.

The other helicopter shadowed them as it came closer. She could see its markings — an eye painted on the side.

Almost out of rebel territory. Almost but not quite.

Wes shouted. "Incoming. Brace."

She banked to the right, trying to maneuver the old bird and take evasive action, but they had taken a missile to the tail of the helicopter. She remembered spiraling downwards. The trees getting closer and her helicopter not responding.

The smell of burning fuel.

The devastation on impact.

Miraculously, three of them had survived.

"Savannah," Laurence's voice sliced into her memories.

She was back in real-time in a millisecond.

"If you head left, we'll pass over an area many of the tourists try to camp at because of its panoramic view. Look, there's a vehicle my men will have to move on to the proper campsite. Sometimes the tourists are their own worst enemies in the park," Lawrence said.

"Ja," Chrystal said, having seen so much evidence of that herself. From their vantage point they could see two people on deck chairs sitting outside their camper van, even at this distance they could make out it was an elderly white couple. "Not them," she said, disappointed. People tended to forget that there were lions, leopards and hyenas in a game reserve, and humans make a real easy meal for them.

"There," Lawrence pointed. "That's the official campsite."

She did a pass over, and then turned around in a wide circle and flew back again.

Sure enough, there was a long-distance overland vehicle stopped, and it was a little away from the others, as if trying to isolate. What was strange was it had only one small tent erected — an overlander would normally have multiple around it, with lots of young adults outside.

"Something is not right with where it's parked," Lawrence said.

She nodded. "I agree. How far behind us are the teams?"

"At least an hour on the internal road," Lawrence said, not removing his binoculars from his eyes. "It's designed to keep the traffic gentle; we've put bumps and turns into it on purpose. Life is supposed to move slowly in a national park. With the rains, some of the special access roads are only partially accessible and then they must use their 4 x 4 capabilities for large sections of it. Once they get back onto the main road, rather than the access ranger roads, they will move faster."

She looked at the sky, on the horizon huge storm clouds were gathering and towered high into the atmosphere. The blackness showed that there was heavy moisture within the clouds, and she watched as lightning highlighted the cloud and those behind it tumbling across the veld. Still in the distance, they would be a formidable foe when they swept across the reserve. "Shit. That storm is intensifying. It's going to hit us before the sun goes down."

Lawrence clicked his tongue. "They are common at this time of the year. It'll be dark by the time it passes. There's a spot we can land safely not too far from here, so we're not in the turbulence. The rain will make the team's going even slower. They can travel when it's dark but are going to have to use low beams to see the animals. Hopefully these bastards won't see us coming and run."

"What are the chances of us going into the campsite tonight?" Chrystal asked.

"Slim. If they're armed, we could create an even bigger problem. There are other visitors at the site, who could be hurt in the crossfire. We have to think about civilian casualties."

"If we go in as a strike force, we should be able to stop any of that," Rowan said.

Lawrence shook his head. "In the dark, I don't want to risk anyone in my park. We can wait, stay close, watch them."

"The problem is that vehicle could move, and then we would have an even more difficult time in getting to it," Chrystal said. "There's only an hour or so to the park's exit, then they're on tar road all the way to Dar es Salaam. If we don't stop them here, we could miss this chance altogether."

• • •

Rowan watched Chrystal as she stood to stretch her back. It was going to be a long night. They were off watch for another two hours, after that it would be eyes on constantly. The others in their team were taking their watches while some rested or talked quietly.

She'd brought the helicopter down in a clearing near the road, only a few kilometers from the campsite, and waited for the two Jeeps to join them before they all set out on foot, walking through the rain, praying that the lightning didn't strike them. They were racing the fading daylight to get into position to keep the overlander under constant surveillance through the night.

She was restless. He could see the small path she'd already trampled into the knee-high grass.

"Come on — sit. There's nothing we can do except watch until the light returns," he whispered.

"I know, but that doesn't stop me from worrying," she said as she sat on the ground right next to Rowan, her body touching his.

He didn't move.

Didn't breathe.

Like a skittish foal who came to its human when a bond was formed. Chrystal's body was trusting him now, even if she didn't admit it to herself.

She faced the campsite, even though she didn't have her binoculars trained on them. "I keep thinking I could take a little peek tonight, in the tent, inside the overlander, then everything would be alright, and we'd know if they were hiding her in there."

He looked in the same direction, at the single but significant acacia tree that blocked their view. "From my conversation with Cherri, she didn't seem like the submissive type of kid, it seemed that she was always trying to escape. Now that Cherri isn't there, we don't know what they've done to her and how they've treated her. Given that the woman we assume was the one who looked after them was reported missing to the police in Zambia, I would assume that they have her with them. I just cross fingers we're not following a false lead."

"God, I hope not," Chrystal said. "I don't think I could handle that right now. Not when I think we're so close."

"I've been doing this for many years and every time I get to a situation like this, I have to remind myself that it's so easy to crash and burn. If they feel threatened, they could kill her. The fact that they're transporting her over land in Africa makes me think perhaps she's still giving them trouble, and they're not used to having an older non-compliant child. They've been trying to avoid places with lots of people until now. Which means after Cherri's escape, they don't trust her to not run away. That's why they are making this long trip, instead of simply flying to wherever it is they're ultimately taking her."

"You think so?" Chrystal asked as she picked at a tuft of grass. Night sounds of crickets and owls were clearly audible.

"Yeah. If they were seasoned professional international traffickers, they would've flown her out of South Africa the moment they had her, and she would've disappeared. I think we have a bit of a maverick on our hands. I also believe that we've underestimated their tenacity to get her to auction. Looking at the lengths that they've gone to, they're desperate to get her to wherever it is; obviously their livelihood depends on it."

"Still no news on where and when this auction is?" Chrystal asked.

"Holly's found some notices about one in Venice in two weeks' time. She hasn't found out exactly where yet. There's been some talk about an exciting opportunity for some 'American cargo' on one of the groups, but that it was 'in danger'. She's trying to uncover identities — we can't be sure it's the same cargo yet, but it's worth her looking into it."

"It must be good to be able to trust your sister with something so important when you're out here, on the ground. I miss that type of trust. I know I have Khulu, and of course Zenzele, and I would trust him with my life, but it's not the same." She took the grass out and tossed it aside.

"I think you've built up an amazing team, Chrystal, they're loyal to you."

"It's not this team I'm thinking about." She took a breath. "On my last venture there was someone on the team who I put my trust in. I believe they let me down. I can't be certain, but I do have my suspicions, and I'm beginning to think I was right."

"You were betrayed?" He stilled, trying hard not to stop her now that she was talking.

She bit the inside her cheek. "I think so, but I left it all behind without sorting it out. Perhaps when this is over, I'll follow this through and let the dead rest. I think that Busi the sangoma might be right," she admitted. "It's time to let them go and let myself be free of responsibility of the five souls."

Rowan kept quiet. He wanted to reach out to her, bring her close to him.

Help her. Comfort her. But Savannah didn't need that. She needed space now to talk through the last experience.

"You were the one who survived. It figures that you think it's your duty to find who's responsible. Survivor guilt," Rowan said.

"No, it's more than that. I feel it here." She put her hand on her stomach. "There's no way anyone should've had a helicopter where we were. Or even know our location, for that matter. Something that I remembered today was that it didn't come out of the jungle; it came from the UN side. When I saw it, it was in the good guys' territory."

"You sure on that?" Rowan asked, leaning toward her, pressing his arm to hers, and feeling the heat of her through the fabric of his shirt.

"*Ja*, dead sure. Nothing I can do about it now, bringing Akina home takes priority."

"And talking about Akina," Rowan said. "It's almost time for our watch. From the looks of that lightning, we're going to be drenched again."

Chrystal stepped carefully on the clump of grass. She could hear the crackle of the older breaking dry thatch, despite knowing the newer green shoots would mask the sound over a distance. She hated that she'd made a noise.

Looking around at the trees for primates or birds that might have woken, who could raise an alarm call.

She slowed her pace.

The sun was not up but there was a slight lightening of the sky, and while she could see shadows around her, honestly – if she stepped on a tortoise, she wouldn't be able to tell the difference between that and a rock.

Hopefully anything alive would move out of her way feeling the vibrations as she walked toward it. They were using the ablution block to mask their approach. There was still about fifty meters between the bushes and the overlander.

Although she could see the vehicle, she couldn't detect movement.

On the ground, was a small piece of white paper. Someone had gone to the toilet, and they hadn't buried their feces. It was fresh. Only a few hours and deposited before the rain last night — the tissue was totally wet. She put her hand over her nose and went to avoid the area but then noticed that the ground had been disturbed. She signaled for Rowan behind her to follow and purposely moved away from the site.

He stepped into the space, matching her footsteps one by one.

She itched to take a torch and look closer at what was in the sand, but her priority now was to get to the overlander. She made a mental note to come back to behind the bushes to check. She veered right and stepped out from behind the low bushes.

Slowly she inched her way, as quiet as a leopard stalking its prey, Rowan close behind her.

She peered into the small pup tent. It was empty.

Together they looked underneath the belly of the vehicle.

Remnants of an older fireplace, but that was all.

No people sleeping beneath the vehicle or around.

Chrystal motioned with her hands that she wanted to investigate the window in the front. Rowan threaded his fingers together, to give her a step to use as he stood in front of where the driver's seat was.

Without hesitation, she placed her hands on his shoulders, and her foot into his hands.

He easily lifted her.

She shook her head and climbed down again, pointing toward the back. Slowly they moved along the outside of the overlander and repeated the maneuver when they had a window to see through.

"Nothing, it's empty," Chrystal said quietly. "Open the door."

Rowan grabbed the handle and pulled. Chrystal was ready to spring inside and up the few steps.

She looked in. It was dark. The light from outside not quite bright enough to penetrate the tinting of the windows.

She turned on her torch and checked each seat.

"No one here," she said. Backing out, she closed the door quietly.

"Perhaps they are sleeping nearer the other campers?" Rowan said.

"Look," she said, shining her torch on the ground. "Tracks. One barefoot, only a child, one larger — but still small, might be a female, and then one large, wearing boots. That's a big deep imprint. A big man. Another vehicle stopped here, and the child and the woman got in." She walked around, and then was on the other side of where a camper van would have stood between them. "The big man's prints disappear here."

"What the hell? What are you saying?"

"They've switched vehicles again and left," Chrystal confirmed.

"How?" Rowan asked, his voice rising.

"I don't know, but the *spoor* says that they left last night during the storm. There's a little bit of rain over the tracks. The storm would've muffled any engine noise, and it was the only time we couldn't see the camp clearly." Chrystal bent down to show him with a piece of grass. "Look, the narrower tire tracks of the other vehicle, come to the inside of the overlander track, and you can see where it's overlayed, imprinting over the thick track, trying to hide it from us. They camped here knowing we could only observe from a higher place, as that was where our camp was. They used that to their advantage, and moved inside where we couldn't see. This man knows the bush. He knows how to hunt and to track."

"What now?"

"Get the helicopter back in the air, we might still see them. At least till they hit the exit gate and get on the tarmac again," Chrystal said. "Zenzele!" she called aloud, now not caring who she woke up or who slept. "Check what's behind that toilet block, something is disturbed the sand. Lawrence, get your guys to check if any vehicle is missing from camp. Run, I need to be in the air. Stat."

"Find whose vehicle was stolen and radio me," Lawrence called to his men, as he ran to the Jeep.

"Come on, Rowan, move. Zane, with me."

She rushed back to where the bird sat. Zane had scrambled in ahead of Lawrence and Rowan as she started snagging her chucks.

Getting back to the helicopter had seemed to take forever but in truth it was probably only about twenty minutes. Even as she became airborne, Lawrence's men were on the radio.

"The old couple who we moved on yesterday and told them to get into the camp. They've both had their throats cut. Their vehicle is missing. It was a 4 x 4 campervan, white with blue trim, from memory the number plate was T 995 AGT."

Rowan shook his head. "How did they know we were onto them?"

"I don't know. We don't know what time they left, the spoor was still fresh, but fresh could mean three hours ahead," Chrystal said.

Lawrence said, "The gates open at six-thirty, when the sun rises."

"Radio your guys and tell them not to let anybody in or out," Rowan instructed.

"Calling Morogoro gate. Calling Morogoro gate. Come in." Lawrence tried the radio.

There was no answer.

"Morogoro gate, come in," Lawrence tried again. No answer.

As they flew toward the gate, Chrystal said, "Shit. Look in the road. Man down."

They could already see that things had gone wrong.

Touching down in a clearing inside the reserve, Lawrence, Zane and Rowan ran toward where they could see men lying face down on the ground, while Chrystal waited. The gates were open and while they could see that the guards had put up a fight, they had been overwhelmed and unprepared for an attack to come from inside the park. Not only were they all dead, but their guardhouse had been ransacked and the gun safe raided.

Leaving Zane with Lawrence, Chrystal and Rowan flew over the reserve border and into Tanzania airspace. She kept low to avoid anyone who was out and radioed into the airport that she was out of the National Park space.

"East?" she asked Rowan as they came to the road. "Dar Es Salaam and a boat which could take them through the Suez Canal, then up to Venice is that way. If it is Venice they are running toward."

"Definitely, if that fails then they will head toward Nairobi, but I don't think they'll have the contacts to get past Somalia and the pirate run, without major help on the ground," Rowan said.

She kept her helicopter flying directly into the rising sun and headed east.

However, seeing not one camper van in an hour in the direction of Dar Es Salaam, she began to make a big lazy turn. "Not enough fuel to go further. Besides we should have seen them by now. I need to head back to the National Park."

"Fuck it. Fuck it," Rowan swore. "We almost had them."

Zenzele's voice came over the radio. "Chopper RZB-86, come in."

"86 here," Chrystal said.

"Request you return to the campsite."

"That's Japanese writing for sure," Rowan said as he looked down at where Zenzele was pointing.

"This is where Akina had gone to the toilet," Zenzele said. A discreet mound of sand had been put over her feces. "She wrote in the sand when crouched. There was her father's cell number and the fact that he had $. There are also some drawings which I think may be Japanese in the sand. Despite the rain, her writing is dug in deep with a stick. She's one brave and smart little girl."

Rowan had his phone to his ear. On the other side was Curtis, Akina's father.

"I can tell you what the marking on the ground means," Curtis said. "The first photo you sent me—"

Rowan looked at the corresponding marking.

ヴェネツィアアート

"That means VeniceArt."

"And the second photo?" Rowan asked, turning his attention to it.

私を売る

"Sell me," Curtis translated, his voice cracking.

"Are you sure?" Rowan asked.

"It's faint and some of them are not exact, she's in a hurry writing it, but that's what it looks like to me. I'll get my assistant to confirm. Clever girl — writing it in Japanese in case they saw it." Pride and emotion were clear in his voice.

"Thank you, we appreciate the translation," Rowan said.

"If this gets to the press, what will they do to her?" Curtis asked, his voice low, almost a whisper.

"Not a good idea to let it leak to the press. They're mavericks, doing things I would never have expected. It's as if they are one small step ahead of us constantly. I think that so far, they have tried everything to get her to this auction. They are keeping her alive so they must think she'll fetch a good price."

"You realize that VeniceArt is a huge auction house," Curtis said. "I've bought several art pieces from there over the years."

"I understand that. We now have an auction house and a city," Rowan said.

"You need to go to Venice. But I cannot bear the thought of abandoning

Akina now that we are so close and making her continue the journey. Can Chrystal carry on looking in Africa?"

"Split up?" Rowan asked.

"You work well in Europe, and you said yourself — she's been good on the ground in Africa. You told me this woman brought a man out of the jungle in the Congo alone. The only survivor of a whole team. If she can do that, she can keep on Akina's tracks. Find her, try and steal her back. But you need to be ready to buy Akina if we must. Get to Europe and find out how you get a buyer's ticket to that auction."

Rowan disagreed. The last thing he wanted to do was split from Chrystal so close to the traffickers. He felt that they had a better chance together, but he would see what happened when they got back to base. He wouldn't be doing anything to jeopardize finding Akina.

CHAPTER 24

Pretoria, Gauteng Province, South Africa

8ᵗʰ April 2016 — 22 days until auction

maCalio and Davinia waited in an old white Isuzu bakkie they had stolen, and then changed the number plates, which had also been appropriated from a different vehicle. They had followed Tomi Patel at a respectable distance until he went inside his mansion gates in Parktown. Once one of the more affluent suburbs of Johannesburg in yesteryears, the streets were tree lined and wide. Houses were large, with big gardens walled in to keep those living there safe.

Many had changed hands, and were being renovated, modernized. Some had been changed into exclusive apartment blocks, others into business premises, but some remained whole, and in the hands of the wealthy who still wanted to be nearer the city.

Davinia moved on the seat.

"Patience, that is what this is about. You wait. You watch and when they least expect it, that is when you take them," maCalio said.

"This Tomi Patel is a gunrunner like maNtuli?" Davinia asked.

"Yes," maCalio said. "You have been watching him well. You followed him from after we told you to watch Elias De Waal."

"Yes. But they are the same, why doesn't maNtuli live in a big house like this?" Davinia asked. "This man is loaded, look at this place, and you know the cars he drives too."

"Because she is not a showoff, and she is clever. With a big house comes big expenses, and it gives you a place your enemies can target. See his cameras on the wall, his security team is inside, and he never leaves without at least two bodyguards close by his side. Where she can walk freely down the street if she wants to."

They watched as a delivery van pulled up outside and spoke on the video intercom, before the gates opened outwards, and the van drove inside.

"Give Patel fifteen minutes, and he'll come out of his house, and head to the gym," Davinia said. "Like clockwork. The same every day."

maCalio smiled and glanced at Davinia. "This is why you followed him, so we had information like this. It is important not only to know who you are collecting the information for, but also not to ask too many questions as to why you are being asked to do what you will do. It's trust between me and maNtuli, and now trust between me and you."

"Why are we poisoning him? Why kill another gunrunner?" Davinia turned her head just to look at maCalio, not wanting to take her eyes off the house for more than a second, in case she missed something. Clever girl.

"He is the man who is directly responsible for maNtuli's supply line problems. Not just here, but everywhere. You are not the only one to send us a picture of him meeting with other people in the chain. He wants to take over her business. Because of Tomi Patel's suggestions, our man at the police armory, Elias decided that he was going to try and set the police on us. Tomi Patel is attempting to take out maNtuli as his competition.

"Remember the tracker that you sent on the train? We have found the man who made that for Tomi Patel. This was not a once off."

"*Eish*," Davinia said.

"Tomi Patel is the problem, so he must be eliminated. Elias knows then not to cross us again. Our supply keeps coming, uninterrupted. maNtuli looks after those who stay loyal to her, long term, and who can perform special tasks for her. End of story."

"I do not believe I ever want to be on the wrong side of maNtuli."

maCalio smiled. As the delivery van left, Tomi Patel's white Porsche Cayenne drove out behind it. There were two security guards with him, one in the back, and one in the front.

"How come we can't ram him and kill him?" Davinia asked.

"That car looks fantastic, doesn't it? Like a regular one, but it is bullet-proof. If you ram it, it would be like ramming a tank. A man like that knows that he's a target, so he takes steps to ensure he's safe from everyday South African pettiness. No hijacking. No bullets get to him. His clothes had Kevlar built into them, so unless you get a shot at his head, no assassinations. But they always forget one thing. He's still a man. We had to find a way to get through all that armor and get to him."

"That car is *jislaaik*; it's beautiful."

"Don't get your heart set on a stupid car, it will lead to death. Come, we go to the gym, you ready?" maCalio asked.

Davinia nodded.

maCalio started the Isuzu and reversed up the road, so that she never passed Tomi's house, and was not caught on his security camera.

At the corner of the gym, maCalio looked at Davinia.

She was dressed all in black, including black plastic gloves and she had removed the Evian water bottle from its bag.

"Wish me luck," Davinia said, then winked as she put her white earphones with a cord into her ears and pushed herself away from the *bakkie*.

She began jogging slowly to where Tomi had come out of the gym, and as was his habit, Tomi took a swig of his water bottle as he came out. He strolled toward his Porsche. Davinia increased her speed from under the trees and ran right into Tomi.

Davinia rolled over onto the tarmac of the parking lot and was on her feet and backing away, a water bottle in her hand, her other hand up in a no harm gesture and was saying sorry, pointing to her headphones.

maCalio could hear her apologies, even before the two big burly security guards reacted.

"So much for muscles if they are so big you can't move fast enough," maCalio said as Davinia carried on running and disappeared into the shadows of the trees.

Tomi waved his security away, water bottle still in his hand.

He walked to his Porsche and slammed the door. Then he started it and backed out of the parking space. maCalio lay low behind the wheel, pulling her beanie down over her forehead.

Waiting.

Tomi followed the same route he always did. He turned away from where maCalio was and drove down the road. maCalio watched the clock on the dashboard, waiting a full two minutes before starting the *bakkie* and driving forward. She turned the corner at the end of the street and stopped.

Davinia walked out from where she was in the shadow of the tree, ran to the *bakkie* and climbed in.

"That man might be rich, but man did he stink," Davinia said as she threw the bottle at her feet. "And he gets into that nice car smelling like a pig."

"Don't lose that bottle, you need to burn it," maCalio said. "And your clothes, anything that came in contact with him. We burn those first, then we can burn this bakkie."

"Such a waste."

"This might be South Africa, but believe me, Tomi Patel dying is going to have every cop in the country crawling over every camera in this neighborhood. He had more than just Elias De Waal on his payroll. We don't want to be anywhere near anything that had any of his DNA on it. We can get another *bakkie*. It's all part of the charm of this job. New cars."

Davinia asked, "Now what happens?"

maCalio smiled. "Watch and learn."

They cruised slowly a little up the street, then maCalio stopped. "Look up ahead, his armor proof Porsche has hit a tree. Even a man like Tomi Patel can't drive a fancy car when he's dead. Today, your job is done."

CHAPTER 25

Mikumi Game Reserve, Tanzania

8ᵗʰ April 2016 — 22 days until auction

The police were crawling all over the damage done at the gate. Cordoned off as a crime scene, there was a lot of talking going on there with Lawrence.

Rowan, Chrystal and her team had quietly disappeared, better out of sight, and out of mind. Now they were standing next to the helicopter, and the Jeeps had all the rangers in them, ready to drive back to base at Rungwe Game Reserve.

"Curtis thinks that we should split up," Rowan said.

"Split up? Is he crazy?" Chrystal asked. "Of all the harebrained things we could do, perhaps that is the worst."

"I agree."

"What if they didn't go out of the reserve?" Chrystal asked. "They created havoc, and then went back inside, to wait it out. They have done things differently, all this time. What if they did that now? The unexpected."

"Hide where you are least expected to be, back in the place where you came from — what are we waiting for? If we fly over them, we can tell if it's them or not."

"They have a few hours on us already, I don't know how far they will have pushed into the reserve."

"Right, so if we load up our guys, and one of the local game guards that knows this place well. Lawrence is busy, so we take someone else, and off we go."

"This is a six-person chopper, but with guns and ammo, better with only four. The fuel will last longer. The others can follow in the Jeeps in case we need them. If we move fast, we start flying in semi-circles from the gate, in the reserve. We should cover a lot of ground before I need to head back to base and fill up," Chrystal said.

"Right, I'll tell Lawrence's guys what we're doing, so they can fill him in when he isn't busy with the police. We have to count Zane out; he's with Lawrence and won't get away from those police for a while," Rowan said.

"*Ja*, so it's you, me, and Zenzele and one other in the helicopter, and then the rest of our team with Desmond, on the ground in the Jeep, coming down the roads as close as they can to where we go."

They had been in the air for over an hour when Zenzele tapped her on the arm. "There," he pointed.

From above, if he was not well trained, he wouldn't have seen the change in the bush, but he did. There was a white vehicle, half-covered with a tree that had been cut, and half covered under a camo net.

"Could be them, could be a researchers camp or even a poachers camp," Zenzele said.

"Not a researcher, they all pack up in the rainy season and go home. The big rains are starting, no one wants to be caught out here in the wet," Bernhard, the local game ranger said.

"Let's go in for a closer look," Chrystal said.

She slowed down, but as she did, a man ran out from the vehicle, and pointed at them. Even at the distance they were she could tell he had a hunting rifle.

"Incoming," Rowan shouted.

She banked trying to avoid the high-powered bullets, putting the bottom of her bird to the incoming slugs. She knew her bird could take a fair bit; not much could bring it down. Helicopters were built robust, and sturdy, to stay in the air. She heard another shot hit them on the undercarriage and turned her tail to the shooter, lifting in altitude to get out of range of his weapon.

Chrystal thought they were going to be okay, then the alarm sounded.

Electronic fluid. The bastard had got a lucky shot and she was leaking fluid.

"Brace for impact," she commanded. "We're going to go down fast."

Her helicopter began to descend.

They were still upright, but the altimeter was whizzing madly as she lost height.

She kept the helicopter as level as she could, but still hit the ground hard. Too hard.

The helicopter bounced on its skids, but she managed to keep it from tipping over.

The engine whined.

She cut the power and switched everything off.

Silence. No explosion.

"Everyone okay?" she asked.

"Fine," Zenzele said.

"I'm good," Bernhard said.

"Zenzele, I'm going to need you to help Chrystal out. Bernhard, you'll need to help me," Rowan said.

Still held firmly in her chair, she began to turn her head to look at Rowan.

"Don't look at me, get your door open and get out," he said through clenched teeth. "Now."

She didn't need to be told twice. She flicked the handle on her door and opened it.

"Wait," Zenzele said from behind her as he got himself out of his seat and out his door, then he was leaning in and reaching for her. "Undo your seat-belt, I've got you. Keep looking at me."

She did as he asked. All the time she could hear the blood pumping through her body. She knew there was blood; they wouldn't be treating her like this if there wasn't.

Rowan was hurt. Images of Wes jumped in her mind. Wes hurt. Blood.

The python who crushed her chest stuck fast. Her breathing shallowed. She gulped for air.

"Don't look," Zenzele warned.

She shut the images down by blinking rapidly. The python still crushing her, she slid down off the side of her helicopter and landed on the ground.

"Breathe," Zenzele said. "No blood here. Just breathe."

And the python loosened its grip.

She was breathing; she was okay. "I'm good, I'm good."

"Okay. Go stand over there, I need to help Bernhard," Zenzele said.

She wanted to help. Rowan was hurt.

Now when she expected detailed graphic images of Wes hurt to flood over her, it was images of Rowan and her together instead. Rowan's smile. Him handing Cherri a teddy bear. Him sitting next to her in the bush, their bodies touching in the rain. She could almost feel the warmth she had drawn from that.

She wanted to be the one to be able to go in and help Rowan.

He deserved it.

But knowing that he was hurt—

The python slithered back.

Her breath was too shallow. She could hear it herself.

"Is he bad?" she called back, keeping her eyes away from the crash. Fighting the python.

"He will be fine," Zenzele called.

She sat down in the grass, listening to all the sounds as the men attempted to get Rowan out from the helicopter. But at the same time trying hard to block them out. There was a crested francolin calling somewhere, followed by another. The doves cooed, and somewhere she could hear the trickle of water.

She was safe from the python.

Zenzele called, "Chrystal, we need you. You are the smallest of us all, and whatever is pinned through his leg is under the seat. If you can go into that space by his feet, and you can see what is stopping us pulling him upwards, then we can get him out."

She got up and took a deep breath.

Rowan needed her.

"You have to do this. There is blood so you need to keep calm," Zenzele was instructing, but his voice had a tone of urgency.

"I'll try, I have to do it," she said.

Images of Wes threatened, and she pushed them back.

Wes was dead. She couldn't help him.

But Rowan was still alive.

She could help save him.

At the helicopter, Zenzele stood next to her on Rowan's side. He gave her his arm to use to help pull her up, then she slithered on her belly inside, but not onto a seat, instead in underneath Rowan's legs.

There was blood; she could smell the metallic scent.

Her breath shallowed. She felt the flick of the python's tongue.

"Stay calm, Chrystal," Rowan said. "Breathe normally. I'm not dying, it's clearly in and out through the thigh. I'm not going to die. I have too much to do still, too much to live for. Besides, I'm too stubborn to die before I find Akina."

She smiled weakly.

The python lessened its grip. Rowan's deep voice was hypnotizing the python, calming her. His words were helping.

"Get in there," Zenzele said as he pushed her further into the small space where Rowan's feet were.

"Talk to me," Rowan said. "Explain what you see."

"There is blackness on the edge of my vision," she said, the python reticulating on her chest.

"Focus on the picture inside that, I need to see what you see. Do you see my feet?" Rowan asked.

"Yes."

"What boots am I wearing?"

She tried to smile at the ridiculous question. "Black boots, combat style, and your Kevlar pants are pulled up slightly. I can see a hairy leg. Did you know you have a small mole on your leg?" Two could play this game.

"Been there all my life," he slurred in an exaggerated Southern American farmer's drawl. "Look further than that, what do you see that is under the seat?" Rowan asked in his normal voice.

She wanted to laugh and take a breath; it was almost normal. "I see a few springs and there's a really thin piece of metal sticking through and downwards. I'll try and see where the end leads."

"Keep going," Rowan said.

"It's come through the chair and bent itself around one of the springs, I'm touching it. Can you feel that?"

"No, he feels nothing," Zenzele said before Rowan could even answer.

"Good, it's quite flexible, hang on, there you go, I have dislodged it. See if you can pull Rowan out now."

"Give me one second," Rowan said, and then Zenzele and Bernhard were lifting him by the arms and pulling him upwards.

"It's moving; it's going up with you," Chrystal said.

"We have him out his seat" Zenzele said, "now we need to get him out the helicopter."

Chrystal let out a huge breath. "Righty-o."

"Stay there. We are lifting him over you," Zenzele warned.

She stayed dead still. "Once you're done, I'll go look for the medical kit."

"Good idea," Zenzele said. "You can start trying to move now. We are down."

She backed out of the space she'd been in and glanced upwards. "One, two, three," she counted before she got out and then into the back, but she glanced at the seat where Rowan had vacated. There was a lot of blood pooled there.

She began breathing shallowly. "I'm going to the back to look now," she said, averting her eyes and pushing through the seats. "I'm looking and there it is, strapped where it should be. Got it. I'm now going to climb out."

"Good. Wait there, I'll come and help you out," Zenzele called to her.

He came back and she had his arms to help her again.

"Is Rowan okay?" Chrystal asked.

"We have him lying on his side. I can bandage a cut on the arm or a rip in someone's leg, but I have never seen something that goes through. He says we need to pull it out, but I told him he must wait for you. You're the only one with any medical training Chrystal, you're going to have to help him."

Chrystal's breathing got faster.

"Start talking. That was working with him, talk. Tell me what to do," Zenzele said.

"If there is a clear straight part of the metal, then we should be able to pull it out, and there'll be field dressing in this kit, we can put on and bandage. There was lots of blood on that seat, but I've seen more and even then, it wasn't arterial blood, so he shouldn't bleed out."

They had got down and while Zenzele had the first aid kit in his hands, he was slowly pulling her toward where Rowan lay.

"Zenzele and I can sing to you," Rowan said. "I'm sure that I can learn the words, maybe Bernhard knows them too, if that will help you?"

"I have to look at this metal in your leg, get it out so that you can move, and we can then talk about seeing if the radio still works, as I didn't have time to send out an SOS, and the guys will have seen us disappear. They won't know where we are. And there is potential that if we don't get this bleeding stopped that you are going to be lion fodder out here."

"Excellent," Rowan said.

"I need to cut your pants away, and get it cleaned before I can do anything else," Chrystal said. The panic threatened and she sent it back deep inside. It was not going to control her. Rowan needed her.

"Do what you have to," Rowan said, his voice strained.

"This part I can do. You look away, I will call you when you can see it," Zenzele said, grabbing a pair of scissors from the first aid kit.

She looked away and sang softly. "*Thula thul, thula baba, thula sana.*"

The python rested. She was going to beat this. She had to for Rowan's life.

"You can look," Zenzele said.

She turned and looked. "You have a thin metal rod from the door frame or somewhere that's gone through your thigh. I think if we pull it from the back side the top end is mostly straight and it will slide through and out cleanly."

"Do it," Rowan said.

"Zenzele you grab that end and wait for my signal. When I say it, you pull hard, make sure it comes all the way through in one go. Understood?"

Zenzele nodded.

"Bernhard, you hold Rowan still. Sit on him so he can't turn over at all. He must stay on his side. Yes, like that, grip his arms down with your legs." She took a deep breath. "Ready, pull on three. One—"

"Ahhhhhhhhh," Rowan screamed. "Fuck, that hurt."

"Yes, but it's out." She grinned down at him as she saw Zenzele holding the whole rod in his hand. They had used that trick a few times during their anti-poaching accidents, not giving the person time to clinch up. She let out a breath. Rowan was going to be alright. The immediate danger was past. A wave of delight washed over her.

The python slithered back into hibernation.

"Here," Zenzele said to Rowan, and then he passed the metal to him, then reached into the first aid kit.

"You really did that, you helped to get it out," Rowan said. "No panic attack."

"So far so good, but I'll keep talking in case." She took the field dressing from Zenzele. "Now, I'm cleaning your wounds, both on the front and the back. You're going to have to be careful how you sit for a bit — that's going to be right where you take weight on a chair." Chrystal said as she looked at Zenzele who passed her more dressings.

Just keep talking, keep me focused on what I'm doing. That was how she was getting through today. She took another breath and carried on doing exactly that.

"Right, those are clean. I'm going to dry them, and lucky, they're not bleeding. I can put on the dressings and wrap one of these elasticized bandages around, that should help with compression too, yippee for a well-stocked kit." She took a much-needed breath. "We need to thank Curtis for money well spent. Right, now you're done. There is a tub of paracetamol in here and some broad-spectrum antibiotics, there you go you can take two of those," she put them into Rowan's hand.

"Thank you," Rowan said.

She continued rummaging in the kit. "Put the others in your pocket, and here's some better drugs for pain. Take two of these." She placed the tablets in his open palm, noticing her hands were steady. A little burst of pride hit her. "You can roll over onto your back now. All done. So now all I have to do is wash all this blood off my hands—" She stopped talking and was looking at her hands. There were smudges of blood, but they were not soaked. She turned them over.

They did not have blood up her wrists and up her arms.

She looked up at Rowan.

He looked back.

She turned to Zenzele. He was staring at her, smiling.

She took the antibacterial wipes from the kit and using two, wiped her hands.

"Looks all clean," she said. "And not one panic attack."

"At last," Zenzele said. "Chrystal is back with us."

Chrystal grinned.

"You did well," Rowan said.

"Talking never helped before, but—" Zenzele said.

"I'm not so sure it was simply the talking, more of a life event combined with a team effort," Rowan said. "Thank you, Savannah, you were there when I needed you."

"*Ja*, right, if it wasn't for you and Zenzele making me talk all the time, distracting me, I wouldn't have got through that at all."

"Come sit, you might not have had a full-on attack, but you are starting to go into shock. Sit next to me, I can help warm you. Zenzele are there any space blankets in that kit?"

He rummaged to the bottom. "*Yebo*, here you go."

She watched as Zenzele passed them two and gave one to Bernhard, before he opened one himself. She looked at Rowan, who despite being in his own world of pain, was helping to pull a blanket around her.

"I'll go check that radio now before I settle," Zenzele said.

Chrystal nodded.

Rowan's warm body settled next to hers, offering her comfort. She felt content sitting beside him. She let herself relax, leaning her body into him as they sat in silence for a long time listening to the sounds around them. The wind as it whispered in the long grass, the birds calling and the crickets chirping — the constant buzz of mosquitoes and flies.

It was good to be alive.

"It's a good thing Chitauro saw us fall from the sky," Chrystal said. "And that he was apparently so adamant the direction they had to drive in."

"Mmm," Rowan said sleepily.

"I have to admit, seeing the Jeep coming toward us before Zenzele even got to radio for help was icing on the cake."

"They definitely were not happy seeing your helicopter on the ground," Rowan said.

"No, but they did well," she said as she lay in a sleeping bag. Hers touched Rowan's on one side, and the back wheel of the Jeep on the other. A stretcher held her off the ground so that creepies like scorpions didn't climb into bed with her.

Their small fire had already died down. There was not lots of wood on hand to burn on the grasslands part of the National Park. They lay slightly away from the others, and they had set up a watch schedule. They were camped in a National Park, where lions, cheetahs and leopards roamed freely, not to mention the hyenas if they were interested.

Their makeshift camp would do until the morning when they would limp back toward headquarters. A mechanic would come out and fix the helicopter, and then fly it back to headquarters.

The white camper van had been gone by the time their Jeep got to them. Whatever hope they had of finding Akina in the park had faded with the light.

"You okay?" Rowan asked.

"I'm doing great. A little shaken. Pissed as hell about the chopper, but great," she said, frowning. "Trying to sort out in my mind how they are always a step ahead of us."

"Luck?"

"No, it's like they knew that we were here. As if they knew we had them under surveillance. But there's no way they could have known. How could they?"

"I've got no answer for you," Rowan admitted. "You sure you're okay?"

"I survived my second helicopter crash and I didn't have a panic attack. I'll take that as a win." She looked over at him. He lay on his side so that he didn't put any pressure on his leg. He reached for her and touched her cheek. The gentle glide of his thumb seemed intimate.

"Thank you," he said.

"I don't quite know how we got through today," she said.

"One small step at a time," he said, cupping her face in his hand.

"Corny," she said, but she smiled. His hand felt good against her cheek. "You know, you never asked anything from me. You told me to get out of the way."

"You needed to get out. I didn't want you having a panic attack inside the helicopter. You know fuel and crashes and all that stuff," Rowan admitted.

"I know, but the last time someone I knew was in a bad way, they asked for my soul," she admitted.

He stilled his hand.

"Wesley was alive when we crashed, but he was badly wounded. Our mark, he miraculously had a few cuts and bruises, but otherwise he was fine, and so was I. The others were all dead. Wes's wounds were critical; he had major stomach injuries, pieces of shrapnel peppered all over and broken legs. I couldn't carry him out and move fast enough with the mark. He knew that and we could hear the guerillas coming. I've never understood why they shoot their round off into the air and announce themselves in advance so that you know how far away they are." She looked at him. His hand was still on her cheek, but it had taken on a slight shake.

"It's okay. I should shut up about now," she said.

"No, you shouldn't. I'm feeling cold."

"That we can do something about — but you are going to get colder before you get warmer. Give me your sleeping bag." She stood up and waited while he got his sore body out from his and passed it to her. She zipped them together, making the two sleeping bags one big one and put it on her stretcher closest to the fire. "Get in."

He climbed in, making sure that he was lying on his good side again. It took him time to move and get into the right place.

"You ready?" she asked, before carefully getting in next to him and putting her back to his chest. She could feel each muscular contour of him as he sucked in his stomach where she made contact with him. She already knew them well enough from sparring with him, but this was different.

Intentionally lying right next to each other.

She could do that.

He had done so much for her.

She could do this for him. Share her body's warmth.

"Better," he said. His breath fluttered on her hair as he adjusted and put his arm under his head.

"Good."

He rested his other arm over her hip and around her waist and drew her closer against his chest.

"You any warmer?" she asked.

"Getting there. Thank you."

She wiggled, getting more comfortable. Then stopped still, realizing what she was doing.

"Then what happened?" he asked, as if his body was totally unaffected by the closeness of hers against his.

"I probably said too much already. We should sleep."

"Probably, but you can't leave me in the middle of that scene. What happened? I need to know."

She took in a deep breath and stared at what was left of the fire. The orange embers smoldering, and the wispy-thin smoke that still raised upwards to the stars.

"Wes knew he wasn't going to survive, and there was no way we would make it if I tried to carry him. Wes was my partner in more than the mission. We'd been together for nearly a year. What started out as a casual itch had turned into a relationship." She paused and then in a voice filled with so much emotion it was barely a whisper, she said, "I loved him."

She wiped a tear from her eye before it could run down her face and onto her arm. "We'd made a stupid pact. To never leave one another behind, but he knew it was impossible. He knew if the guerrillas got hold of me, there was no telling what I'd have to endure. And if they got him alive, they would torture him no end. We were in a bad place. He asked me to help him die, with a promise to cut out his heart and take it home to Zimbabwe, his country of birth, to the Zambezi River and throw it into the Victoria Falls."

"That's the place that the sangoma told you to go, isn't it? The Smoke That Thunders?" Rowan said, but she could hear the tone in his voice was strained.

"Yes, it is." She sighs.

Now it was her time to shake. The tremors started small, but they got more noticeable. She attempted to pull away. He ran his hand over her hair as if tucking it next to her head, then he held her again, only this time, he tightened his hold, securing her against him. He held her close. She was sure his body curved around hers, protectively despite the confined space of the stretcher.

"And did you? Did you help him?" he urged.

"I told him I loved him, but I couldn't do it. He told me he loved me too, and he held my hand in his. He shot himself while I held him because he knew that no one would survive without him dead. He expected that I would do the second part of the pact. I tried, I really tried." She couldn't stop her shakes.

No amount of trying to hold her muscles still would stop them.

Rowan still held her tightly against his chest, but now he brushed his chin over her hair, and she could feel as he tried to wrap his body around hers, gently putting pressure with his leg over hers. Reassuring her he was there. That she was safe now.

"I tried to do as he asked. Because he wanted it. But do you know how hard it is to cut out someone's heart? Someone you love? To mutilate their body? I thought if I cut up underneath his ribs, I would be fine. And then my hands were in there, deep in his chest and I couldn't tell where his heart was, where his lungs were. I couldn't simply cut his heart out." She drew in ragged breaths.

"It was a mess inside there. And they were coming closer. I could hear them shooting blindly, hooting, trying to flush us out. My hands were all bloodied, inside his chest. There was blood everywhere. And still I couldn't find his heart. I have cut up so many animals hunting before and here I was, unable to locate the heart of the man I loved."

Her whole body was shaking violently now, and she was beginning to take shallow breaths.

"Shh, it's okay. It's not happening now. It's a memory. It's over, it's over, keep talking. You're doing great. Just keep talking," Rowan said, patting her arm as he held her.

She put her hand over his and held onto him tight. "Instead, I took his bandana, his favorite one he always wore around his neck when we went on any mission and I soaked up some of the blood from his heart area. Then I kissed his lips for the last time, and I left him. I left my Wes there for the guerillas to defile and do whatever else sick things they do to dead people, and I ran through that jungle with my mark, and didn't look back.

"We ran and ran, and even after we were out of the jungle, I made the mark keep going. And even when we were safe, I kept running because I couldn't get far enough away from what I had done." She took a deep breath to try and control her emotions, but the small sob still escaped.

She felt the soft kiss on the top of her head. In her hair. He didn't try and find skin, just kissed and then lay there, holding her. There was a long silence before Rowan said, "I know that you say you loved him, but that was one fucked up individual to ask you to do something like that. I don't think anyone has the right to ask someone to do that. I know that you're still hurting from losing him, and I finally know what happened to you, but be assured that I'd never ask you to do anything like that for me."

CHAPTER 26

Mikumi Game Reserve, Tanzania

9th April 2016 — 21 days until auction

Rowan walked into the garage at the Mikumi Game Reserve rangers' headquarters and saw pandemonium.

Chrystal had the hood of the Jeep up, and all the doors open. Pieces of the Jeep were lying all over the floor. She was on a bodyboard underneath, her legs sticking out. Zenzele was under the second vehicle, doing much the same. He swore as he hit his head on something.

"What are you doing?" Rowan asked.

"Looking for a GPS tracker. There must be one on something we have. Someone knew our location," she said. "And if we don't find it here, then we need to go back to the chopper and check that."

"If you say so, but why would someone way up here want to know where we are?" Rowan said.

"I don't know, but I shouldn't have been so trusting. We should have searched everything he gave us when we got it in Zambia. We should have made sure it was all clean. Taken no chances," she said, bringing her trolley out and standing up. "The only thing in common with my two missions is

Jason. Both times I got my helicopter and guns from his supply chain. Both times, someone sabotaged the mission."

He heard Zenzele move out from under his Jeep to listen.

"They shouldn't have known we were there. The helicopter looked commercial. They saw us fly away. We wouldn't have looked tactical. We were downwind from their camp, and far enough that they wouldn't have heard us, and couldn't have seen us. How did they know to move during that storm? Unless someone knows where we are?" Her hand movements were exaggerated again, but her face showed determination.

"Good point. Who would profit most from this? Would your old friend sell you out? What's he got to gain by it? Besides, if he misbehaves you can get the big-bad maNtuli to sort him out. I think it's more likely that they got lucky. That's all. We're going to follow them, and we'll catch them. But I'm not against your pulling everything apart to make sure our operation hasn't been compromised."

"We'll catch them," Chrystal said with a determined tilt to her chin.

"Does this mean we can stop stripping these vehicles?" Zenzele asked.

"Once Chrystal's satisfied, we need to start packing to leave. We're still hot on the trail of one little girl," Rowan said. "But it's about to get easier."

"What are you thinking?" Chrystal asked.

"Something they didn't put much thought into — running into a city area. Means cameras. Lots of them. Even in African cities, there are webcams, traffic cameras, red-light cameras, lots of digital footprints we can access and search."

"Really?" Chrystal said. "How?"

"Hopefully they haven't had a chance to steal new plates. Holly has a program running through all the webcams she can find in Dar Es Salaam now. Trawling for both their plate and the type of vehicle. They also have a whole system of traffic cams in place that haven't been switched on 'officially', so she's borrowing that. If they're there, Holly will find them and work out where they're going."

"Next time maybe lead with that," Chrystal said. Her shoulders relaxed a little.

"I wanted to know what you were doing. How long before we can get those Jeeps back together and get going?"

"Twenty minutes tops, we were almost finished searching."

Fifteen minutes later, they were loading the Jeeps. Chrystal stood next to Rowan. She put a glass jar filled with water in his hand, inside two electronic devices had gone swimming.

"Might still be one in the chopper. I have shown Lawrence what to look for. He doesn't want that baby tracked once it's fixed, it'd give the poachers too much of an upper hand."

"You really think it's Jason?" Rowan asked.

"He's the common factor on both missions, so it's a logical conclusion."

"It's never great finding out that someone you thought you could trust has crossed you," Rowan said.

"Makes sense now that I think about it, but I don't see what he gets out of it. Something is still missing. I think the saying goes: You don't bite the hand that feeds you."

"Let it percolate in your head a while," Rowan said, "your mind will sort it out. In the meantime, we need to get moving."

"There's something else. I have been thinking that there's a big airport at Victoria Falls for a detour on our way back to South Africa."

"Why?" asked Rowan as he pointed to Zenzele to load the last bag of gear into the Jeep.

"I need to visit. I can hire a car and drive over the bridge. I'll need to cross to the Zambian side to get close to the top of the falls, there's no access to it on the Zimbabwe side. I think with everything that's happened, there is something — that I need to do. A promise I need to keep."

Rowan stood straight up. "Depending on what we find in Dar Es Salaam, it could be soon, it could be after we get her back, but we'll go."

"I'll go. Just because I told you doesn't mean you have to be there," Chrystal protested.

"You pulled me out of a helicopter crash. You helped pull a metal pole from my leg. You confronted one of your worst fears. You had to live that experience twice — it's because of you that we were able to walk away from the crash—"

"*Ja*, but—" Chrystal said.

"No buts. It took real inner strength to do what you did, and you need to

214

understand that no matter what you've done and under whatever circumstances — I'm here for you. You need to forgive yourself. Even the witch was telling you to let the ghosts go," Rowan said. "But our priority right now is to find Akina. Then we can visit your falls."

"You're right — Akina comes first. This ghost has impacted enough of my life, and my priority is the living."

CHAPTER 27

Dar Es Saleem, Tanzania

Akina touched the curtains by the window in the hotel. Sure, it wasn't a five-star luxury like she was used to, and there was no hotel phone sitting beside the bed. But it was a million times better than what she'd had for the last goodness knows how long. There were two single wooden hand-crafted beds with thick foam mattresses and cotton bedding. Colorful mosquito nets had been strung above them. And there was an en-suite, with a shower and an old cast iron bathtub with running hot water. The air-conditioner hummed, causing vibrations along the windowsill and through her hands. She looked outside.

All she could see was a hedge of bushes, through which she could just make out a wall with the plaster falling off. If she pressed her head to the glass and looked sideways, she could see a few black and white pigeons strutting around in the dirt. A small brown hen had speckled baby chicks wandering behind her as she scratched in the pots that held a few green flowers. The windows had louvers and there were burglar guards, keeping her in, more than keeping anyone out.

Levi had chosen their hotel well.

No one was going to pass by that she could call out to for help.

There was nothing in the room to tell her where they were — not even the paper from the takeaway container that Tahaan had brought to them had a place identifier.

She heard a plane and looked out the window and upward to see if she could see the tail or anything on it that she recognized but couldn't see it at all.

Iesha lay on the one single bed reading a magazine that had been under the bed's leg to straighten it. Old and tatty, it was the first piece of literature that they had seen the whole trip. When she looked at the cover, it said Dar Life. Inside she found it referencing Dar Es Saleem, Tanzania. She had never been there before, but she knew sort of where it was. She was a long -long way from Cape Town.

"Why don't you lay down on a nice soft bed while you can and enjoy the cool of the air-conditioning?" Iesha asked.

"Because I don't want to get comfortable. If I look too much like I like a place, then Levi will find some other way to punish me."

"Fair enough," Iesha said.

"Do you think we have stopped traveling?" she asked, moving along to the small desk that was in the room. She opened the drawer. There was a pen refill inside with no outer casing. She dug it up out of the crack with her fingernail and slipped it into her pocket.

"No." Iesha licked her finger and turned the page.

Her heart beat hard in her chest. She was sure that if Iesha looked up, she would be caught. A pen meant she could write something. Leave another crumb. "Do you know what's happening next? Did Tahaan tell you anything?" She tried hard to keep her voice steady.

"No. To both questions."

She walked over to the bed and flopped down. "I think that this is worse than being in our box all day. At least there I know that at the end of the day we'll come to a stop. Here we seem to sit in the hotel room all day. And there isn't even a TV to watch movies. All I can think about is what will happen to me when Levi and Tahaan get me to wherever we are going, and exactly who'll buy me. What do you think? Do you know where we're going?"

"I think that you should enjoy this hotel room while you can. Enjoy the air conditioning, and nice takeaway food we are getting. We are still captive, and there is no way out. We can see what tomorrow brings, maybe we will still be here, who knows."

"Don't you want to escape?" Akina asked.

"I do," she said, flicking another page of the old magazine.

Akina tried again. "But you are still too scared to run away, because they have your daughter?"

Iesha clicked her tongue in a disapproving manner. "Until I know she's dead, or they show me proof she's safe and where she is, I'm as much a prisoner as you. You think I want to carry on looking after you on a long journey? You're wrong. I never wanted to leave my village in Zambia, much less travel to wherever we are."

Akina sat on the bed and reached over; she took the magazine from Iesha. "But if we can get away, then my dad will help us. All we have to do is call him. He will send money; we have to get away from Levi and Tahaan."

"Give me back that magazine." Her voice was flat. Irritated.

Akina gave it back, but she'd closed it. "I wanted to make sure you were listening to me."

"I'm always listening to you," Iesha said, looking at her, but not opening the magazine again. "And I wish the world worked like you think, little Akina. Your daddy is never going to find you or me. He'll never send money. You'll never get away from these men, or those they sell you to. And you can kiss your freedom goodbye. You'll be learning the prostitution trade soon enough. These men are selling you. You understand that, don't you? They are taking you on a sea journey to sell you far, far away. And there is nothing you can do about it."

Akina's mind reeled.

Her a prostitute — not while she had a heartbeat!

She would never give up trying to get back to her dad. Once she'd seen a documentary of the street prostitutes in South Africa and knew what they did, and with whom. Her dad had watched it with her, and explained things, saying that it was important that she knew some of the hardships some people faced. Now *she* was about to become one of those people. She had to get a note out to someone about her situation. It was time to give more thought on how, because if she got to this auction Iesha spoke about, her life would be forever ruined. She would be ruined. Would she be strong enough then, to keep fighting? Already she felt like perhaps the birds had been eating the crumbs she was leaving, and no one was getting any word to her father to save her.

She was truly on her own.

The sun had set, and the sky was dark, the lights from Dar Es Salaam twinkled in the distance invitingly. Rowan's phone rang and he answered it before it rang a second time. "Curtis?"

"I got a call. She was at the Crested Crane Guest House, in Dar Es Salaam. She left a note. The cleaner found it and called me."

"Did you record the call?" Rowan asked.

Chrystal pulled to the side of the road and motioned to Zenzele and Zane to keep quiet.

Rowan put the phone on speaker.

"I'll send the recording when we get off the call, and the photo of the note. It's written on a magazine margin in brownish ink, but there is no mistaking that it's a plea for help. The cleaner said she found it inside the pillowcase. Apparently, they checked out early this morning—"

"She took all day to phone you?" Rowan asked.

"Said she was scared to call from work. She said she might get fired and she needed her job to put her own kids through school."

Rowan ran his hand through his hair.

Chrystal mouthed, "Fuck!"

CHAPTER 28

Dar Es Salaam, Tanzania

10th April 2016 — 20 days until auction

There were two sides to Dar Es Salaam.

The tourist glitz and glamor, the high-rise buildings and smart five-star hotels, all built on top of an ancient slave trade city. You could walk around the atmospheric ruins of Bagamoyo and visit the 13th-century mosque; you could buy Tinga Tinga paintings in the local markets and purchase authentic certified tanzanite in all its splendor; and you could frolic on the local beaches or climb into one of the many safari vehicles that would whisk you away from the city to the airport to fly to the Serengeti for a big five experience.

And then there was the reality of the local people who lived on the fringe of the tourist world, in the slums and shanty towns that surrounded the city. Where wood fires burnt constantly, causing a thick smog to hover all day over the corrugated rooves, and the smell of poverty ingrained itself into the skin of the people.

Those who were born in the interior of Tanzania and who had abandoned the rural farmlands of their ancestors to seek out a new life in the city. Those whose ancestors were probably the ones traded during the 19th century at the very same 'resting point' and found themselves on their way to Zanzibar in chains, on a one-way voyage to the 'civilized' world.

In Dar Es Salaam, the rich lived in extravagance and the poor barely survived.

Looking around the motel, Chrystal could understand why the traffickers had headed for this guest house in this city.

The building was like a jail.

They didn't need to worry that anyone would come running to help Akina should she scream. From the high walls outside to the bars on the windows, there was no way a child was escaping.

They had booked three rooms in the same guest house, asking specifically for Akina's room.

It had been allocated to them.

The site was secure. They could process it later if needed.

Other than going into the reception area where Zenzele paid for the accommodation and got the keys, no one else had been near the rooms.

"Rory and Chitauro, you stay here, keep watch. If you see anyone go into them, make sure you get a photo and make sure they stay in the room. Preferably alive so we can ask questions," Chrystal said.

Rory grinned.

"We'll text and let you know our hotel across town when we get one," Chrystal said, "but right now we are off to Tandale, one of the largest informal settlements, to visit with the maid."

They sat across the table from the woman, Janda, amongst a noisy crowd of locals.

"This is the note," Janda said as she passed the paper to Chrystal.

They'd arranged to meet her in a nearby bar, aptly named, *To What Place*, to avoid any suspicion being brought on her in her home.

Shanty towns were infamous for people talking about each other, no matter where you were. When everyone lived on top of each other like that, gossiping was rife.

"Thank you," Chrystal said, taking the note, and reading it, she turned it over. The magazine had been carefully folded and then torn so that only the margin was in use — the long page strip had small pieces missing from age and a stain on it too. Akina's note was written in tiny letters with a pen with drying ink, but she'd managed to scratch out her message.

"Definitely her — same words. *My dad has $*. Look at this on the back," she said to Rowan. "It's smudged but read this."

VeniceArt. Sell me. Prostitute? Bad people: Levi. Tahaan. Iesha. The Mother Bitch? Sea journey. Help me Dad.

"I can see why you didn't say that aloud," Rowan said.

"Put the note where it's safe," she said, and watched as he put it in the top pocket of his shirt, and then buttoned the flap down.

"You're sure that there was nothing else in the room?" Rowan asked.

"That room was clean, like not even a hair left in the basin. It was as if someone cleaned it before me," Janda said.

"Can I get you anything?" the young waitress asked, walking up to their table.

"Sure, we'll have a share meal for all of us," Rowan said. Then he looked to Chrystal for help.

"Plates of Mishkaki, are they nice here?" she asked Janda.

Janda nodded. "It is very good from this bar. They chargrill the meat, but don't overcook it and make it dry."

Chrystal nodded. "Good, let's have some *mbuzi*, and add a big helping of *ugaliugali* for us all to share. Also, some bottles of Serengeti Premium Lagers all around, and cokes too. Can you run us a tab and we'll pay in cash at the end?"

"Of course," the waitress said, and then putting the pen into her braided hair, she walked away.

"Thank you," Janda said, when she'd left them. "Dinner was unexpected, but I appreciate it a lot. With three kids, I don't get to eat here often."

"Our pleasure. We still have a lot of questions, but why do that on an empty stomach?" Rowan said. "What was all that you just ordered?"

Chrystal smiled. "Some beef, chicken and goat meat, chargrilled on an open fire with a cornmeal porridge. Much like the Zimbabwean's *sudza*, although sometimes they can use cassava flour up here, it gives it a different flavor. It's worth eating here, we won't get any bad stomachs from the food. Look at all the local patronage, and they are eating as well as drinking. You don't get crowds like this coming back if they get sick eating your food."

"Fair point," Rowan said, then he turned his attention across the table. "Janda, why do you think someone cleaned the room before you got in there?"

"Everything was neat. Nothing was out of place. Even the bath towels were refolded and put back on the rails, even though they were wet. The shower had been wiped and the bath, there was no water ring. Even the toilet, it was clean. They had also re-made the beds. Even though I have to strip them, it was like they had made sure everything was tidy as they could, to ensure that nothing was left behind. But I found the note. It was inside the pillowcase. When I shook the pillow out to change it, it fell onto the bed. When I read it, I felt sick."

"There have been so many people along her journey that haven't bothered to call. Thank you for reaching out and at least seeing if it was a trick or not," Chrystal said.

"I wondered that. A call to America is expensive. I put the number in WhatsApp. In the end, it was only airtime. The man, her daddy, he kept thanking me for calling, and took all my details and he said a lawyer will be in contact with a reward. It wasn't a trick. The lawyer, he already called. He made an appointment to see him in the city tomorrow. He even sent me credits for my phone so I can buy a ticket on the taxi. I think if the daddy can do that in a few hours, he can save his daughter. That girl, she is very very lucky to have him for her father."

Rowan was at the hotel, on his computer with Holly and his American team, trying to see what ships had left that day, and if any had manifests to say they were sailing to Venice.

It was a long shot.

Now they knew how she was getting to Venice but were no closer to knowing what ship she was on.

And there were plenty to choose from.

Dar Es Salaam was one of the busier ports in Africa, with a lot of trade. To make it even more complicated, the government had begun building a new bigger port known as the Bagamoyo Port project, and while it wasn't finished, there were some ships in that harbor.

Holly had tracked their stolen 4 x 4 camper, with changed plates, to an abandoned lot adjacent to the shipyards. As with any vehicle deserted in an African city, the street urchins were already stripping parts off it.

A local *dhow* could take Akina to any of the vessels in the Tanzania Sea. Or if they were good at sailing, to one in the Kenyan sea.

Rowan stood looking at the screen. "There's no use even going to the docks, we're a day behind them. She's long gone. The ship has sailed, with her on board already. No way did they wait in that hotel room for nothing if they could have been on the ship. They have slipped on as it was casting off."

"We were so close," Chrystal said, showing her finger and thumb with no space in between.

"We're done here. It's time to regroup in South Africa. Holly is tracking those ships that left today by satellite. She's also monitoring the ones off the coast in case she was taken to one by a local *dhow*. We'll know as they approach Italy if any of them do. We know where she's going. A ship from here to Venice will dock in twenty days, that means we have under three weeks to get ready, gain access to the auction, and rescue Akina when she gets there. We concentrate our efforts in Venice."

CHAPTER 29

Leopard Hill Farm, Thabazimbi, Limpopo Province, South Africa

15th April 2016 — 15 days until auction

Chrystal looked at the big gates and high electric fence that maCalio had already installed around the property. A little box on the gate had an inter-com. Chrystal got out. She knew she was taking a chance but being different and having a backup plan had always been what got her through. She'd called ahead and left a voice message saying she was going to visit but had arrived not knowing whether maCalio was there or not.

She pressed the intercom.

A male voice answered. "*Yebo*?"

"I'm here to see maCalio," Chrystal said.

"She's not here today."

"Please tell her Chrystal from Saliebos Farm wants to see her. I'll wait by the gate for her to come here."

"You wait?"

"*Ja*, I wait," she said, smiling and waving, knowing that maCalio had a camera on her. She pointed to the car and then got back in. Turning the key so she could listen to the radio while she waited. She pushed her seat all the way back and put her feet up, knowing that curiosity would get the better of maCalio and she would come and talk to her.

If she was here.

Of course, she could be wasting her time, maCalio could legitimately be away on business. It was a chance that she was prepared to take.

maCalio's curiosity would get the better of her after their last meeting.

It took half an hour before maCalio's Land Cruiser pulled up next to Chrystal's open window. Her cat jumped up on her dashboard and walked across, behind the steering wheel.

maCalio had parked so close that Chrystal couldn't get out of her Cruiser. maCalio watched Chrystal with no expression on her face while the gate closed behind her. She was so close that Chrystal could hear the loud purr of the cat.

"About time," Chrystal mumbled, sitting up straight.

"I told you not to come back without an appointment. I am busy," maCalio said.

"I called ahead. Don't you get your messages?" Chrystal asked.

"I see you got back in one piece."

Chrystal stared back at maCalio. "I did, but we haven't got the right girl yet."

"Right girl?"

"We got a child that was traveling with her. She's coming to South Africa soon. We've had to move on to plan B to get our hands on Akina."

"Why do I get the impression you are going to ask me for something?" maCalio said.

"Not ask you. Suggest. If I asked you, then I would owe you a favor in return. Isn't that how it works?"

"Fine. Suggest it to me then," maCalio said.

"We have information putting her at a human auction. You know many people. Would you perhaps know someone who can get us an invitation to this event in Venice, so we can attend the auction where she's being sold, and we can buy her?"

maCalio's cat jumped into her lap. She stroked it, and Chrystal could hear the content purr from her Cruiser.

"I take it that your Zambian connection did good?" maCalio asked as she fussed over the cat, and if it was possible, the cat purred louder.

226

Chrystal wondered why maCalio had ignored her question. "*Ja*, he did. Mostly."

"Your old friend. Such a nice man until you get to know the true person underneath his pretty blue eyes." maCalio stopped petting her cat and met Chrystal's gaze. "Perhaps you should ask him to get a bidder's tag. That is his market. Not mine."

"How is Jason Adams going to be able to get a bidder's ticket to a human auction?"

"My sweet Chrystal. You really are not a cutthroat mercenary at all, are you? And of this I am glad. I think I like that we live in the same area, you have heart to look after your community, and we never have to meet on the battlefield. Do I need to spell it out for you?

"Who do you think supplies those miners and their executives with all their pleasures in Northern Zambia? You should ask him for the details of that one yourself. When you speak to him, tell him that this will pay off a little of his debt that he owes maNtuli for helping you. You might wait until he helps you get the girl back and has returned to his shit hole in Mpika, before you give him this fragment of information. I don't think you will part as friends after that, but I don't think you should kill him either. He might still prove useful to both of us, one day. Now, I was on my way to Checkers, you know there always seems to be no samp in my pantry."

maCalio waved at her and then drove off toward Thabazimbi.

CHAPTER 30

Venice, Italy

Akina had been to Venice many times before, but she hardly recognized it from where she was now. Standing high up in her cabin on the container ship that had brought her from Africa, she looked from the small glass window. The cruise ships that she'd been on before were parked tail to nose in the distance, dwarfing many of the buildings. Between her and the cruise ships, giant iron yellow cranes with red-striped hoists lifted freight from the cargo ships, placing their loads on the docks, or loading goods into the steel ships' waiting jaws, while men in hard hats shouted to each other.

Where she'd previously seen thousands of tourists on her visits to the City of Canals, with sun hats and cameras, now she only saw industrial beasts with workers in hard hats and fluorescent clothing that scurried around like mice.

Above their ship, a flock of swallows gathered, dancing across the sky in a rhythmic swarm. Pulsating. They were free, like she should be. She could almost hear them singing their chorus, except she couldn't, not in her cabin hideaway. It was deceptively quiet for being on a ship, especially since Iesha had disappeared. She hadn't found anything to write on in her small cabin, and even if she had, she knew that the people on this ship would never help her.

They were loyal to Levi.

She heard the familiar sound of the lock in the door. Tahaan's bulk filled the doorway before he passed through and stalked toward her.

She backed up against the cold steel of the cabin wall.

Levi came into the room as Tahaan grabbed her. She could see the syringe in Levi's hand.

"Struggle all you want. The more tense you are, the more it'll hurt," Levi said. She could almost swear there was a snarl on his lips, like a hyena.

Gritting her teeth hard together, not wanting to give Levi the satisfaction of knowing that both the sting of the needle and the medicine he gave her burnt like fire, she stared at him, until the edges of her vision blurred and then there was only darkness.

"Come on young one, time to wake up," a gentle voice said.

She opened her eyes, and saw a nun standing over her, patting her arm. She wore a habit and robes of dark blue.

"That's it, you can open those eyes now," she said, her voice soft, comforting.

Looking around the room, Akina's heart sunk. Levi and Tahaan were still there, seated in chairs on the other side.

She wasn't out of danger.

"That's it, here have something to drink, it'll help the nauseous feeling," the nun said, pushing a cup to her lips.

Akina struggled to sit up. The nun helped her.

"You need to go now," the nun said, turning to look at the men. "My sisters and I have her and will take it from here."

"A word, Sister, in private," Levi said.

The nun nodded. She smiled at Akina and left her, following the men out the room.

Akina heard the click of a lock in a door.

She scrambled up, and on legs that were still unsteady, made herself check the window.

While light came in through pretty lace curtains, the glass behind was heavily frosted, so no one could see in. She checked the frame and found that the windows were screwed shut. The holes where the indents of the brass fasteners were filled with dust and grime, so it obviously had not been done recently. She went to the small dressing table and rifled through the drawers, but there was nothing. Not even a single sheet of paper to line the bottom.

The nun stepped back into the room. "There's nothing for you in those. Even if there was, it would not be of any use to you.

"You are more highly strung than most of the children who pass through here. They are already reconditioned by this time, but Levi says that you're an unusual case. It was good to hear that Mother said not to harm you. I think that man would have caused scarring if given free rein over another human body." The nun shuddered her whole body, then looked at Akina. "I'm talking too much. I need to take your measurements and get you bathed and ready for the photographer."

"The photographer?" Akina asked, as the nun used a tape measure around her body and entered the measurements directly into her phone.

"You do not think that we would subject you to seeing all those people interested in you, in person, do you? Through this door please. I have started running a bath." The nun opened an interconnecting door with a key that she produced out her pocket when she slipped her phone back in.

Akina wished she had taken a few streetwise lessons and was able to steal the phone.

"Get undressed and stand on the scale. Then I'll help you wash."

"What? Here, with you watching?" Akina asked.

"God made us all the same. Tell you what, if you have something I have not seen before, then you can splash me with the water, how does that sound?"

Akina tried hard to respond with a smile, but it was so hard. She didn't know who she could trust, and obviously this nun knew Levi, so she couldn't trust her, even if the nun was trying her best to put her at ease.

"Do you have a name?" Akina asked.

"Sister. It's better for you to not know who anyone is. It'll make it easier in the long term with what is to come," Sister said.

"And what is that?"

"After your bath, I'll get you dressed and looking tidy, the photographer will take your pictures. You'll be here for a few days. There's a TV to watch movies, and an en-suite so you can go to the bathroom. Your traveling days are almost over. Once the auction has taken place, I'll fetch you to take you to your new owner."

Akina frowned, the word *owner* rattling around her head.

Akina slipped her tattered shirt over her head; her jeans and underwear came off next. She lowered herself into the warm water, and as some of the dirt on her skin washed away, so did a little bit of her hope.

It had been so long and her dad hadn't come.

She pulled her knees to her chest, wrapping her arms around her legs and for the first time in a long time, she let herself cry.

CHAPTER 31

Kitwe, Zambia

20th April 2016 — 10 days until auction

Savannah walked into Jason Adam's bar for the second time in a month.

"Hello gorgeous, you back so soon?" he said, walking toward her with a big smile on his face.

She smashed her fist into his nose, and then let rip with a series of punches before he had a chance to defend himself.

He covered his face and shouted at her, "What the fuck? Stop it! I don't know what you think I did but stop it. I'd never hurt you."

"But you'll sell women and children," she shouted, punching him in his chest again.

"Fuck it, wait, stop. Just stop."

"I'll stop," Savannah said, "but only because it's not bringing me the joy I hoped it would." She gave him one last punch to the jaw, then shoved him in the chest, making him stumble back.

"You have a hell of a right hook," he said. He turned his back on her and scrambled behind the bar. She watched as he got a bucket of ice out and a bunch of serviettes off the counter. Looking in the glass shelves' mirror, he made sure the blood was washed off his face in the basin. He made an ice compact and held it to his face.

He walked to where she stood and took out a bottle of whisky. He poured two glasses and passed her one.

"I'm not drinking with you, you piece of shit."

"Fine, I'll drink yours too," he said, tossing them back one after another. "You're obviously pissed at me. What have I allegedly done?"

She drew up a stool and perched on it. Her foot tapped repeatedly. The adrenaline still pumped through her body, white-hot. She watched as he did the same, still holding the ice to his nose, carefully keeping the bar between them.

"You're selling kids for the sex trade, while I'm trying to rescue one from that very fate. How many kids' lives have you ruined trafficking them to the miners?"

"It's not a part of my business that I'm proud of, but if I didn't do it, someone else would, and he might not be as nice to them as I am. So yes, I deal in prostitution in kids. But I haven't seen the one you're looking for."

"You wouldn't have. She's off to an auction in Venice."

"Fuck. You sure?"

"Yes. When we got shot out the sky in your helicopter, it kind of put paid to catching her on African soil. So now we're going to try buy her at auction, in Venice."

"Who's we?"

"You and me. You owe me."

"Fucking hell, Savannah, are you mad? The people at an auction like that will eat you alive. Do you have any idea of the stakes to buy into an auction like that?"

"That's not your concern. All I need from you is to organize the tickets for us."

"You're asking for more than I can deliver."

"Jason, that eye that you paint on all your goods — the helicopter that fired on us in the Congo two years ago. It was one of yours. Which means the missile that downed us in the jungle that day was also sold by you.

"You played both sides when we went in to save that mark. You sold out your best friend. You're the one who was responsible for Wes's death. So, you're going to close this shop, get your passport and get in my helicopter. We have a little girl to save. Even if you don't want to do it for me, do it because you want to show that there's some decency left in you, and that you're not a total piece of shit."

"I was supposed to be the one to go in that day, remember? We spoke about it."

Somewhere at the back of her mind, an inkling of that came back to her.

Forgotten, until he'd mentioned it.

"You weren't supposed to go in at all. I was taking the pickup. Wes didn't want you in that area. You went anyway. Yes, I sell goods to different factions, but I sure as hell never sent a helicopter after my best friend, not when I was supposed to be the one fetching him. It should have been me in that crash, not you."

Why had it taken her two years to remember what Jason had just told her?

She felt like a fool.

It made her question so many things.

The fact that both her last missions hadn't resulted in the outcome she expected.

Wes dying.

Her trying to keep such an insane promise to Wes. Before Rowan had commented on it, she hadn't given it much thought — what he'd asked of her.

But now she was aware of it; aware that what he'd asked was beyond her, then and more so now.

She shuddered at the thought of his bandanna that she had kept with her for so long.

Jason's comment about the fact he was supposed to be there, not her for their extraction.

What else had Jason said that she hadn't heard?

She had a lot of talking to do with Jason, and the sooner the better.

CHAPTER 32

Venice, Italy

27th April 2016 — 3 days until auction

Venice. City of canals. The City of Masks, with its two faces.

Rowan saw none of the beauty as he checked in with Zenzele once again hunkered down near the VeniceArt building.

Right now, Zenzele was whispering. "Two people exited the art gallery auction house. They are walking down the street. I'm relocating to the small alleyway next to the building."

Rowan nodded. Scaling the old architecture was easy for Zenzele who climbed like a cougar and hung to buildings like a Rocky Mountain goat.

In no time, the three clicks on the radio signaled Zenzele was back on the roof. Wearing brick-colored clothing, he blended into the tiles he lay on.

The sensor Zenzele had put on the window allowed them to hear the conversation inside. Now, they sat in silence listening to the chatter of the secretary and the Director as they spoke about the auction taking place on Saturday. If it wasn't for Akina telling them who was running the auction, they would not have been able to survey the ground and find out so much information in the days they had been there.

. . .

"Brigitte," the Director Matteo said. "I know you hate having anything to do with these people, but I need you to drive out to the old Canossian's convent estate in Treviso and see Brother John. There's a discrepancy in one of the lots for Saturday. It's made its way onto an international watch list this morning and having something like that could put everything in jeopardy at this auction. Tell Brother John that he can accept one of the pre-auction bids, but we can't have the child's picture in the catalog."

"You're talking of the one with the extremely pale skin?" Brigitte asked.

"Yes," Matteo said. "Kidnapped stories are about to hit all over the place. Apparently one of the newspapers in England took a shine to the child's picture and is doing their best to get the story out there. Some kids just get all the attention, while others are allowed to silently slip away without so much as a newspaper article about their pathetic lives."

"I told Brother John that it was too soon after the kidnapping to bring him to auction," Brigitte said. "He was adamant the child went in."

"Well they're coming out. Issue an update. I don't care what Brother John says. No amount of security will save us if we flaunt the children brazenly. This new practice of theirs must stop. They're putting us all in danger."

"You hearing this?" Zenzele whispered.

"Yes," Rowan replied.

"The girl was a forgivable case," Matteo said. "Her mother managed to somehow get it in all the newspapers and everywhere on social media, even though they would not normally feel the snatching of a female child newsworthy. But the boy is too hot, the British Press—"

Zenzele said, "Shit, not Akina."

Rowan said, "Shhhhh."

"You know that her father is a sheik with too much money," Brigitte said. "It would probably be a feather in the seller's cap to have their girl at auction, but it also could attract attention. The boy is out this auction. The girl will be handled as a silent auction, selected bidders only."

Rowan whispered, "They are taking the boy totally out. Interesting."

"I was hoping it was Akina," Zenzele said.

"Me too."

"Where is Treviso?" Zenzele asked.

"About forty-five minutes away by freeway."

They could hear Brigitte's stiletto heels as they clicked-clicked across the wooden floor to her desk where she got her bag out from the drawer. "I'll go and break the news, but you're right. I'm not happy and you're going to have to make it up to me."

Some real art buyers walked into the gallery ending the conversation as Matteo turned to greet them, while Brigitte left the building via the back door.

"We have a secure tracker on her Mini Cooper?" Rowan asked, as he stood up.

"*Yebo*. You think we should follow her?" Zenzele said.

"I'll meet you on the road."

Zenzele read the directions from the map as Rowan drove their hired car. "Map says that Treviso is near the main airport for private and chartered airplanes." He shook his head, who would have thought that his life was in the small town of Thabazimbi, in South Africa and yet, after rushing all over the African continent, he was in Venice, Italy. He knew that when Chrystal went away, she often flew places, but this was beyond what he had ever imagined.

"Make sure you keep an eye on her car moving too, don't get lost in the map," Rowan warned."

"I am watching. Brigitte's GPS turned into a property and seems to be waiting on a driveway. We should see her as we get around the next corner. "

They caught up and had eyes on her vehicle again.

Rowan slowed and pulled into a parking. Taking his computer out, he opened it and began typing. "This makes the third building that we have connected to the traffickers. Chitauro, is almost as good at you are urban hiding and is still stationed outside the first premises we found in Lido when Brigitte drove there too."

"That was also near an airfield," Zenzele said.

"And it has all the public waterbus routes available to it, and direct access to the water. So easy distribution. Chitauro's recordings from inside that house have been interesting. Definitely children there, but no sign of Akina." Rowan continued to type, the sound loud in the car. "What number is that showing as?"

"One thousand and two," Zenzele said. "Are Zane and Ian still listening to that second apartment in the Campo San Polo area, on the Grand Canal? Do they think there are only administrators there? No evidence of children?"

"Nothing conclusive yet," Rowan said.

Brigitte still waited. Her tracker not moving.

"Watch her," Rowan said. "This from my Google search on the address: The complex is a 15th-century monastery with a huge tract of open land around it. All that remains of the original Canossian nuns is a statue in the front of the main convent building. Everything inside these walls has been modernized within the last twenty years. The huge communal gardens of the original monastery has been preserved, as has a little gatehouse apartment."

"Movement," Zenzele said.

They watched as the large iron gates opened and her little Mini Cooper disappeared into the estate. Zenzele jumped out the car and jogged a little along the fence until he found a place where he could scale it easily and was inside in seconds. The estate was made to look secure, but to any man from Africa, it was clear that it was only a facade. This was no fortified property. The walls contained window boxes, with footholds, and there were no cameras mounted on the walls or in the large trees that he could see. Zenzele jogged along the internal road and soon saw the Mini Cooper outside of what looked like the building that used to be the stables.

Painted pristine white with black trimmings, the huge box had large tinted blue glass windows for privacy. He saw Brigitte walk through the front door which looked like it had been imported from Zanzibar. It was large and empowering. As ancient as the slave trade was there, they had brought the stigma with the door. Zenzele took a look around the perimeter, making sure he checked for cameras as he went.

On the opposite side of the building was a large canal with water that looked stagnant. It was covered with green slime and water lilies floated on its surface.

He looked back to the building that Brigitte had entered, making sure that he was pressed against the wall, hiding low behind the hedge that surrounded the building. The windows were heavily tinted so he couldn't see inside. When he went in the house's furthest side between the stable building and what he thought was the old servants' quarters, he could see children's playground equipment.

The front door opened, and Brigitte came out again; she stood by her car and lit a cigarette. The front door opened for a second time and a man in old-fashioned Francesca priest robes came out of the house and joined her. He handed her an envelope to which she smiled and opened her door.

She drove away without looking back.

The monk watched her every move out the gate before he turned and walked back into the house.

"How fast can you get back out?" Rowan asked.

"Two minutes tops. I think this place deserves a deeper look and some listening devices. Would be better done in darkness."

Rowan had reached out through his international contact at the Hague, Sem Meijer, who'd introduced him to Riccardo Ricci, the *Capo della Polizia* — who was the Commissioner responsible for the *Polizia di Stato*. The State police.

The policeman sitting opposite him certainly did not embody every reason that Rowan usually worked without police and federal agents. They were either disinterested in solving crimes or wanted to rush into every situation guns blazing and basically annihilate any chance he had of recovering the children.

Riccardo was different.

He wanted to nail the traffickers as badly as Rowan did.

"The whole affair will be swept under the carpet by our politicians so fast. No way is Venice allowing anyone to add the City of Slave Traders to its tourist label," Riccardo said. "You have the experience in this area, but even you have to admit that this is now bigger than anything you have dealt with before. I'm happy to help you any way we can, under the banner of the Hague, owing to the nature of what you have exposed."

"I've never been involved with something this big. Now we're in, and we have some details that will enable us to save these kids, not only Akina, but all of them." Rowan said. "They don't have to suffer the slave trade. They're humans, not animals."

"Sì," Riccardo said. "I think it's important that the *Polizia di Stato* have these recordings to listen to and anything else you can pass on. When this is over, we can use them when we bring these people to justice. What do you need from me?"

CHAPTER 33

Venice, Italy

30th April 2016 — morning of auction

Chrystal and Jason were the last to be reunited with the team in Venice, and before today had spent their time holed up in the headquarters collating the information that Rowan and her anti-poaching guards had fed back, ensuring they had everything ready for the auction day event.

Now they got to do the final reconnaissance with Rowan as they drove past VeniceArt.

"I have to admit this looks nothing like what I expected, even the photos never prepared me for this," Chrystal said. "Actually, a bit of a letdown from the name to reality. From the outside, the building doesn't even look like an art auction house in Venice, and certainly not one where they are about to hold a gala event."

"I agree. The roads here are terrible. They're barely wide enough for two cars to pass without the mirrors touching. And there is no parking on the street. Not to mention that more than half of the pavement is taken up by overgrown bushes." Rowan said.

"You sure this is where it's happening?" Jason asked, peering out the window.

"It's the right place," Rowan said. "This little six story high, brown brick building is a slave trader's headquarters. You've studied the blueprints that Holly sent through. They use the top five floors to display normal artworks and the ground floor to host people for auctions. One large space with columns holding up the rest of the house."

Jason nodded. "Any update on security?"

"Zenzele has confirmed the layout when he'd crawled all over the outside during the night. A feature of the house that came as a surprise is that it's attached to the building next door — someone has tried to blend the two buildings together, making it one structure." Rowan said. "There was no visible door leading to the access between the houses, and yet the same VeniceArt company owns both, according to the title deeds. The strange thing is that there are no security cameras in that second building that we could find. Where we would expect it to have security everywhere, given the art house is right there and attached."

Rowan slowed down even more.

"You ready for this Jason?" Rowan asked.

"As ready as I'll ever be," Jason admitted.

Rowan clenched his fists around the steering wheel. "You can see from the program that Holly secured that Akina is Lot #12. You need to secure her, then leave if you can. Be there earlier than planned — there's a pre-auction cocktail party you're expected to attend."

"I take it Holly still had no success trying to get a second ticket?" Chrystal asked.

"It's not the type of event you can put a plus one on the invitation," Jason said. "Anyway, I'd rather you don't show your face there. You'll bring attention to us, and it could compromise the rescue. The people who deal in this trade will think nothing of killing you if they ever come across you again. While I'm aware that you can look after yourself, I'm also conscious of the fact that most traders in our profession are male."

Chrystal said, "I still don't get how no one ever notices these kids moving around Venice?"

"Based on what we saw out at Treviso, Zenzele thinks they move them as school sports teams—" Rowan said.

"Most of the bidders are in the Middle East, Russia, Vietnam and Malaysia, where people are far less likely to ask questions," Jason added, in a voice devoid of emotion. He was back in soldier mode.

"But when do they deliver them? Who delivers them?" Chrystal said, her voice rising in volume and pitch. "I get that there are many canals and boats. Surely the kids don't want to go with yet another stranger, so why don't they try run, go to one of the authorities?"

Jason put his hand on her arm and squeezed before letting go, but all the time his eyes were watching the scenery outside "If they are anything like the kids I deal with, by the time I get them, they would rather cooperate and be safe, then risk another beating or worse. The buyers at the auction specifically are the elite, I don't believe for one moment anyone will question that there's an extra child in the house even for one night." Jason looked at Chrystal.

"Sicko's," Chrystal said.

Jason continued talking. "Since Holly gave me access to the dark web auction chatroom, I've been able to catch up in the last few days. I'd imagine that many of the people who come to an auction like this are legal adoption houses representing private citizens whose options of adoption have been exhausted. They know the only way to get a child is to buy one illegally. Papers can always be fabricated. These would be the lucky ones who don't end up sex slaves but find themselves in a loving home."

"But many will end up in the trade," Chrystal said, frowning.

"While auctions like this happen all the time, this particular auction's only held once a year and it's for really high-end children and extremely valuable virgins. This one is targeted at a select clientele, and there are only eighty lots up for auction. It's the crème de la crème of merchandise out there that they have to offer. It'll show in the process, and it will show in the quality of who's being auctioned. Each of the lots has something special or unique to offer," Jason said.

"These poor kids." Chrystal shifted in the seat. "Classified as 'special' making them a target for predators."

Rowan ran his hand through his hair, a clear sign of his frustration. "I agree."

"Me too, believe it or not," Jason said. "You saw in the program that Akina is being promoted as being multilingual and above normal intelligence. Many of the clientele can benefit from somebody like that close to them. She's almost twelve, which means they can have her on their arm in only four years when they go out in public. Until then she can be part of any entourage that moves around. Think of the business application of having someone who can translate for you in multilingual meetings, without having that person know that you have a translator. Or have her listening in to all that's being said in an office where they think you don't speak their language."

"A translator, not a sex slave?" Chrystal asked.

Jason nodded. "She could be either, or both. I think The Circle who have put her at auction has experience in trafficking. She's a known kidnapped face, and yet she's still at auction. I think the client they are looking to sell to is someone with a beef to grind with her father— who will be prepared to use her against him. I don't believe that she's there as a 'normal' item at all."

Rowan stopped to let an old lady cross the road in front of them, and Chrystal took the opportunity to look back at VeniceArt House. She could understand a little about the children going to families who desperately wanted to be parents and were continually coming up against bureaucratic red tape. Still, she didn't understand how Jason was so complacent about the fact that some of these children were there to be sold into the sex slave industry, and they would stay there until they died. Their life would be a nightmare of the worst kind.

Sure, they were mercenaries, and their code was a little askew of what most people thought was normal. They took on the jobs that the 'good guys' were prevented by law from doing, but she'd always thought that he was the moral guy.

Rowan's phone rang and he pushed answer on the dashboard.

"I just saw you go past," Zenzele said.

Chrystal smiled.

"Welcome to my part of Venice, my friend," Zenzele said. "Hope you get to see more than me today. I am very well acquainted with this roof and the pigeons who visit each day."

Chrystal smiled. "Good to hear your voice and to know you're watching."

"With the eyes of a bateleur eagle. Knowing what animals are at the waterhole is good when new predators begin to arrive," Zenzele said, and his voice dropped a pitch.

Chrystal frowned as Rowan turned left at the bottom of the street.

"I see them," Rowan said, and ended the call. "Look, security moving in for tonight, that man is a new addition. Looks like our last drive-by was done just in time."

"You're leaving Zenzele up on the roof?" Chrystal said.

"He's got the whole area mapped out from up there. Like the others in the team, each can watch and listen to their 'eggs' as they have taken to calling them. Your guys are as good in the city as in the African bush with tracking, surveillance and concealing themselves. You taught them well."

CHAPTER 34

VeniceArt, Venice, Italy

30th April 2016 — the auction

Jason straightened his bow tie as he exited the chauffeur driven car that had stopped on the street outside VeniceArt. This was it.

The team were out there, but they couldn't be with him inside.

Zenzele had given them a rundown on the boxes of security gear being carried into the building through the back door, and with the cameras inside, they could see that the security was now as tight as any bank.

He dropped his hand and walked the short distance to the door. Taking a deep calming breath, he opened the heavy wooden door with his head held high and walked into the auction.

Brigitte gave him a bright smile from behind the reception desk that had been set up. Beside her was a scanner. He handed her his phone.

It beeped. "Welcome, Mr. Adams. Nice of you to join us tonight."

He smiled as she passed him what looked like a paddle with a number clearly printed on it and his phone. Not bothering to pocket it, he walked to the x-ray scanner, tossed the two items and his wallet in the small basket and walked through.

"Thank you, Sir," the security personnel said, passing him the plastic container so he could retrieve his possessions when he exited the other side, and walked to the bar set up in the corner.

"Whisky on ice," he said, and when the young bartender put one shot in the glass, he indicated another. Taking his drink, he headed toward the side of the room where he could observe everyone.

Like him, no single person looked different, and yet they were all there to participate in a trade that had been outlawed internationally for the good of humankind.

No one was legally allowed to buy another person.

He looked around the room.

No art was on display. Two large screens dominated the wall that all the chairs faced. In between them was a lectern with a microphone, and a table next to that. There was no raised platform for the auctioneer, nor a viewing cage like at an animal auction. The upright chairs were arranged in rows, but widely spaced so no one was sitting on top of another. Everywhere he looked, there was space.

He sipped his drink and kept to himself.

No one was mingling; the cocktail party was just an excuse to get everyone in the door on time.

The VeniceArt Director walked into the room. Jason tracked him as he went to the lectern in the front and spoke clearly into the microphone. "Please, take your seats. A final catalog has been sent to your phones. The auction will begin in five minutes."

Jason sat in a seat on the right, near the window with a clear view of the front door. He also had clear access behind the chairs to the corridor that led to the back door, should he need it. Some skills taught to him in the Marines were never wasted. He looked at his phone and pressed to access the file. It was slow. The minutes ticked by as he watched the download.

There was a general hushed hum of low talking as they waited.

"Thank you to everyone present," the Director said. "The doors have now closed and the internet jammers have been activated."

On the flight to Venice, Chrystal had mentioned that Holly thought there was a strong possibility that the auction house would do something like this.

He was truly on his own.

He didn't think the listening devices on the outside of the windows would work.

He took a breath and looked at the app. He scrolled through.

Akina was not there.

In her lot had a 'Sold before auction' label.

"Fuck."

Chrystal was going to lose her shit when she found out, of this he was certain. He took a deep breath and looked around.

Time for Plan B.

He had to find a way to let them know. Akina's life depended on it. And she was his only way to try and get Chrystal off his back.

With the front door now closed, he looked to the corridor. A menacing Russian looking security guard stood there, blocking that route.

There was no way out without bringing attention to himself.

He was trapped inside the building for the duration of the auction.

He turned to the window, hoping that Zenzele could see him and realize that he was trying to communicate. He didn't know if Holly would have got a copy of the auction lineup from his phone before they shut down communications.

He tapped his finger on his phone in Morse code.

... --- .-.. -.. .-.-.- / -. --- - / ....-. . .-.-.-

Sold. Not here.

Jason adjusted his seating, again.

The Director announced, "Lot #80," as they finally got to the last lot.

"Pre-auction bidding closed at one million and fifty thousand—"

A man wearing a blue Arab Shemagh, raised his paddle.

"We have sixty thousand."

"Seventy," a Chinese man said, raising his paddle.

"Ninety," the Arab man said. Once again, his paddle raised.

The Chinese man shook his head.

"One million, and ninety thousand, going once, twice. Sold." He indicated with his hand to the Arab man. "This concludes this year's auction. The Wi-Fi will now be enabled so all lots can be paid for before you leave the building."

Jason stood up. There was nothing further he could do here. Walking as casually as he could toward the exit, the first to leave; he knew once he left, all hell would break loose.

"Sorry to see you didn't purchase anything, Mr. Adams," Brigitte said.

He took a chance. "I was particularly interested in Lot #12. But, that's how this business goes, it's a pity she was not here tonight."

Brigitte dropped her voice. "I'm not supposed to say anything, however I hear that she went for three million dollars, but it was outside our auction."

"I would have paid more," he said. Then he shrugged and leaned a little toward her, also making his voice lower, but no less audible. "I wonder if the purchaser would be interested in further negotiation. It would mean a tidy profit for them on their investment. A quick profit. Offer them five million, and your commission on top of that, but open to negotiation. You know how to reach me."

Brigitte seemed taken aback that he would still be trying to purchase something that was off the auction already. But she recovered with a smile, picked up her phone. "I'll pass on your message. And be in touch, should they reconsider."

"I would appreciate it," Jason said, giving her back his paddle.

He walked out the front door. Onto the road. Free at last, he breathed in the Venice air.

It wasn't over. They might still get her—

His exiting of the building was the signal that the *Polizia di Stato* were waiting for.

Riccardo had coordinated with a special task force for such urban maneuvers as this.

The raid on the VeniceArt House had begun.

They had people stationed at the three houses where there were children too. He'd been part of taking down a huge child trafficking ring and should have been proud, but all he felt was a sense of foreboding. Jason looked around. The police, in full riot police gear, were running from their vehicles and down the side of the building opposite VeniceArt toward him. Glancing to the left, the street had been cordoned off in an instant. Satisfaction that he'd been part of the effort to rescue the kids with the police in Italy would have to do for now. It was the feeling of doing right that he'd first had when signing up to the Marines, before learning that not everything they did was heroic.

Before choosing a different path.

The shot that hit him in the chest took him totally unprepared. Jason slammed into the concrete. He couldn't breathe. He knew the bullet had taken out parts of his chest. Without help, his lung would collapse in seconds.

He wondered how long it took a man to bleed out in this situation.

Then Zenzele was there, lifting him and dragging him away toward the house next door.

He heard another shot. It missed them, but hit the concrete nearby and ricocheted, obviously trying to herd them in a different direction to where they were heading.

"Fuck," Zenzele said as he reached up and opened the door.

Another shot. The doorknob splintered.

Snipers don't generally miss their shots. Not the professionals anyway.

Zenzele lay on the ground and kicked the door. It opened.

Jason's arm was being pulled, and slowly he was being dragged into the house. His chest burnt even more now, as if something was in there cutting him from the inside.

The sniper couldn't get them here.

What was happening?

They were the good guys; his mind couldn't comprehend that he'd been shot. It wasn't supposed to happen. It wasn't in the plan.

"We got your message," Zenzele said.

"She's not lost." He tried to talk, but could feel the blood bubbling up. "We can still buy her, she was sold for three million, outside of the auction, but I offered five, she's still in play."

"Maybe, but I think they're on to you. Why else would they be shooting at you?" Zenzele said, pulling him further into the room and turning him to lie on his side of the bullet wound.

Blood poured thick from the exit wound and saturated his suit. Froth bubbled from Jason's mouth.

"Direction of the police sniper..." He coughed on the blood. "Why?"

He could hear the terrible sucking sound of a damaged lung. Zenzele was using his knife to cut at Jason's clothing, pushed a wad of the cloth into the exit wound, and then put pressure on the wound. "None of it matters now. I have you. There is a hospital close by, they will fix you. Hang in there, Jason. Hang in there—"

He was cut off as the police switched on their sirens and stormed into the building next door.

CHAPTER 35

Venice, Italy

30th April 2016 — after the auction

Zenzele shook his head, watching the ambulance leave, its lights flashing.

"It's not your fault," Rowan said, standing next to him. "You did everything you could. Pulling him into the building, giving him cover. Who the fuck shot him is what I want to know?"

"Me too," Zenzele said. "Jason said it was from the direction of the sniper. Why would the Italian police shoot him? He was on the same side as them."

"I don't know, but we'll get an explanation from Riccardo. This isn't over."

Rowan put his hand up to Zenzele to stop talking as he listened to the microphone in his ear.

"News from Chitauro, in the Lido area. He says that the police stormed the building, and there were shots fired. Buses have arrived outside, so they have rounded up the children there. He's been allowed to watch the children being loaded by the police but hasn't seen Akina."

"Any news from Ian?" Zenzele asked.

"They went into the Campo Sa Polo apartment, but there was no one there.

They've left police there to watch over the place, keep it intact, and safe. I'm still waiting to hear from the insurgent team with Chrystal and Zane at Treviso."

Chrystal stood next to the police car. Leaving the canals behind for the Venice countryside was proving interesting. She and Zane had been outside the property's perimeter when the police initially assaulted the building, then they had gone in closer, as discussed with Riccardo beforehand. They would be present at the clean-up, but not take part in the actual breach.

She watched as the police marched multiple Brothers from the building. A few plain-clothed people were also brought out and loaded into the waiting police vehicles in handcuffs.

"Arrogant assholes," she said. "They all wear the same expression on their faces, of disbelief that they have been caught."

Transport buses were arriving, passing through the gates, and driving into the police area. Lights still flashed. An ambulance arrived, the two paramedics running into the building without their stretcher after talking with the coordinating policeman.

Riccardo stood with him now. He'd gone in on the initial breaching of the building, but now he was outside, helping with the ensuing chaos.

Her heart beat steadily.

Waiting.

A fire engine arrived, and Riccardo walked to it and talked with the driver. They drove closer to the building, parked before the team exited, and walked into the building without their gear.

The firefighters began walking the children out. This had been in their breach plan, knowing that some of the children would be petrified of any form of authoritative figure with a weapon, so a more neutral option had been chosen to escort the kids. The children in this building were young, mostly between six and ten years old. Even from a distance, Chrystal could see their faces. Not one had luggage with them, and all were dressed alike. A blue T-shirt and blue shorts — dressed as a team.

Silent and obedient.

Chrystal watched closely for Akina. She didn't need a picture for comparison, her face was burnt into her memory.

The last fireman came out, and the police followed behind them.

Riccardo looked at her.

She shook her head. He nodded, then walked over to where they still stood. "You want to take a closer look inside the buses?"

"I would, thank you. I know that there was no Akina but one of the children, there is something about her..." Chrystal said.

"Take as much time as you need, especially if any of them look familiar. It could be a break we need. If it weren't for you guys collaborating with us, we wouldn't have known this was happening in our own city. At least now we could save this lot. Take another look. Make sure."

Chrystal walked with Riccardo to the first bus and climbed inside. She ambled toward the back studying each child carefully, committing each face to memory.

The children had been arranged one child to a seat. She looked into their faces and saw such disillusionment at the world already. One child looked back at her, making eye contact. "Did you see this girl at all?"

The child took the picture and studied it, and then she shook her head and passed the picture back.

"Her name is Akina. Are you sure you didn't see her?"

The child shook her head and looked downwards.

She climbed off and then onto the second bus and made her way slowly down toward the back. About halfway, she stopped.

A small black face looked downwards, trying not to attract attention to herself. Her hair was neatly braided, and someone had taken time to put traditional beads into it.

The familiarity grew...

Chrystal cleared her throat and the girl lifted her head.

She would recognize those blue eyes anywhere.

"Can you show me your hands, little one?" she asked in Zulu.

The girl looked at her, and then slowly lifted her hands. Her baby finger's last joint to her nail was not missing.

The kidnappers had given them an ear from a different child, not Akina. Another special child, without a mutilation. They were following animal husbandry rules after all.

"Hello Liyana, I know your *úgógo* Busi, from Thabazimbi in South Africa. I was hoping to find you here."

Liyana looked at her in disbelief. "You really know my *úgógo*?"

Chrystal nodded, squatting down next to her seat. "She's a special sangoma, she's got blue eyes like yours. Only cloudy. Old. I have been to her *ndumba*. There's a picture of you on her wall next to an old skull of a wilde-beest. You don't have these pretty braids in your hair, but you're wearing a pink dress and smiling. I see you grew that missing tooth since the picture was taken." The girl smiled with watery eyes. "I know she's going to be happy to hear that we have found you. That old sea bean seed necklace of hers will click together loudly as she dances in joy to have you back."

Liyana launched herself against Chrystal. "Please take me home. Please take me away from here. Please take me home to Busi."

Riccardo stared at her as she held the child to her.

"I need you to be brave a little longer. I need you to look at this picture, and tell me if you have seen this girl?"

Liyana took the photo in her hand. It shook but she stared at it carefully. "Before we came to this building, we went to another place, there was water outside the door, like a river. We could hear lots of pigeons on the windowsills. She was there. She sang about Sunflowers and everyone dying except her. But then she would sing our names too, she called me Liyana-Lilly in her song. But the Sister told her she had to stay at that place, she wasn't moving with us."

"Can you tell me anything about the Sister?"

The girl looked at her blankly.

"Did you notice anything different, what she was wearing?"

"Her *umgexo*, it only had three big beads. The *umgexo* my mother has lots and lots of beads."

Chrystal nodded her head. "And what else? Why did you call her Sister?"

"Because she wears clothes like the Sisters at church, long skirts like the Zionist who meet on the hill outside our village, but hers were blue. And the man that was there called her Sister. She let us keep the light on at night."

Shivers ran down Chrystal's back, and into her trousers, as goosebumps danced up her arms.

A sense of dread.

She knew that clothing too well.

"What color was the blue, light like the sky or dark like deep water?"

"Dark water," Liyana said.

"Zuga Mission Church clothing," Chrystal said. Dreading her next thought, that somehow Stella-Rose might be involved.

Same clothes.

Same church. Rowan's words rattling in her head: It's either a mistake or a coincidence, and I don't believe in those … *Stella-Rose, what have you got involved in? And how could you do this if you are?*

Liyana said, "I don't like water because I can't swim."

Chrystal smiled and smoothed her hair. "Maybe when you get home, your *Gogo* can take you for some lessons. And what about the place you were first, was it a church?"

"No. It had lots of steps going up, not like here."

"Outside the windows?" Chrystal asked. "Could you see anything?"

"No, but we could hear church bells."

She looked up at Riccardo.

"There are one hundred and seven bell towers in Venice alone," he said.

Chrystal stroked Liyana's face. "Were the bells loud or soft?"

"They didn't hurt my ears," Liyana said proudly.

"We'll search any other properties in this church's name. We'll find her," Riccardo said.

Liyana curled closer into Chrystal, hugging tightly. "Can you stay with me until my mummy or my *Gogo* fetch me?"

"I'll stay a while for now, but I still have other children to find. See that little girl in the picture, she's still missing. I need to go and help her."

Liyana nodded. "You must find her so she can go home too."

Chrystal looked around at all the others, and it struck her what was so different about the children. Despite the terrifying conditions and the fact that they had been rescued, not one child was reacting to the situation.

No one spoke.

No one cried.

The bus was silent.

These children were broken.

Chrystal drew in a ragged breath.

"Still no Akina. She's not in the building, not on the buses and not at the auction. Surely they didn't ship her out so fast when she was sold?"

Rowan stood close beside her as she sat in the chair that Riccardo had offered her in the police debrief. She could feel him there.

Riccardo said, "The strike force managed to round up all those people attending the auction. Seventy-seven children were saved. We have to be happy with that."

Chrystal pushed back in her chair.

Rowan placed his hand lightly on her shoulder. His fingers were warm. She chose to lean into the heat. He squeezed lightly, as if to let her know that he had her back.

Rowan cleared his throat. "Missing were Lot #25, the white, blond-haired boy. Lot #42, a willowy black Sudanese teenager. And Lot #12, Akina."

"So we still haven't found the target you came for," Riccardo said.

"There has to be another stash house. We can't stop now," Rowan said. "This is the frustrating part, we know we did good, but it wasn't good enough. That was a lot of children, and we can only hope that they will now be taken care of, but Akina is still out there. We're so close, and yet so far—"

"Any news on if Jason's offer of five million might have got through to the purchaser before they were raided?" Chrystal asked.

Rowan nodded. "Holly said they had passed it on in the web chatter. The offer is out there... Sem has assured me that they'll work through each of the people in that chat room and their profiles. They'll piece together who all those people were, and they'll be held accountable."

"It's too slow for Akina. She'll disappear completely by then," Chrystal said.

"Sem is good at his job, and it's good to have the ICC working with us. But I agree, we must have missed someplace. Three of them," Riccardo said, and took a map off the wall and laid it on the table.

"I can't keep looking at maps," Chrystal said.

Rowan began to lightly massage Chrystal's shoulders. "Remember when I first came to you, and you accused me of clinical coldness? It's time for some of that. We can't let our emotions out until we have her back safely with her father. There must be something more. We need to keep picking through each of the clues, she'll be there."

Chrystal relaxed into Rowan's warm hands.

She felt a featherlight kiss on the top of her head. She wanted to stay there, lift her face up and kiss him, but this was hardly the place or the time. There was still so much to achieve, she couldn't be distracted by anything personal.

Rowan's phone buzzed in his pocket. "Sem?"

"We have a location. I'm sending it through now." Chrystal leaned in, trying to listen. Rowan hit speaker.

"Tell Riccardo to come too," Sem's voice held urgency. "Intel says children are on the premises, two of them match the description of the other missing kids, but a third is also there—"

"Akina?" Chrystal's eyes were wide as she whispered the name.

"We don't have enough information to confirm—" Sem said.

Rowan was already standing. "We're on our way."

CHAPTER 36

Venice, Italy

Akina stood near the window. She couldn't see out, but she could tell it was nighttime. Watery images of lights seeped through the glass, and she traced each one with her finger.

She used to think night lights were pretty, but that was before all this happened.

Now she knew whoever her father had sent had failed.

They hadn't arrived in time.

Sister had said she was being transported to her new home and had bathed her and dressed her in sports team clothing.

Now she waited.

There was nothing in this room she could use to save herself, or leave a note, nothing to inflict an imprint onto the putty around the windowpane even, to leave her name.

Perhaps wherever she was being sent, she could get away there.

She knew her dad would never give up searching, she just had to keep trying.

Unlike the younger kids she had seen, she had good memories and she knew however long it took, she would keep trying to get back to her dad.

If she could get away, she knew her way home.

She didn't want to be a prostitute, made to do horrible things with strange men and women.

She didn't want to be owned by anyone and have to wear a collar like a dog.

She didn't want to be some exotic pet.

Her hands began to tremble. So much uncertainty again... she sang her song quietly.

"Sunflowers, sunflowers growing up so high
We're all pretty maidens
We all have to die
Excepting Akina-Aster
Because she's the only one,
Such a shame, such a shame
We'll never see her face again."

Tears threatened and she dashed them away. She would not allow her captors the victory of seeing her cry.

She. Would. Not.

Night noises came up from the street below. She put her head against the glass.

In the quietness, she heard the thud, and felt the glass vibrate with the impact.

She pulled her head away and put her hand on the glass.

It was still.

But noises came from in the apartment somewhere, a man shouting.

Raised female voices.

Screaming.

Chaos. A chance of escape.

She tried her door. Locked.

The Sister opened it from the other side.

"Quick, Akina, we need to go. Levi's come back for you." She grabbed Akina's arm and dragged her toward the back of the apartment.

She pushed on a panel with her free hand and the wall moved to reveal a hidden spiral staircase.

Akina's heart pounded in her ears as she started down the steps with the Sister.

The descent was a slow, difficult one once the panel above had closed and the steps were in darkness.

Right now, the person she hated most in life was Levi.

If he wanted her back, that would mean that he'd bought her. That he'd do things to her, that before he hadn't been allowed to. She could hear him louder now. Shouting above.

She threw up.

It splashed on the Sister's robes but they carried on down the steps. Levi's voice slowly faded behind them.

Then there was a different noise — sirens in the background.

The Sister stopped. Akina bumped into her back.

The sirens were getting louder.

The Sister stayed motionless on the steps, as if uncertain of which way to go.

Akina took the opportunity to push past her and carried on down the steps.

"Wait. Wait. It's not safe out there. Levi might be there," the Sister said, just as Akina reached the door at the bottom.

"Levi is out there!" Sister shouted.

The name broke Akina's momentum.

She didn't want to come face to face with Levi.

Carefully she opened the door.

And stopped.

Levi was just outside the main apartment complex. She would know his silhouette anywhere. As quietly as she could, she closed the door.

"He's there, at the exit," she said.

The Sister opened the door just a crack. "We can't get out that way. Go back upstairs, if he's down here, then we can go back up there, there is another way off the roof." She pointed back upwards.

Slowly they made their way back up the stairs.

She trudged back up, away from Levi.

Pandemonium was breaking loose as they came out of the hidden panel.

There was a man in full black fatigues. He had the other Sister kneeling at the end of his weapon and another man was using thick tie straps to bind her hands behind her back.

Akina froze.

The Sister grabbed her arm and yanked her back toward the hidden stairs.

"Polizia. Polizia." They had seen her, and the man was pointing to himself, and lowered his gun.

He said he was the Police, but how could she trust him?

If these men were with Levi, she was in trouble.

She was caught like a rat. She had to get away.

She ran with the Sister for the hidden door.

The policeman grabbed her and pulled her out the grip of the Sister. His hands were like steel bands as they wrapped around her arms.

"No, I'm not going back to Levi," she screamed and bit him. "Let me go."

She fought with everything she had.

Another policeman had the Sister and was making her lie face down on the floor.

"Stop. I'm the police. We're here to save you," he said in English as she struggled against him, trying to kick him, trying to get away. "We're the Police, Akina. Stop fighting me."

She stopped struggling.

They knew her name.

But so had the horrible Levi after a day or two of her being taken.

She renewed the fight.

"*Soggetto protetto*," he said, and then slowly lowered her onto her feet. "Don't run, we're here to help you. I'm putting you down. But you have to stop struggling."

More policemen came in, one with the other boy who'd been in the apartment with her, and the other with a tall black girl who hadn't spoken much.

The first policeman was holding the boy tightly, as he too was struggling.

Fighting.

Screaming.

"You can't trust the police any more than the animals who stole us," the boy said, still fighting. "Fight. Get away. Fight for your life!"

The darker girl was oddly subdued. Not fighting at all.

A woman followed by a man rushed into the apartment, they were also dressed in black, but were not armed.

"Akina. Confirming it is Akina," she said.

Akina looked at the woman, and the man.

261

"Your father, Curtis Wilson, sent us, we have been looking all over the world for you."

"My father sent you? A woman?"

The boy stopped fighting. Akina watched the policeman put him down and step away.

Akina looked at the woman.

She had the bluest eyes and her face was deeply tanned. Her hair was covered by the helmet she wore, but she took it off as Akina stared at her. She placed it on the floor. "He sent us. My name is Chrystal, this is Rowan." She signaled to the man next to her. "It's good to finally find you."

Akina looked at him, his green eyes unmistakable, shimmering with moisture. "Hello Akina, I'm Rowan."

She didn't need to look at him again as she launched herself at him. To be near someone she knew was a friend. "I know you. I know you. My dad has a picture of you in his office. You saved his life once. You're the soldier that he sent to save me." She laughed and she cried, filled with so many emotions. She pulled back and looked at the man. "What took you so long?"

CHAPTER 37

Somewhere high above Africa – heading south

3rd May, 2016 — Three days after auction

The TV was on in the private jet that Curtis had arranged to fly them back to South Africa. Akina, wrapped in a blanket, curled up on her father's lap was not asleep, and not awake, caught in that land between. Every now and again she would jolt upright, and then hug her father again, sink into him and cry.

Shocked. Exhausted and sleep deprived, she was handling the situation in her own way.

Rowan sat beside Chrystal, the tray table between them sporting two unfinished glasses of champagne and an empty plate where the hostess had given them a cheese and meat platter.

"In breaking news, the Italian police and their specialist task force have raided an auction house, and other residential premises in Venice suspected of funding a radical terrorist group. The suspects were from several nations, all known for aiding terrorists, and their investigation continues. And next the weather—"

"No mention of the children," Chrystal said. Glancing at the sleeping child in the seat opposite her. Permission to travel with Liyana because of their connection had been easily obtained once Curtis had shown up and begun throwing his weight and influence around. She slept under the thin blanket and clutched another stuffed toy that Rowan had taken time to find.

"As we expected," Rowan said. "But at least we've got some new leads to follow in South Africa. We still need to find out who kidnapped Akina, and who bought her. Only then can Curtis have some closure."

She stood, wanting to pace but the plane wasn't big enough. She stretched instead before sitting down again, and pulled her legs beneath her. She rolled her head, thankful that the plane had larger seats than a commercial flight.

Chrystal needed to find answers.

Tears welled unexpectedly in her eyes. "The last time I flew, Jason was with me, and we talked about so many things that my mind had blanked out. I miss him, isn't that weird."

Rowan reached for her, and then pulled her into his lap. "I know that their police apology is never going to be enough for the loss of your friend."

She relaxed into him, putting her head on his shoulder.

"It's been a big few days." He patted her back, but then the pats turned more toward massages. Lazy exploration.

She lifted her head and touched her forehead to his. "I know that they said that because of the rush everyone wasn't briefed, but it's unacceptable that their dual-nationality sniper shot him just because he recognized him as an arms dealer in their conflict in the Congo."

Rowan looked into her eyes as she lifted her head a little so she wasn't seeing him with four eyes.

"Jason was not the person I thought he'd become," she sniffed. "But, in the end, he did the right thing. What's going to happen to the kids he was 'running' back home? I don't know what will become of them now—"

"One child at a time. Let's finish this investigation, then we can think about other kids in peril."

She nodded.

"You okay?" he asked.

"*Ja.* Thanks." There was so much more she wanted to say, so much more she wanted to do, like run her hand over his shoulders and sink back into his warmth, but for now she had to pull up her big girl panties.

There were still so many questions on the Akina case unanswered. And there were those niggles that had become loudspeakers in her head too, about Stella-Rose, that she needed to bring to Rowan's attention.

She lifted herself back into her own seat. Putting physical distance between them. "I've been thinking. What's the link between Curtis and the kidnappers? Other than Akina?"

"Pass. They're your thoughts, you tell me," Rowan said, turning toward her.

"Corruption." She could hear him breathe, he was so close to her. She closed her eyes, trying hard to remove the picture that it set off in her mind — of what could have been just moments before. *If* she had taken the chance instead of moving away...

She'd missed having a partner at her back. One who she trusted.

But it was more too. Only she couldn't allow herself to think on that now—

"There is someone they both deal with, or dealt with, who's corrupt," Chrystal said.

Curtis said in a low voice, "Plenty of people on that list."

Chrystal stared at him. He'd been listening the whole time. She was suddenly shy, glad that she hadn't taken Rowan's compassion further. "This is a two-pronged theory. Remember what Busi said — she warned me of a snake, but also to 'look in the shadows.' We're not looking only for the actual kidnappers, but the puppet master.

"We need to see if Akina can shed any light on who she talked to. She loves you, Curtis, that's evident, but there must be others whom she confides in."

"And the second?" Rowan asked.

"We need to go through that list of people Curtis gave us again. We're looking for another type of link, one that might not pop out, but be more subtle."

"Whatever you need. I have to find out who did this to my daughter," Curtis said.

Chrystal saw Rowan smile, but it was a sad expression. She felt the same — Curtis had been through hell and back. Yet he'd been patient and trusted them to do their job. To find his daughter.

Now it was time to hunt the perpetrators so they could never do it again. Bring the full extent of the law down on them.

"Any news from the police? How long before they match the transaction for her sale to one of the people?" Curtis asked.

Rowan shook his head. "They said that the transaction had taken place outside of the auction's database. We know that Brigette was being cooperative, while the Director, Matteo, wasn't. But Riccardo hasn't given up. He owes us a huge debt, we wouldn't have been there had it not been for Akina, and they wouldn't have broken the whole circle if it wasn't for you not giving up on your daughter."

"And I'll never give up trying to find who stole her and bring them to justice," Curtis said. There was stress in his voice, threaded with steel-like determination.

"We have a small lead, but I'm not sure of it. I can't believe I'm thinking like this," Chrystal said, her heart beating against her ribs, hoping that her instincts were wrong, just this one time. Dreading that it came back so close to home. "We know from Akina that they kept referring to someone as The Mother Bitch. And she was found in a building that was owned by the Zuga Mission Church. Can you think of any link between these religious people and someone you would have connections to through your anti-corruption work in South Africa? I can't help but feel there's a link we've missed?"

Curtis was quiet, deep in thought. "I guess if the Church was involved in child services, that would fall under the South African Minister of Social Development, Health and Welfare, Thulas Masutha. I met him in New York a few years ago to discuss increasing cross-nation adoption and how to keep corruption out of it. He's a keen cook and got Akina started after meeting him. I also dealt with him on a couple of other occasions, but none of those were against him, it was always working with him and his team."

"Nothing about adoption and children except the original consult?" Rowan asked.

"No," Curtis said.

"You know, I think Akina and Thulas might still talk to each other when she makes some dish or another. She calls him to tell him about it. I mean, she used to talk to him. I'd forgotten about that."

"You've had a lot going on. Sometimes it takes distance and time to remember little details. I know that firsthand," Chrystal said.

They had to look closer at Stella-Rose. She had believed in her innocence, but now there were too many coincidences to simply ignore. Closer scrutiny was unfortunately going to be necessary.

"I can't afford to take time to remember," Curtis said. "We have to bring them to justice."

Rowan nodded. "I know it's hard at this point to stay positive, but someone also paid three million dollars for Akina. They will not simply let her go. Chances are they'll come after her if they knew who she really was. I know a firm in Pietermaritzburg who I'd trust to protect her. It won't be easy being under 24/7 personal guard but she'll be safe until we settle this."

CHAPTER 38

Leopard Hill Farm, Thabazimbi, Limpopo Province, South Africa

5th May, 2016 — 5 days after auction

"It's Chrystal from *Saliebos*. I'm here to see Busi and maCalio. I have an appointment," she said, after she'd pushed the intercom at Leopard Hill farm. This time she'd called ahead and secured a time.

"She's driving out," the voice said.

"It's now or never," Chrystal said. "Hopefully it's the first one, we could do with a break round about now."

"She can either help or tell us to take a hike," Rowan said. "I have to admit I have never consulted a sangoma before, let alone twice in one job."

maCalio's Cruiser came into view and the gate opened. She parked close to where Chrystal stood and wound down her window. "Why are you bothering me again?"

"Nice to see you too, maCalio," Chrystal said as she stood next to her Cruiser and leaned against the door where Rowan was still sitting. He raised a hand in greeting.

maCalio looked at him but offered no other acknowledgment that he was there.

"Hello Busi," Chrystal said, greeting the old woman who sat beside maCalio in the passenger seat.

"Madam." Then Busi looked at Rowan, and she nodded to him.

"Where's your cat?" Chrystal asked.

maCalio looked down. "A snake got it. But Rikki saved my life again. This time it was a boomslang. She is buried under the fever tree where she can watch the weaver birds that she loved to bring me as gifts."

"I'm sorry to hear that," Chrystal said.

"I am not. That snake would have killed me instead if Rikki had not leaped on it. If something dies in your place, that is a good thing? It means you are still living."

Chrystal couldn't fault her logic.

"Now — why are you here?" maCalio asked.

"Two things. I wanted to give Busi this gift we brought back from Italy," she said, going to the back seat and opening the door.

Liyana jumped out, like they'd discussed, and revealed herself. "*Gogo!*"

Busi beamed, but the shocked look on her face was priceless.

"*Mzukulu!*" She scrambled out of the Cruiser and was running, faster than Chrystal thought possible for the old woman. When they met, Busi hugged Liyana and lifted her up, swinging her around in a circle. Tears of happiness ran down Busi's face as she clung to her grandchild. "My beautiful granddaughter. You are really here!"

"This is why I do it. For moments like this," Rowan said.

Busi was holding up Liyana's hand and kissing her full fingers. She shuffled her feet in the sand in the way that Ndebele women do when they are excited and thumped them down in a dance movement.

Only after this was over, did Busi look up, still holding onto her grandchild.

"*Siyabonga gakulu,*" she said, tears still running down her face.

"She said thank you very much," Chrystal said to Rowan as he was taking a small case from the Land Cruiser's trunk and putting it into maCalio's one.

Chrystal passed over a blanket that she bought in Venice. "This has a picture on it of the Rialto bridge; it was near where Liyana was found. And I wanted to tell you in person that she's a special girl — without her, three other children might have been lost. And I brought you a chicken, so you can celebrate together over a feast."

"Don't curse us," Rowan muttered. "Remember we're the good guys."

Busi laughed and her whole face crinkled up with its age lines, as she showed her gums where teeth should have been. "*Siyabonga*. You did not need to give me another chicken," Busi said, "you already got my grand-daughter back, and that was a big enough *bonsella*. My daughter will come now. My family will live with me, under my protection. Not in the village."

"That's good news," Chrystal said. "We're glad that we could help. It's a good thing I had maCalio's number, so she could tell you."

"I think I will change that number now," maCalio said, as she too wiped her eyes.

Chrystal smiled. "I wanted to say thank you, Busi. I haven't gone to Victoria Falls yet, but soon."

Busi clapped her hands together. Her beads around her neck clunked. "When you are ready, it will be so. But know that the golden *inkonkoni* is not finished with you. There is still those who were responsible to be brought to justice."

Chrystal frowned. "I know. We're not giving up. We'll find them. I was wondering if you could use your sangoma talents and tell me where to find those responsible?"

Busi shook her head. "I cannot. That way is blocked to me. This is your journey, and you must find them and get justice. The spirit of the golden *inkonkoni* is restless, it is still inside of you. Part of you. If you look closer to the one you do not want to look at, you will find them. You need to learn to be fierce like the *inkonkoni*."

Chrystal frowned. "I don't understand."

Busi clicked her tongue. "You already know one, but you choose to ignore. But soon, you serve justice. Another will be much changed because he was caught. He is a proud man of power. The people trusted him. They were wrong."

"We'll carry on the search as soon as we can." She reached out and touched the old woman's hand. "Now that your granddaughter is safe, it would help if you could tell me who approached you about hiding the girls in the first place. We need to break The Circle so this can never happen again."

Busi looked at her. "I cannot. But know that I will deal with that person, and the owl will call their name."

Chrystal warned, "Not many people really believe anymore that when an owl calls your name, you will die. That is only a superstition."

Busi looked her in the eyes. "They will believe. I will make sure of that. Even now they will be counting their days walking on the earth."

"I can't change your mind, and let the law handle them?" Chrystal asked.

Busi spoke slowly. "Sometimes it is better for those who don't believe in the law to be punished from beyond the law."

Chrystal reached forward and touched her arm. "Be careful. We can't have you going to jail now your granddaughter's home. She needs you."

Busi smiled, putting her hand over Chrystal's and patting it.

"And the other thing?" maCalio asked.

"That question is for your ears only," Chrystal said.

Busi turned to walk away.

"Put those things in the Cruiser, I'll pick you both up on the way back. No need to carry heavy gifts," maCalio said.

Busi smiled and Liyana helped her to put her gifts into the Cruiser before she ran back to Chrystal and hugged her. "Will I see you again?"

Chrystal looked at Busi. "If it's okay with your *Gogo*, I can come visit sometimes. And you're always welcome to see me on my farm. Any time. You be good."

Liyana hugged her again. "Thank you for coming to save me."

She waved at Rowan but was still a little wary of men, before joining her granny who waved to them. They turned and walked slowly to the gate hand in hand.

Together.

maCalio opened it and the old sangoma and her grandchild with the matching blue eyes, began to walk down the long path homewards.

When they were sure she was out of earshot, Chrystal said, "I wanted to tell you that Jason Adams was killed while we were in Venice."

"That is old news," maCalio said.

"But the policeman who shot him was ex-Congolese. He recognized Jason."

"Jason was many things, but above all else he was an arms dealer," maCalio said. "It is a basic business rule, demand drives supply."

"True. But before he died, Jason realized that someone was trying to clean out your spiders and disrupt your network." She passed over the bag she held and spilled its contents into maCalio's hand. "I found these in the vehicles Jason supplied, and while I wasn't able to retrieve the one from the helicopter, I think there was a GPS tracker in that too."

"Interesting," maCalio said, turning the devices over and looking at them.

"On the plane to Venice, I even showed him these thinking that he might recognize them. He denied seeing them. We both came to the same conclusion. maNtuli has a problem up there that needs sorting out. Before it gets out that the supply line is not secure, and you lose all your clients."

"I am not a stranger to this design of tracker. I know who was trying to destabilize maNtuli here in South Africa, and I have already taken care of it. Tomi Patel met an unfortunate but necessary end. I guess now we must look further afield to make sure the webs are clear of any debris he left behind."

"You knew there was a problem?" Chrystal said, her voice rising.

"Of course. But I am also a businesswoman, I can always get one job sorted for me by another if the need arises. Why do you think the weapons you required were such a reasonable price?"

Chrystal raised her eyebrows.

"Do not worry, I knew you would find the truth, even if you were not happy with helping an arms dealer. You need to know that I have your back. We women, we need to stick together. Build each other up, not tear one and other down, unless the woman is a snake — then she can die."

"Do I want to know? Who and where or what?"

"Probably not," maCalio said. "The child who started this all, she was found and is safe?"

"She is," Chrystal said, nodding as she walked to the driver's door of her Cruiser and climbed in. She leaned across Rowan and spoke out of his window. "Until next time, maCalio. As always, it's been — fascinating."

"Hopefully there will not be a next time," maCalio said.

Chrystal started her Cruiser and waved as she drove away.

CHAPTER 39

Pandora Timbers Mission Orphanage, Thabazimbi, South Africa

8th May 2016 — 8 days after auction

Mother Stella-Rose Naude heard a scratching at the door of her bedroom. It wasn't a rat or a mouse — was it a person running their nails down the old wood? She looked out her window. The curtains were open as always, and it was the darkest hour before the sunrise, when the sun hadn't woken yet and the moon was too weak to illuminate the sky.

Stella-Rose smiled. It was probably one of the new aspirants, unsure if she should knock properly or not. She climbed out of bed and walked barefoot to her door and opened it. Looking around, there was no one in the passage. She stepped out into the vacant space to look further and kicked something.

On the floor in the corridor outside was a bundle of leaves, woven into a basket. She picked it up and looked inside. It held owl pellets, fragments of bones and skulls of its last few meals.

She knew what this was.

A hex from a sangoma.

All she had to do was wait for the owl to call her name.

Shaking, she carried the nest into her room. Slamming her door, she took a deep breath.

She was a woman of religion; she didn't believe in African superstitions anymore.

Stella-Rose believed in her God, and that he would protect her. She threw the curse in her bin, and dropping to her knees, she grabbed her *perle sacre* from her bedside table, and one bead at a time, she prayed with her necklace.

"Protect me Father." She kissed one of the beads.

"I serve you Father, it's in your name I do what's for the good of the church." She kissed the next bead.

"To my place by your side soon as a *Divina-Saint*, if the owl calls my name, then may I be by your side faster." She kissed the final bead.

She bowed her head as she called on her God in prayer to protect her, so that she could continue to worship him, and do great deeds in his name.

Finally, she stood up.

She looked at her bin. In a few hours, she would take it outside and burn it.

Witchcraft had no place in her Mission. It was a holy place.

But when she got back into her bed, her mind was awake, and as she looked at the darkness outside, she remembered that she and Chrystal used to call this time the '*Tokoloshe* hour' from tales of the creatures that Elijah, one of the old workers on *Saliebos*, would spin.

Elijah believed in spirits and that the *tokoloshe* were real.

He would hang bags of herbs around his house to ward off the evil spirits, and perform rituals at the dam, to keep the souls of the dead from rising up. He would dance around a campfire, gyrating and chanting, to remove the negative spirits from the farm, and to welcome all those traveling who were not going to cause any harm.

He would tell them tales of the *tokoloshe* who would come out of his swamp, steal naughty children, and drown them in the dark water. And of huge owls that if they called your name, you knew that someone had put a sangoma's curse on you and your time on earth was ticking to an end. Or if you saw an African mask on a wall, and let down your guard, the spirit inside would jump into your body and possess it. You would forever be lost to this world, and unable to enter the spirit world — you would simply cease to exist, the spirit stealing your very soul.

How something so small like a noise and a hex had reminded her of that old man Elijah, she had no idea. She didn't even remember what had happened to him, and when he had gone from the farm, if he'd died or decided to move on to a different place. Had she even been home when that had happened? Probably not.

But she lay there thinking about how her life was so different to his.

Everyone would remember her.

Her church would exult her. She would be a *Divina-Saint*.

CHAPTER 40

Marakele National Park, Thabazimbi, Limpopo Province, South Africa

10ᵗʰ May, 2016 — 10 days after auction

Levi took a steadying breath, then squeezed the trigger.

The impala ram dropped to the ground. Even before he walked to it, he knew it was dead. "After all, I was taught to hunt by the best."

He stood over it, looking at its glassy eye staring up. He pulled his 9mm from his belt and emptied the magazine into it.

Rage and uncertainty for his future burnt deep in his soul.

Once again at a crossroad.

Grateful that he'd been able to shoot the impala today. If he hadn't, there was a danger he would beat his wife to death, and as she'd pointed out the last time, he was close to having the gangs discover who he was, then they would want a cut of everything.

Levi hadn't worked so hard to give those bastards anything.

But things were not supposed to have gone quite the way they had over the last few months.

He looked at the tree where he'd carved a simple F into the bark. In the years it had grown, it was still at tombstone level. This big camel thorn tree marked the spot where he'd killed his father so many years ago and buried him in the park where his father had taught him everything about poaching.

It had been his first step after prison to becoming his own boss.

And years since he'd returned — until the Japanese Doll came into his life.

He would visit the Mission station, deliver the kids or take delivery, and then get the hell out of the town where he'd spent his childhood.

Today he was visiting his old man. One final goodbye.

He would be starting over. Changing his name. Again.

Only this time, he would change his country too.

His share of three million American dollars could buy him a quiet life in a different place in Africa, or even a place like Jamaica. Beach. Fishing. Freedom.

Five million would have been better, but things had happened — if he'd only got her again... but — he hadn't, so no use torturing himself. His share of three million was still decent money for one scrawny brat.

He took his hunting knife and cut the impala's throat. He watched the blood soak the ground, and within a few minutes, the flies of the Limpopo province heard he was having a pity party and they buzzed around. Slicing holes in the back legs, he threaded a stick through and hoisted the impala into the camel thorn tree, wedging the stick between two branches. He hummed as he skinned the impala, and then he opened it up, letting the guts spill onto the skin.

It was soothing to be using his hands and performing a job he'd done so many times before. Ensuring the intestines were all out, he pulled the skin away to the side, separated the liver from the rest of the offal. Only then did he get his small fire ready.

"Nothing like fresh liver." He took the small frying pan he'd carried with him and, slicing the organ, put it in the pan. Frying it in its own fats, he cut off pieces as it browned and ate them.

He sat for a while watching the small flames turn to ash and begin smoldering. Digging in the soil with his boot, he flicked sand over the coals so that it didn't start a wildfire. He took his pan, and wiped it with his handkerchief, packed it with his 9mm and 22 rifle before beginning the hike back to where he'd left his *bakkie*.

He would do what he'd always done, divvy the money out, ensuring his business partners could be counted on for future days. Future profits.

His blood lust quenched, in his salute to his father who'd shaped his life. He drove toward the gates.

Marakele National Park had once again lived up to its Tswana name. It was his 'place of sanctuary'.

The game guard pulled his phone from his pocket and dialed his neighbor and friend on the farm next door. "Zenzele, remember after that ear incident, you asked me to call you if I ever saw that man who was asking questions. The one who spent a long time in the park all alone? He was here again. He was driving a white *bakkie*, number plate is EFG 931 GP. He signed his name on the paper as Levi Louw, from Pretoria."

CHAPTER 41

Saliebos Farm, Thabazimbi, Limpopo Province, South Africa

10th May 2016 — 10 days after auction

Chrystal turned to Rowan. "Zenzele was on the phone with the guard at the gate of the National Park. He identified a Levi Louw. Levi — the name on the paper from Dar es Saleem, and the name Akina and Cherri keep saying of the man who had them—"

"Don't get too excited. It might be nothing," Rowan warned.

"We need his driver's license so we can show his picture to the girls."

"We've been promised improved cooperation from the South African police, let's ask our liaison officer," Rowan said, as he opened his laptop and began typing an email relaying all the info. This could be the piece of the puzzle they needed to find who took Akina, and who bought her. He hoped so.

He pushed send. "Now we wait for Detective Oliver Motsisi to reply."

Rowan's laptop tinged. "Now that is service," Rowan said as he opened the email. Chrystal came and put her hands on his shoulders, leaning down as she joined him to read it.

There was a driver's license and a photo of a white man, his address, and his rap sheet.

Poaching.

Murder while in jail — downgraded to self-defense.

The man had changed his name after leaving jail, and then he seemed to have no other run-ins with the law beyond a noise complaint by a neighbor in his posh neighborhood.

He ran a successful company, a fleet of cargo trucks, and had residences in Cape Town's Hout Bay as well as in Hartbeespoort outside of Pretoria.

Interesting though were the hospital reports that were attached; suspected wife abuse, but she refused to press charges, so there was nothing they could do.

They looked at the photo of her bruised face.

Chrystal sucked in an audible breath and gripped Rowan's shoulders hard.

The woman could be her sister — even her twin.

"Khulu," she called, "can you come here?"

Rowan said. "You can't frighten him, there could be an easy explanation—"

Khulu came into the lounge. "You called?"

"You want to sit down for this," Chrystal said. "When the social workers got you to come pick me up, did they make any mention of another child?"

"Only you," Khulu said. "I checked with them at the time, and they confirmed you were the only child she had."

"Look at this," Chrystal said, and she turned the laptop toward her grandfather.

Khulu put his glasses on. "It can't be. They said only one." He carried on looking at it. Then he shook his head. "No. She's a fake. Look at this, her hair is bleached. Black roots. You don't have any. Neither did your grandmother. Pure natural golden. And look at her nose, it's too thin at the end, almost like a surgeon has shaved too much off. Who is she?"

"The wife of the man we think took Akina. Too much of a coincidence to have him in the nature reserve and in Dar Es Saleem. We're going to pay her a visit," Chrystal said, pointing at the screen the whole time.

Rowan's phone rang. "Hello — hang on Oliver, I'll put you on speaker. Okay, you're on—"

"He looked interesting, so I kept digging. I've emailed you his bank account details. He had a deposit clear in his account just shy of three million US dollars from a bank in the Cayman Islands."

"Three million?" Rowan said, raising his eyebrows.

"Forty-five million rands. That's a lot of money. Fourteen million transferred to an account in his wife's name. Twenty-eight million he withdrew — and then deposited as cash half to a Mr. Tahaan Abeo and Pandora Timbers Mission Orphanage. Because of the amount, the bank flagged the transactions."

"Son of a bitch, it's them," Rowan said.

Chrystal sank into the chair. And there it was, the link confirming what I've been dreading. *Stella-Rose is involved.*

It was time to face the facts. "I was just so close that I refused to acknowledge it — I have to face it now. Mother Stella-Rose Naude from Pandora Timbers Mission Orphanage, Nicola's daughter and my childhood best friend, was in it from when we first suspected at the hospital, Rowan. All this time — even Busi had pointed toward it. I just couldn't believe it. She is 'The Mother Bitch' Akina referred to."

"Don't blame yourself for believing the best in people," Rowan assured her. "The question is, will knowing it's her get in the way now?"

Chrystal shook her head. "No, but I do have to know how she could do this to innocent children."

Rowan reached over and took her hand in his. "I'll go with you. We can do this — together."

"There's more," Oliver said. "Half of that donation was withdrawn again as cash. The nuns walked out the bank with seven million rand in cash."

"What?" Chrystal said.

"The bank sent me the surveillance videos of the four women who carried it out. I've sent you the link and the picture of Tahaan Abeo," Oliver said.

Rowan took his laptop from Khulu, started the video download and opened the picture of Tahaan. "Got it, I'll send these pictures to Curtis. See if Akina recognized them, and we'll print it and go see Salin and Cherri."

"Call me once you've shown it to them. I'll get some warrants ready and assemble a team," Oliver said, and then disconnected.

CHAPTER 42

Pandora Timbers Mission Orphanage, Thabazimbi, South Africa

11ᵗʰ May, 2016 — 11 days after auction

Chrystal quickly assessed Stella-Rose's office. The room was bright, but dominated by the huge wooden cross that sent a shiver down her spine — or maybe it was the lack of reaction Chrystal's childhood friend was showing to seeing her.

Stella-Rose sat at her desk, and didn't bother standing as Chrystal and Rowan were shown in.

"Been a while, Chrystal," Stella-Rose said from behind her desk.

Her slightly slumped posture told Chrystal that she was weary.

Tired.

Distracted.

Interesting, she thought, as Stella-Rose didn't make any eye contact with her or Rowan but continued looking away to the side of their faces, as if the cross on the back wall was judging her every move.

"That it has," Chrystal said. "This is Rowan, he's been looking into Akina Wilson's disappearance."

Stella-Rose acknowledged Rowan with a nod of her head.

Chrystal couldn't read the expression on her old friend's face. But she did notice the lines at the edge of her eyes twitch when she'd mentioned why Rowan was there.

"Sit," Stella-Rose said, motioning to the chairs. "What do you want?"

Chrystal didn't sit and looked directly at her. "Do you have any knowledge of Akina Wilson's kidnap and sale?"

Stella-Rose stared at her, then her eyes flicked to Rowan. Back again.

"We know about her sale that netted you fourteen million rands deposited into your account," Chrystal said.

Stella-Rose sat back in her chair. Her shoulders slumped further.

Then she straightened up, as if dragging the courage needed from deep within to face off with the enemy.

Chrystal said, "I'm sure you have an explanation, and we'd love to hear it."

"That was a kind cash donation to the Mission."

"And the video we have seen of you withdrawing seven million of that in cash yesterday? Is there an explanation for that? Half the donation liquidated. A strange way to run a charity."

Chrystal watched Stella-Rose swallow. Then take a deep breath before she answered.

"I have nothing to say to you, or anyone else. I only answer to my God," Stella-Rose said, lifting her chin defiantly.

"Fine. I wanted to give you the opportunity to tell us what happened. Talk to me, like the friends we once were, so I might understand how you got involved. Tell me what's going on? Before Detective Motsisi and his colleague get in here with their warrant for your arrest."

Stella-Rose glared at her. "It's like I said, I only answer to my God."

Chrystal watched the jut of Stella-Rose's jaw. It was as if they were teenagers again, and they were standing near the *bakkie* and she had told Khulu the truth about the fire. That gesture had been there then. And ever afterward. She knew that look — when her best friend in the world then ground her teeth and said no, she meant it.

"Damn it, Stella-Rose, don't be so stubborn. I'm trying to understand you. Trying to help you," she said, her voice rising slightly.

"I don't need your help," Stella-Rose said through clenched teeth. "I didn't ask for your help. Never again. You lost that right years ago—"

"We're talking about child trafficking here," Chrystal said as she tried hard to bring her temper back under control. "And you being involved in the kidnapping of Akina Wilson. Along with the donation of fourteen million rands you received for her sale into your account. How could you get involved with something like this? If you needed money to help run the mission, Khulu and I would have helped you. We even offered to lease your land, to give you income to get this place going. But selling children? You're the one that's supposed to protect them, and you sell them instead. How could you?"

Stella-Rose stood up and slammed her fist on the desk. "Do not preach to me!" She made eye contact with Chrystal. "I did what needed to be done. Your family taught me that lesson well. Sacrifice one so that another can have the perfect life."

Chrystal frowned. "What the fuck are you talking about?"

"You turned on me when that fire was an accident," Stella-Rose said. "You stood with your grandfather against me, and I was sent away because of that. Your precious Khulu paid for it all. My boarding school, the holiday camps, even my university fees until I found the Sisters. It was him who ensured I didn't come home, didn't cause any more trouble on his farm."

Chrystal shook her head.

So much for this being about the children. Stella-Rose was going to bring all the old hurts, and past up all over again.

Perhaps this time, they would get to the bottom of it. Before she was sent to jail.

"You're wrong," Chrystal said, deliberately keeping her voice even. "I heard them arguing after you had gone. He wanted you home. Your mother wanted you in a better school. He was paying your way because your mother insisted that as a gifted child, you needed more than what was offered locally, and she said that he was unfairly holding you back just because I was just–normal. It was always your mother who wanted you away, not Khulu. He paid so that you got the best, even gave you a generous living allowance. I know that because I saw it in the farm books. Not because he told me, and I know it was not to keep you away. My grandfather tried to do the best for you, even if your mother refused to have you home."

"That's not true. It was because of the fire. I burnt half the farm, and he could never forgive me. He hates the sight of me. He sent me away from everyone I loved and cared for," Stella-Rose said, her voice rising even more.

Chrystal looked at Stella-Rose. All these years she had believed her version. It was going to take a bit to convince her otherwise. But then a small niggle started in her stomach.

This wasn't about them.

How many more children that had been in Stella-Rose's care had been trafficked like Akina?. Stella-Rose was deflecting away from that. Making it personal for Chrystal, and not about the children. While the misunderstanding was understandable: the trafficking was unforgivable.

"That's rubbish," Chrystal said quietly. "Let me tell you in no uncertain terms that was never what Khulu wanted. I remember clearly begging with him to stop paying your bills, because I wanted you home. Do you know what he said? "While you are my responsibility, Chrystal, the hardest thing I have to accept is that Stella-Rose is not. Nicola makes the decisions for her, even if they're not the ones I'd make." He even wanted to know if he should come with me today, to mediate between us as he could never understand the animosity that had festered up. But then neither did I, until now."

"Oh dear, at your age. Poor girl. You are still too attached to your grand-father's shirttails to see it. You have never grown up. He sent me away from you. I was the housekeeper's child and I paid the full price for that fire."

"We both know that's not true," Chrystal protested.

"You think he's so upstanding and so perfect. You didn't even turn on him when he sent your precious boyfriend Eric away, paid him everything out of your farm savings — it was all in the newspapers."

Chrystal shook her head again. "I can't believe someone as intelligent as you was taken in by that news-fodder. A defense lawyer's theory that was thrown out of court, when that shit was sentenced to jail for stealing. You're sick, Stella-Rose. Your mind is twisting things. Only looking at half-truths—"

"I'm sick? You got to be kidding. Look at you. How perfect did your life really work out to be? Other than your grandfather, exactly who do you have in your empty life my sister— Chrystal? Or as you like to be called— Savan-nah. Who stands with you? No one.

"You even killed your teammates to save yourself getting out of the jungle on your last mercenary mission. Everyone except you and your cargo died. How convenient that no one could say anything else about the attack. If there even was one. Now you come in here, asking me to answer your questions? I'm not at war with anyone, my God absolves all my sins. Who absolves you from yours?" Her chest heaved.

"I have chosen the Sisters of the Zuga Mission Church as my family, and by prayer they will be with me. Don't you get it? I don't need you. I don't need my mother or even your grandfather to help me. I have my God, and my Sisters. You never knew me then, and you certainly don't know me now."

Chrystal stood, and Rowan went to step between them, but Chrystal put her hand out and cautioned him to stay where he was.

"You're right." Her voice was softer. Defeated. "I don't know you. Perhaps I never did. I'll grieve for the sister I had, not what she became. The press will run your story and you will be known as the nun no one could trust, and there is so much social media these days. My heart breaks for your mother, that you are subjecting her to this. I don't know how Nicola will deal with all of what is about to come out. Child trafficking, in my book, that is unforgivable. This was calculated. This wasn't a mistake. It took planning and execution to succeed, and all you say is 'sacrifice was needed'. I'm not even disappointed in you, I'm shattered that you have so little of the value of the soul of a child. Another life—"

"You have no right to talk to me about another life, and the value of a child," Stella-Rose shouted, putting her hand on her stomach.

"I have every right," Chrystal said, said while she didn't shout her voice was even. Deadly. Controlled. "You abused these kids' trust. They came to you for shelter, for care and protection and you sold them into a life of hell. How many, Stella-Rose? How many did you sacrifice for your own greed to be successful in your darling church?"

Chrystal waited while Stella-Rose said nothing. Just stared at her.

"I'm done," Chrystal said. "I still can't fathom why I still believed in you, that you were not that person. And yet, looking at the evidence, you were. I can tell you now that neither Khulu nor I will post bail for you. I think that given everything you have done for your church, the least they can do is pay to defend you in court. I'll always miss the sister from my childhood, but not what she became. Goodbye and good luck, Stella-Rose," Chrystal said, and walked out the door.

"Your turn. Good luck," she said to Detective Oliver Motsisi and his colleagues who were standing right outside. "Rowan, I'll be outside when you guys are finished."

Chrystal turned her back and headed out the door. Her chest heaved, tears burnt in her eyes and she grieved the sister that was now certainly lost to her.

Stella-Rose walked into her room. The policewoman stood guard outside her door. Waiting. Respect given to her only because she was a Sister of God.

She knew she would never return.

The church lawyers would arrive and they would post bail. She would be flown back to Italy for a few years, and then dispatched somewhere else in the world that needed her.

The church looked after its own.

Packing only those items most precious to her, her bible that contained a picture of her child from all those years ago, in her arms. Even though it had died, the Sisters had said that a photograph often helped the grieving mother.

Underwear, two spare uniforms and a small toiletry bag went into the suitcase, before she reached into her little box of keepsakes that she kept right at the back of her wardrobe. One last photo. It was taken before the fire at *Saliebos* — when she and Chrystal were not at each other's throats.

It was of their family. Ben, Chrystal, her mother and her, all sitting on the veranda at the farmhouse. It was her birthday. She was blowing out the candles and wishing that things could always stay as they were. She'd loved her life then, before she really understood that she was the *housekeeper's daughter*.

That they were not a family.

Her heartbeat increased as she attempted to get her breathing under control. Stop the tears she knew were going to fall.

She held the photo close.

Wishes were for dreamers. She was a realist.

She looked at the sangoma's curse in the bin — she hadn't had a chance to burn it yet.

Well, the sangoma could dream on.

The owl couldn't call her name if she was not in the same area as it now, could it?

She stopped at the open door and looked back one last time at the place she'd been happy to call home, before she walked out of her room.

The female policeman still stood outside.

They made their way slowly down the passage, carrying her small suitcase. While her steps were silent, the policewoman's squeaked loudly beside her. Too soon they came to the main exit near the front door. She looked around one last time.

The walls were pristine and white. They did not show a mission in trouble, and neither must she.

This was her path she'd chosen to walk with her God. She lifted her head in pride, just as a courier *bakkie* drove in.

Detective Oliver Motsisi stepped into the driveway and stopped the driver.

"*Dumelong*. I came to collect a parcel. For Minister Thulas Masutha," the driver said.

Stella-Rose looked skywards. *Could it get any worse?*

"Here?" Detective Oliver Motsisi asked.

"*Yebo*, I always collect here for him," the driver said.

"Right. Let's see what you're collecting," Oliver said.

The courier walked up to Sister Mary-Jane who was standing wringing her hands. She pointed to a pile of boxes sitting just inside the front door.

Oliver walked to the first large box. He took his pen from his pocket and slipped it into the tape and opened the flaps. "Cash. A lot of it."

Rowan walked forward and looked at the pile of boxes. "And now we have the missing link we've been talking about. The payoff to the possible mastermind. Minister Thulas Masutha."

Stella-Rose silently cursed Thulas Masutha for always insisting on cash for their deals, and she laughed that the stupid policeman thought that Thulas was the mastermind. The minister didn't have an original thought in his head, other than cooking another meal to look like a recipe in a book.

She cursed Levi for his deposit into her account instead of a direct delivery of cash like normal.

The money should never have gone into her account.

Levi had left an electronic trail.

"Sister Mary-Jane, please take care of things while I'm gone," Stella-Rose said. "Sister Vannini has been delayed returning from her annual leave in Venice, so you'll need to take over as Acting Mother, until the church can send someone else to take my place."

"Yes, Mother Naude," Sister Mary-Jane said, taking the bunch of keys that Stella-Rose passed her. "Is there anyone I should call?"

"Perhaps Father Godfrey. Ask him to send me the church's lawyer. His number's in the phone book in the right-hand drawer of my desk."

"I will do that, Mother."

"Thank you, and bless you, my child," Stella-Rose said as she made a sign of a cross and kissed the top of Sister Mary-Jane's head that bent to her.

She held her case and walked, back straight and head high, to the police vehicle.

While they had not arrested her or put her in handcuffs, she knew there would be no returning.

She got into the back seat and looked forward.

From the mirror hung a small fluffy owl.

CHAPTER 43

Hartbeespoort Dam Area, North West Province, South Africa

11ᵗʰ May 2016 — 11 days after auction

Levi heard a small noise that woke him.

Metallic.

The dogs began barking.

He reached for his 9mm pistol that slept under his pillow. Checking his wife was in bed with him, he shook her and whispered, "Get in the bathroom. Lock the door. Someone's trying to open the gate."

She fled and he heard the click of the lock.

Scraping metal signaled that the gate had been manually opened, and the dogs went quiet. Either the intruder had thrown poison-laced steak for them, or slit their throats, either way, they had done their job. But he would miss them. The rottweilers always seemed happy to greet him when he came in at the end of the day.

He glanced out the big window of their bedroom that framed Harties dam. The sun was up. No burglar would be attempting to enter the premises in the light.

Police.

"Fuck," he said, shrugging into pants as quickly as he could, throwing on a shirt and pushing his feet into takkies. He opened the balcony door at the same time he heard the thunder of the breach ram against the front door splintering the lock and wood. Pulling the *Trellidor* slightly open, he slipped out. The sun hitting him in his eyes, he looked downwards and reached to where he'd ensured that he had a downpipe for escape.

He'd always had a plan for escape in every home he'd constructed over the years, and until today, had never had to use it.

Shimmying down, he could hear the police identify themselves inside, loud and proud, and he knew they couldn't see him as he clambered the three levels of artificial sandstone blocks and landed softly on the paving stones in the garden. He could stay in the shadow and slip over the bottom boundary wall if he kept close to the pool wall.

If he covered the razor wire with his shirt—

He had other clothes stashed further up the road.

His wife screamed as they smashed another door in his house.

Turning, he ran a few steps into the shade of the pool wall. Stopped. Realized that there was movement coming toward him.

Squinting, Levi finally comprehended that what he looked at was one of the Special Task Force trailing his rifle at him, moving quickly up the same slope that he'd planned to go down.

"Fuck," he said, pulling his 9mm from the trousers band.

He took its safely off and let rip with two shots.

The man dropped.

He ran forward. Downhill was his only escape.

He hadn't noticed another man behind the first; they had been moving in perfect tandem. The second shot him in his leg. The pain burnt, but he kept running, trying to aim at the policeman as he dodged from side to side. The next bullet brought him down as it smashed its way through his other thigh.

Levi landed hard on the pavers.

His gun skid out of his grip. He attempted to crawl after it.

If he could only get away.

The first policeman was obviously wearing a Kevlar vest as he appeared to gain his breath, and launched himself in a huge leap, smashing Levi in the face with his rifle and knocking him out.

CHAPTER 44

Pretoria Police station, South Africa

13th May, 2016 — 13 days after auction

Akina took a deep breath.

"I know you've been through so much," Chrystal said, "but the police need you to identify the men. We'll be with you the whole time. They can't see you through the glass. There will be other men in there with the monsters, so take your time. Make sure you point out the right one."

The lights were turned off in the viewing room. The only light came through the one-way glass separating them from the line-up area.

Akina began to shake. "Da-a-d, what if he gets me again?"

"He won't," Curtis said, hugging her tightly. "He'll go to jail for life for what he did to you and the other children."

Chrystal bent at the waist so that she was eye to eye with Akina. "Facing your fears after an experience like this is often harder than living through them. But you can do this. You can. I believe that you can; you are stronger than all of them together—"

Akina took another deep breath before she turned around to the glass, holding onto her dad's hand.

"Do you recognize any of the men?" Oliver asked.

Akina looked from man to man.

Left to right.

"You sure he doesn't know I'm here?" she asked.

"Pinky swear," Chrystal said as she held out her hand with only the little finger sticking out.

Akina held out her other hand to Chrystal and shook on the promise.

"That man is Tahaan. He drove us all over, before we tried to run away, and then Levi came," she said as she pointed him out. "He's shaved his silver beard off. But it's the same man."

"You're doing well, my angel," Curtis said.

"Number Five, step forward," Oliver said over the intercom.

"Remember," Rowan said. "He can't see you. You're safe here; they can't get to you anymore. You sure that's the man?"

Akina nodded.

There was no mistaking him. She'd lived under his thumb for most of the time. Tahaan was the one who'd cut her arm and removed the GPS tracker. She rubbed her scar.

"Take them away, bring in the next lot," Oliver said. "Let's get it over with as quickly as we can for her."

"It'll all be over soon," Curtis said. "Take deep breaths. It'll help calm you."

She took a moment to control her breathing. Making sure that it was normal, despite her heart racing.

She wanted this over with.

Watching the back of the first group of men as they were taken from the room, she wondered why Tahaan hadn't looked back.

Had she picked the wrong man?

Surely not?

The Tahaan she knew would have looked back to make sure whoever had pointed him out knew that he'd be coming from them.

She exhaled sharply as the next group was brought into the room, recognizing Levi instantly.

"It's okay, it's perfectly natural to have a response to facing the evil again after being safe away from it, but you can do this," Rowan said.

She nodded. She would never forget the man who had almost destroyed her.

"Number three is Levi," Akina whispered before Oliver even asked her.

"Number three, step forward," Oliver said over the intercom. Then to Akina, "Are you certain?"

Akina looked at Levi as he used crutches to move forward. The side of his face was badly bruised, and he had a black eye. But the was no mistaking him.

Not the tattoos sticking out from his shirt or those on his face.

Not the arrogant look on his face.

This man had cut off Cherri's ear.

He'd almost beaten her to death when Cherri had got away.

He had left her with the nun in Venice to be sold as a human slave.

She would always bear the scar from where he burnt her.

Anger rolled up from her stomach and across her chest.

Hurt. Humiliation.

Unimaginable anguish for what had happened to her at his hand.

The hot tears of relief that she was away from him and every dark thing that he touched ran down her face, and she let them fall on the floor.

He was in police custody.

She finally knew that she really was safe.

"I'm glad someone hurt him. I wish they'd beaten him more and then killed him." Akina dragged her eyes away from Levi to see Chrystal smiling down at her.

Oliver was tired. He'd been at this for over twenty-four hours with no sleep.

"Tell me again, Mr. Louw, who did you sell Akina to?"

"I told you; I don't know what you are talking about," Levi said.

"Fine, another night in jail." A small knock sounded. Oliver went to the door and opened it. He stepped outside, so that Levi couldn't hear the conversation.

"There's a suggestion from his wife. Mrs. Louw thinks that perhaps he'll talk to Chrystal Booysen," one of the other detectives said.

"Why?"

"Interesting backstory here. One you'll soon understand. But you will need to let her in there, no way anyone else will get the reaction from him. Trust me on this one."

"Fine," Oliver said. "Bring her."

He waited outside the room until the detective brought Chrystal to him. He had to admire her; this was a woman who could probably outshoot, outrun and most likely outmaneuver his every move, and yet instead of being out there fighting for the highest bidder, she was in their police station, having fought to find one little girl. Despite the odds, it was as if she and Rowan had found a sandstone brick in the middle of the Kalahari.

"Look," Chrystal said as she opened her file and showed him a few pictures. "I visited his wife. Let's say Mrs. Louw was surprised and leave it at that."

He looked between her and the pictures, and then he smiled.

"Usually, I wouldn't let a civilian into this room, but you clearly have the skills, and can look after yourself. I'll be close by, but I have a feeling you were born to play this role today. Keep out of his way, make sure he doesn't get hold of your pen or anything that can help him in any way. Understood?"

"Clear as a bell," she said.

Chrystal took the interrogation chair.

"You got to be kidding me? What is this? A joke? You bringing in spectators?"

Oliver could see that his body language had changed. He sat up straighter. His shoulders back.

"Do you know Ms. Booysen?" Oliver asked.

"She looks familiar, but I don't know her," Levi said.

"She has some questions for you." Oliver rubbed his hands over his face. "Can you at least try and answer them?"

"Perhaps. Depends what they are," Levi said.

"I've never met you in person before, is that correct Mr. Louw?" Chrystal said.

He leaned forward for a second, and then he leaned back in his chair as if checking his behavior. "That's right, yes."

"Can you tell me who this is?" she asked as she put a series of photos on the table in front of his handcuffed hands.

"My wife."

Now Oliver could see him starting to move uncomfortably in his chair. He was interested in the pictures, whether he wanted to show it or not.

Chrystal leaned toward him. "Think hard on every picture."

Levi looked at her. "I told you, my wife." He moved in his chair again and began rocking.

"Do you recognize this photo?" she asked, putting down another picture. This time he stilled.

There was a long pause before he spoke. "My wife, when she was younger?"

Oliver looked at the older photo and then at Chrystal.

"That's my wife too," he said as he slammed himself into the back part of his chair. His expression didn't change.

Oliver could have sworn it was Chrystal.

"She changed a lot don't you think, between this photo and that one?" Chrystal said. "Now, she looks almost exactly like me, don't you think?"

"Coincidence," Levi said.

"And this one?" She put down a more recent photo of his wife, this time with bruising from recent plastic surgery.

"My wife. And I had to pay for all that plastic work, the stupid bitch."

He was calling his wife names, now that was an interesting development. She brought back the last picture.

"So how do you think Dr. Miller, the plastic surgeon, got this picture of your wife, years before she looked a little like that?"

"No fucking clue," Levi spat out, and he glanced at Oliver, then looked back at Chrystal.

"Do you know who Dr. Miller said gave him the picture?"

He shrugged.

"You. He says this is what you asked him to make her look like," Chrystal said. "The woman in this picture. That's me. I even remembered the day that Eric took it — it was shortly before he stole the farm's savings from our account and landed up in jail. Incidentally, the same jail you were in — I believe you were there, together, before his demise."

Levi rocked more. Flicked his thumbnail and his fingernail together. "What does this have to do with anything?" Levi asked. "Time's up for the police. They have to put me in front of a judge, and he'll grant bail. My wife will post it, no matter how much it is."

Chrystal sat still in her chair. "Wrong on both accounts. Your wife gave me a message for you. 'You're not my *Skattie*. You're dead to me. I'm keeping that money you put into my account, the house in Harties, and all the trucks, at least. I will not be posting your bail. You'll hear from my divorce lawyer shortly.' I think those were her exact words. No wait, she also said something along the lines of, but I'm paraphrasing this part — at least now she knows who you like using as a punching bag, the woman in the photo and not her. It made her life mean a little more."

He jerked against the restraints, his face red. "You bitch. What did you say to her? She is not getting a divorce from me."

"You pathetic man, after all the times you pulverized her face, you still think she has to ask for your permission? No one wants to be confronted with the original when they have been made into a replica," Chrystal said, and she stood up. "I guess the reality is no bail, which means back into the prison system and a happy reunion with the old gang members. Shame. Poor Levi, always the victim in his own eyes."

Now he was physically fighting his restraints.

Chrystal leaned halfway across the table, and without changing the volume of her voice, she said, "You could always roll on your partners. Tell us who paid you for Akina Wilson in Venice? Help the judge, they might take it easier on you — cooperate with us. Don't be the fall guy."

Levi looked at her.

"I don't know."

Chrystal smiled. "I hear that there are certain gang members, already getting an erection over the fact that you're coming back to them."

He glared at her.

"A judge can put you in a different prison. If you give us the information we want — tell me who bought her outside the auction."

He stared at her. Eyes running over her from head to toe, his expression pure lust.

Oliver had to give her credit, she didn't even flinch. Although he was sure she wanted to punch Levi's nose into his brain.

"Different prison?"

"Sure," Chrystal said, leaning closer to him and lowering her voice.

Even to Oliver, she sounded sexy as hell. He shifted the weight from one foot to another and held his breath. There was an extradition on these kidnappers already. The Hague was going to process them, not South Africa. Technically, Chrystal wasn't lying.

"The director of the auction, Matteo, bought the Asian brat. He told me we wouldn't get nearly as much at auction, then after he bought her, that slut of his Brigette sent a note that someone would pay five million." Now he'd started talking, it was as if he couldn't keep the anger inside.

"Five million US dollars. I got to the house to fetch her back from them, but those Nuns, they hid her away, and then the fucking Italian police arrived and stormed all over it. I don't care if he rots in jail. He stole two million dollars from me."

"And there you have it," Chrystal said as she turned and walked out of the room.

Slam dunk.

That round goes to the police, for now, until they can find out from Brigette and Matteo who the real buyer behind them was, Oliver thought as he watched Levi deflate and slump in his chair.

Chrystal walked out of the interrogation room and leaned against the wall. Levi Louw's shirt had been unbuttoned, when she'd leaned in close, she'd seen his neck. There was no mistaking that the tattoo of a crystal in prime position represented her, not with the evidence from his wife that he'd been pretending all these years, that his wife was her.

And she had no idea he even existed.

A stalker in the dark.

And the words of Busi came washing over her: "Beware of the one who wears you on his skin. He is a *nyoga*, and he watches you, always."

CHAPTER 45

Victoria Falls, Zambian Side

25th May, 2016

Chrystal stood at the edge of Victoria Falls. Millions of gallons of water rushed past her and down into the gorge below. She looked over the 354-foot drop down over the edge into deep pools.

This was what Wes wanted.

She had to keep this part of her promise, even if she couldn't bring his heart home.

The thunder of the water drowned out everything, even the birds' song, but she could feel the warm African sun and the soft droplets of water that kissed all over her face. They ran together, forming rivulets on her skin.

She looked down.

Water dripped from the bottom of her Kevlar pants on to her boots, and back into the water stream to plunge down again.

"You can do this," Rowan said beside her, his hand lightly touching her back. "I'm here. You're not alone."

She turned her head and looked into his green eyes and knew that she was doing the right thing.

It was time.

Not only to say goodbye to Wes and keep her promise, but to turn that new leaf.

To embrace life again.

Rowan's head came down and he kissed her, just lightly at first, testing her lips, making sure she was okay with the contact, then deeper. He held her close, then slowly, lightened the kiss.

"I have faith in you. Let go of the past. Time to step into the future." He touched his forehead to hers then let his arms fall beside his body. She missed the contact and warmth of his hands immediately. "I'm right here when you need me."

She took in a deep breath and pushed all thoughts aside.

Rowan was right.

Today was about Wes. About her. About the past.

Rowan belonged to the future.

She needed to heal in order to continue to function as a decent human going forward. And the way to do that was to say her final goodbye.

Let go of something that no longer belonged to her.

Wesley.

She turned toward the water.

Taking the small box from her pocket, she removed a leather pouch. Held it to her heart, then to her lips. She kissed it before sprinkling the powder that Busi had given her.

Finally, she knelt beside the pool of water. Lowered the dried blood-soaked bandanna. Slowly, she put her hand into the water.

It rushed over the pouch, soaking it.

"I kept my promise, not in the way you wanted, but I brought you home," she said. "You're safe, Wes. You sacrificed your life for us, but I didn't want to let you go these last two years. I wanted you close, not only because I loved you, but also to remind me that I had been loved. I was more than just Savannah. You'll never know what it took from me to keep my promise to you but know that I'm setting you free. I've kept my promise to bring you home, to your home country, to the place where you were happiest as a child. The place you always talked about returning to one day. Your day has come, and although there'll never be a white cross on this watery grave, I know that you'll be here in the bush, with your tiger fish, elephant and hippos that you loved so much.

"You need to know we found the bastard who betrayed us. Being honest, it wasn't about us at all. It was all about gun running. We just got caught in the crossfire." She took a deep shuddering breath and looked across the river.

An elephant had stepped out of the lush bush and had waded into a pool on the edge. It looked at her, its trunk smelling the air, checking on her. Urging her to continue talking.

To make her peace.

"If that's you, Wes, know that I need to free my heart and forgive myself for trying to do what you asked of me. I love you, Wes. You'll always hold a special place in my heart. Forever." She opened her hand and watched Wesley's bandanna get swept away in the water, and slowly gain momentum from the rock pool to plunge over the edge of the falls.

She washed her hands in the cool water of the falls as if removing the last of his blood. "*Mosi-oa-Tunya* holds your soul now. May Nyami-Nyami protect you and open your eyes once again to the beauty that is the real Africa. The Africa where you are free."

EPILOGUE

The sangoma's song

Busi looked at the rusted tin box in her hands. Hidden inside, she knew that the golden *inkonkoni* still scowled.

She whispered to it, "I know she is not finished. And I understand that I need to give you to the children's champion to make sure that you are safe. There are rumblings here. The drums beat for change. The earth bleeds and trouble is coming.

"Remember when I first buried you, when I settled at Leopard Hill farm? It was my haven, away from the world, after my husband died. I put you deep in the ground so that no one could steal you away from me. Now I need to rejoin that world. My daughter and my granddaughter need me. You will not be safe with me.

"The time has come for you to travel with the champion. She has a modern safe in her house that you can hide in, so that no one steals you and puts you in a museum or a glass case. One day she will understand the legend, one day I will get to tell her the whole story.

"But I promise you, I am coming back for you, my beautiful golden *inkonkoni*. Once she no longer needs your wisdom and strength inside of her, once she has finished protecting the children. You must stay with her until the war drums stop. Then I will come back. It is my duty to pass you to the next sangoma. But now is not the right time — you are needed here with the champion."

She tapped the box once. "You take care of her. Help her. She has done more for our people's children than I knew to expect from her."

Busi walked to outside Chrystal's room, placed the box on the floor at the base of her door and tapped lightly so that only she would hear. Then she walked out the house, and back into the night.

She turned around only once and shook her *ishoba*.

The dogs began to bark, and the night noises returned. Lights came on.

Chrystal had found the box and was reading the note she'd left:

To Chrystal of the Savannah, our children's champion

Look after the Golden *Inkonkoni*. She is sacred to my people.
The war drums still beat.
Her place is with you for this fight. One day I will return when
    there is peace to pass her to the next in succession.

Keep her safe.

Your friend,
Busi

GLOSSARY

baie – Afrikaans – very

bakkie – South African Slang, a Pick Up truck, a 4x4

Bar-One – like a Mars bar – caramel and chocolate bar.

Bonsella – Ndebele – Present. Gift.

Capo della Polizia – Direttore Generale della Pubblica Sicurezza - Italian - The Commissioner of Police – Director General of Public Security.

Cha– Zulu – No

Dhow – a ship with slanted triangular sails. Of Arab origin.

Divina-Saint – Italian – divine – saint – (like a saint, wanting to be godlike for the purpose of this book).

Ingqwele - Zulu - Champion.

Inkonkoni – Zulu – Wildebeest

ishoba – Zulu - Wildebeest tail hair used as a wand by a sangoma to swish away bad spirits.

Jislaaik – A South African expression. Pronounced "Yis-like", it is an expression of astonishment.

Lackeys – Afrikaans – junior workers

Mosi-oa-Tunya – *Ndebele* – 'The Smoke that Thunders' is the name for Victoria Falls.

Nyami-Nyami – *Ndebele* – The snake god of the Ndebele that protects the Zambezi river.

Nyoga – Zulu – snake

perle sacre – *Italian* – sacred pearls – a beaded prayer necklace.

Polizia di Stato – Italian – Italian State Police – responsible as an arm of the police force for policing duties, to cities and large towns, and with its child agencies. It is also responsible for highway patrol (*autostrade),* railways (*ferrovie*), airports (*aeroporti*), customs (together with the *Guardia di Finanza*) as well as certain waterways and assisting the local police forces.

Skattie – Afrikaans - A term of endearment like darling.

Skinder – Afrikaans – for gossip.

Sunlight soap – a washing bar of green soap used for body and clothes, everything from washing dishes to making your stomach work. A miracle cleans and fixes all, soap.

Takkies – South African slang – Trainers, joggers.

Trellidor – South Africa trade name of a concertina style security gate.

Ubaba - Zulu – Father

úgógo – Zulu - Grandmother

Vrot – Afrikaans - rotten

Waai – South Africa slang – let's go.

Zamalek – South African Breweries, Carling Black Label beer – After the soccer World Cup in 2010, South Africans have renamed the brew because its label sports is the same red and black colors as those of the top Egyptian team, Zamalek.

FACT VS FICTION

While the golden wildebeest legend is not a traditional story — it's fictional — the golden wildebeest statue was modeled on the Golden Rhinoceros of Mapungubwe, which is real.

The golden wildebeest is a rare variation/mutation in color from the blue wildebeest.

Child trafficking is real. "Statistics released by the South African Police Service Missing Persons Bureau for 2013, say that a child goes missing every five hours in South Africa. 77% of children are found. 23% of the children are never located. Trafficking in children is a global problem. UNICEF estimates there are as many as 1.2 million children being trafficked every year."
~ Forgood.co.za

THULA BABA

A traditional African song

Thula thul, thula baba, thula sana,
Thul'ubab uzobuya, ekuseni.
Thula thul, thula baba, thula sana,
Thul'ubab uzobuya, ekuseni.

Kukh'inkanyezi, zi-holel' ubaba,
Zimkhanyisela indlel'e ziyak-haya,
Sobe sikhona ka bonke bushoyo,
Bayathi buyela. Ubuye le ikhaya.

Thula thula thula baba,
Thula thula thula sana.

Thula thul, thula baba, thula sana,
Thul'ubab uzobuya, ekuseni.
Thula thul, thula baba, thula sana,
Thul'ubab uzobuya, ekuseni.

Kukh'inkanyezi, zi-holel' ubaba,
Zimkhanyisela indlel'e ziyak-haya,
Sobe sikhona ka bonke bashoyo,
Bayathi buyela. Ubuye le ikhaya.

Thula thula thula baba,
Thula thula thula sana.

Thula thul, thula baba, thula sana,
Thul'ubab uzobuya, ekuseni.
Thula thul, thula baba, thula sana,
Thul'ubab uzobuya, ekuseni.

Kukh'inkanyezi, zi-holel' ubaba,
Zimkhanyisela indlel'e ziyak-haya,
Sobe sikhona ka bonke bashoyo,
Bayathi buyela. Ubuye le ikhaya.

Thula thula thula baba,
Thula thula thula sana.

Thula thul, thula baba, thula sana,
Thul'ubab uzobuya, ekuseni.
Thula thul, thula baba, thula sana,
Thul'ubab uzobuya, ekuseni.

Kukh'inkanyezi, zi-holel' ubaba,
Zimkhanyisela indlel'e ziyak-haya,
Sobe sikhona ka bonke bashoyo,
Bayathi buyela. Ubuye le ikhaya.

Thula thula thula baba,
Thula thula thula sana.

Hush, hush, hush-a-bye little man, be quiet baby,
Be quiet, Daddy will be back in the morning.
Hush, hush, hush-a-bye little man, be quiet baby,
Be quiet, Daddy will be back in the morning.

There's a star that will draw him home.
It will illuminate his path home to
Where we are. All will urge on,
They'll say, go back. He returned to this home.

Hush, hush-a-bye baby
Hush, hush-a-bye baby.

Hush, hush, hush-a-bye little man, be quiet baby,
Be quiet, Daddy will be back in the morning.
Hush, hush, hush-a-bye little man, be quiet baby,
Be quiet, Daddy will be back in the morning.

There's a star that will draw him home.
It will illuminate his path home to
Where we are. All will urge on,
They'll say, go back. He returned to this home.

Hush, hush-a-bye baby
Hush, hush-a-bye baby.

Hush, hush, hush-a-bye little man, be quiet baby,
Be quiet, Daddy will be back in the morning.
Hush, hush, hush-a-bye little man, be quiet baby,
Be quiet, Daddy will be back in the morning.

There's a star that will draw him home.
It will illuminate his path home to
Where we are. All will urge on,
They'll say, go back. He returned to this home.

Hush, hush-a-bye baby

Hush, hush-a-bye baby.

Hush, hush, hush-a-bye little man, be quiet baby,
Be quiet, Daddy will be back in the morning.
Hush, hush, hush-a-bye little man, be quiet baby,
Be quiet, Daddy will be back in the morning.

There's a star that will draw him home.
It will illuminate his path home to
Where we are. All will urge on,
They'll say, go back. He returned to this home.

Hush, hush-a-bye baby
Hush, hush-a-bye baby.

ACKNOWLEDGMENTS

As always, it takes many people to make a book happen.

Thank you for being there, my long-suffering writing friends, especially Gayle Ash, Robyn Grady, Amy Andrews, Rachel Bailey and Alli Sinclair. Whenever I need my writing butt kicked, these are the people to do it.

My online sprint partners Joss Wood and Katherine Garbera. Thanks for keeping the momentum going.

Thank you to Richard Morton and the Morton family from Tembani Wildlife in Thabazimbi, South Africa, who embraced this author like she was family and shared so much of themselves with me, including their Golden Wildebeest.

To Steve Delport and Amanda Marler who treated me to an amazing dinner, and one of the best ox tail stews ever! And they introduced me to Matthew Marler, who I shamelessly pumped for information on armored vehicles. Any mistakes are mine — and in no way his. I constantly smile every time I think of Zamalek beers, and the shock on his face that I didn't know what they were.

Mel Kruuse, for being an all-over amazing person. Driving literally thousands of kilometers so I wasn't traveling alone, taking so many photos and videos while I talked and talked. For just going everywhere and doing everything we could. You were such an important part of my research team during my South Africa solo trip in 2020. I had a ball with you as my co-conspirator — we need to do it again one day!

Helicopter pilot Gary Fonternel, for his help and expertise in his field.

Clay Stafford and the Killer Nashville team, for awarding this book in its unpublished state a Claymore Award in 2022 for Best Action Adventure. Nashville people were so lovely and hospitable, and it made me so proud to be a part of the writing family that spans across the world.

My independent team: Thank you guys — every single one of you!

Editing by the amazing Sali Powers (who introduced me to Voxer and all things voice messages) and final proofreading by Madeline Ash (whose eagle eyes for details slay me...), both from Creating Ink. If there are mistakes now, they are all mine – not theirs!

My beta readers: Jane Alexander, Sam Eeles, Petro Grobbelar, and Jen McDowell. Thank you!

Debbie Kahl for checking my Japanese.

Josie Montano for checking my Italian.

To all my readers, who have hung in there with me over the last three years, checking in, asking how I was, asking me where the next book was. The contact with every single person was so important on this journey of the new book, and on my expansion into independent publishing. Thank you from the bottom of my heart.

My sons Kyle and Barry, who both grew over six feet tall, giving me a signal that this was the right time to write this story. I love you guys and your belief that other than singing badly, I could do anything else I wanted to.

My husband Shaun, for 'wrapping me in cotton balls' when it was needed over the last three years, and then standing beside me to 'break out' once I was strong enough again. For challenging me, constantly and learning new computer skills so I can continue to write what I want to. Love you — always!

Shadows Over Africa

MY BROTHER–BUT–ONE

**An epic saga exploring the violence
And traditions of rural Africa.**

T.M. CLARK

ISIPHO RODNEY NUBE

1941

'The earth rejects your sacrifice. Like only a few children before him, this white son of yours has lived. You have offered him for three days and nights, yet he survives. The cats do not want him, nor do the scavengers. Even the sun has not taken his life. Pick up your baby, Moswena,' the sangoma instructed, 'he has earned his right to life. You must take him back to your breast, before you offend the earth and she sends drought or floods to our tribe.'

The first-time mother snatched the naked baby from the flat rock and cradled him in her arms. Immediately, the albino began to scream, his skin badly sunburned. With haste, she arranged her son in a *kaross* made of soft animal hide and secured him on her back. She rocked back and forth to quieten him. She knew children must not scream in the sangoma's presence.

The sangoma turned to her and without warning, lashed out savagely with his *knopkierie*, hitting her on the front of her body. Blood seeped from the lacerations as the sangoma rained down his personal disgust. She kept her front exposed to him, knowing that if the large knot of wood at the end of the stick hit her son, his skull would be smashed.

'He might have escaped his death today, Moswena, but life will not be kind to you now that he lives. The tribe will hate you and this child. He's a bad *tokoloshe* that brings destruction and death to all around him. The white people will never accept him as anything but a *kaffir*, so do not look to them for help. Tomorrow, you must leave this kraal forever. You are cast out for giving birth to such a child and bringing shame to our tribe.'

The tears streamed down Moswena's face, but she kept her eyes downcast. She knew better than to argue with the sangoma. He was the tribe's almighty healer, the doctor, and the link to her ancestors. Her people would never protect her from him; he was almost more powerful than their chief. When he was finished with her, she turned her back to him and trudged down the kopje, the well-worn red dirt path towards her *ikhaya* in the kraal.

He rushed past her, almost tripping her up in his haste to tell the tribe about the banishment. To instil fear into anyone who attempted to help the outcasts. Moswena straightened her back as she passed the dense thornbush fencing that signalled the perimeter of the kraal, and moved inside.

No one looked at her, their faces averted. Already she wasn't welcome. Her own mother and sisters could not come near to comfort her or help, for the banishment made her invisible even to them. To acknowledge her presence meant they would also become outcasts. This was tradition; the sangoma's whim was law.

Moswena entered her hut. She lowered herself onto the small grass mat she'd woven as a wedding present to her new husband and sat in the traditional position, legs out straight, crossed over at the ankles. A single tear ran down her left cheek. She tried not to think of the man she still loved. Her hands shaking with the pain and anger burning inside her, she took her son from her back and brought him to the front of her battered body. He lay against her, unmoving, and didn't attempt to latch onto her engorged breast. Three days without her milk being suckled had brought her great pain. Pain as she'd never experienced before—worse than any beating she'd ever received—and heat hotter than any summer she'd lived through. Her breasts felt as though red coals had been laid on them. The new beating she'd received from the sangoma had made the ache worse. Huge angry welts rose on her copper skin.

She fought the pain. Her baby's fluids were of greater importance. She squeezed her nipple and warm milk jetted out in an arc, showering his small face and running down his neck. As the pressure eased, he was able to latch on and feed. Spots of black and purple swirled and closed in around her as the pain ravaged her body. Moswena pushed it away with a deep groan in her throat, curling her fingers and toes and straightening them again.

Once her son was content and sleeping, she stood up and looked down at her legs. Her bare calves no longer bore the ribbons of gut and fur, decorations that an unmarried *tombe* wore. They were bare.

Just like her *ikhaya*, and her heart.

A husband dead in a great war with the Zulus somewhere far away, and a son no one wanted.

Banished.

Her husband had paid a large *lobola* for her just a few months ago. Twelve cattle. The whole tribe had celebrated with a party. A prize ox had been bled and then slaughtered.

Now she was a nothing. A no one.

Dead to everyone living, except her tiny son.

She smeared some root *umuthi* over her baby's skin to ease the discomfort of his sunburn. Satisfied she'd helped him as much as she could, she packed her meagre belongings: her husband's assegai, a few skin skirts and treasured beads. She gathered what little food there was and placed it carefully in her cooking gourd. She rewrapped her son in the *kaross* and tied him onto her back, with only his head poking out from the soft skins and tightened the leather below her breasts. Lastly, she rolled up her grass sleeping mat.

Balancing her life's possessions on her head, Moswena stepped out of her *ikhaya*. No one looked at her. With confidence and purpose, she walked to the fire pit in the communal area and picked up a burning stick. No one stopped her as she strode back to her hut and lit the dried thatch roof. By the time the other villagers realised she'd started a fire in the centre of their kraal she was walking away.

As she climbed the kopje where her child had recently lain open to the elements, she looked back at the large kraal she'd called home since her birth. Slowly she smiled. Other huts near hers had caught fire, and the flames were spreading. She watched as the villagers who wouldn't look at her scrambled to put out the flames. With delight she noticed that the sangoma's hut was burning. He tried to beat it out with a wet cattle skin. None of his black magic could help him now.

Adjusting the bundle of belongings on her head, she raised her voice so her son could hear.

'Come, *Isipho*, my gift. We must search for a friendlier home.'

ZOL NDHLOVU

1966

Zol heard himself breathe. He wasn't dead. He needed to shinny up a tree before the hyenas found him.

A blood-red blur and pain ended his attempt to open his eyes. His fingers hung limp, broken. He gently rubbed the palm of the opposite hand against his fingers to count them. One, two, three ... ten. At least they hadn't cut them off. He probed his face with the back of his hands. His cheekbones weren't shattered but his face was swollen and disfigured from the beating he'd taken. Hesitantly, he slid his hands around to his ears. Relief swept through him; they were still there.

Rising to a sitting position, he checked his toes. Broken, but still there. Nothing had been hacked off; he was lucky. Taking a deep breath, he used one hand to lift the other and attempted to straighten his right index finger.

He passed out.

In the darkness behind his closed eyelids, Zol regained consciousness. He sat up to take the pressure off his bruised shoulder, and after a few attempts he managed to stand. He hobbled forward, gently freewheeling his arms about, hoping to bump into a tree to seek refuge in.

He heard an animal snort nearby. Not a hyena or a leopard. It sounded more like a zebra. Zol wished he could smell through his rearranged nose, but broken and swollen shut, it was no use. He crept forward, figuring the animal would move out of his way. But he felt warm fur on his arm and the animal breathed deeply, as if its nostrils flared against him, and he heard a snort.

Leather. He felt leather. He'd stumbled into a domesticated animal.

Groping more, he felt a knee-length leather boot, and a rifle carrier ...

Stories of the Dragoons of Angola and their demon horses who would run through fire and buildings had been recounted in the training camp. They were part of the Portuguese army. Images of slaughter and chaos flashed behind his closed lids, and he dropped to his knees, praying to his ancestors, to the Christian God, Jesus, and to Allah all at once.

A deep laugh cut through the silence of the bush.

He was in trouble. Today, he was going to die.

'East is in the opposite direction, boy,' the man said. 'And it doesn't look like your ancestors were doing any watching over you either.'

Leather creaked as a weight shifted then a muffled thud signalled the man had dismounted.

'Move over, Vic,' the man said to his horse as he rummaged in a saddle-bag. The sound of enamel crockery clanging together was loud. Then the splash of liquid, a foreign noise. A cup was held against his lips. The cool liquid soothed his parched throat. Zol drank deeply.

'Slowly, boy. Slowly. Where are you heading?'

He was going to die anyway. He had nothing to hide from this man who spoke Swahili and his demon-horse, so he opened his mouth and told the truth. 'Home.'

The man gently touched around his eye. Zol flinched, both from the contact and the pain. He sucked a quick breath in through his teeth.

'Not broken, but darn close. From the blackness of your skin, you are far from your homeland. Where was home?'

Zol dropped down onto his haunches. 'Lake Tanganyika. That was before they came and took me away. I was trying to get back.'

'Lift your face to the sky.'

Water cascaded over Zol's head. The man blotted the blood from his eyes, then his cheeks. Zol opened his eyes a slit, his vision was still blurred, and the pain of a million daggers stabbed into his brain. He closed them again and hung his head in defeat, still blind to what the man looked like. His voice was deep and rich, but he spoke Swahili almost as if it was his native language, although some of the pronunciation of the clicks in his dialect were louder than needed, formed with the side of the mouth, not his tongue. But obviously a man who spoke many languages well.

'You can forget using your eyes for a while. Who left you to die?'

Zol took a deep breath, uncertain how to answer the stranger who helped him. He dreaded being kept alive for information and then slaughtered later. This was how it felt to be an animal caught in a snare. When your life is held in the palm of the hunter.

'Don't lie to me, boy. Who did this?'

'My comrades.'

'That figures. They stole your pack and shoes too?'

'They took them as punishment for deserting.'

'Thought so. Hold steady ...' The man held Zol's left hand in both of his and pulled the pinkie finger straight.

Zol saw blinding stars.

'Welcome back,' said a rich voice with a slight accent.

Zol remembered where he was.

He lifted his hand to his face. Bandages covered his eyes and his fingers were bound. Splinted straight. Reaching down, he found the same with his toes.

Dread clenched his stomach, uncertainty about his life niggled in his head. He'd heard that the men with the iron-shoed demons massacred entire villages, even ran down children with their horses. Why was a man like that helping him? He trembled as renewed fear raked through him.

A large warm hand fell on his shoulder. 'Easy, easy. Come, drink this soup. You need to get strong again.'

Zol breathed deeply. What if the man wanted him strong so that he could hunt him down again when he drained the information from inside his head? Testing his theory, Zol volunteered, 'I don't know any information. Soon you will kill me anyway.'

'That depends on you, boy.'

Zol wondered about that, but already the man had shown him compassion beyond anything he'd received outside of his village.

'Tell me about when they took you. How long ago was that?'

'Three moons ago. I am fifteen summers old.'

'Only fifteen years old. Go on.'

'The communist freedom fighters drove through our village. They made promises to my mother.'

'Guess you know now they don't keep them?' The man snorted like his horse, and the horse answered him with a snort of her own. The air was filled with a rich belly laugh. 'Yes, Your Highness. It's been just you and me for too long.'

Zol wondered about this man who was tending to him like a veterinarian would an injured animal, straightening his bones, bandaging his wounds. He communicated with his horse as if she were human. Perhaps the stories of the demon-horses had been exaggerated. Or perhaps not. But this man wasn't trying to harm him.

'They executed my cousin for refusing to join them. Right there, near the cooking fire. They put a gun to his head and shot him when he said he wanted to stay and be a fisherman. I didn't want to die.'

'Good choice.' The rim of the tin cup pressed against his lips again. 'Drink. It's cool enough not to burn you.'

Zol drank. Feeling hard biscuit touch his lips, he ate too. Swallowing was difficult.

Refilling the cup with water, the man again held the rim at his mouth. 'Where did they train you to fight?'

Zol sipped the water. It slid down his throat easily, clearing away the biscuit. 'They took me to a camp far away from my home. They taught me how to fight and shoot. They taught me how to kill people and how to move in the bush like an animal. They made the fisher boy into a man.'

The man snorted again. 'Killing people doesn't make you a man. You are just a boy with a gun.'

'They told me I was ready to fight for freedom, and gave me a full pack of rations and boots on my feet.'

The air around him swirled as the man took the empty cup and walked away, this time to refill it from a pack on his horse. A sound of a different container opened and shut. The horse stomped one leg as if irritated, or to dislodge an unwelcome bug.

'Here you go, Vic. You know I'd never forget you.' Zol heard the man patting the horse, his voice soothing. When he returned, he put the cup at Zol's lips once again. 'Drink. You need liquids. It's sweet. It'll help.'

Zol drank the sugared water.

'So tell me, how did you manage to get all the way down Africa to the Caprivi Strip?' He took the empty cup and sat on the ground, a dull thunk signalling the direction of his resting place close by.

'It took many days in a cattle truck. But as soon as the others began to disperse into the bush, I left. I was going home.'

'That's a long walk, boy. Lots of unrest between here and there, and you probably had no money.'

'Anywhere is better than with them.'

He felt the man touch his forehead, his hand cool as he lifted the bandage to gauge his temperature. 'So, do you want to run back to your village, a coward and a deserter? Or do you want revenge on these men who have caused you such harm?'

Zol knew the answer. A deep hatred for the men who had taken him from his home burned low in his belly. Joined now by a raw revulsion for the albino, the leader of the group of men who'd left him for dead in the bush. It was the albino who had broken Zol's fingers and toes, one at a time, and laughed while he crippled a fellow human. A comrade.

In reality, he couldn't just go home. Not now. They would find him again. Perhaps after another beating they might take him back to their camp for retraining. Or they might kill him on sight. But he knew deep in his gut that he wanted the men responsible for his cousin's death dead. That would be better than fresh summer mopane worms in winter. 'Revenge.'

'You make good choices. A survivor. Like me. What's your name?'

'Zol Ndhlovu.'

'Zol.' He felt his arm being clenched in a manly grip. 'A good strong name for a man about to change his life. I'm Charlie. My horse is Victoria. Don't ever cross me, or you're dead. Welcome to the Decker family.'

CHAPTER 1

1995

Scott Decker watched Kevin's plane buzz the impala grazing on the airfield's short grass. The honey-brown buck flicked up their white tails and scattered in all directions, as if a giant predator was after them. The baboons scavenging alongside the runway easily loped away on all fours. Once into the safety of the thicker bush, they turned to bare yellowed teeth at the intruder.

The Cessna straightened up, circled around once, and touched down on the grass. Bumping its way along the runway, its engine changed pitch as Kevin eased off the throttle and coasted to a stop.

Scott shook his head, smiling that Kevin had inflicted his oldest plane on yet another of the new volunteers, giving them a false picture of what were acceptable standards in Africa. Most of the international volunteers were so green on arrival that they didn't look further than the cracked windscreen and peeling paint. But the engine on the old Cessna was in tip-top condition and serviced by the same top-class aviation mechanics who serviced their fleet of charter jets.

Kevin hopped out and walked around to the passenger's side. He unbound the door from the outside and yanked it open. 'Told you my bush mechanics would work. Wire is the backbone of Africa. It holds everything together.'

Scott chuckled as he climbed out of his blue four-wheel drive *bakkie*. He watched as Kevin offered his hand, and a woman stepped down onto terra firma.

Scott walked closer. 'Hey Kevin.' His attention was focused on the blonde, her eyes as green as the new grass after a fire. A bright red t-shirt, varnished red fingernails and long shapely calves that extended from a knee-length khaki skirt to red socks that stuck out of neat ankle boots, everything about her screamed city-girl. He would bet his ranch that her toenails matched those flashy fingernails.

The aircraft hold clanked open and Kevin dropped a crate onto the runway. 'Your supplies came through. Give me a hand, Scott. A storm's been on our tail all the way. I need to tie my plane down ASAP.'

'Just a minute.' Scott was still focused on the woman in front of him. 'Where's my volunteer?'

Kevin jerked his thumb at the woman.

She slid her dark glasses up the bridge of her nose. 'Hi. I'm Ashley Twine.'

Surely there had to be a mistake, he thought. He would never have given permission for a female volunteer to join his program. Women and the African bush simply don't fit together. No way. Caught totally off guard, with a scowl on his forehead and a headache already drumming at the base of his skull, he stared at her.

She took her sunglasses off. 'Ashley Twine,' she repeated a little louder, 'reporting for duty.'

Scott's heart dropped. 'But you're female!'

He noticed her outstretched hand drop to her side and confusion cloud her eyes as she straightened her back, gaining a few centimetres in height as if preparing for an argument.

'You don't say?' One perfectly groomed eyebrow rose as she spoke and her megawatt smile sent shivers down his body. Her Australian drawl was as alluring as her smile. Given the right circumstances, he could listen to her talk forever.

But she was not what he needed this week. He ground his teeth. How had he made such a gigantic mistake?

Kevin rescued him, filling in the uncomfortable silence. 'Don't mind Scott. Usually he's a real hit with the ladies, with those big baby blues 'n' all.

Give him a chance to get used to that halo of blonde hair and he won't let you go home after your month of volunteering is up.'

Okay, perhaps not exactly rescued—Kevin had just sunk him deeper than the Chinhoyi Caves. The drought project was too important to be messed up. He'd had too many experiences of being let down by females in his life, and no way was he going to let yet another one disappoint him. Females all followed the same well-established pattern: they came; they attempted to stay; but ultimately, they hated his Africa and left.

'Kev, get back in your ramshackle tin box and fly her back to The Falls. She was supposed to be a man who can fix things. I need the water pumps in Hwange repaired fast, not a lesson on how to apply nail polish.'

'Excuse me. I *am* a mechanical engineer. I can fix anything.'

Scott looked at Ashley. She was probably around five foot eight, with legs that went on forever. He swallowed as he tried to remember everything her résumé had said about her. Her qualifications he recalled clearly, but nothing about Ashley being a female. In hindsight, he should have asked for photographs.

'I would have thought that beggars couldn't be choosers in the volunteer field, Mr Decker. You seem to have forgotten something here. I co-own a successful engineering business in Brisbane, and I've paid to come to Zimbabwe to help the animals, not be judged for my gender.'

She paused as she put her glasses on, and then pushed them up onto the top of her head as if to let the words sink into his thick head. 'In my field I've come across grumpier men than you. So, I'm going to ignore those Third World chauvinistic comments.' She flashed another smile. 'Believe me when I say, I really can repair those boreholes in Hwange National Park. You advertised for a miracle worker to restore them to their former glory. I'm your answer. So what if I'm female and I wasn't born with a little dingle-dangle between my legs?' Two eyebrows rose this time.

Scott stared at her. A dingle-dangle?

Kevin shook his head. 'Be reasonable, I couldn't head back now even if I wanted to; that storm's nearly on us. Deal with it. *Nicely.*' He deposited Ashley's designer luggage at Scott's feet, the rebuke about forgotten manners delivered in a friendly but firm manner.

Scott continued to stare at Ashley. He recognised that he was physically attracted to her, just as the elephant were attracted to the marula fruit, despite the fact the fruit were bad news. He could develop an addiction to having a woman like her around. But he could do without the wake of destruction she was sure to leave behind her when she returned to Australia.

He regretted his lack of manners and realised he'd pushed past the point of being downright rude. 'We don't usually have female volunteers. Our living quarters are set out for all-male volunteers. There are no locks on the doors. I can't put a female in digs with those guys, you'll have to move into the main homestead with me.'

He looked at her again, studying her face in detail. Eyes spitting like a desert cat, challenging him. But she was here, and the pumps needed attention. Professional reasoning won.

'Okay. For now. If you prove you can fix things, you can stay. But if you turn out to be a useless city slicker out for a cheap adventure thrill, you're back on a plane to Australia. Understood?'

'Yes, sir.' She saluted, her mouth curving into a smile as she laughed, mocking him.

He shook his head, but couldn't help the small smile that sneaked onto his lips. His Australian Princess was going to be a handful.

'Zol, this is Miss Ashley.' He introduced the black man with grey hair who had materialised at his side. 'Please get her luggage into the *bakkie*.' Scott turned back to her. 'Miss Twine. With that attitude I take it you are still a Miss?' He couldn't resist. He knew his comment would needle her, but he wanted to know if she was single. He watched her jaw clench, and regretted the way he had asked as he saw hurt flash across her face.

One week. He would give her a week, see what she could achieve, and then deal with the fallout. He would put money on her not lasting one week in the bush before scuttling back home.

'Scott Decker, I give you one week's probation to see if I want to stay and work in your project. Or I might just take that safari everyone told me I should take instead of a working holiday.'

His jaw dropped open. What? Was she psychic too? He had no comeback.

Ashley smiled at Zol. 'Nice to meet you.'

'Ma'am.' Zol nodded and returned her smile.

Kevin heaved more cargo into the *bakkie*. 'Hey, can you give me a lift to the lodge? You'll save me getting wet out here waiting for Tessa.'

Scott shouted above a low rumble of thunder somewhere not too distant in the veld. 'We can make a plan. Zol, come and help us with the lodge supplies.'

When everything was loaded into the *bakkie,* Scott opened the passenger door and motioned for Ashley to get inside. She gave him a glare to freeze hell, but complied. Kevin attempted to follow her.

She pointed to the seat. 'There's no seatbelt in the middle.'

Scott positioned himself behind the steering wheel. 'So?'

'It's not safe to travel with no belt.'

'This is Africa. Nobody cares. Move over, put your right leg over the gearshift so Kevin can get inside. Zol's going to get wet.'

Already he regretted giving in to *Ms* Ashley Twine.

Ashley turned her head to the back, where Zol sat on top of her suitcase. 'Surely he isn't going to sit out there?'

'Zol, get off Miss Ashley's fancy suitcase. Sit on the beers,' Scott shouted out the window. 'Is that better?'

'No. I meant he can't travel out there.'

'There is only room for three in the front. Where else do you expect him to sit? This is how we always travel. He's been on the back since I was just a boy. He's used to it. Anyway, it's easier for him to open the gates.' He started the engine with an unnecessary roar and cut off any further complaints.

Scott turned the *bakkie* around and headed off in the opposite direction, changing gear into second as the vehicle picked up a little speed.

The *bakkie* coasted to a stop in the driveway at Zebra Pan Lodge and Kevin climbed out. Scott shifted himself out of the vehicle and turned to watch as Ashley unwound herself from the middle seat and clambered, not too ladylike, out after him, her movements a bit stiff and slower than before. With her flight from Australia and the time zone changes, he knew she was exhausted. He'd seen her struggle to watch the road and stay awake for her first experience in Africa, and the rocking of the *bakkie* hadn't helped her. She'd almost dropped off to sleep more than once on the short trip. He closed the door quietly behind her.

Tessa walked up to them and hugged Kevin. 'Sorry, my *bakkie* broke down. Sipewe has only just got it started again.'

'Not a problem, Scott detoured here instead.' Kevin linked his hand in hers and turned to make the introductions.

'Ashley, this is my fiancée, Tessa. Ashley is Scott's newest volunteer.'

'Hi.' Ashley put out her hand.

'Hey,' Tessa said, shaking it. She looked over Ashley's shoulder at Scott standing behind her, and smiled. 'Good luck to you being the first female in his pack.'

Ashley glanced around at Scott and saw him drop his hands from what looked like a time-out gesture to Tessa. She turned back slowly. 'I guess I'm going to need it. Thanks.'

Tessa smiled.

'Come on, Sipewe,' Kevin called. 'Help Zol get the *bakkie* unpacked.' His simple instructions defused the awkward silence.

Unloading the supplies took little time and soon they were done.

'Good luck,' Kevin said to Scott as he walked towards the *bakkie*.

Scott smiled. 'Thanks, but I figure I need more than luck. I truly got off on the wrong foot with this one.'

He opened the driver's door. Ashley was already in the passenger seat, and he heard the loud click of her safety belt. He slipped behind the wheel.

Zol tapped on the roof to signal he was ready to leave.

'Cheers Kev, Tess,' Scott said, and began his journey home.

He watched Ashley's head nod.

'Put your head back on the headrest. Sleep. You can barely stay awake. I understand your tiredness, jetlag drains your last drop of energy when it finally gets hold of you. Lay down. It's a while to Delmonica, I promise to wake you if I see anything interesting, but I suspect it will just be bush and more bush.'

'I'm fine,' Ashley said, then yawned. 'I'll admit, I'm dog-tired. But what if there are elephant, or warthogs, or anything other than bush? I'll miss it.'

'You have a month to see it all.'

She looked at him. 'A week, remember?'

'Ah yes, a week. But potentially a month. Seriously, your CV looked brilliant, on paper you were exactly what our project needs. But I wasn't lying when I said I wasn't equipped for female volunteers. This is a first. It's going to be a steep learning curve for all of us.'

'That's okay.' She rotated her head to get rid of the stiffness that was setting in. 'I like a challenge. So, about the pumps? The advert for the Hwange Water Project didn't really say much about it, only that you were looking for mechanics to fix old diesel pumps, and that the work was mainly in Hwange National Park. The national park bit was what attracted me.'

'The drought has been harsh, the pumps are old and they keep breaking. The game knows where there's water, and they congregate around those areas. In order to graze the park at a manageable regeneration rate, we usually switch off a few pumps and the animals move on to the next section, giving the vegetation time to recover. We rotate the pumps regularly.' He glanced at her, and although she was listening, she was looking eagerly through the windscreen, watching. He smiled.

'But many pumps are now beyond local help. The Parks Board no longer has the funds to sink into them, and the pumps are being discarded and not replaced. The game is impacting on the drought-ravaged vegetation. We are getting parts of the national park that look more like TTLs.'

'TTLs?'

'Tribal trust lands. Areas the African population were given to live during the Independence years, and where they over-grazed the vegetation and caused deserts.'

'So, how did you get involved in a project inside the park if your ranch is outside the national park area?' she asked.

'My ranch is the first privately owned land backing onto both the hunting concessions and Hwange National Park. Concessions are land leased by the government to a group for a purpose, and that land then brings income into the park. So when they shoot anything, a cut of the price goes to the national park to help with the conservation of the species.'

'You shoot animals on your ranch?'

'Sometimes. We shoot for rations, but we don't trophy hunt on Delmonica. We have fenced the land and brought in more game. Our main farming activity is still stud Brahmans, and training game guards against poaching.'

'So, you need the pumps fixed to give water to the animals in the park, so they can be shot?'

'No; I wish it was so simple. The biggest problem is the poachers. When you have an overabundance of game in one place, the poachers are ruthless in their pursuit of those animals. They become easy pickings. That's the reason I got involved in the Hwange project: from the anti-poaching side. Zol and I began the volunteer program to restore the pumps. We believe that by fixing one problem, other problems will solve themselves. If the game redistributes, the poachers will have to work harder to find it, thereby helping us with our poaching problem.' He looked at her to see if she was still paying attention, and saw she was watching him, not the surroundings.

'The system was simple until now. We built two rondavels for the men to sleep in, and put in an adjoining shower block between them. We have a maximum of four volunteers at any time, who pay their keep to stay at the ranch. But the labour and expertise that they bring for a month are free, so the project can afford to fix the pumps with the donations it receives. Simple, until your arrival. You will have your own room and en suite in the main house.'

'Well, thank you for not putting me in a shared room with a male volunteer. I do appreciate my own room and bathroom.'

Scott remained silent.

Ashley took a breath, beginning another conversation. 'Your advert said Zimbabwe is still in drought conditions, but I could only find newspaper articles referring to your worst drought as being in 1991 and 1992?'

'Been reading up about us? Good. The worst of it was then, and we had a small reprieve with rain in 1993. But last year, the drought was back with a vengeance. We had less than our fifty-year average in rainfall again, with just on 500mm. Our average is supposed to be closer to the 750mm mark.'

'That's not a lot of rain.'

'No, but we are being hopeful, with a few showers this year already, that maybe this year the drought will break. But until it does, the pumps need to be fixed, and animals need to be watered. We have seen so many animals die because of the broken pumps.'

'That's sad,' she said. 'It seemed like a simple enough request of a volunteer.'

'Mm,' Scott said. 'Simple is not always solvable.'

'That is so true.'

He watched her turn to study the road ahead, and she appeared lost in her own thoughts. He switched his attention back to the road and the long drive home to Delmonica, the first and only love of his life.

Bordering on the northwest of the Hwange National Park, his ranch was his life partner. Even after all this time, and everything that had happened during his thirty-six years, his land had been the one constant. When his mother had decided she hated the isolation of the bush, and took away his little sister, Alex, the ranch had been a salvation to a young boy who found himself left alone with his dad, Charlie. Its wide spaces, wild animals and hard work kept his mind busy.

He remembered the day Charlie remarried, and then the day his step-mother Sarah left, taking his stepbrother Dale away too. But when Sarah died, in his grief, Dale had come home, losing himself for days in the solace of the African bush. He knew Dale hated going away to attend university in Cape Town, as Delmonica had claimed his heart too. But unlike the women, he would be back. Dale would come home, looking to the land to settle.

There was no getting away from this chunk of dirt.

Alex was lost to Delmonica. She was lost to Africa, now living in England. And despite his attempts to stay in contact with her, he had failed. Another female gone from his life.

But Dale was more like him: Africa pulsated in their bloodstream.

Just like it had in their dad's. When Charlie had been shot during the war, Zol had brought him home to die. Home to Delmonica.

The seat creaked as Ashley shifted her body, seeking out a more comfort-able position. His attention was ripped from the past and focused on her. She fiddled with the seatbelt across her creamy neck. Damn, his life for the next month would be a living hell.

Now that the surprise had passed, and he knew her a little, her stubborn-ness left him in no doubt she would rise to his challenge, and, given her glowing résumé, he should be happy she was here to help. But he had bigger problems. Thanks to the sell-out by the British and their Lancaster House agreement, Zimbabwe's land was being redistributed under the guise of equality between blacks and whites. The idea was that a willing black buyer and a willing white seller applied for economic help from Great Britain, and the land ownership was transferred to the new black owner when the money was approved. Scott had been approached to be bought out and had refused to sell his birthright. Putting half of Delmonica into Zol's name now looked like it had been the best way to dodge that bullet.

But there was trouble brewing. The white commercial farmers' union was shouting warnings that the government was not happy with the small number of sales, and there were rumours that it wanted to begin an acceler-ated land reform to transfer land quickly into the hands of the majority black population. He needed to concentrate his efforts on keeping Delmonica in his possession and all his people safe.

He didn't need a female complicating his life.

They never survived the isolation of the bush and there was no way in hell he would ever give up his ranch. Not even for someone like Miss Glamorous Painted Nails.

Find out where to get your copy at
books2read.com/MyBrotherButOne

ALSO BY T.M. CLARK

ADULT BOOKS

Shadows Over Africa series

- Child of Africa
- Cry of the Firebird
- My Brother-But-One
- Nature of the Lion
- Shooting Butterflies
- Song of the Starlings
- Tears of the Cheetah
- The Avoidable Orphan

PICTURE BOOKS

- Slowly! Slowly!
- Quickly! Quickly!

www.ingramcontent.com/pod-product-compliance
Lightning Source LLC
Chambersburg PA
CBHW020931260626
47169CB00006B/1675